The minute Daniel Pierce the bachelor auction runway, heart-pounding, juices-flowing hormonal overload.

He strolled the catwalk like a *GQ* model, one hand stuffed in his pocket, his jacket hitched back behind it. He had the body and the attitude to pull it off. The face could have been carved out of granite. Except for the eyes. The eyes were piercing, dark and intense, and more than a little predatory.

Half the women sat back in their seats and rethought their plans to bid on him. A little danger in a man was exciting, but little didn't seem like an adjective that applied to Daniel Pierce. In any way.

Vivi should have been busy taking stock of her surroundings and formulating a plan, but her eyes were glued to the stage. Sure, the sense of helpless inevitability ranked somewhere below tingling nerves and throbbing body parts for sheer volume, but it managed to make enough noise so she couldn't forget that the man on the catwalk was in mortal danger. And he didn't look like he'd be inclined to believe her . . .

PRAISE FOR

Tag, You're It! and *All Jacked Up*

"Razor-sharp repartee and sexy humor add fun to this high-stakes game of hide-and-seek."

—*Romantic Times* (four stars)

"A fast-paced, bumpy ride with some surprising twists and turns that keep you on the edge of your seat. The chemistry . . . was HOT." —*Romance Junkies*

"Full of suspense and excitement. Sure to get your pulse racing and keep your interest all the way through."

—*Romance Reviews Today*

ACE
IS
WILD

Penny McCall

BERKLEY SENSATION, NEW YORK

THE BERKLEY PUBLISHING GROUP
Published by the Penguin Group
Penguin Group (USA) Inc.
375 Hudson Street, New York, New York 10014, USA
Penguin Group (Canada), 90 Eglinton Avenue East, Suite 700, Toronto, Ontario M4P 2Y3, Canada
(a division of Pearson Penguin Canada Inc.)
Penguin Books Ltd., 80 Strand, London WC2R 0RL, England
Penguin Group Ireland, 25 St. Stephen's Green, Dublin 2, Ireland (a division of Penguin Books Ltd.)
Penguin Group (Australia), 250 Camberwell Road, Camberwell, Victoria 3124, Australia
(a division of Pearson Australia Group Pty. Ltd.)
Penguin Books India Pvt. Ltd., 11 Community Centre, Panchsheel Park, New Delhi—110 017, India
Penguin Group (NZ), 67 Apollo Drive, Rosedale, North Shore 0632, New Zealand
(a division of Pearson New Zealand Ltd.)
Penguin Books (South Africa) (Pty.) Ltd., 24 Sturdee Avenue, Rosebank, Johannesburg 2196,
South Africa

Penguin Books Ltd., Registered Offices: 80 Strand, London WC2R 0RL, England

This is a work of fiction. Names, characters, places, and incidents either are the product of the author's imagination or are used fictitiously, and any resemblance to actual persons, living or dead, business establishments, events, or locales is entirely coincidental. The publisher does not have any control over and does not assume any responsibility for author or third-party websites or their content.

ACE IS WILD

A Berkley Sensation Book / published by arrangement with the author

PRINTING HISTORY
Berkley Sensation mass-market edition / August 2008

Copyright © 2008 by Penny McCusker.
Cover design by Rita Frangie.
Interior text design by Laura K. Corless.

ISBN: 978-0-425-22298-0

BERKLEY® SENSATION
Berkley Sensation Books are published by The Berkley Publishing Group,
a division of Penguin Group (USA) Inc.,
375 Hudson Street, New York, New York 10014.
BERKLEY SENSATION and the "B" design are trademarks of Penguin Group (USA) Inc.

PRINTED IN THE UNITED STATES OF AMERICA

10   9   8   7   6   5   4   3   2   1

To Debbie—
Gone from our lives but never from our hearts

chapter
1

VIVIENNE FOSTER SLIPPED THROUGH THE DOORS OF the Oval Room at the Fairmont Copley Plaza Hotel, easing into the shadows next to a potted palm in the corner by the cash bar. Any Boston native, not to mention most New Englanders, would be familiar with the Oval Room. It was historically significant, artistically important, architecturally stunning, and socially desirable. But estrogen charged? Definitely not an everyday occurrence, and one those who normally frequented the Oval Room would have pooh-poohed at.

But not Vivi. She'd been prepared for this. And she'd come anyway. Glutton for punishment, that's what she was.

"What can I get you, darlin'?" the bartender asked her.

Vivi peered through the foliage and discovered him standing in her neck of the woods, at the end of the bar.

"Trying to keep a low profile here," she said under her breath.

"Something tropical," he decided, eyes on the greenery, not getting with the skulking program. "Piña colada? Mai tai?"

Vivi gauged the level of sexual tension in the place. "How about a fire hose?"

The bartender grinned. "What kind of fun would that be?"

"Planning to console the losers?"

"One or two of them, anyway."

He winked and headed off to fill a drink order for the aforementioned potential losers, which would be any number of the rich, bored socialites crowded at round tables, some of them with their chairs turned backward so they didn't have to crane their necks to see the rainbow of men lined up across the low stage erected at the opposite end of the room. Every few minutes one of the men would be trotted forward, and the socialites would go into a frenzy— bidding, of course, since it was all in the name of charity. Tax write-offs were clearly not the fringe benefit they had in mind, though, and since the ratio of debutantes to beefcake was about twenty to one, and there was enough combined heat to set off the overhead sprinklers, the bartender—not to mention husbands, fiancés, limo drivers, and shower massagers—stood a good chance of getting lucky.

It was exactly what Vivi had anticipated, except this version came with sound, and it was already giving her a headache. She tried to shut out the cacophony of shouting, laughing, shrieking female voices, concentrating instead on the men being auctioned off. Tall men, short men, stocky or slender, in every skin tone from Michael Jackson to, well, Michael Jackson. They were all handsome and fit, all well-respected members of the Boston business or social communities, all decked out in evening wear and encouraging smiles. Or nearly all.

One man stood at the end of the line, a little apart from the rest of the male smorgasbord. It wasn't distance that separated him, though, it wasn't his clothing, or his stature in the community.

Vivi recognized Daniel Pierce from his photo, but she hadn't been prepared for the impact he made in the flesh. Not his flesh, hers.

The emcee announced him, and proceeded to give a simpering commentary, probably laced with vital statistics and sexual innuendo. All Vivi heard was *wah, wah, wah,* because the minute Daniel Pierce began to make his way down the bachelor auction runway she'd gone into slack-jawed, heart-pounding, juices-flowing hormonal overload.

He strolled the catwalk like a *GQ* model, one hand stuffed in his pocket, his jacket hitched back behind it. He had the body and the attitude to pull it off. The face could have been carved out of granite. Except for the eyes. The eyes were, well, piercing, dark and intense, and more than a little predatory.

Fully half the women sat back in their seats and rethought their plans to bid on him. A little danger in a man was exciting, but little didn't seem like an adjective that applied to Daniel Pierce. In any way.

Vivi should have been busy taking stock of her surroundings and formulating a plan, but her eyes were glued to the stage, and what she was feeling could best be described as "fatalism." Sure, the sense of helpless inevitability ranked somewhere below tingling nerves and throbbing body parts for sheer volume, but it managed to make enough noise so she couldn't forget that the man on the catwalk was in mortal danger. And the man on the catwalk didn't look like he'd be inclined to believe her.

So she'd have to make him.

It wasn't going to be easy.

The elegant lines of the tuxedo couldn't camouflage his strength, and it wasn't just the muscles flexing when he walked, it was the way he carried himself—arrogant, in charge, take no prisoners. There was a distinct unevenness in his stride, but the expression on his face dared anyone to feel sorry for him.

Vivi wasn't about to make that mistake. Underestimating him—or overestimating herself—wouldn't be wise, either. She had a feeling Daniel Pierce was going to defy prediction. Not a confidence-inspiring thought—but in the absence of confidence she'd always found impulse a pretty good substitute. As impulsive as a woman like her could be, that is.

Before the urge to overthink matters could get the better of her, she eased out of the shrubbery. And into Freak Central. While her mind had been wandering aimlessly in the interest of procrastination, all the men but Pierce had been auctioned off and joined their buyers in the audience. The bidding had opened on Pierce, and women were bouncing in their chairs, hands in the air, shouting each other down. Even the ones who'd decided not to bid were caught up in the craziness, egging their friends on to make even bigger fools of themselves. Vivi saw a woman duck under her table and figured the action was going to head the Chippendales route any moment.

She took another good, long look at Pierce, wondering how he'd fooled these people into thinking he wanted anything to do with them. Or maybe that was part of the attraction. The sad truth was that women always wanted the guy they couldn't have.

Well, Vivi didn't want him. She didn't want anything to do with him. But she was leaving with him. One way or another.

The current bid had already topped what she could afford, but she'd known before she got there that she wouldn't be able to buy her way out of this one. The contest was down to a trio of picture-perfect examples of Boston society, a brunette, a blonde, and a redhead with a girl-next-door face, the body of a Playboy Playmate, and six figures worth of jewels at her ears, neck, and wrist. She upped the bid by two hundred dollars, but it was the look that passed between her and Daniel Pierce that told Vivi the redhead was going to outlast the others. Because it was rigged, and he was calling the shots.

What he didn't know was that no one controlled their own destiny. Not even Vivi, and she had a hell of a lot better chance at it than he did. Under normal circumstances. Circumstances, however, weren't normal, and free choice was only a fond memory.

The back of her neck was prickling like heat rash at a fat

farm, and she felt an urgency to do *something*. The compulsion was stronger than any cautioning thoughts, stronger than the conclusions she'd drawn about Daniel Pierce's character from seeing him in person, strong enough that she was already at the edge of the stage before she realized her feet were taking her there.

"I need to talk to you," she said when he looked down at her.

He didn't reply, at least not verbally. His gaze panned down from her face and over her body, lingering in all the obvious places before he looked up again. Their eyes met, and she jolted. He'd felt it, too; she saw his reaction though he was quicker to hide it, his gaze lifting to the audience of still-screaming women as if Vivi didn't exist. Of all the reactions she'd expected from him in this situation, being dismissed wasn't high on the list.

"I'm not too happy about this, either," she said.

He turned to her again, his eyes narrowing on her face. "What do you want?"

To be anywhere but here. She didn't speak, though, and not because she didn't know what to say. Stage fright was more the issue. The room had grown still, and Daniel Pierce's eyes weren't the only ones on her.

"Please take your seat, miss," the emcee said.

Vivi ignored her. "You have to come with me," she said to Pierce.

"Miss, the bidding stands at just over three thousand dollars."

Vivi glanced over at the podium in time to see the woman pass a look over her and dismiss her—not as Daniel had done, without judgment or malice. This dismissal was meant to be an insult.

Vivi laughed softly, not the least offended. If she'd wanted to be one of these tight-assed, snobby, better-than-thou society witches and have a career as arm candy, she could have accepted one of the half-dozen marriage proposals that had come her way in the last seven or eight years. "Well, you put me in my place" was all she said.

The indignation ratcheted up, the politeness down. "If you'd like to have a conversation with Mr. Pierce, you can take your seat and place a bid. If you can afford it."

"Shut up," Vivi said sweetly.

The woman hoovered in a breath and pasted on a glare, beckoning someone out of the shadows behind her. Vivi caught movement, a flash of silver, and realized a police officer was in attendance, probably to guard the donations. Or provide riot control.

Vivi rolled her eyes. "I'll be with you in a minute," she said to Pierce, and turned to the cop, but not before she caught the amused lift of Daniel's brow.

She looked over her shoulder at him. No smile on his face, but there was a definite shift in his attitude. He wasn't sure of her, but the gleam in his eyes told her he was going to sit back and see how she handled herself. So he'd know how to handle her.

Lawyers, she thought as she shifted her focus to the more immediate threat, ranked right below cops on the list of people she despised most. It was unfortunate how often she had to deal with both.

The cop pulled his cuffs out of the holster at the small of his back as he approached her. "Come with me, ma'am," he said.

"I haven't done anything wrong."

"There's disturbing the peace," Pierce observed blandly from the stage.

Vivi gazed out over the sea of silent, staring faces. "It appears to me that I reestablished the peace. You were seconds from getting hit in the face with a thong. You should be thanking me."

He didn't say anything, but there was no gratitude in his eyes. A little reluctant humor, some impatience and curiosity, but no gratitude. Not that Vivi was expecting any.

"I really need to talk to you," she said, feeling a little impatient herself. "It's important."

Daniel reached into his breast pocket, pulled out his

wallet, and handed her a business card. "Call my office and make an appointment."

"It can't wait."

"Then tell me now."

She considered the rapt audience, the now-avidly attentive emcee, and the cop with his eager expression and shiny bracelets. "Can we go somewhere else?"

"I'm in the middle of something, in case you haven't noticed."

"You're not the type of man who enjoys this kind of ridiculous spectacle."

"Maybe not, but this ridiculous spectacle happens to be for a good cause."

"Are you talking about the charity or your campaign for political office?"

His gaze turned even more intense, and there was an assessing manner to it, a looking-below-the-surface quality that made her want to squirm. He didn't trust her.

Vivi couldn't blame him. But she had to give him credit because he held out a hand. She took it, long enough to let him help her up onto the stage, then she let go. He wasn't any more eager to prolong contact, but Vivi made the mistake of rubbing her tingling palm on her jeans. Daniel Pierce noted it with a slight smirk.

"That's some ego you have there, Ace," she observed blandly. "You get tired carrying it around?"

His eyes dropped to her chest, lingering on the orchid tattoo peeking out of her tank top. "No. You?"

Vivi resisted the urge to cross her arms over her C cups. "I've learned to live with the burden."

"Any time you want some help with that, you have my card."

"I think I can handle it by myself, thanks."

This time his smile was quick and genuine, and she could all but hear him lingering on the word *handle*. She liked the idea, too, any idea he might have that involved *handling*. "How about we discuss something else," she said before her racing heart and tingling palm could gang up on her self-control and make her do something she'd regret. "Like why I crashed this party."

His smile faded away, his brow knitting in consideration as he gestured to the curtain hanging at the back of the stage.

"Where are you going?" the emcee all but shrieked.

Vivi whipped around. She'd forgotten they had an audience. The audience, unfortunately, hadn't forgotten about her. If it had been Texas, there'd have been a lynchin' in the works. Boston debutantes had their manicures to worry about, and they probably couldn't tie a decent knot between them, anyway. And since they didn't want to frown and cause themselves wrinkles, the worst they could do was look down their rhinoplasties at her.

Daniel couldn't have cared less about the mood in the room and what it might do to his market value. He wasn't too concerned about the emcee's hand-wringing, either. "We won't be long," he said to her, "auction off someone else."

"There is no one else," she wailed, but she stayed put at the podium, watching the two of them disappear behind the curtain.

"How do you know I'm considering a run for office?" Daniel asked, not wasting any more time on witty banter about her body parts. In fact, body parts seemed to be the furthest thing from his mind, except maybe her brain. He was definitely interested in what she was thinking.

Vivi would have found that a refreshing change from most of the men she met, if she'd had the time to waste convincing him she was serious. As things stood, she couldn't afford to do anything else. "If you wanted to help the charity, you'd send them a check," she said. "You're here to ingratiate yourself with the right kind of people, and when I say *right*, I mean rich and influential, which," she hooked a thumb in the general direction of the emcee in her vintage Chanel suit and tasteful but expensive pearls, "these women are."

Daniel crossed his arms. "Fascinating. Go on."

Vivi studied his face, but he looked so politely interested she decided she must have been mistaken about the undertone she thought she'd heard in his voice. "I wouldn't have expected your aspirations to run to politics," she continued. "Don't get me wrong, I think you'd make a great politician. I mean, you have all the right credentials—law degree, camera-ready face, perfect body with what, ten percent body fat?"

"I can feel my ego inflating."

She snorted softly. "You can't help your face, and you exercise daily because you like good food and good wine once in a while. And because of your leg."

"You don't pull any punches."

"Neither do you," she said, ignoring the warning in his tone, the second warning he'd given, because he needed convincing, and she didn't know any other way to do it except to make him believe in her. "You fight your battles in a courtroom, but it doesn't stop you from wanting to go after justice more directly. Probably another reason you work out every day. Kind of like walking an aggressive dog—tire it out and it's easier to control."

"Sounds like you researched me."

She shrugged, hoping he couldn't see the nerves jumping around under her skin. Or hear them in her voice. "You sleep on the left side of the bed," she said recklessly, "you don't like cauliflower, or cats, and you wear boxer briefs."

"Correction, you're a stalker."

The emcee poked her head through the opening in the curtain just in time to hear that. She stayed long enough to gasp, then her head disappeared.

Vivi's voice hadn't carried to the audience; the emcee made sure hers did, and if those at the back of the room had missed it, the front-row seats were happy to pass along Daniel's assessment of her character. Either that or there was a hell of an echo in the place.

Even worse, the word "stalker" was a label the cop could understand. And act on. He stepped behind the curtain, caught her left wrist, and clapped a handcuff on it before she could deny the accusation. She twisted her other arm out of reach, looking at Daniel, although why she should have expected him to help her she had no idea.

All he did was watch, his eyes speculative, challenging. Get out of this, Houdini, he was saying.

But Vivi was done proving herself to him. Vivi was ticked off. He wanted to see what she was made of? Fine. She stopped struggling, sagged back against the cop too suddenly for him to stop her when she grabbed his gun and wrenched it out of his holster. She pulled her arm free, handcuff and all, whirling around to point the pistol at Daniel.

His eyes never left hers, one corner of his mouth quirking up in grim amusement.

Until she thumbed off the safety.

chapter
2

THE WOMAN WAS A MENACE. SHE'D HIJACKED HIM from the middle of a charity event, called him names— Okay, politician was hardly name-calling, and he was considering running for a public office of some sort. In his crazier moments. And he had accused her of being a stalker, but at least she fit the part. Take the way she cocked her head from time to time, like the voices in her brain were having a conversation she didn't want to miss. If that didn't shout "stalker" Daniel didn't know what did. Unless it was the gun.

It wasn't the first time he'd had a gun pointed at him, and by a hell of a lot more dangerous types than this woman appeared to be, with her shaking hands and the making-it-up-as-I-go panic on her face. As long as there wasn't a serial killer among her other personalities, he figured he was safe. And not bored, which was probably the most confusing part of this whole thing. Since the day the High and Mighty at the FBI had sidelined him because of his injury, he'd been bored. And angry.

He'd spent months in rehab, trying to get his leg back to prime working condition. When he'd realized ambulatory was the best he could hope for, there'd been the years in college, upgrading to a law degree so he could still be a part of the justice system. He'd succeeded because failure had never been an option—until he became a federal prosecutor and his fate had been put into the hands of judges and juries.

The juries he could forgive; they were just regular people who were fooled by the lies and tap-dancing of slick defense lawyers. Judges were another story. Judges had to be reelected, so they walked a fine line between the law and public perception, and that included their verdicts. More often than not, it hadn't worked in Daniel's favor, so his win/loss ratio wasn't all it should have been, and unless it improved he likely wouldn't be an assistant U.S. attorney for much longer.

All that left for him career-wise was politics, which sounded like the perfect job for a man who'd only ever wanted to make the world a better place. Politics, however, bore a striking resemblance to the world's oldest profession, and since Daniel wouldn't sell himself to the highest bidder in order to keep his job, he probably wouldn't last long at that, either.

That added frustration to the bored/angry mix. His job was the only thing he'd ever really loved, and accepting that he'd never be a field agent again had been hell—and not just from a professional standpoint. Trust was something that would never come easy to a man who'd learned that suspicion was the only way to stay alive. There were a couple of people he'd consider friends, but he kept as much of himself to himself as humanly possible. And although he let an occasional woman into his bed, he rarely let one into his life. He liked it that way. Women were trouble—clingy and demanding and manipulative.

Including this one. She might be desperate or crazy enough to pull a gun on him when she didn't get what she wanted. And he might find that interesting enough to play along until he found out what she was up to. But then he was kicking her out of his life, just like all the others.

Of course, there was a pretty good chance she'd be

going to jail, especially if she shot someone—on purpose or by accident.

She moved to one side so she could keep both him and the policeman in sight, swinging the gun as she went. The emcee, standing between the two men, ducked for cover.

"You going to shoot me, or them?" Daniel asked her.

She looked down and swung the gun back to point at him. "You, unless you do what I tell you."

Her hands were steady now, so were her eyes. She might be in over her head, but it was sink or swim. No turning back. And a cornered nutcase was always more dangerous.

"You have a name?" he asked her, keeping his voice calm and his expression pleasant.

"Vivi," she said.

"You wanted to talk to me, Vivi, so why don't you let the others go and we'll talk." It sounded lame even to him, so he wasn't surprised when she rolled her eyes.

"I know you're just humoring me until you can come up with a plan to catch me off guard. Unfortunately, we don't have time for a standoff." She shifted her eyes to the cop and held up her wrist with its chrome bangle. "Unlock this," she ordered him.

He edged forward, his gaze on the pistol.

"You really don't want to try it," she said, probably because she saw the same thing in the cop's eyes that Daniel did, an intention to act that might take the form of calling her bluff. "I know how to use this." She cocked the gun to prove her point. "And I will."

The cop decided she might be serious. He unlocked the cuff and stepped back.

"Not so fast, Officer . . . Cranston," she read off his badge. "Lock one of the cuffs around your wrist." She fielded his glare, waited while he did as she instructed. "Now you," she said to the emcee.

The woman drew herself up. "Do you know who I am?"

"No."

"Cassandra Shaw Scott Hanson Martindale Winston Hobbs."

"Still not ringing any bells, but I can see why you've had all those husbands."

"Every one of those husbands has been a leader in his field, and I spend my time doing charitable works, assisting the poor and downtrodden of this community. If you put down that weapon and surrender yourself to this nice, young officer, I will make sure you receive the best representation possible before you are found guilty and trundled off to jail."

"You'd really help me?"

Cassandra folded her hands primly, gave a little sniff of distaste, and nodded.

"Great." Vivi pointed to the floor. "Have a seat."

"I will not!"

"Officer?"

The cop didn't waste any time trying to play negotiator. He plucked the petite woman off her feet and deposited her on the floor, where she sat in shock, sputtering her indignation and making threats in well-modulated tones.

Vivi didn't have any qualms about appearing undignified. She raised her voice and gave a few more terse instructions that resulted in the cop and the socialite being handcuffed together, around the underpinnings of the stage.

Daniel stood his ground and enjoyed the show. Not that he was getting a kick out of Cassandra's plight, or the cop's. Mostly he was running out the clock because it was only a matter of time before someone looked behind the curtain.

"We need to get moving before someone looks behind the curtain," Vivi said. "And I'll need your cell phone."

Daniel slipped his hand in his pocket, cussing under his breath because he didn't have anything but a wallet and phone. But he hadn't routinely carried a gun since he'd become a lawyer. He really missed carrying a gun. Throwing the book at criminals just wasn't as satisfying.

Not that he would have used a gun on Vivi, but it would have been nice to have options. He handed over his cell phone, and watched her slip it into her back pocket.

"Step down from the stage," she said, "and keep your hands where I can see them."

"You're just going to leave us here?"

Daniel glanced down at Cassandra. "If she takes you with her, she'll have to point the gun at you again."

Cassandra looked at the gun, then at Vivi, and sighed heavily.

Daniel knew just what she was thinking, too. Vivi was holding a gun, and it was possible she'd use it. But it was hard to take seriously the threat of a woman who looked like she should be headlining at the nearest strip club. True, Cassandra's imagination wouldn't be running to G-strings and pole dancing, but any straight male this side of the grave would see—and feel—what he did.

Clouds of dark, curly hair surrounded a beautiful face, dusky skin, amber eyes just slanted enough to make them exotic, and what fantasies weren't set off by her lush mouth were sparked by her stripper's body. And when he thought *sparked* he meant it, since he felt like someone had lit him on fire.

In the tiny part of his mind that hadn't fallen into his jockeys, he knew he should be concentrating on getting her out of the hotel before anyone got hurt. Including her. But he was too busy fighting off an attack of teenage-strength lust.

"Come on," she said, bouncing on her toes, antsy.

It took a minute for her meaning to batter through the brick wall of attraction he felt for her, and then he had to wrench his eyes up to the crown of her head before he could translate her instructions into action and formulate a plan. Such as it was.

He hopped down, ready for the pain that shot up his bad leg. He winced, though, made sure she saw it on his face as he stumbled forward, half bent at the waist and reaching forward as if to catch his balance. She wasn't fooled. She stepped back and brought the gun up so the barrel was practically buried in his left nostril.

"That still cocked?"

"Yep."

"Just checking." He straightened and backed off a step so he could see something around that big black hole. But she wasn't watching him. Her eyes were unfocused, and he saw her cock her head slightly. Before he could do more than think about disarming her, she snapped back. She climbed up onto the stage and peeked through the curtain just as a male voice shouted, "Everyone stay calm."

Of course, all hell broke loose. Men yelled, women screamed, chairs thudded over as people jumped to their feet. Daniel joined Vivi at the curtain opening and saw two men in black, right down to the guns in their hands and the ski masks covering all but their eyes, at the other end of the Oval Room. One of them was busy securing the doors, the other looked like Jerry Lewis, darting a couple of steps in one direction then the other. Both hands were flapping in the air, including the one holding the gun, and he was yelling instructions.

The crowd ebbed and flowed like a school of fish, herding away from the guns but not paying any attention to what the guy was saying, which probably had something to do with the fact that nearly everyone in the place had a cell phone out. If it was one thing these women could do, even with their manicures, it was speed dial.

The other guy finished with the doors and turned around. Daniel could have sworn he was rolling his eyes. "Shut up," he roared, and when that didn't work, he fired a shot into the floor. If the guy believed that would get him what he wanted, he must not have had a lot of dealings with women from the upper echelons of Boston society—or women in general—because the screaming rose to a level that could have shattered all the glass for a five-mile radius. Human ears were at real risk, but Daniel wasn't worried about ears so much as the bodies they were attached to. And not just from the guys with the guns. There was a better than even chance someone was going to get trampled.

"I hope nobody gets trampled," Vivi said at his shoulder.

"You a mind reader?" Daniel wondered out loud.

"Something like that," she said, which might have gotten his attention if he hadn't been focused on the gun she was pointing at him. Again. "It's time to go."

"If you're going to shoot," he said, "do it, because that's the only way you're going to stop me from going out there."

"Nine-one-one is probably choked with hysterical calls by now. It's only a matter of time before the police arrive." And Vivi was wondering how—or if—she'd manage to get Pierce out of the Fairmont and keep herself out of jail, too.

Especially since he was hardly being cooperative.

He walked away from her. She followed, not bothering with the gun since he wasn't paying attention to it anyway and shooting him, while it had its attractions, would defeat her purpose. There was a table at the end of the stage with water for the bachelors when they'd been waiting for their moment on the auction block. Daniel whipped the cloth off the table, sending bottles flying, and took it over to the two people still handcuffed at the back of the stage.

"As soon as we're gone, unlock the cuffs and get out of here," he said to the cop. "You'll be safe as long as you keep your heads down. And stay quiet." He directed the last comment to Cassandra. She didn't look very happy, but she nodded.

Vivi caught the edge of the tablecloth and waited until he turned to face her before she let it go. "You can't go out there."

He looked at the gun still in her hand. "If you want to stop me you're going to have to use that."

Standing on the edge of the stage, Vivi was only a few inches taller than Daniel. She still felt like he was looming over her. She held her ground anyway. "If you go out there, you're going to die."

"Then give me the gun."

Vivi said, "Okay," and when he bent to toss the cloth over Cassandra and Officer Cranston, she gave him the gun. Across the back of the head.

He folded like an amateur at a table full of poker pros.

"If you want to keep him alive," she said to the cop as she jumped down from the stage, "you'll keep him here."

She popped the clip out of the gun and pocketed it, dropped the gun in Officer Cranston's lap, and slung the tablecloth over the three of them before she headed for the exit door a few yards behind the stage. She didn't look back.

VIVI WAS DOZING IN DANIEL'S LINCOLN WHEN HE CAME out of the Fairmont around two A.M. He didn't look surprised to see her.

"You really ought to lock this," she said when he slid into the passenger seat.

"Nobody bothers my car. It looks like a mob ride."

"Or a hearse."

"I was going for image."

"Sure, big, black and boring screams government employee."

"I'm guessing you didn't wait all this time to insult my car."

"No, but it seemed like a good icebreaker."

He rubbed the back, of his neck. "I think you already covered that."

"I didn't hit you that hard."

He gave her a long, silent stare full of attitude.

Vivi caught herself fidgeting and stopped. "So what happened in there after I left?"

"Everything was dark for a while—no wait, that was while I was unconscious."

"Hey, you have a sense of humor. They teach you that in law school?"

"It's homegrown. But it comes in handy with some of the criminals I run across." The expression on his face said he was including her in that lineup.

It shouldn't have bothered her. But it did. "You going to answer my question, Ace?"

"The name is Daniel Pierce."

"So I've heard."

"Then use it," he said, rubbing the back of his neck again.

"The whole thing, first and last, or should I call you Mr. Pierce?"

He gave her a look.

"Just give me the *Reader's Digest* version," she said. "Ace."

"Fine, condensed," Daniel said, taking the high ground on the nickname. They weren't going to be together long enough for it to be an issue. "By the time I woke up, the police were there and the gunmen were gone, along with most of the auction attendees. I convinced Mrs. Hobbs—"

"Who?"

"The nice lady you handcuffed."

Vivi could have argued with the term "nice," but she was in long-story-short mode, feeling an urgency again.

"Mrs. Hobbs agreed to keep her humiliation private."

"What about the cop?"

"No such luck."

"I would have thought he'd be glad to have his gun back."

"He was, and I assured him the FBI will handle you."

"The FBI." Vivi sat back in the driver's seat, not liking that notion. But the FBI wasn't there yet, and she didn't see any reason why she couldn't avoid them, just like she'd slipped past the notice of Boston's finest.

"Officer Cranston was relieved about the gun," Daniel continued, "and since he'd gotten the handcuffs off, I had come to, and the bad guys were gone with no one getting hurt, he was looking pretty good by the time his coworkers arrived."

"And that wasn't enough for him? He couldn't just pretend he never saw me?"

"I'm almost sure there's no chapter on turning a blind eye in the police manual."

"Cops are such sticklers for the rules."

"Not a lover of law enforcement, huh?"

On the contrary. In fact, Vivi could have told him that the law, specifically the FBI, was the very reason she'd crashed the party tonight. But it was too soon. He didn't trust her—she'd hardly given him reason, after all. If he knew exactly why she was so frantic to save his life, he'd trot her off to jail and throw away the key. And he'd end up dead, too.

"Your turn," he said. "Why were you in there? And why are you here?"

"Take a look out there," Vivi said, having caught a quick flash of movement through the windshield.

Daniel had parked on the top level of a structure across Dartmouth Street from the Fairmont. It was five levels, or maybe six—the slanted floors always confused Vivi—surrounded by taller buildings, and very poorly lit.

Daniel peered through the windshield, lingering on a denser, man-shaped piece of darkness at the edge of the roof before he searched the shadows beyond each of the other windows. There was an SUV parked on the driver's side, and cars to the left and behind, so admittedly there wasn't a lot to see. "The other guy must be behind a bigger vehicle."

"Nope," Vivi said, eyes closed, concentrating. Until she heard the rattle of keys. "We have to get out of the car." And since she knew he would argue, she reached over and plucked the keys out of his hand.

He tried to get them back, predictably, and as much as she enjoyed grappling with him like teenagers in the front seat, there was more to worry about than hickeys and un-planned pregnancy. Namely, the van that screamed up to block in the Lincoln. The driver's door opened, but Vivi didn't wait to see who was coming out. Not that it was a mystery anyway.

She fumbled the key into the ignition, hands shaking, heart pounding so loud she barely heard the engine catch, and she completely freaked out when she pushed her foot forward and found nothing but empty air. It took her a few precious seconds to realize that Daniel was close to a foot taller than she was, and then to scoot herself forward in the seat.

This time she found the gas pedal, simultaneously slamming the car into reverse as she jammed her foot to the floor. The car traveled all of six feet, crashing into the van and sending the guy standing between the two vehicles into a panicked dive for his life.

Daniel reached for his door handle, but she said, "No, this way," fisting her hand in his jacket and hauling him out the driver's door just as the windshield on the passenger side exploded.

He dropped into a crouch, ignoring the screaming of his crippled leg and cursing himself for giving up the practice of keeping a gun in the glove compartment of his car. Because he'd never expected to be in this position again.

And he probably shouldn't be enjoying it, but he was. The adrenaline rush, pitting his wits against the bad guys, protecting an innocent . . . Okay, Vivi what's-her-name wasn't innocent, and there was the possibility they'd both be riddled with bullets at any moment, which kind of blunted the rush, but it got him moving.

He curled his hand around hers and weaved between the vehicles, working his way down the levels with her in tow, trying to circle around to the hotel. The structure was mostly full, so it shouldn't have been that difficult to make it back to the Fairmont in one piece. Except the hit men seemed hellbent on preventing that.

Daniel flattened himself against the side of a minivan on the first level, easing over until he could see through the van's windows, peering in the dark toward the hotel. A suggestion of movement caught his eye. All he could make out in that direction was an indistinct patch of deeper darkness, but it told him a lot. None of it encouraging.

In the brightly lit Oval Room, the two had looked like garden variety thugs who'd gotten lost on their way to hit the local gas station for a few bucks and a six-pack of beer. In the gloom of the parking structure, it was a different story. They blended almost seamlessly into the night. Even their guns seemed to suck up what little light there was and give nothing back, no chrome or nickel to reflect the weak overhead lights, and the steel of the barrels must have been scuffed and blackened. Definitely a professional hit. The question was why? And how did Vivi know about it?

It was a question for later, one he intended to be alive to ask, which wasn't as simple as it sounded. His car was blocked in, and even if they broke into another, the gunmen would be on them before he had time to hot-wire it. It was after-hours for the office buildings around the Fairmont, and the gunmen were between them and the hotel. Which left only one option.

"Give me the phone," he whispered to Vivi.

"Can't," she said, "I left it in your glove compartment."

He slumped, shaking his head.

"I didn't want you to accuse me of stealing it."

"You tried to kidnap me, and you were worried about petty theft?"

"How about we save this discussion for later."

"I'll add it to the list."

"If we're still alive."

Daniel glanced down at her, but all he got was a face full of hair. Really nice-smelling hair. Soft, too.

She looked up at him, their eyes met, and even in the dim light her dusky skin took on a nice warm glow. Some parts of him were pretty warm, too, warm enough that he took a step closer to her. She didn't move away. And even though he knew that part of what was burning through his bloodstream was adrenaline, he still put her up against the side of the van and moved in close, felt her breasts skim his chest as she relaxed into him, her breath catching . . . just as a bullet plonked into the van right by Daniel's head.

They jerked apart, Daniel pulling Vivi into a half-crouch and shoving her ahead of him to the rear of the van.

"We have to get to the hotel," he said, keeping his voice low and his eyes off her so he could put his mind back on the life-and-death part of the program.

"Did you forget about the guys in black who were shooting at you a minute ago?" she asked him, a little snap to her voice.

"You mean the hit men?"

"They weren't Johnny Cash fans."

A bullet pinged off the roof of the van. Daniel dragged her behind the truck next to it. "If you don't keep your voice down," he whispered, "the next one's going to be in you."

"They're not shooting at me."

"That doesn't mean they won't hit you."

Vivi didn't reply, but in the glare of the overhead lights, Daniel saw her tip her head and stare off into the gloom. It looked like there was a war going on inside her, her expression running through emotions faster than he could put names to them.

Just when he thought she was about to start talking to herself, she took off. Daniel had no choice but to go with her, ducking between cars and SUVs, straining his ears for the sound of footsteps. Or gunshots.

"What the hell are you doing?" he demanded when he caught up to her and hauled her to a stop.

"Running away from the men with the guns."

"Where are you running to? We can't hide from them forever. The best we can hope is that someone heard the shots and called the police."

He didn't need light to get the full effect of the look she shot him. Police would be the last thing she'd want, not that they'd get there in time. Not before he and Vivi ran out of cars to hide behind, anyway, and once that happened they were screwed.

"Any suggestions?" he asked her.

"You mean besides wait them out and hope the cavalry arrives in time?"

"I mean besides sarcasm."

"Yeah." She sighed. "I know how to ditch them." She took his chin in her hand and turned his head until a neighboring building was in his line of sight.

Daniel didn't say anything for a full thirty seconds, and then it wasn't something particularly nice.

"Swearing isn't going to get us out of this."

"Christ deliver me from clueless women."

"Are you done now?"

He felt his teeth grinding together and slowly unlocked his jaw. "We have to cross at least a hundred yards of open street to get to the hotel door," Daniel said. "There are lights. We're going to get shot."

"We'll run fast. And zigzag. Like they do on TV."

Daniel shoved a hand back through his hair. He'd kept his sentences short and simple. He'd used irrefutable logic, but did she get the point? No. "I thought you wanted to save my life."

"That was before I actually met you."

Footsteps slapped the pavement, heading in their direction, and the shooting started again. She fisted a hand in his jacket and towed him, while he fought for balance on his bad leg, toward a towering office building.

"There'll be a guard inside," Daniel pointed out, as they came to a halt behind a pickup truck at the front exit of the structure. "He's not going to let us hide in there. We'll be trapped in a lobby fronted by glass, and those guys out there will pick us off at their leisure."

"We don't have a choice."

Daniel met her eyes, fathomless in the darkness, and came to the same conclusion. It was quiet again, but he knew the hit men were closing in on them. "We'll have to run for it," he whispered, his voice close to her ear.

She shivered, and it sidetracked him—right up to the moment he remembered their lives were on the line. "Stay out of the light as much as possible."

"Don't forget the zigzagging."

"Just run!" He gave her a light shove, and she took off.

He lagged behind, protecting her. The good news? It wasn't far to the building. The bad news was that the shooting started almost before they hit the open expanse of Stuart Street behind the hotel, and one of the hit men was between them and every other building entry in the vicinity.

They ran down Dartmouth instead, keeping close to the

parking structure until they hit St. James. Daniel would have stopped and looked both ways. Getting flattened by a bus was even worse than a gunshot wound. Gunshot wounds might be survived. Buses were usually final. Vivi wasn't worried about buses. She dragged him straight out into the street and across to Copley Square, a sea of concrete with no cover whatsoever. The hit men had to wait for traffic to clear, but it didn't hold them up long, and then they were in the Square, too, and bringing their guns to bear.

And then Daniel heard the helicopter. And there was no way to hide from an air attack.

chapter
3

"GET YOUR ASS IN GEAR, RADAR," DANIEL SHOUTED
back to Vivi.

"Radar?"

"You knew the helicopter was coming."

"I didn't, not specifically. I just knew we needed to get
into that building."

"It was a safe bet, considering half the rich women on
the East Coast were at the auction."

"Fine, it was a lucky guess. How about we make the
most of it?"

Daniel gave her the kind of look that made hardened
criminals squirm on the witness stand. Her eyes widened,
as if she'd just remembered where they were and why, not
to mention the part where they were together because she'd
held him at gunpoint. She looked like she was thinking
about running in the opposite direction, and he wouldn't
have blamed her for it. Instead, she linked her fingers with
his, and they ran back across St. James and onto the small
stretch of lawn in front of the Fairmont.

They went instinctively into a crouching run, which

saved them from the guys chasing them, and since the helicopter only whooshed by overhead without guns bristling out of any doors, the most they got hit with was a hellacious downdraft. More important, the gunmen dove face-first into the ground, which was not only satisfying, but reassuring, since they clearly believed the copter was a threat to them. That would mean it was manned by good guys, or at least neutral guys. And it seemed to heading to the same building Vivi had been trying to get him into since the gunmen showed up again.

They hit the door of the high-rise and burst inside, dropping to a walk almost immediately for the benefit of the armed guard. No point in making him any more suspicious than he already was.

"The building is closed," he said, one hand resting on his gun, the other beneath the counter, probably hovering over the trip button to a silent alarm.

Daniel looked over his shoulder. It was pitch-black outside, but he knew the hit men were out there, lurking. If the guard turned him and Vivi away, they'd be dead the minute they walked out the door.

"We need to get to the roof," Daniel said.

The guard was predictably resistant to that idea. "Got specific instructions about who goes up. You ain't on the list."

"Who is?" Vivi asked. "On the list, I mean."

The man shifted his gaze to her, sweat popping out on his upper lip. Good thing he hadn't spent any time with her, Daniel thought. Beauty only excused so much. But the guard was blissfully ignorant of her detractions as, dazed by lust, he said, "Mr. Hobbs," amazingly without drooling. "He leases the top five floors of this building for his brokerage firm."

"I know Preston Hobbs," Daniel said. "Call up there."

Vivi smiled and nodded, and the guard picked up the phone without any further urging. "There's a guy down here, claims he knows Mr. Hobbs," he said into the phone, his eyes never leaving Vivi's face.

"Daniel Pierce," Daniel said quietly so as not to break his focus.

The guard repeated the name, then hung up the phone, a measure of respect creeping into his attitude. "Elevator One," he said, "you can go up."

Daniel felt Vivi slip her hand into his again and take off, so that he had no choice but to go with her or fall over. They ran into the hallway leading to the elevators just as the lobby doors burst open.

"Hey," the guard shouted, "you can't come in—"

Zzzzzzzzzzzzzt.

Daniel looked over his shoulder and saw the hit men Taser the guard. He ducked into the second elevator and back out almost immediately, diving into Elevator One as bullets smashed into the marble wall behind him.

"What was that all about?" Vivi demanded as the doors slid shut and the elevator hummed into motion.

"Slammed my fist into the control panel," he said, pausing to catch his breath. "I managed to light up at least a half dozen. If we're lucky, it'll leave without the hit men, but even if they make it on, they're going to have to stop at several floors on the way up."

Her breath whooshed out, and she leaned against the back of the elevator, closing her eyes.

Daniel reached over and felt the back of her neck. She hunched her shoulders and tried to duck away. He let her turn into the corner, then stepped up behind her, thinking if they weren't face-to-face he could keep a lid on his hormones. That was before she looked over her shoulder, gave him a slow, sultry smile and said, "Kinky" in a voice that was one-tenth humor and nine-tenths aural sex. "Want me to spread 'em?"

"I'm not looking for weapons." He took her arm, turned her around and ran his hands down between her breasts, not noticing her curves, the warmth of her skin beneath the loose T-shirt, the way she trembled under his touch—

"Are you done?"

His gaze jumped to hers, and when he noticed his hands were resting on either side of her rib cage he pulled them away and stuck them in his pockets. They weren't quite steady.

"I'm here to keep you alive, not provide a cheap thrill," she said, too wrapped up in her own upheaval to notice his.

"I was looking for wires," he said. "Either you're working with someone or you can see the future."

"Door Number Two."

"Shit," Daniel said under his breath. "You're that kook who kept calling my office."

"I'm not a kook. If you'd bothered to talk to me you'd know that."

"I'm talking to you now, and I think you're a kook."

"That's because you forced me to kidnap you."

Daniel turned to stare at her. "I forced you?"

"Yes." She sighed as the floor numbers climbed into double digits. "But I knew you would."

"Of course you did. There's just one problem. I don't believe in psychics."

"Tell me something I don't know."

"According to you that's not possible."

"I don't know how you got to be this way, Ace."

Daniel limited himself to a visual reply.

Judging by Vivi's expression, she got the message. There'd be a reckoning. If they lived long enough.

The elevator stopped, the doors whooshed open and they raced out, running through the maze of cubicles and offices, heading for the far end. That, Daniel figured, was where the executive office would be, and the executive office would be where they'd find the stairs to the roof.

When they got there, Daniel locked the door behind them and jammed a chair under the knob. "Won't hold them long," he said, hoping like hell they were in the right place, because if they weren't he'd just signed their death sentence.

"Well?" Vivi said, standing by the middle of three doors behind the massive desk that dominated the room.

Daniel hunched his shoulders, disgusted with himself for feeling relieved because the *psychic* wasn't second-guessing his decisions. But sure enough, when he pulled open the door marked EXIT it felt like they were standing at the end of a wind tunnel. They could already hear the sound of the helicopter, and when they'd navigated the flight of concrete stairs, they found it waiting, blades rotating, ready to take off.

Daniel went across the roof, half hunched over. He checked to make sure Vivi was behind him, then pulled open the side door of the helicopter.

Cassandra Shaw Scott Hanson Martindale Winston Hobbs looked out at him. "Come right in," she shouted over the whine of the blades. "I'll be happy to take you anywhere you'd like." Her gaze shifted to Vivi. "But not her."

"WE HAVE TO MAKE THE CALL."

"No."

The elevator dinged, the doors opened, the first of seven lights on the panel went out.

"This thing's going south, Hatch."

"And who's fault might that be, now?" Hatch said, his broad Boston accent mixed with a trace of Ireland in the phrasing, the combination marking him as a Southie.

"It's nobody's fault," Flip said. He and Hatch had grown up side by side in South Boston, considered and rejected all forms of legitimate employment, and gone the easy route—which wasn't so easy at the moment. In fact, it could get downright ugly.

"It's our fault," Hatch corrected Flip. "That'll be how it shakes out."

The elevator went through its ding/open doors/light out routine again. Flip jammed his hands on his hips and huffed out a breath, tapping one foot impatiently.

"Asshole," Hatch said. "We're not going to make it to the roof before Pierce does. If he wangles a ride on that bird, it's all over for us."

"Wangles?"

Hatch repeated his character-assessing commentary without losing his train of thought. "If You Know Who finds out about this before we report it, we'll be nothing more than a couple of cheap headstones and fond tears in our mothers' eyes."

"The only thing my old lady ever cried over was an empty bottle," Flip griped.

"I'll take that as a yes," Hatch said. He pulled out his cell phone, waited until the elevator went through its bump-and-grind routine and his bodily orifices unlocked, then dialed.

"Hello." The voice was female and pleasant. Hatch knew it was only a come-on, like a worm on a hook. And he had no choice but to bite.

"I need to talk to—"

"I'll put you right through."

Best to get it over with, he thought, barely waiting for the next voice to come on the line before he launched into a rundown of the night's events. The debacle at the bachelor auction was met with "botched," the hide-and-seek game in the parking lot termed "incompetent," and the fact that they were seconds from a rooftop helicopter of indeterminate origin was met with a long, stony silence that had Hatch thinking of frostbite. Or being shot in the head and stuffed into a walk-in freezer.

The elevator hit the top floor, finally. The doors opened on an expansive office space, beautifully appointed, sparsely lighted, completely devoid of human life. Pierce and the woman he was with were nowhere in sight, but Hatch knew from the slight vibration buzzing through his feet that the helicopter was still on the roof.

He knew by the words coming through the phone that they weren't going to see it firsthand.

"There's no telling who owns that helicopter," the boss said in the same kind of broadly accented, Irish-shadowed voice, "but it'll be one of them rich, better-than-thou Beacon Hill snobs."

Hatch decided that was obvious—and best kept to himself. The fact that it would take a crowbar to pry his jaw open could only be a benefit.

"Back off" was the terse instruction. "And Hatch?"

"Um-hmmm," he managed to force out.

"Fuck up again and it'll be the last time."

chapter
4

DANIEL SHOUTED SOMETHING TO THE SECOND PER-
son in the helicopter, keeping one eye on the stairway to
the office door.

Vivi didn't bother with the office. There was no need,
for one thing, and she was busy staring back at Cassandra
Hobbs for the other. It was childish, but Vivi refused to be
intimidated. Cassandra might have the power to leave her
stranded on the roof like a shooting gallery duck, but at
least she looked away first. The fact that she crossed her
arms and huffed her way into a sulk made it even more
childishly amusing. Too bad it only lasted until the other
passenger touched Cassandra's arm and said something
along the lines of letting Vivi into the helicopter.

Vivi deduced that because Daniel wrapped his hands
around her waist and boosted her up and in, following
close behind so she had no choice but to scoot into the
other seat. She picked up the headphones lying there before she sat down, slipping them over her ears and taking
stock of the woman in the seat across from her—clearly
Cassandra's daughter, in looks if not in temperament.

Same fine-boned features, same slender build, completely different attitude. The younger woman watched her with a long, level gaze that was less bug-under-glass and more wait-and-see.

"Alex Scott," she said once they'd had a chance to size each other up. "Your former hostage is my mother."

Vivi took the hand she offered, the handshake as firm and no-nonsense as Alex's demeanor. It was nice that she wasn't automatically resenting Vivi for her mother's sake, but she wasn't accepting her either. Vivi could respect that. And she could be just as big a person. "I'm sorry you had to be handcuffed," she said to Cassandra. "I just couldn't think of any other way to—"

"Kidnap this poor man?"

"Save his life."

Cassandra looked out the window, making a big show of studying the empty rooftop. "From whom?"

"The two guys with guns who were chasing us," Daniel said, then instructed the pilot to lift off.

"Not so fast," Alex countermanded. "If there are men with guns—"

"They're gone." Vivi's comment netted her a warning look from Daniel. Like that was going to keep her quiet. She opened her mouth. He gave her another look and she had second thoughts that went something along the lines of *best to let him run the show. For the moment.*

"I don't know if they're gone, but I'm pretty sure we're out of danger," he said, switching his attention back to Alex and notching his expression down to pleasant—or as close as he could get. "Shooting me would get some press and the attention of the FBI. Shooting down a helicopter that's almost surely carrying someone wealthy and well connected would be monumental stupidity. Aside from the FBI, the FAA, and the press, there's no telling who else would decide to get involved."

Alex mulled that over for a moment, calm and deliberate, before she instructed the pilot to lift off. Whether it was her own judgment or Daniel's she was bowing to, she'd be just the kind of woman who would appeal to a man like him. Vivi didn't let herself wonder why it set her teeth on edge. "Weren't you bidding on him at the auction?" she asked Alex.

"Only to save him from the man-eaters in there. We haven't known each other for long, but I like to think we're friends."

Daniel returned Alex's smile. "Any more than that, and I wouldn't have to wonder who's trying to kill me," he said. "I didn't know you and Tag were in town. You shouldn't be."

"Try telling him that," Alex said, then gave Vivi a bare-bones explanation. "Tag was an FBI agent. We met on a case. Daniel is prosecuting it."

"Not if my witnesses don't make it to the stand," he said. "The two of you should get out of Boston. Especially with what happened tonight."

Alex leaned forward and wrapped her hand around his wrist. "You think Anthony Sappresi is behind this?"

"No. Sappresi's a lot of things, but he's not a fool. Killing me would just get him a new prosecutor. Taking out the witnesses, that would destroy my case."

"I won't let someone like Sappresi scare me."

"Don't be scared, be cautious."

Alex sat back, her expression mulish. She didn't look like she was inclined to take his advice. Vivi had no choice. She'd stopped breathing at the mention of Tony Sappresi's name, to the point where she was seeing black spots. Thank God nobody was paying attention to her at the moment, was all she could think, especially Daniel.

"If Tony the Sap would have an FBI agent killed," he was saying to Alex, "a witness is small change."

"Tag isn't worried, although I wouldn't have had to go to the auction if I'd stayed in Africa."

Her smile seemed to take Daniel off guard, enough that he relaxed back into his seat and went with the change of subject. "You're still hoping she'll ditch Tag and marry someone normal?" he said to Cassandra.

"You're still single, I believe."

"Sure, but it takes a gun to get him out on a date," Alex said.

"Only if it's a lunatic who claims to be abducting me for my own good."

Alex popped up a brow. "You appear to be having a lot of fun for someone who's been abducted at gunpoint by a lunatic."

Daniel crossed his arms, refusing to dignify that with a denial. Not that it would be a very convincing denial. He *was* having fun. It'd been a long time since he'd felt so . . . alive. The excitement of being in the field again, that's all it was. Nothing to do with the woman in the seat beside him, he assured himself, resisting a sidelong glance in her direction.

"I know how you dislike these things," Cassandra said, waiting politely for him to focus on her again. "I was so grateful you agreed to participate. I didn't want you to have an unpleasant experience, so I suggested Alex bid on you."

"He already had it arranged," Vivi said. "The redhead."

"I didn't realize you knew Patrice Hanlon," Alex said.

Cassandra sniffed and muttered something that sounded like, "New money," but no one was paying attention to her.

"She was involved with my last case as an agent," Daniel said. A case that had caused her considerable personal grief since it had been her brother who'd ended up with a life term in prison.

She hadn't held it against him, though. Over the years, Patrice had come to be not just a friend, but a valuable resource on the Irish mob, her family having once been prominently involved. The fact that she wanted more than friendship wasn't lost on Daniel. But he'd managed to pretend it was.

The conversation had hit a lull, which was fine with him, except for the way Alex was studying Vivi. "So where is Donovan tonight?" he asked before she could take the discussion in a direction he didn't want it to go.

"Tag is off doing something with his family. I'm boycotting them until they stop asking when we're getting married." Her gaze cut to her mother's, one eyebrow lifting. Whatever Cassandra had been about to say, she thought better of it.

Daniel had to admire her control. There'd been a time—not too long ago—when, if not for Tag Donovan, Daniel might have tried his luck with Alex Scott. She was beautiful, well connected, and most of her conversation consisted of facial expressions and body language. When she actually spoke, she never minced words, and she didn't wait around for a man to read her mind. She made her thoughts and feelings known in no uncertain terms.

Vivi was nothing if not cryptic. Sure, she was beautiful, and sexy, but in the short time he'd spent with her, she'd been contrary, unreasonable, frustrating, and irritating. He didn't care for the way she kept cocking her head and gazing off into thin air, either. It was creepy. And she was too damn calm. People were shooting at them; she should have been panicky and clinging. Not that he wanted her to cling. The last thing he needed in his life was a helpless woman. Unless it was one with a hidden agenda.

Her eyes snapped back into focus, and she smiled a little, looking smug when she caught him staring. He hated smug.

"Drop us off in the park," Cassandra instructed the pilot, "then take Mr. Pierce and his . . . friend anywhere he wants to go."

Almost before she finished, the pilot started his descent into a park not far from the Fairmont—still within Boston city limits.

Vivi was clearly puzzled.

"Mother likes to arrive at these events in a manner befitting her station," Alex explained.

Cassandra waved that off with a perfectly manicured hand and a supercilious expression. "I simply prefer not to wait in traffic."

The helicopter set down. Alex climbed out and the driver of a waiting limo helped Cassandra to the ground. Vivi tried to slip out immediately after the other two women. Daniel took her by the arm and pulled her back in, holding on while the limo driver shut the door.

"Sorry you gave that cop his gun back?" Daniel asked, seeing the look in her eyes.

"I've done what I wanted to do. I'll go and—"

"Get arrested."

The pilot broke in over the headphones, asking where they wanted to go. "The FBI building in D.C.," Daniel said. "Call Mike Kovaleski, tell him Daniel Pierce is on the way in. He'll okay it."

A flare of panic crossed Vivi's face before she hid it.

Daniel almost felt sorry for her. Almost. "It's either the Boston P.D. or the feds."

"Or you could let me go, seeing as I saved your life."

"You pulled a gun on a U.S. attorney, not to mention the Boston cop and the wife of a very influential man. The locals aren't going to care that there were two hit men after me. The feds are your get-out-of-jail-free card."

"Why would you want to help me?"

Daniel sat back and looked out the window. "I'm asking myself that same question."

"VIVIENNE FOSTER, AKA VIVIENNE TOTCHKA, AKA Madame Totchka. Oh, sorry, that's the grandmother's alias. Not that it makes a difference." Mike Kovaleski pushed back from the computer, not his favorite tool no matter how much data it spit out, or how fast. He missed the days when information didn't travel at the speed of light, the bad guys didn't commit crimes without ever leaving their newly— and loosely—democratic countries, and the geeks weren't running the world. "No known groups or affiliations."

"How about cults?"

"None of those either," Mike said. "But I don't trust her."

"Of course not," Daniel said, "she's Russian."

"They're just lulling us into a false sense of security," Mike maintained. "Soon as we let down our guard, *bam*."

"Back to communism?"

"I'm just saying."

"Right, not letting my guard down."

"Wise-ass. That's what happens when you go to law school instead of sticking it out here."

"Not exactly my choice," Daniel reminded him.

"Yeah, dumb fucks upstairs with their medical reports and insurance advisors. Probably don't have a dick between them, and if they did they couldn't find it with a flashlight and a book on anatomy."

Daniel grinned, flipping the chair in front of Mike's desk to one side so he could get off his bad leg and keep Vivi in sight while Mike kept muttering things like "putting people out to pasture," and "pencil-neck college boys with manuals for brains."

They were in Mike's glass-fronted office, in the FBI building, surrounded by agents and researchers and the people who cleaned the floors, which was mostly who was there at that time of night. But still, it was a pretty safe place to be when somebody was trying to kill you. If you hadn't brought one of the lunatics along.

His eyes were drawn back to the lunatic in question, but he wasn't feeling threatened. There was still that little spike of lust when he looked at her, but mostly what he felt was relief. She'd gotten him out of an uncomfortable situation, after all, being auctioned off like a side of beef. And okay, the way she'd gone about it left something to be desired, but damn, he thought, looking around, it was good to be back, even under these circumstances. Hell, who was he kidding, especially under these circumstances. Nothing like a halfway decent death threat to make his day.

"I don't think she's dangerous," he said, his eyes still on Vivi. She turned around and looked at him, like she'd done every time he'd thought of her.

"Apparently she leaves a hell of an impression, though."

Daniel wiped the smile off his face and gave Mike his full attention.

"She's been in some trouble," Mike continued, squinting

at his computer screen long enough to refresh his memory. "One arrest, charges dropped."

"Fraud?"

"Yeah. Not one of your more violent crimes. I think you're right about her potential threat level."

"She didn't hold you at gunpoint."

"You telling me you were afraid of that little slip of a thing? With that face? And that body?"

"Want to check for a staple in her navel?"

"Not Hugh Hefner," Mike pointed out unnecessarily, then ran down the non–Playboy Bunny facts they knew about her, which wasn't much. "She knows how to use a gun, and she claims to be a mind reader, which we both know is a load of hooey."

Daniel nodded, thinking hooey was a pretty good way to put it. But . . . "She knew there was a hit out on me."

"Yeah." Mike managed to convey a lot with that one word. But then Mike had been his handler, and Daniel figured they'd worked together long enough to both be asking the same questions and drawing the same conclusions.

Like once they ruled out clairvoyance, ESP, gut feeling, and guesswork, the only thing left was direct knowledge. But from whom? How involved was she, and why warn him?

"Ran a check after you called me from the helicopter," Mike said. "Nothing on the taps, nothing in the air, no rumors. Far's I know you're completely off the radar of anyone who'd·want you dead. Or at least they're not talking about it. 'Cept to her."

"She put her own life on the line," Daniel felt a need to remind them both.

"True enough," Mike said, "so what's in it for her?"

"Maybe she was just doing a good deed."

"Fraud with a heart of gold?" Mike snorted. "I don't buy that psychic crap, and neither do you. The only way she could've known there was a contract out on you is if she heard it firsthand from the author or the contractor."

Mike was right, Daniel knew it, but it didn't sit well.

Vivi Foster didn't seem like the sort of woman who'd be mixed up in the kind of criminal activity that would involve killing a federal prosecutor. Then again, she didn't look like someone who'd bilk innocent people out of their hard-earned money—even when they asked for it. But she'd copped to that much.

"Any way you look at it," Mike said, "she's dirty."

Daniel couldn't have agreed more, but his version of dirty had nothing to do with rap sheets or criminal activity. His version of dirty would have broken decency laws in about thirty states and gotten them both arrested. Without realizing he'd turned, his eyes met hers and there was heat there, and knowledge. And a challenge. *Bring it on, Ace,* she was saying, *but don't expect an easy victory.*

Something flared inside him, something he hadn't felt in a long time. Lust, he decided, for her, for the chase. Especially for the chase. If she understood anything about him, she'd know a good pursuit would be more of an aphrodisiac to him than anything else in the world . . .

Of course, he thought, however she'd discovered it, she knew that about him. And she was using it. "She can't be trusted," he said, "but that doesn't give us cause to hold her."

"The gun gives us cause."

"There's more to be gained from letting her go. Call off the Boston P.D."

Mike blew out a breath, scrubbing his hands back through his marine-cut hair. "I'll take care of it. All of it."

VIVI SAT OUTSIDE OF MIKE SOMEBODY-SKI'S OFFICE, thoughts muddled, nerves jumping, hopped up on adrenaline and having a hard time working past any of it long enough to get some halfway decent impressions. Except the ones that came through her physical senses.

Daniel and the fed were in a closed room and far enough away to keep her from hearing much of anything, so her ears were no use. That just left her eyes, which was a problem. Not because her chair was situated to put her back to the windows. But because every so often she'd glanced over her shoulder, and each time her eyes had met Daniel's. That was where the trouble started.

She ought to be seizing the chance to get a read on him. But there was the physical jolt to get past first, that instant buzz of attraction she couldn't prevent no matter how she braced herself. Before she knew it, she'd be thinking about how amazing he looked in a tuxedo—or rather half out of it.

His jacket hung open, and he had a really, really good body. Muscular. Everywhere. She liked that he'd lost the tie and undone the top couple of shirt buttons. She liked that he had chest hair, not so much that she had an urge to ask him if he hibernated in the winter, but enough to make her wonder how it would feel under her palms. She liked his five-o'clock shadow; she liked the way his limp gave him just enough vulnerability; she even liked the way he looked at her like she was crazy.

She loved the way his hands felt on her.

She could still feel the slide of his fingers, the heat of his palms burning her alive even through the thin, maddening cloth of her T-shirt, almost as hot as his eyes when they went all intense, as if she were the only other person in the world. If he so much as kissed her with that kind of focus, she'd never be the same again, and if they made love . . .

But they wouldn't be making love, or kissing, or even touching again, for that matter. They weren't going to see each other after tonight if Daniel had his way. That much was clear from the way he was watching her. It wasn't particularly pleasant, or reassuring, even though she tried to remind herself that at least he had a sense of humor.

The other guy was another story. The other guy was a humor black hole. He was watching her, too, except he looked like he was posing for Mount Rushmore. She turned back around, and though she knew there was no way he was still staring at the back of her head, physically it felt like he'd reached out, curled a hand around the nape of her neck, and was squeezing. It didn't take a psychic to know why.

For starters they'd gotten her name out of her. Not that she'd fought very hard to keep it a secret, and even though she'd given them the legal one, Vivienne Foster, she knew they'd find the business alias she used. That being the case, they'd have read her police record. Even that didn't bother her; the worst of her past wasn't in there anyway.

What bothered her was the certainty that Daniel and his FBI straight man were using her history as an excuse to treat her like the enemy. Not that it surprised her.

She looked over her shoulder, met Daniel's eyes, and felt like she'd caught fire. She didn't know how he'd gotten from suspicion to sex but there was no question what was on his mind, and now that she'd tuned into it, she had no choice but to let it run its course. It didn't take long. Daniel went from lust back to mistrust with a speed that made Vivi envy his self-control, especially as she couldn't match it. She spent a little more time battling back her libido. The most she could manage was a slow simmer, and she got there none too soon.

The door beside her opened, and she shot out of the chair, whipping around to find Daniel, looking grim, just closing the door behind himself. The other guy was still sitting behind his desk, doing his imitation of granite.

Daniel wrapped his hand around her elbow and escorted her away from Mike's office.

"Where are we going?"

"Just follow me and keep quiet—and you might want to be grateful the FBI isn't arresting you."

"Why aren't they?" she asked because she figured he'd expect it.

"Let's just say warning me about the hit men balanced out the rest of it."

And they planned to have her followed, hoping to find out how she'd known about the attempt. "Doubters," she muttered.

"Still sticking to your mind-reading con?" he asked, stopping at the first bank of elevators they came across.

"Are you so sure it's a con?"

"The people who sued you thought it was."

She followed him onto the elevator, watched him punch the button for the ground floor. "The people who sued me heard things they didn't like."

"And the ones who arrested you?"

"Were cops." Which said it all, as far as she was concerned. Cops were taught to believe only what they saw with their own eyes and heard with their own ears. So were FBI agents and lawyers.

She'd learned as a child, at the foot of her gypsy grandmother, that Don Quixote might have been noble, but he'd been a fool, too. Unfortunately, she needed Daniel to believe her, so she had no choice but to tilt. "People come to psychics because they want to know if they're going to fall in love, or strike it rich, or get that dream job, but they don't really want to hear the truth. They want me to reassure them that everything's going to be okay, no matter what I see."

"And you always tell the absolute truth."

"Do you?" she shot back. "You never get up in front of a jury and skew the facts to make a defendant look even more heinous? You never omit evidence that doesn't bolster your own case?"

"I'm trying to get criminals off the street."

"And I'm trying to be as honest as I can." Except for those rare occasions when she saw something horrible in someone's future. She couldn't bring herself to make predictions about death. Instead she tried to steer the subject away from that particular path. Except in Daniel's case.

"Making a prediction means handing someone the knowledge to change their own future," she said. Or not. In her visions, she'd seen Daniel die in the Oval Room during the bachelor auction. Clearly that hadn't happened. It didn't mean she'd altered the ultimate outcome. "Revealing what I see today doesn't mean it will come to pass, but it doesn't prevent anything, either."

"That's a handy dodge."

"Spoken like a true skeptic."

"You have an alias," he pointed out, as if that justified his disbelief.

"I use my grandmother's name in the shop because it makes good business sense not to have to build a new reputation."

"Doesn't make it any less dishonest."

Big surprise, she thought. The elevator dinged for the first floor, the door opened, and Daniel got off, clearly expecting her to follow. She did, of course. What other choice was there?

"You've been arrested," he felt a need to remind her, "and sued."

"And your point is?"

"It doesn't say much for your rate of return."

"I'm not a mutual fund."

"What you do isn't all that far off."

"Being arrested and sued has nothing to do with my 'rate of return.' People get predictably angry when I don't tell them what they want to hear." And some of them weren't in possession of the most stable psyche's to begin with. Best, she decided, not to point that out to Pierce.

"So tell them only good things."

"Now you're suggesting that I lie? What would that do to my rate of return?"

Daniel apparently felt that was a rhetorical question because all he did was turn down another boring corridor, one that led to a back entrance. Or maybe it was a side entrance. Either way there was a man in a black suit waiting there, young enough to be stuck with babysitting duty, old enough to have learned comportment from Daniel's friend upstairs.

"This agent will make sure you get back to Boston," Daniel said.

Vivi caught him by the sleeve and hauled him to a stop. "You're just letting me go?"

"Yep."

"And the Boston P.D. isn't going to show up at my door?"

"Only if they're selling tickets to their annual ball. But I'd steer clear of Officer Cranston if I were you."

"You're going to take precautions, right?" she asked him.

"Yeah. Taking precautions."

He curled his hand around her wrist, and for once she had no trouble ignoring the skin-to-skin tingle. "I went to a lot of trouble to save your life."

"Okay, but it's my life."

"But—"

"Good-bye." Just to be sure she got the message, he transferred her wrist to the other guy's hand, then turned on his heel and walked away.

As if it was his decision to make.

chapter
5

DANIEL'S GUT WAS TALKING, BIG-TIME, AND WHAT
it said was, "trouble." It didn't stop him from following
through with his plans. After all, he'd been feeling some
level of alarm since the moment Vivienne Foster had bull-
dozed her way into his life and told him he was up for a hit.
And then two guys had tried to kill him.

He hated to admit it, but he was spooked, over the woman
more than the hit. Having a target hanging on his back was
nothing new. Being stalked by an obviously deranged woman
who claimed to be a psychic in order to hide her connection
to whoever wanted him dead was.

And he'd decided not to think of Vivienne Foster tonight. Or ever again—

"This is you taking precautions, Ace?"

—which was pretty hard to do with her sneaking up behind him. "Still in stalker mode, I see."

"No FBI tail," she said, sticking to her own agenda,
"you aren't armed—that I can see anyway—and you're on
foot in South Boston."

"I have a date."

"With a bullet? 'Cause this would be a good place to get in the way of one."

She had a point. An FBI shadow wasn't going to prevent him from catching a bullet, though. Neither was the clutch piece strapped to his ankle, but it was reassuring. Having Mata Hari following him wasn't. He didn't know if she brought the trouble with her or just showed up at the same time, either way it was the wrong neighborhood to be tempting fate. She was right about that much.

Some of South Boston had been invaded by young professionals, but it was still a stronghold for what was left of the Irish mob, which was constantly at war with the Italian Mafia to see who was going to run the Boston underworld. The war had been at a slow simmer for the last couple of decades, the Italians running drugs and numbers in their neighborhoods while the Irish families carved up chunks of South Boston and held them by right of might. It was an uneasy peace, elastic, stretching to allow a wily and enterprising man to make his way to the top, snapping back to crush those who weren't worthy.

Daniel and Vivi were walking through one of those chunks, a narrow South Boston street crowded with old brick buildings. Maybe not the wisest choice to be on foot, but he wasn't expecting another attack. This engagement wasn't on his calendar, work or home, and no one else knew he was here except the woman he'd come to meet. And Vivi Foster apparently, which pretty much destroyed his confidence, since there was no way of knowing who'd told her where to find him.

"You're wondering how I knew where you'd be tonight."

"Let me guess, the voices in your head told you?"

"They're not really voices, they're more . . . impressions, suggestions. They help me to get in touch with whatever feeling I'm having."

"I'm in touch with a couple of feelings right now."

"Then there's my grandmother," she continued with a

you-asked-so-spare-me-the-sarcasm shrug. "I actually talk to her a lot."

Daniel's eyes cut to hers, he couldn't help himself. "Your grandmother is haunting you?"

"She's not jumping out of dark corners shouting 'Boo!' if that's what you're asking. She doesn't even talk back. It's more of a Jiminy Cricket sort of thing. You know, a conscience, like I ask myself what would Madame Totchka do in this situation? And it helps guide me. Unless I have a vision, which is what happened in your case. There's not much interpretation required with a vision, just figuring out who, where, and what. And 'what' isn't usually a problem, either. Especially not with you."

"I take it back. You're not just a kook, you're crazy." And she was trying to draw him into her insanity. "There's medication for that, you know."

"Predictable," she observed.

"Is there any way I can convince you to go away?"

"You could get a restraining order, but you won't."

Nope, Daniel thought immediately, not his style. Restraining orders were for people who didn't have any other resources or skills. Women with drunken exes got TROs, so did kids being bullied in school . . . He caught Vivi's smug little grin and scowled. "There are other ways to deal with stalkers."

"You could shoot me," she said, "but you don't have a gun—at least not one you can get to easily. You could pick me up and stuff me into a cab, but cabs don't frequent this neighborhood."

"I could carjack the next slow-moving vehicle, drive you out to some rural area, and hope you can't find your way back."

"Hmmm, the unwanted puppy treatment. Might work if the carjacking portion of the program didn't go against everything you stand for."

"Breaking the law seems like a small adjustment to make in your case."

"You don't make small adjustments, Ace. You don't make any adjustments. That's one of your problems."

Vivi Foster was the only problem he had at the moment. "How about if I ask nicely? Would you go away then?"

"I might, if your teeth weren't clenched. And if you actually asked me."

Daniel unlocked his jaw. "Would you please stop following me?"

She didn't say anything, but a glance at her face answered his question. She was bubble gum on the bottom of his shoe. Until he found a way to scrape her off.

He turned a corner, slowing as he came to a storefront pub in the middle of the block. Despite its rundown appearance, Cohan's had people spilling out the doorway and congregating on the sidewalk in the early evening twilight.

"You're not eating here," Vivi said.

Daniel ignored her, fighting his way inside and taking a moment to familiarize himself, and not just with the furniture. Some of the waitstaff—the male waitstaff since the mob hadn't heard of equal opportunity—would be armed, though you'd never know it to look at them. There'd be armed guys in the kitchen, too, who weren't even trying to blend in. And no one was getting past the dragon at the front door without her permission.

"Pierce," she repeated when he gave her his name. Her voice was blurred by the lilt of Ireland and heavy with displeasure, "that'd be English, wouldn't it?"

"It's American," Daniel said. "I'm looking for Patrice Hanlon."

The glare cooled down to subarctic.

Vivi caught him by the arm. "You can't have dinner here. This place is a gang stronghold. Half the waiters are carrying guns."

"I'm aware of that. The question is: How are you? Grandma spill the beans?"

She snorted softly. "Their suits could be cut a little more generously."

"Not much of a deterrent if people don't know they're packing."

"But—"

"I'm having dinner here. You're not."

"But—"

"Prosecutor!"

They both turned toward that booming voice. A tall, stocky, ginger-haired man in his late forties strode toward them, a huge smile on his broad, freckled face, and a shrewd glint in his blue eyes. He held out a hand wide as a dinner plate.

Daniel took it, shifting so he stood in front of Vivi. No point, he told himself, in anyone making a connection between the two of them—although he didn't take the time to ask himself why he'd rather she stayed unmarked by a man known to use whatever weapon fell into his hands in order to get what he wanted.

He went through the whole who-can-squeeze-harder routine, more for the sake of his bones than his ego, giving all his attention to the man trying to crush his hand. It wasn't wise to do otherwise. "Flynn," he said by way of acknowledgment.

"What brings you to our humble establishment?"

"Lawyers have to eat, just like everyone else."

"Not having Italian for supper tonight?"

"I'm saving up."

Joe Flynn let out a laugh that drowned out even the prodigious noise of the Irish crowd. "You get a guilty verdict for that wop bastard, Tony Sappresi, you can eat free in South Boston for the rest of your life. Give that son of a bitch a one-way ticket to the federal pen and you can write your own check in this city. You've a hankerin' for City Hall, or just to be a hero in Washington, it's yours."

"That didn't work out so well for John Connolly," Daniel said, referring to the FBI agent who'd used Irish mob boss Whitey Bulger as an informant back in the '80s. Not such a bad plan, if not for Connolly's looking the other way while

Whitey broke every city, state, and federal law on the books, then tipping him off before he could be arrested. Whitey had never been caught; Connolly hadn't fared so well.

"You want to think about your future, Pierce. Boston'll be a cold city for someone dense enough to piss off the Mafia and the mob, too. My boys're lookin' kindly on you at the moment, seein' as you're removin' a thorn from our side—"

"Your boys? You must be talking about the handful of thugs who steal cars and terrorize little old ladies for you, because there's no way the mob families will line up behind one leader. Too many egos."

Flynn held his gaze a moment, then laughed. "Things change, Boyo. You'd best keep that in mind." He glanced over at Patrice, smile gone, the sparkle in his Irish blue eyes turned to a hard glitter. "Your friend is waitin' for you."

"Still no love lost, I see." Patrice's maiden name was Flynn; Joe was her uncle. And Bobby, her brother, had been the reason Daniel had almost died seven years before.

Patrice had lined up on the side of law and order, not taking an active enough part to testify against her own brother, but trying to make amends for the fact that it was Bobby's bullets that had narrowly missed Daniel's heart and shattered the bone in his left thigh. It might as well have been Patrice who'd shot him, she took it that personally.

Any other family would have modeled their behavior after hers. Patrice's family labeled her a traitor.

Daniel hadn't been any happier to have her hovering over him day and night. He'd been in pain all of the time, and pissed off about everything. It had been awkward to have a constant reminder of the unwanted detour his life was taking. It had been even worse the day word came down that Bobby Flynn had died, victim of a jailhouse execution, less than two years into a life stretch. By then, Daniel had given up trying to kick Patrice Hanlon out of his life. By then, she'd become the closest thing he had to a friend.

It still didn't sit easy on Daniel, but he couldn't avoid the label—and it was better than the one Patrice wanted.

"She's got balls showing up here, I'll give her that," Joe said. "Best watch who you socialize with, Counselor."

"I'll take that as a threat."

Joe measured him for a moment, then boomed out another laugh and walked away, slapping backs, shaking hands, looking for all the world like a man running for office.

Judging by what he'd said, he was, but there wouldn't be campaign speeches and polls in this kind of election, and anyone stupid enough to vote "no" wouldn't live to fill out a ballot. If Flynn was successful in uniting the Irish mob, God help the city of Boston.

"Who was that?" Vivi wanted to know.

Daniel let his head drop to his chest. "Just when I managed to forget you were here."

"It looked like he was threatening you," she said, still in one-track-mind mode.

"And you're wondering if he tried to have me killed the other night."

"It crossed my mind."

"Joe Flynn doesn't want me dead. As long as I'm prosecuting Tony Sappresi, this is probably the safest place I can be in the city."

She didn't look convinced, and she wasn't getting his point.

"So you can go home. Unless you want to answer some questions."

She rolled her eyes. "Are we back to that again?"

"Yeah, and we'll keep coming back to it until you tell me how you knew there'd be a murder attempt two nights ago."

"I told you already. No matter how many times you ask the question the answer is going to be the same."

Impressions and visions, she meant, probably with a little bit of Grandma thrown into the mix. Daniel would have rolled his eyes, but he wasn't sure how to take her anymore. If she'd wanted him to believe her, she would have come up with a more convincing line than "the spirits told me," because that sounded crazy, and she didn't seem crazy—most of the time. But if she was crazy, she'd probably be hearing voices and think they were real when they told her he was about to be killed, and she'd be crazy enough to try to warn him. But that would mean she wasn't crazy because the voices were right about the murder attempt . . .

"I'm sorry I asked," he said, his head beginning to hurt from trying to squeeze an ounce of logic out of a sea of insanity.

"I told you you wouldn't believe me."

"And I told you to go home, but you're still hanging around. I'd say that makes us even." He turned to find that the dragon at the door had switched to hostess mode. She was waiting patiently for him, a menu in her hand, new respect in her attitude. She probably wasn't the only one in the place to have noted Joe Flynn's warm greeting. And Daniel wasn't above taking advantage of it—in a strictly limited capacity.

"Miss Hanlon is right this way, Mr. Pierce," she said. "Will this young lady be joining you?"

"No." Daniel took the menu from her, and added, "I can find my own way."

"I guess I'll need a table for one then," Vivi said.

Daniel stopped, turning back to the hostess. "She's Russian," he said, and had the satisfaction of watching the dragon show her claws again, the Russian mob being even more hated by the Irish mob than the Italians.

By the time he made it to Patrice's table, a quick but thorough check of the place showed him Vivi had been evicted. Something told him he hadn't seen the last of her, and it wasn't coming from the spirit world. Sure, there was a voice in his head, but it was the voice of experience. The really fatalistic voice of experience.

* * *

COHAN'S WASN'T VERY BIG, BUT THEN FEW OF THE REally good, family-owned pubs in South Boston were. The front wall of the place consisted of windows, clear glass, curtainless, unadorned by expensive hand-lettering. Why waste the money when it was only a matter of time before someone got tossed through them? The inside was just as lackluster, one big room with the bar and kitchen at one end and the restrooms at the other. In between were tables crowded almost on top of one another, all of them occupied, the bar two-deep in serious drinkers.

The atmosphere grew murky away from the windows, a stew of dim lighting and smoke haze, not to mention a cacophony consisting of music, televised baseball, and heated conversation that involved violence on both sides of the Atlantic Ocean.

Cohan's served Irish food, Irish whiskey, and Irish politics. Before the uneasy peace on the Auld Sod, they'd have collected gun money for the IRA. Nowadays it was charity for the war orphans and widows left behind. It was the sort of place Daniel would've met an informant or chased a suspect into.

Patrice Hanlon was a paradox, at once clearly a member of this community with her auburn hair, creamy skin, and blue eyes. A closer study marked her as an outsider, clothing and shoes costing more than most of these people made in a week. She sat alone at a table for four, on the side with the banquette built against the wall. That left the seat across from her, or the seat beside her. Daniel hated having his back to the room. The alternative was worse than death.

"Patrice," he said, bending to give her a kiss on the cheek before he sat opposite her.

She covered her disappointment with a bright smile. "They're wondering if you're carrying. Or if you're my lawyer."

Daniel glanced around, noting the absence of conversation nearby, and the presence of speculation. "It's the suit." He shifted slightly, enough to let his jacket gape open and prove to the other diners that he wasn't armed. "I came straight from work."

"Even though you didn't want to."

"I shouldn't be here, and neither should you." He'd tried to explain that to her on the phone, but she'd been insistent. Since he knew firsthand just how stubborn she could be, he'd given in to the inevitable. That didn't mean they had to be there any longer than necessary.

"We're perfectly safe here," she said.

"You've been away for a long time."

"I still consider this my home, even though I wanted more."

And she'd gotten it. Married into it, rather briefly as she'd been widowed less than two years in. She'd decided to stay in that other world at first, and then she hadn't really had a choice . . .

"You're thinking of Bobby, aren't you?" She closed the menu, placing it just so on the table. "I could tell by the pity."

"It's not pity, it's regret. If I'd handled the situation differently, he never would have gotten a shot at me to begin with."

"You didn't have a choice. Neither did I. Bobby chose, and the rest of us had to react accordingly."

Not quite true, Daniel thought. He'd stumbled upon Bobby Flynn dealing to the neighborhood kids. He should have backed off, he should have let local law enforcement handle the situation. Instead he'd blundered in, determined to save at least a couple of youngsters from drug addiction. All he'd done was get himself shot and help Bobby Flynn graduate from small-time dealing to attempted murder. He'd ruined his own career, and ultimately he'd gotten Bobby killed.

"So . . . You haven't asked me why I was so determined to keep our date tonight." Patrice waited a beat, smiling at his reaction. "Your virtue is safe from me."

"My virtue is long gone."

"That's even better."

Okay, now he was beginning to get uncomfortable. "You were about to explain why we're here."

"You already met him," she said.

Daniel followed her gaze to the bar, where Joe Flynn was standing a group of men to a round of beers.

"He's moving to unite the mob," Patrice said, leaning forward to keep her voice down. "I thought you'd want to know, considering what happened the other night."

"Flynn said as much to me a few minutes ago," Daniel told her, "but I don't see what it has to do with the other night."

"Taking out an assistant U.S. attorney would buy a lot of street credibility."

"Owning one would be better, especially one who used to be an FBI agent. That's if he can even pull off a coup like uniting the mob, which I doubt."

"I wouldn't be so sure," Patrice said, sitting back in her seat. "He's making big promises. Some of the families are listening."

"Shit," Daniel said and would have apologized if he hadn't said it under his breath.

"He's talking about stepping into the void that'll be left when you put Tony Sappresi in jail."

This time Daniel kept his one-syllable reaction to himself. "I'm sure the Mafia has already decided how they're going to fill that void." Which, if Flynn got what he wanted, meant Boston was going to suffer a crime wave that would make the eighties seem like a grade-school dodge ball tournament. Most of the casualties would come from the ranks of organized crime, but a whole lot of innocent citizens could get caught in the line of fire.

"Isn't that the woman from the other night?"

"Huh?" Daniel focused on Patrice's face again, then twisted around to see what she was looking at. And there, peering in the front window of the pub, was Vivi. "Yeah," he said, facing forward again, even though he knew Patrice would be smirking at him. Instead, she laughed softly.

"What?" he asked her.

"Dinner theater. You're just full of surprises tonight, Daniel."

"I'm sorry."

"I like it."

"Great." He opened the menu, ignoring the tingle that told him Vivi was still staring at his back. "I'll memorize some Marx Brothers for next time."

chapter
6

"HEY THERE, GORGEOUS, HOW'S ABOUT HAVING A drink with me?"

"No."

"Dinner?"

"No."

"Well, if you're not hungry, and you're not thirsty . . ."

Vivi straightened up and turned around. "How about you go inside and get a sticky note, or a Magic Marker, or a bunch of half-cooked pasta, anything you can use to spell out the word *NO* in big letters on my back so I won't have to say it to another annoying . . . man," she finished, because "drunken Irishman," which was what she really wanted to say, would have gotten her yet more attention, but of a far worse variety.

The man held up his hands, palms out, backed slowly away, and said, "Don't get your knickers in a twist, luv, I was only askin'."

Him and about a dozen other guys. But at least this one hadn't wanted to know the going rate.

The blue jeans and plain white tank that had looked

casual and unremarkable in her mirror at home seemed to be acting like a "for sale" sign. True, the hem of the T-shirt and the waistband of the jeans didn't exactly come into contact, and both were fairly form-fitting, but no tighter than any other woman's in the vicinity, so why did she get singled out for hooker status . . . Okay, she knew the answer to that, but she wasn't blaming herself for this. She was blaming Daniel Pierce.

It didn't really matter what she wore, or what her bra size was. If not for Pierce she wouldn't be here, exposing herself to a bunch of beer-soaked walking libidos. And was Daniel grateful? No. He was distrustful and mean, not to mention stupidly overconfident. She'd saved his life once already, and what did he do? He sent her packing. Again. She ought to go, she thought, just walk away and let the arrogant, pig-headed, walking suspicion of a man deal with whatever the evening had in store for him.

The back of her neck prickled, and a ball of urgency formed in the pit of her stomach, making her nauseous at the idea of leaving Daniel to his fate.

She turned back to the window, muttering, "Give it a rest already, I'm staying," and cupping her hands around her face to cut the sunset glare.

Daniel was still sitting there across from the redhead who'd been bidding on him at the auction. Vivi didn't like it. She wasn't too happy about being chased out of the place by the old bat at the front door, either, but she really didn't care for Daniel being out in public like . . . this.

He ought to be at home, keeping a low profile, not sitting in a South Boston mobbed-up pub surrounded by armed waiters and facing a man-eating redhead who did him favors and looked at him like she was expecting repayment. Horizontally. Several times.

"Oy, Cupcake, how 'bout I buy you . . . dinner?"

Vivi glanced over and got a face full of beer breath, and a way too up-close look at a man about her height with fuzzy orange eyebrows and fuzzy orange muttonchop sideburns. That was the extent of his hair growth, except for a fuzzy red fringe around his bald pate. "Dipping into your pot of gold?"

"Wha'?"

"I think they're running out of beer."

His bleary eyes went wide, he drained the mug in his hand, and hustled back inside. Head down, leading with his beer glass, burrowing through the crowd spilling out of Cohan's front door.

Vivi watched him disappear, thinking maybe she shouldn't be so picky. Her love life was the closest thing to a practical incarnation of speed dating there was. Okay, the dates lasted more than eight minutes, but not much. Just until the guy she was dating discovered her . . . avocation. Not that she blamed them. The second a man suspected she knew what was going on inside him, especially when he wasn't quite sure himself, he ran in the other direction. True, most men didn't believe in her "abilities," but feelings were nothing to mess with.

She looked in the window again. Nothing had changed, except Daniel decided to turn around and scope out the place, including the front window and who might be peering through it. Vivi managed to fade back into the crowd, at least enough to keep Daniel from seeing her before she came up against something that wasn't moving and smelled like beer. The fuzzy-faced drunk, she discovered when she turned around.

"Why haven't you passed out yet?" she grumbled. "You look like you've drunk enough beer to fill Boston Harbor."

"There's plenty more where this came from." And in case she wasn't sure what "this" referred to he lifted his mug to show her, and beer sloshed onto his shoes. He peered down, brow furrowing all the way back to the nape of his neck.

"There's plenty more where that came from," she reminded him before he made an attempt at beer retrieval, "right in there."

He got that lightbulb-over-the-head look and started for Cohan's, turning back before he'd taken more than a step. "Hey, that's how you got rid of me last time."

"Really? Just by mentioning beer?"

He gazed down at his glass again, saw that it was below the halfway mark, and mumbled something about being right back.

Vivi watched him go, no second thoughts this time. First, she liked her men a bit taller—and less fuzzy. Second, he didn't have what it took to be a stalker. For starters, he needed to be able to concentrate longer than ten seconds. Probably his skills of concentration would improve as his beer intake went down, but that was a different problem. That was a problem she wasn't qualified to deal with. Another day or two of following Daniel Pierce around, and she could probably give lessons on how to be a stalker, but alcoholism would still be outside of her skill set.

She went back to her surveillance, just in time to see Daniel turn around again. She ducked out of sight, and when she eased back to peek in the window he wasn't sitting at the table anymore. But someone was breathing down her neck.

"Oh, for Pete's sake." She whipped around and came face to chest with Daniel.

Her breath wheezed out, and parts of her that should have been completely buzz-free were singing like electric wires in a thunderstorm. She'd never understood the fascination with toes as a sexual body part, but hers were definitely curling. And when she managed to get past her own reaction, she could tell he wasn't unaffected, either. "Changed your mind about dinner?" she asked him. *Or anything else?*

"What the hell are you still doing here?"

"Increasing my stalker skills so I can get a gig at the Learning Annex."

"What?"

"It's a long story. What are you doing out here?"

"That should be self-explanatory."

"It's a free country. I can eat wherever I want."

"You're not eating, you're staring in the window and freaking out the people who are eating."

She pressed her nose to the glass. "They don't look freaked out to me." They didn't look like alien spaceships erupting from the bedrock would freak them out. Bostonians were tougher than that, no matter what heinous slander Steven Spielberg tried to perpetrate on a gullible populace.

"The voices in your head sounding off again?" Daniel wanted to know.

"Something like that." She turned back, and there, behind Daniel, was the leprechaun. She went with impulse, slipping her arm around Daniel's waist and plastering herself to his side, and okay, there were other advantages, but mainly she was really tired of fending this guy off and nothing else had worked.

She didn't expect Daniel to play along, especially not by slapping a hand on her ass. Not that she was complaining, she was just surprised. And aroused. She slid him a sideways glance. He was looking down at her, half-smiling, a challenge in his gaze.

She might have taken him up on it— Correction, she wanted to take him up on it, with every nerve ending in her body. But she could see he knew that, and his ego was doing cartwheels. And since the drunk had taken himself off, there was no way to salvage her self-respect but to reach back and pluck Daniel's hand off her butt. Much as she regretted it. "Way to step up, Ace."

"You saved my life. I'm saving your virtue."

She popped up an eyebrow.

"It's the thought that counts." He turned to go back inside.

Vivi still had hold of his wrist, and she didn't let go. "Please don't," she said.

For once he didn't look harassed or irritated. He looked puzzled. "I don't understand why my life is so important to you."

"It . . . just is."

"This is ridiculous," he said, shaking her off.

"If you go back inside there'll be another attack—"

"Right, and I'm going to die."

"No"—Vivi hooked a thumb over her shoulder, in the general direction of Cohan's dining room—"your girl-friend is."

"Her name is Patrice Hanlon. And she's not my girl-friend."

"Your choice, not hers."

He raised one eyebrow and flattened his mouth, back to irritated.

She couldn't help but laugh a little. "It's not mind read-ing. It's not even feminine intuition. It's the way she's looking at me."

Daniel peered over the top of Vivi's head. Sure enough, Patrice was staring at them, and if looks could kill . . . And how the hell could Vivi see Patrice's expression when she had her back turned to the window? "Annoying," he said, although it went beyond annoying, wandering somewhere into the Twilight Zone. "And stop showing up in my life."

"Okay."

He halted, mid-stride and mid-argument. "Just okay?" he said, turning back to her.

"My grandmother always said you could lead a jackass to water."

"You mean horse."

"Not in your case."

"Cute. Good-bye."

She crossed her arms.

"Suit yourself," Daniel said, and went back inside.

Vivi had to give him credit. He crossed the room and sat down, never so much as glancing over his shoulder. From the looks of things he wasn't telling Patrice about her, and Patrice didn't like it. She put on a polite face, but her eyes, before she shuttered them, weren't so polite. Vivi hadn't enjoyed it the first time she'd been on the receiving end of one of those looks. She didn't like it this time, either. It made her feel like retaliating, and since the retaliation she had in mind furthered the rest of her agenda, she didn't see any reason to hold back.

She ducked inside, slipping past the dragon at the door by

hiding behind someone taller than her—not hard to do since three-quarters of the adults in America were taller than her. She found what she was looking for right next to the kitchen doorway, no ESP necessary. Where else would they put the fire alarm, she asked herself, pulling the little red handle and slipping into the crowd before she could think of any one of the hundreds of reasons why it was a bad idea.

There was a moment of stunned disbelief, composed of sudden silence and people looking at each other while they connected the *whoop-whoop-whoop* sound with potential mortal danger. Then there was chaos. Diners shot from chairs, knocking them over, drinkers milled around at the bar, torn between abandoning their source of alcohol and saving their lives. Most of them chose some combination of the two, carting pint glasses and beer mugs with them as they headed for the door, where the exodus hit a bottleneck and, compliments of liquid refreshment, took on more of a party atmosphere than a panic.

Except Daniel. Daniel wasn't partying or panicking. Daniel was standing beside his table at the back of the room. He had his arm around Patrice's shoulders, but he wasn't shepherding her to the door. He was studying the melee. Noticing the absence of smoke. And looking for Vivi.

His height might allow him to see over the crowd, but hers allowed her to blend in and sneak out. She only went as far as the opposite side of the street, and when Daniel finally came outside, she kept her eyes on him. It wasn't easy. Pedestrians and people from the neighborhood had joined the crowd from Cohan's. The Boston Fire Department had already arrived and blocked the street so traffic was at a standstill, and the Boston P.D. had cordoned off the area to keep the onlookers back, all of which compressed the crowd to the point where it would be difficult to move, let alone get a clear shot at anyone.

Again, except Daniel. Being that he was a U.S. attorney, the cops had allowed him and the redhead inside the danger zone where he was surrounded by a nice, big clear space. Making himself a nice, big target.

To give him his due, he wasn't standing out in the open like a complete idiot. He'd deposited Patrice by the fire truck, and he was keeping the bulk of it between him and the crowd. On the other end of the street, a line of cops was holding people back. Daniel should have been safe.

But something shivered over Vivi's skin, raising goose bumps before it settled in at the nape of her neck. She resisted the urge to hunch her shoulders against it. It was all she had to guide her and she used it like the announcer in a game of hot/cold tag, working her way methodically through the crowd until she saw two guys doing the same, all three of them heading toward Daniel's position.

"Daniel," she shouted.

The volume of the crowd was set at dull roar, and he was deep in conversation with the fire chief, but Patrice turned around. With death bearing down on him, Vivi couldn't be picky. She pointed at the two men closing in on the police line and mimed a gun with her thumb and forefinger, a universal sign that any four-year-old would have understood.

Patrice, however, decided to stare blankly at the gunmen. Vivi panicked, throwing herself at the tape line, screaming Daniel's name and looking like a threat. Or a distraction. The cops converged on her position, leaving a gap in the line, which the hit men headed straight for. And if she hadn't completely lost her ability to read body language, they were both reaching for guns.

Patrice, genius that she was, decided that instead of telling Daniel he was about to be shot, it would be better for her to drag him to the ground. Except he outweighed her by about seventy-five pounds. She managed to pull him off balance, thanks to his bad leg, so the shots went wild, at least one of them ricocheting off the fire truck.

The firemen dove for the pavement, the crowd freaked and scattered, taking the hit men with them, and Patrice slumped into Daniel's arms.

The cops had pulled their guns, but they didn't have a chance in hell of catching the shooters. So they focused on Vivi. "I didn't do anything," she protested.

"Where have I heard that before?"

"Officer Cranston." She stopped struggling, closing her eyes for a minute and wondering when her luck had gone sour. When she opened them again, Daniel was there.

"I'll take it from here," he said to Cranston.

"This time I'm arresting her."

"For what?" Vivi and Daniel asked in unison.

Cranston didn't answer, but he was thinking pretty furiously. Vivi wasn't sticking around to see what he might come up with. She would have preferred to disappear from the scene entirely, but she had her pride, and Daniel was giving her no choice but to go with him.

The paramedics on hand had sprung into action, so Patrice was lying on a gurney, one of the paramedics starting an IV in her right arm, the other bandaging her left.

"Gunshot wound to the upper arm," one of the paramedics said. They started to wheel her toward the ambulance, but she held out a hand to Daniel.

He took it, and for the first time Vivi noticed the blood on his shirt. And the look in his eyes. Whether or not he was in love with Patrice Hanlon, Daniel clearly valued her, and while he might not blame Vivi for the fact that Patrice had been shot, he wasn't letting her off the hook, either.

"They gave me something for the pain," Patrice said to Daniel, and although her voice was weak, her resolve wasn't. "I'm not going anywhere until I know what's going on. You can start with an introduction."

Daniel took a deep breath, held it for a second or two, then let it out. Explosively. "Patrice Hanlon," he said, "Vivienne Foster."

Since both of Patrice's hands were occupied, Vivi returned her smile and murmured a "nice to meet you," all the while trying to get a read on her. She was blocked, though, probably fuzzed by painkillers.

Patrice barely spared Vivi a glance. She had a death grip on Daniel's hand, and it was crushed to her bosom. "I'm sorry," she gasped out, "I should have warned you, but when I saw the guns I just froze, and then . . ." She closed her eyes and took a shuddering breath. Going for the Oscar, Vivi thought, as the woman released Daniel's hand to clutch instead at his shirt. "Did the police catch them?"

"No."

"You need to get somewhere safe," Patrice said. "Whoever it is, they must be serious to start shooting in a crowd like this."

"All you should be worrying about is yourself."

She waved him off with her uninjured arm, looking over at Vivi. "Are you trying to help him?"

"So she claims," Daniel answered for her. "The jury's still out."

"How are you trying to help him?" a man asked, shoving a microphone in Vivi's face.

"Manetti." Daniel sounded like he was chewing on something particularly disgusting.

"Pierce," the reporter shot back in the same tone, then turned his back to confront Vivi again, minirecorder and all. "I don't believe we know each other."

"Rudy Manetti," Daniel said.

"You left out one side of that introduction," Rudy pointed out.

"Hey, you caught that. Good for you."

"Well, then, no pleasantries." He shoved the recorder in Daniel's direction and pasted "investigative reporter" on his face. "Do you think Anthony Sappresi is responsible for the murder attempt on you two days ago?"

"He's your uncle. You tell me."

"I'm not the one who's prosecuting him for something he didn't do."

"Are you moonlighting for the *National Enquirer*? Because that version of reality ranks right up there with two-headed aliens and the squash that looks like Jesus."

"I'll take that as a 'no comment.' "

"I'm sorry, did you ask a question?"

"No, but here's one for you: Is she the woman you went

backstage with at the charity bachelor auction two nights ago?"

Daniel didn't answer, but Vivi noticed that when the reporter shifted, so did Daniel, keeping her and Patrice firmly behind him.

"Not talking about the woman," Rudy said. "How about the tablecloth?" When Daniel maintained the silent treatment, he prompted, "The one you were hiding under."

Vivi had to give Daniel credit, he held his temper. "I was unconscious, not hiding."

"Pretty convenient for you."

A cop hustled over and planted himself in front of the reporter. "You need to get behind the tape," he said.

"Someday the cops won't be around to run interference for you," Manetti said.

"Apparently that's not today." Daniel turned his back and walked right by Vivi without acknowledging her. It didn't stop her from following him.

Patrice wasn't getting with the Ignore Vivi program. "Who are you?" she said to Vivi, "and how did you know someone was trying to kill Daniel?"

"Just some nutcase," Daniel said, again before Vivi could answer. "Claims she's a psychic."

"Well," Patrice winced, squirming to find a more comfortable position on the stretcher. "If she predicted this, I'd listen to her."

"I really need to get her to the hospital," the paramedic said to Daniel. "Are you going with us?"

"Yeah."

Vivi caught his arm before he could walk away. "What happens after the hospital?" she asked him.

"Look it up in your crystal ball."

"If I could do that, I'd know who's trying to kill you and this would all be over."

"It is over for you. I can take care of myself."

"You couldn't stop your girlfriend from getting shot."

Daniel took that like a slap in the face, going white-lipped and narrow-eyed.

"I know I can help you figure this out," Vivi said, making an attitudinal adjustment before she ran him off entirely. "If you give me a chance."

He stared at her for another moment, smoldering, and not in a good way. "My office," he bit off, "first thing in the morning."

"Mr. Pierce?" the paramedic prompted, holding the back door of the ambulance open.

Daniel climbed in, leaving Vivi behind without a backward glance or another word. He didn't need one, the look on his face had been threat enough. No need to worry about running him off anymore—if she didn't show up in the morning, he'd come looking for her, and when he found her it wouldn't be pretty.

chapter
7

"MIKE SENT YOU."

"Yep."

"You're not a spook anymore."

Tag Donovan sat back in his chair, grinning. "Apparently I'm irreplaceable."

Daniel sat back as well, but he wasn't nearly as relaxed. Or amused.

"Mike says she keeps slipping past the guys he's putting on her."

"Yeah," Daniel said on a heavy exhale. It had been a long night, which he'd spent at the hospital, talking to the cops and doctors, waiting for Patrice to be released. Thankfully it was only a flesh wound. He'd gotten her home and settled, then gone home himself to take a shower and head for the office, fueled up on caffeine and fury.

Tag had been waiting for him when he arrived. Tag, however, wasn't either one of the people Daniel wanted to talk to. Vivi was number one, but Vivi was absent. Predictably. Number two was present, via speakerphone, and not sounding any happier about the situation than Daniel felt.

"Her landline is tapped," Mike said, "no cell, and I put an agent on her."

"Who? Mr. Magoo?"

Daniel ignored Tag.

So did Mike. "She gave him the slip," he continued. "Claims he never took his eyes off the front door except to blink, and she still poofed."

"That supposed to be funny?"

"My guy says she didn't go out, but about an hour into his stint, here she comes waltzing along from up the street, arms filled with groceries, and goes into her place."

"Maybe she was never inside to begin with," Tag put in.

Mike snorted. "I wouldn't put an agent on her who was green enough to make that kind of mistake. She was there, and before you ask, there's a back door, but it opens on an alley. No reason to go out that way."

"Unless she knew the front was being watched," Daniel said.

"He swears she didn't make him, but that's the only explanation."

No, Daniel thought, but it was the only explanation he was prepared to believe.

"So then I put two guys on her," Mike was saying. "Not exactly in the budget, but I figure if somebody wants you dead bad enough to hit the Oval Room, they won't wait long on the second attempt."

"She ditch them again?" Tag wanted to know, clearly getting a kick out of it.

"She took them coffee."

"Christ, Mike, who'd you get to watch her, Laurel and Hardy?"

"They were good guys," Mike shot back, going from frustrated to pissed. "So I put six new guys on her, two at either end of the alley behind her place where she can't possibly see them, rotating the other guys out front in teams of two."

Daniel blew out a breath, trying not to be impressed. Or

worried. But there was no way around it, Vivi had slipped by four agents in order to show up at Cohan's.

"My boys swear at least two of them were eyes on at all times. Nothing happened until about eleven last night."

Which would have been after the attempt, Daniel added silently to himself, after he'd sent her home and headed off in the ambulance with Patrice.

"The agents in front of her place said she pulled the same act on them as the first agent. They never saw her go out, but they saw her coming back in. She made sure of it."

"She must have a way out of that place you don't know about," Daniel said.

"I'm not a complete moron," Mike rasped. "I had the building checked out before I put the first agent on her. One door and some windows in the front, same in the back. Sides are common walls with the buildings next door. No doors, no windows. Same with the basement."

"How about the roof?"

"No exit."

"So how did she get out, Mike?"

"I don't know, but I don't like the way she smiled at the agents on her way back in. Like she's telling us she can ditch her tail any time she wants. Like she knows what we're going to do before we do it."

"You going *Outer Limits* on me?"

"I'll put some more experienced guys on her."

"Maybe Mulder and Scully are available," Daniel suggested.

Mike snorted out a laugh. "I was thinking more along the lines of Tag Donovan."

Daniel grinned, looking over at Tag. "He did fall out of a plane, with no parachute, and live to tell about it."

"And if it makes you feel better," Mike said, "I can draw a big *X* on the file before I give it to him."

* * *

THE U.S. ATTORNEY'S OFFICE WAS LOCATED ON BOSTON
Harbor, across the Fort Point channel from downtown
Boston and the West End. The Joseph John Moakley Courthouse was fairly new and interesting enough, a redbrick
semicircle with a huge curved glass front facing the harbor
and the downtown area. The outside was nothing compared
to the pretention inside. Supposedly, the judges' chambers
were outfitted with Jacuzzis and saunas, so apparently those
robes were hiding a lot of wrinkled skin.

Vivi had her own wheels, but she rarely took them out
for a spin, seeing as the vehicle they hauled around had belonged to her grandmother, and that made it more of a me-
mento than anything else. The fact that it was a 1952 Ford
truck, built like a tank—a flatulent tank—generally had
something to do with her reluctance to take it on the road.
People liked to look at it, but they rarely appreciated being
behind it. So she'd taken the T . . .

And she was stalling again, standing in front of the courthouse, waiting for fate to provide her with a reason not to go
inside. Fate, however, wasn't coming to her rescue. Fate was
like that, never around when you needed it.

It took a lot of disgustingly peppy thinking, and one of
her stronger impulses to get her to the front door. Once she
got that far she had to go inside because standing there
trapped in paranoia made her look like a criminal. Feeling
like a criminal was bad enough, no point in advertising it.

She didn't know about the Jacuzzis, but the place was a
sea of marble, and a beehive of activity. By the time she
got to Daniel's office, she was having trouble breathing.
Being in a place bulging at the seams with cops and judges
and people who had the power to put her in a ten-by-ten
room with a stainless steel toilet and a closed-circuit surveillance system did that to her. But his assistant showed
her in, and Daniel put her at ease immediately by getting
right to the interrogation.

"How did you ditch the agents at your place?" he wanted
to know.

"I walked right out the front door."

"Somehow they missed that."

She shrugged. "People usually see what they expect to see. Especially men."

"They didn't see anything. How did you get past them?"

"I read people, remember? Do you really think staring at the front of my building for hours on end didn't put your agents into a stupor at some point? Combine that with heavy foot traffic and it was child's play."

Daniel sat back in his chair, clearly pissed off. Well, so was she, and they hadn't even gotten to the important stuff yet. "Are you always this pigheaded?"

"How did you know about the hit last night?" he oinked. "And keep it on the physical plane."

"Funny, I was just thinking that."

"Who. Told. You?"

"Why do you keep asking that question when you already know you're not going to like the answer? And does it really matter?"

"It matters when a complete stranger saves your life."

"Why? If you knew someone was going to die, wouldn't you try to do something about it?"

"If you're some kind of psychic superhero who goes around warning people when they're about to get hit by a bus or eat bad shellfish, why haven't I heard about you before?"

"This isn't normal."

"You're telling me."

"For me," Vivi qualified, looking him square in the eyes. "This isn't normal for me. In fact, this is the first time something like this has happened."

"So why do I get the feeling you're hiding something?"

Vivi swallowed back a denial. "You don't believe in feelings."

"I don't believe in ESP, clairvoyance, psychic visions, or spirit guides," Daniel countered. "There is no sixth sense, nobody's talking in your head except your alternate personalities, and there's nothing on the 'other side.' Nobody comes back to suck blood, give advice, or knock on the roof of your car along deserted dirt roads. When you're dead, you're dead."

"Sometimes people don't get that," Vivi said, "and you can't tell me every action you take is backed by cold, hard proof. Don't you ever do something because of a hunch?"

"Hunches are just educated guesses, the kind of instinct that comes from time on the job."

"Going with your gut."

Daniel bumped up a shoulder by way of agreement.

"And your gut tells you I'm lying?"

"Holding back. You saw the two gunmen. What did they look like?"

"Dark hair, average build—"

"Dark hair and dark skin? Like Italian?"

"I wasn't trying to identify their ethnic background," Vivi said, taking to her feet. Moving always helped her work through stress, and remembering last night's events was definitely stressful. "I saw them coming so I tried to get your attention. You couldn't hear me yelling over the crowd noise, but your girlfriend did."

"Stop—"

"Calling her your girlfriend, I got it, Ace."

"And stop finishing my sentences," Daniel grumbled. "And stop calling me Ace. It's irritating."

"Everything irritates you. Not a great personality trait for a prosecutor. You really ought to work on it." One look at his face told her exactly what he thought of that idea. "Look, I saw them coming through the crowd, and I yelled for you, but you were busy playing Big Shot with the fire chief. I managed to get your date's attention," Vivi did the same thing she'd done the night before, pantomiming a gun with her hand, "but instead of cluing you in to your imminent death your girl— Patrice tried to drag you to the ground, which kept you from getting shot. But not her."

Daniel sent her another look, and she realized she didn't exactly sound sympathetic. "I'm relieved she's not dead."

"But it's her own fault she was wounded."

"It was the hit man's fault," Vivi said like she was talking to a particularly dense two-year-old. "But Patrice might have avoided it."

"I guess she's not as good at thinking in a crisis as you are."

"True."

"Not that you're all that good, since it didn't occur to you to yell 'gun' or call the cops."

"The cops were already there," Vivi pointed out, "and if I'd yelled gun in that crowd, the hit men wouldn't have had the only weapons we'd have needed to worry about."

She was right, and Daniel hated that she was right.

"Look," she said, slapping both hands on his desk and leaning halfway across to make her point, "everything happened so fast, and all I could think about was keeping you in one piece."

"I'm flattered." He'd aimed for sarcasm, but he missed. It might have ticked him off more if he weren't approaching spontaneous human combustion.

She was wearing one of those tight little tanks over a pair of low-rise jeans, and since she was still leaning over his desk, there was skin everywhere. Really nice, smooth skin over really nice, rounded curves. One of those curves was adorned with an orchid, pale pink and lavender with pale green leaves twining down, disappearing into fantasyland.

It took real effort to drag his gaze off the greenery. Their eyes met, and she shoved away from his desk, which might have helped if he hadn't immediately honed in on the tattoo at the small of her back. He'd seen it when she was pacing, but he'd been running on anger then, and anger was strong enough to cancel out lust.

The anger was gone, though, and the tattoo was right there in his face, disappearing below the waistband of her jeans and taking his brains along with it. It was some sort of spiritual thing he couldn't identify because he only caught the twin tips of angel wings. Wondering what the rest of it looked like drove him even crazier, like a mystery wrapped in a puzzle, surrounded by . . . Okay, the metaphor had

disappeared behind a testosterone haze. There wasn't anywhere he could focus that didn't wreak havoc on his concentration, and when she turned around and his brain did
kick back in, he didn't particularly like the thought that
came to mind because what came to mind was the possibility that she *was* innocent. And if she was innocent, then she
must be telling the truth.

And if he believed that, there was no point in getting his
head examined because the diagnosis would be terminal
stupidity.

"How the hell did you get mixed up in this?" He didn't
even realize he'd said it out loud until she answered.

"I have no idea what I'm mixed up in," she said, dropping into the chair across from his desk once more. "You're
the target. I just hijacked the signal off the cosmic telegraph."

"Cosmic telegraph?"

She grinned and it him right between the eyes, her
beauty, her playfulness, her sincerity. His gullibility, if he
fell for any of that.

"I thought you'd like that," she said. "And it'll save me
from hearing some sarcastic future version from you."

"Translation: You're going to keep stalking me."

"As long as I can ditch your agents."

Daniel took a minute to find some patience. He didn't
know why he'd expected this to go differently. Must have
been delusional. Or optimistic, which was so much worse.
He wasn't even sure, at the moment, of his ability to keep
his hands off her, if they had to spend any time together.
And this time he was picturing them around her neck.

"So who do you think is trying to kill you?"

It took him another moment to process the change of subject, and by then she'd managed to become irritating again.

"I'd've expected you to put some thought into this by
now," she said. "Maybe it's Anthony Sappresi. Maybe it's
his nephew, that asinine reporter who was so angry you
were prosecuting Tony. Or that Irish guy you ran into last
night."

He sat back, hands steepled, studying her.

"Mount Rushmore," she mumbled with a sigh. But her eyes were sparkling.

Even that irritated Daniel. They weren't having any private little jokes, they weren't going to be friends, and he'd be damned if he let her walk away thinking partnership was even a remote possibility. His life was on the line, and her motives were murky at best. "All I need from you is information."

She sat back, eyes on his face, deliberating. It was unusual for a woman who'd barely given a second thought to holding him at gunpoint. "What do you think I want from you?" she finally asked.

"I don't know."

"That's the problem, isn't it? You can't categorize me. I'm not a defendant or a witness, and you don't have friends, so I must be a suspect."

"You are a witness," Daniel corrected her. "One who can't or won't tell me anything useful. *That's* the problem."

"I'm no different than any other innocent bystander."

"You weren't there by accident, and there's nothing innocent about you."

Her eyes narrowed. "You're right, I wasn't there by accident. I have to live with you, dying, in my head, over and over. Do you think I could ignore that just because you were a stranger?"

She came out of the chair again and took to her feet. Daniel kept his eyes off her ass. He kept his eyes off the rest of her, too, until she turned and he could see her face. That was dangerous enough, considering she was still looking sincere.

"I didn't really expect you to take me seriously the first time," she said, "or the second, but maybe you could try to keep an open mind at this point." She must have caught the look on his face, and she must have enjoyed it. She fought back the smile, but she couldn't stop the sparkle. "I guess I should have brought a crowbar. If nothing else, I could have hit you upside the head with it."

Didn't sound like a half-bad idea, Daniel thought. He felt like he was beating his head against a brick wall anyway. A crowbar might be a nice change. As for the possibility of him suddenly deciding to believe her, it would take more than a couple of blows to the skull.

"Did it occur to you that while you're focused on me, you're not looking for the real culprit?"

"I prosecute culprits for a living," Daniel said. "Do you really think I haven't considered the possibility that one of them is behind this?"

"Not just your current cases. You should also make a list of the felons you've sent to the big house."

"The big house?"

"And all the people who have been wrongly accused. They'd be ticked off, too."

"I try not to wrongly accuse people."

"Well, sure, but it happens, right?"

Daniel flexed his shoulders, twisting slowly to work out the tension. Of course he'd thought about his cases, and he had every intention of combing through them. Since all he did was work, nothing else made sense. "I have a list," he finally admitted. "Care to trim it for me?"

She rolled her eyes. "Still convinced I know who's behind this?"

"I don't believe you're channeling Grandma—or anybody else, for that matter. That only leaves one possibility: Either you know who took out the contract, or you know one of the hit men."

"Well, this was a big waste of time," she said, gathering up her purse.

"I have everything under control," Daniel said.

She opened the door, turning back before she walked through it. "All evidence to the contrary."

chapter
8

VIVI WAS GONE, ANOTHER MEETING WITH NOTHING accomplished. Except Daniel was even more confused than before. There was nothing in her official records connecting her to anyone who'd want him dead, and the agents Mike had put on her couldn't stick long enough to figure out if that had changed. Maybe she'd hooked up with some low-level Mafia grunt or mob patsy. Maybe pillow talk was how she'd learned about the hit.

Daniel didn't like the idea of Vivi and pillow talk, so he tabled that in favor of the other obvious connection: her job. The kind of people who'd put out a contract hit on him tended to be superstitious. It wasn't out of the realm of possibility that she . . . counseled one of them. It was definitely something to look at. First opportunity, he'd have Mike send somebody in to check her books, if she kept any.

In the meantime, he had to stop being a complete idiot. Vivi was right that he'd pigeonholed her. He was stuck in lawyer mode, treating her like a suspect. She might turn out to be one, but interrogation was only effective when there was leverage, and the best leverage in the world was proof. Which he didn't have. Coincidence wasn't proof, neither was suspicion. Or skepticism. So he didn't believe she was getting messages from the Great Beyond, what did that matter? He had to think like an agent, and an agent would play along until he could pin down her source of information. Or until he could gain her trust.

Meanwhile, Anthony Sappresi.

Like Daniel had told Vivi, he was looking at his cases, open and closed, won and lost. Tony Sappresi was open and ongoing, and even though Daniel could think of a hundred reasons why the man would be a moron to have him killed, Tony's intelligence might not rise to that level.

Daniel was prosecuting Sappresi for murder, with a side of attempted kidnapping. Alex Scott was supposed to have been the kidnap victim. Tony had been unsuccessful, thanks to the fact that Alex was nobody's victim, and Tag Donovan was watching her back. The murder victim was Tom Zukey, FBI agent and Tag Donovan's partner.

Alex's ex-fiancé, Bennet Harper, had sold Tony a share in a treasure map, then pinned the failure on Alex when the payoff didn't come through. Long story short, Tag had busted the case wide open, and Bennet Harper had rolled on Tony Sappresi for the murder to keep himself out of jail. Harper was currently in witness protection, with Tag and Alex waiting in the wings to testify, and Tony was going away for a long, long time.

And damn, Daniel thought as he turned his rental car into Sappresi's neighborhood, wasn't it good going in to know his case was a slam dunk?

Tony's house sat on a quiet street in Savin Hill, one square mile of real estate that overlooked Dorchester Bay and traced its roots back to the months before Boston was settled. Currently it was crowded with one- and two-family homes, the more expensive of them boasting views of the water.

Real estate rarely went on the open market in Savin Hill, more often moving by word-of-mouth. Rumor had it Tony's wife had taken a fancy to the Victorian house where they currently resided. Coincidentally, the owners had decided to move not long after. Tony's neighbors probably weren't pleased to have a capo living next door, but none of them were stupid enough to say it out loud.

And none of them were stupid enough to walk into Sappresi's house uninvited.

"You got balls, Pierce," Sappresi said when Daniel was shown into the man's home office, "I'll give you that."

Daniel looked over his shoulder.

Sappresi waved off the henchmen, not missing Daniel's inference. "I'm guessing you're not here to insult me, especially since the law would frown on . . . what's this called? Ex-parte communication?"

"The law frowns on murder, too."

"Sounds like I should be calling my lawyer. He finds out you're here, maybe he can figure a way to make my infraction go away."

"Killing an FBI agent is a little more than an infraction." Daniel sat, choosing a chair that not only put his back to the wall, but was firm enough for him to get out of in a split second, even with his bad leg. "But you're free to call your lawyer," he sent another glance at the guy still standing in Tony's doorway, "if you're that worried about talking to me all by yourself."

Tony snorted. "My mouthpiece says your case is Swiss cheese."

"He's telling you what you want to hear. It's part of the service." And probably some sort of personal pep talk on the lawyer's part, reassurance that he could win the case and not miss his next birthday.

"He could be right if you happen to get dead before I go to trial."

"You've heard about the contract."

"Just what I read in the funny papers."

"Now's the time you tell me you aren't behind it."

Sappresi shrugged. "Killing the U.S. attorney who's prosecuting my case would be complete stupidity. If I was going to hedge my bets, I'd take out the witnesses."

"Not if you can't find them."

"Donovan and the woman wouldn't be that hard to track down."

"And Bennet Harper?"

"Witness protection?" Sappresi laughed, almost silently, just his belly shaking and a puffing sound coming from his mouth. "You're pretty naïve for a former fed and acting U.S. attorney. Maybe that's why you keep losing your cases."

"I don't see how I can lose this one."

"If you're still alive to try it. Way I hear it, odds aren't in your favor."

"The evidence won't change whether or not I'm there to present it." But his murder would prejudice any potential jury on the East Coast, considering Sappresi would be the prime suspect. Then there was the speedy trial issue, and while another prosecutor was getting familiar with the case something unfortunate could happen to the witnesses. "I imagine your defense team has a pretty strong incentive to win."

"Maybe you should be talking to my lawyers," Sappresi suggested again.

"Maybe I should be talking to Andalucci."

That did it. Tony wasn't looking smug anymore. Bringing up the underboss in charge of the Boston capos was taking all the fun out of Tony's day. "I haven't talked to Niko since my arrest."

"He's not worried about what you might say?"

"You know how this works as well as I do."

A capo ran his crew without instruction or interference, as long as he ponied up his cut of the profits and didn't screw up. Tony had screwed up. Big-time. And he knew it.

"You're a loose cannon, Tony. Andalucci's going to be as happy to see you in jail as I am. Hell, I'm doing him a favor putting you away. It'll save him from having to deal with you himself."

"First," Sappresi said, holding up his thumb, "if I was behind this I wouldn't have botched the job. Second," up went his forefinger, "I ain't the only one who'd like to see you dead."

"Care to elaborate?"

"You want information from me, you gotta have something to trade," Sappresi sneered, "which you don't. Ain't nothing in this life free, and I only take debts from people I think'll be around to repay them."

TAG RANG UP DANIEL ABOUT FIVE MINUTES AFTER he'd cleared Sappresi's place. "Call Mike and get the other agents back," he said.

"You lost her."

"Not exactly. I picked her up when she left the courthouse, just like we discussed."

"And?"

"And then I bought her lunch."

Daniel slammed his palm into the steering wheel but his voice was even. "She made you."

"Personally, I think she's going to make any tail. There's something spooky about her."

"Christ, Donovan, not you, too," Daniel said, thinking who'd have believed a conversation with Tony would be the high point of his day?

"We had a long talk."

"And you bought her story?"

"She told me Tom said, 'Hi'." There was a bit of a hesitation, then, "And he's sorry he didn't listen to me."

"Shit."

"That was my reaction, too."

"It wouldn't have been that hard for her to find out your partner was killed in the line." And a blind woman could have seen Tag was blaming himself for it.

"She didn't know I was shadowing her," Tag said. "Hell, I didn't even know it until this morning. When did she have time to research me?"

Daniel mulled that information over, not liking where it was taking him.

"I don't think she means you any harm," Tag said.

"She knows more than she's letting on."

"Could be, but maybe she's afraid of someone."

That put Daniel completely off his stride. Vivi had always seemed so confident and so fearless, it hadn't occurred to him that she might be afraid to tell him who was behind the contract.

"She said she was going home," Tag said into the silence. "Says she's been neglecting her clients lately, and she has appointments back-to-back all afternoon."

Daniel felt a smile coming on. "You're not one of them, are you?"

"No," Tag said, sounding glum, "I know what's in my future. My mother keeps renting reception halls, and one of these days Alex is going to shoot her."

"You're letting her carry concealed without a permit?"

"It's a shotgun. She was carrying it when we met, and if she gets pissed off she doesn't make any effort to conceal it." And Tag disconnected.

Daniel laid on the horn and sped around a driver who'd swerved into his lane, resisting the urge to run the jackass off the road. He took a deep breath, wrestled his frustration under control, and speed-dialed Mike. "Put the agents back on her," he said.

Mike responded by laughing uproariously, which didn't do much for Daniel's temper.

"And maybe you could find the time to send a guy into her place to check her books, see if there are any interesting names in there—when you're done rehearsing for your new job as a sitcom audience member. Wouldn't want to interfere with your retirement plan."

"At least I'll need one."

"WHAT'S SHE DOING?" DANIEL ASKED ONE OF THE LATest pairs of agents assigned to watch Vivi.

"Sitting in an ancient pickup truck, watching your place," the guy reported via cell phone.

Daniel lived on a narrow street in an old neighborhood of custom homes. His house was a Cape Cod, two bedrooms down, along with the normal complement of living and cooking areas. It was professionally decorated, spotlessly clean, and completely soulless. The upstairs consisted of one big room he'd converted to an office himself. Mismatched furniture, cluttered surfaces, an ancient sofa, and a minifridge. Ninety percent of his time at home was spent there. Being a target fell within the other ten percent. No exits upstairs—unless he wanted to jump from one of the dormers.

The front of the house was graced by a large bay window. Daniel went to it, pulled back the curtain, and there was Vivi, sitting in a vehicle with a bulbous hood, and a steel grille and bumper that had seen some serious action in the last fifty years. She'd parked about a half block away, facing the house, slouched down in her seat, and looking like she'd settled in for the duration.

"She alone?" Daniel wanted to know.

"Yep. Nobody came to her shop and she didn't go out— or at least she didn't come back in."

"Wait, she didn't have any customers this afternoon?"

"No visitors, no friends, no pizza delivery."

Which Daniel found strange, since she'd made a point of telling Tag she had readings all afternoon.

"Two calls on her landline," the agent was saying. "Neither call lasted more than a minute and unless they were talking in code, the conversations had nothing to do with you. She didn't leave the place until about an hour ago, when she walked to a lot not far from her house, got in the truck, and drove to your house."

"Who is the truck registered to?"

"Her. Former owner Katerina Totchka."

"The grandmother," Daniel said absently, wondering what the hell Vivi was doing camped outside his house. And afraid he knew. "Thanks," he said to the agent on the phone, "you guys can take off."

"But—"

"I'll keep an eye on her tonight."

There was silence from the other end of the line, the kind that included some sort of wink-wink, nudge-nudge routine. Daniel might have felt a need to set the record straight if he wasn't busy considering the possibility of imminent death. It had been a couple nights since the last attempt, and his gut was telling him to expect trouble. So was Vivi's presence. She'd attended both of the previous murder attempts so her being there struck him as prophetic, which might have been troubling if it hadn't suited his purposes.

With Vivi keeping secrets, his only other hope was to get a firsthand look at the gunmen. That meant being a target. Having a couple of feds parked down the street would be counterproductive to that goal, which was why he'd cut them loose.

Sure enough, about fifteen minutes after Vivi's shadows took off, an unremarkable SUV slid up to the curb and two guys got out. They wore black, no face masks, not expecting him to survive to ID them. They didn't bother to hide from the neighbors, either, not that the neighbors could see much of anything, surrounded as Daniel's house was by hedges that had been neatly clipped when he bought the place. Seven years ago. Gardening wasn't exactly his strong suit.

The two guys split at the curb, one taking the front, the other heading for the back. This time Daniel was ready for them, armed to the teeth, fully prepared to wound one or both of them if that's what it took to get some answers.

He took up a position in the archway between the front room and the kitchen, giving him a clear view of both doors, ready for whoever came inside first.

They set the place on fire instead.

The house was brick, the windows were vinyl replacement, but the doors were wood. Really flammable, original-to-the-house, seventy-year-old wood. Daniel was perfectly placed to see the smoke curling under the front and back jambs, and completely trapped.

There was no basement, and the windows upstairs only

faced front and back. There were windows on the first floor end walls, but they weren't going to do him any good. All the hit men had to do was take opposite corners and they'd each be able to cover two sides of the rectangular structure.

The house was rapidly filling up with smoke, leaving him two choices, go out and get shot or stay in and die of asphyxiation. What he did was dive out of the way because he saw headlights coming straight for the bay window. About a mile of ancient Ford pickup hood crashed through the front wall of his house, glass and wood exploding in a cloud of plaster dust and smoke.

"Get in," Vivi yelled.

Daniel struggled to his feet, cussing as his bad leg tried to give out. He managed to drag himself to the passenger door of the pickup, but it was blocked by debris. Vivi slid over and fought to crank the window down, barely breaking pace when shots sounded, shattering the driver's side window.

Daniel plucked a brick from the rubble and lobbed it over the top of the truck, in the general direction of the gunman, then another before bellying through the truck's passenger window. "Punch it," he said. Then, "hold it," because she was already back in the driver's seat and jamming her foot to the floor, and his legs were still hanging out the window. One of them was already close to useless. He wasn't keen on making them a matched set.

The tires spun, long enough for him to muscle himself the rest of the way inside the truck, long enough for the front gunman to get off a couple more shots. Long enough for Daniel's life to flash in front of his eyes.

The truck finally plowed itself clear of the house debris, the bullets went wide, and Vivi yelled, "Hey, my grandma left me this truck." She was a little wild-eyed, looking like she might run over the shooter, and while that wouldn't hurt Daniel's feelings, odds were better the guy would manage to hit one of them. Probably him, seeing as he was the intended target. And somewhere along the line he'd lost his gun.

So he reached over and cranked the wheel around, adding a couple of nice lawn ruts to the wreckage before they bumped down the curb and into the street, still going backward until they hit the cross street.

"I'm driving," Vivi screeched at him, wrenching the wheel out of his hand, and jamming the truck into first.

It shuddered, gears grinding before the engine caught with an irritated grumble, coughing and stuttering like an old man clearing his throat in the morning. It finally started to wind up, and by that Daniel meant make noise. The thing was pretty close to deafening, more sound than fury since zero-to-sixty was taking . . . Hell, the thing would shake itself to pieces before it even came close to sixty.

"I could run faster than this," Daniel yelled to Vivi.

"Should I let you off here?"

"I don't think it's going to matter." He glanced over his shoulder. The SUV was bearing down on them, and the men inside were probably reloading.

"Stop with the negativity and give me a suggestion."

"Next time run over the guy with the gun."

She gave him a look, but she didn't waste her breath making comments like "too late" or "there may not be a next time," mostly because there was a black BMW parked in Daniel's cul-de-sac and it chose that moment to pull away from the curb. Vivi honked her horn and flashed her lights, and when those didn't have any effect she put the gas pedal to the floor. She caught the Beemer just behind the front tire, the weight of the truck punching it out of their way.

"Your neighbor has a death wish," she yelled to Daniel. "I hope they don't come after you for the damage."

"They won't come after me, they'll come after you. And it's probably not—"

Daniel lost the rest of that sentence because Vivi decided to take the first turn on two wheels. She was going for last minute, he figured, but since it took her entire body to muscle the manual steering, she didn't catch anyone but him off guard. He slammed into the passenger door, which saved his life since a bullet came through the back window right where his head had been.

They wound up and down the neighborhood streets, bullets pinging off the truck, front porch lights popping on. There were enough cars parked on the street to keep the SUV from coming up beside them, especially with Vivi swerving from side to side. But they had to get out of the residential area—

"These guys don't care where they're aiming," Vivi said before the thought could fully form in Daniel's mind. "We have to get out of the neighborhood."

"And do what? This thing couldn't outrun an old lady with a walker."

"This thing saved your life."

"You saved my life."

"So far," she mumbled, her eyes on the rearview mirror. "We get out on the open road, and we're all dead."

"Are you including the truck?" That earned him another look. But she didn't deny it. "The open roads around here aren't exactly open."

"So we lead them out into traffic and what? Hope they get into an accident with some poor, unsuspecting driver?"

"You have a better idea?"

"No."

They both ducked down as a fresh barrage of lead came at them.

"The spirits picked a bad time to take a night off."

"I don't talk to spirits," Vivi said, "but if I did they'd have a hard time making themselves heard over the commotion."

She tried to shut out the pounding of her heart and the panic tap-dancing on her nerve endings. She tried to ignore the roar of the truck's engine, the gunfire, and traffic, the feeling that Daniel was sitting there waiting for inspiration to strike her and save both their lives. Inspiration was having a hard time battering its way through the panic, so she did what she always did—fell back on impulse, taking the first turn at random. She found herself on a four-lane road heading toward one of the bridges that spanned the Charles River.

"You're heading into downtown Boston," Daniel pointed out.

"I know that."

"It's not the best place to avoid injuring innocent by-standers."

"I know that, too," Vivi said, and she had no intention of leading two men with guns into an area that would be jammed, on a balmy summer evening, with people on foot and people in cars, all of them going nowhere fast. "Can't you think of something besides criticism and second-guessing? For a guy with your history, you're pretty stingy with helpful ideas. You used to be an agent, remember?"

"You used to be calm in situations like this."

"Still not helping."

Daniel didn't say anything, which was surprising enough to make Vivi glance over at him. He was looking at an eighteen-wheeler ahead on their right, and she had her hands full, what with the SUV determined to come up alongside them. The fact that they were probably going to start shooting was almost as big a problem as running out of room—as in two lanes, three vehicles, one of them being really big and not likely to give way . . .

Before she could finish that thought the solution popped into her brain, as crystal clear and fully blown as if she'd just seen John McClane kicking ass on the big screen.

Step one, slam on the brakes. Her pickup might not have the greatest acceleration, but it was damn good at stopping. The SUV flew past them just like it was supposed to, slow-ing down when the driver realized what had happened. By then Vivi had the gas pedal to the floor, and the truck had shuddered its way up to about fifty miles per hour, fast enough so that she was able to swing in behind the SUV. And inspiration was talking loud and clear again.

She swerved every time they did, managed to keep the truck moving fast enough to stop them from pulling the same stop-and-drop ploy she'd used to get behind them.

Waiting for the right opportunity, waiting while the hit man in the passenger seat of the SUV turned around and pointed his gun at them, waiting until the semi in the right lane wasn't more than a few yards away.

"Stay . . ." Daniel started, then, "don't let . . . Get right up—"

"—behind him," Vivi finished. "Got it. Hold on." And she jammed her foot to the floor, leaning forward and willing the truck to *move*. It gave a little hiccup and leapt forward, pulling off enough speed so that when her front bumper impacted the SUV's rear bumper and the driver's eyes met hers in his rearview mirror, she could turn the wheel just so and drive the SUV into the side of the eighteen-wheeler. Speed and physics did the rest, not to mention the fact that the SUV's hood was just the right height to fit under the side of the semi. Snugly.

Metal crunched, glass exploded out of all the SUV's windows, air bags went off. The SUV stuck, tire rubber burning as the semi dragged it down the road sideways, air brakes shrieking when the driver figured out what had happened and tried to stop. Vivi sent the pickup in a little jog around them and sped away from the scene of the accident.

She knew she had a stupid grin on her face, but she couldn't help it. She'd saved Daniel's life, her own, too, and she was feeling pretty good about it. Until she got a look at his face.

chapter
9

DANIEL STILL LOOKED... IRRITATED, ANNOYED, HA-rassed. Dyspeptic. For the life of her she couldn't figure out why he was so cranky— Okay, he'd been shot at, again, and his house . . . Better not to think about his house. He was alive, right? That was the important thing.

She risked another glance at his face. He didn't look all that grateful.

"She drove a pickup through the front of my house," he said into the payphone.

"It didn't do my grandmother's truck any good," Vivi pointed out, "since you're keeping track."

Daniel's eyes cut to her. His expression was set to pissed off, just in case she hadn't gotten that from the tone of his voice. "Then she ran the hit men into an eighteen-wheeler." He listened for a second, said, "Yeah, I'm still alive," and then he hung up. "Mike says the hit men are still alive, too—at least they were when they fled the scene of the accident."

Vivi took the first deep breath since she'd rammed them into the truck.

"They tried to kill us," Daniel reminded her.

"They're just doing their job. And if they die, whoever hired them will just send somebody else."

"First you won't shoot them, now you're squeamish about death by car crash?"

She lifted her eyes to his. "And you think it's because I'm working with them."

"You have to admit it sounds bad."

"It could be that I don't want to be responsible for anyone's death. Even someone I don't like."

He chose to ignore the look she sent him. And the argument for innocence she made. "Mike is going to have my house boarded up. I gave him a description of the hit man I saw when he was shooting at us outside my house, but it won't do him any good. Too generic. He told me to lay low, watch my back."

"You mean, like take precautions? Gee, what great advice."

"We can't go to my house," he said, taking all the fun out of her I-told-you-so moment.

"We?"

"And we can't go to yours since they've probably run your plates by now."

"What, you're just going to ignore me . . . Wait a minute, they know where I live?"

"Not yet, but it won't be long." They were parked at an outdoor payphone, and Vivi had gotten out of the truck while Daniel talked to Mike because she needed to walk off the aftermath of the car chase. Now the nerves came back full force, along with a knot in the pit of her stomach.

"Get in the truck, Vivi."

She turned, stared blankly at him for a second before reality kicked back in. Then she took a minute to process what he was saying. And what it meant.

She couldn't go home. Daniel was right about that much, and since what she needed was to go with him anyway, and he wasn't dumping her, she was actually getting what she wanted. But she didn't like it, and not just because she didn't have a choice. Being a psychic didn't exactly put her on the road to riches—at least not the way she did it. Heck, she was barely on the rutted dirt lane to making ends meet. She worked hard keeping her head above the financial water. She'd already gone a week without working. It wouldn't take long for her to end up in the poorhouse.

Seeing Daniel sitting behind the wheel of her grandmother's truck helped lighten her mood. She could have warned him, but Daniel was a show-me kind of guy.

He turned the key. Nothing happened. So he turned it again. "Why do I get the feeling the problem isn't mechanical?" he asked.

Vivi shrugged. "You insulted Maxine."

Maxine? he parroted silently, just his mouth moving, then aloud, "I knew I shouldn't have asked that question." And he turned the key again.

Maxine made a sound that would have been termed a raspberry if Maxine had been human. Then the engine turned over once, and the truck lurched forward a couple inches, steam hissing out of the radiator.

"You mocked my grandmother, too."

This time Daniel kept his head down and his mouth shut. Gathering his patience.

"You should try apologizing," Vivi suggested.

That brought his head up. He stared at her for a second, then reached for the key again. He snatched his hand back just as quickly, shaking off a nasty shock.

Vivi crossed her arms on the open driver's window, grinning.

"It's just static electricity," Daniel said.

"Go ahead, try it again."

He thought about it, the stubborn idiot.

"Maxine's not going to let you drive her, Ace."

"You're telling me the truck is possessed?"

Vivi tipped her head to one side, this time communing with her sense of humor. "I didn't say a word."

"At least not that I could hear," he muttered, eyes narrowed.

"Getting a little paranoid?"

By way of response he slid over to the passenger's side. Vivi climbed into the driver's seat, turned the key, and Maxine cranked right over, settling into a loose, rattling shimmy in rhythm with the rough idle of the engine. "Where to?"

"Somewhere over the rainbow, apparently."

"I'm not a witch."

"Good thing," Daniel said, "otherwise my house would have fallen on you."

"Yeah, and I'm not wearing the right kind of shoes for that."

She followed his directions to a part of Boston she'd never been in before. It had seen better days, that was for sure. Mortar was crumbling on the old brick buildings, windows were broken or boarded up, graffiti was everywhere, and either X-rated or gang-related. The overall attitude was apathy, nobody on the street except working girls, dealers, and buyers of one or another commodity. The rest of the neighborhood stayed behind locked doors and looked the other way.

Vivi turned the pickup into the no-tell motel Daniel pointed out, the engine giving a little derisive-sounding cough and shudder as she steered it into a parking space in the back where it couldn't be seen from the road. Not much chance the hit men would be trolling for them in this neighborhood, but it never hurt to be careful.

Daniel was wearing worn jeans, a faded T-shirt and an unmistakable air of authority. Probably no one recognized him as an assistant U.S. attorney when they walked into the tiny lobby, but the half-dozen men lounging in front of the ancient television definitely took him for the john and her for the flavor of the night.

She found it amusing, the more so when she realized Daniel didn't. "I can set them straight if you like," she said to him.

"No point in you being any more memorable than you already are."

"Well, we can't have that." She sidled up to him at the desk, plastering herself against his side and keeping her face turned into his chest. Her hands were busy, too, but she kept them above his waist. Playing the hooker was kind of fun, feeling his muscles quiver under her palm was . . . interesting. Letting herself get caught up in the moment would be a mistake.

Once he'd paid for the room and put his wallet away, she headed for the elevator, swinging her hips and crooking a finger at him.

"Way to be forgettable," he said, taking the opposite corner of the elevator.

"This being the kind of place that charges by the hour, I figured memorable would have been me keeping my distance."

"Not from where I was standing."

THE ROOM MET ALL VIVI'S EXPECTATIONS. FADED WALL-paper, musty draperies, and a bed that had seen hard duty. Even with the threadbare chenille spread pulled up, she could see the dips and sags. If she hadn't been coming down from a major adrenaline rush, nothing could have induced her to get within a mile of that bed. Not even the memory of Daniel's muscles under her palms, the scent of him when she'd had her face pressed to his chest . . . On second thought, best to add him to the list of reasons why the bed was a bad idea.

The rest of the room was minimally furnished, no chair, no table, a small nightstand with a lamp perched on it. No drawer so no Bible. Even the Gideons had given up on the place.

"I'm going to take a shower," she said, thinking maybe if she gave herself a good scrubbing she'd feel better about everything . . . And she didn't need that little nudge at the edge of her thought processes to know she wasn't kidding anyone, including herself. It wasn't crashing her grandmother's truck into Daniel's house that had her on edge. It wasn't being shot at, either, or ramming the hit men into that semi.

It was Daniel. More specifically, it was spending the night alone with him in this room, with one bed that made her think of sex. Sure, it was tawdry sex, but at the moment she couldn't think of one reason why a little tawdry sex would be bad. No money would be exchanging hands, and it had been so long—

"I thought you were going to take a shower," Daniel said, his voice sounding a little strained.

He was probably thinking about tawdry sex, too. The notion didn't do much to reassure her. One of them had to have some self-control, and it might not be her.

"Right," she said, "on my way," and she escaped into the tiny bathroom. A shower might help lower her body temperature, but it wasn't going to do much for what was causing the heat, namely the generally dirty direction of her thoughts. A gallon of soap and a hinged skull wasn't going to sanitize the pictures in her mind. She had to settle for cold water, shivering under the paltry flow as long as she could bear it. Then she rinsed out her bra and panties, hung them over the shower rod and stepped out. No towel, she realized, and it wasn't the kind of motel that provided robes.

She'd never been one to balk at a little nudity, until there was a really bad purpose for it standing on the other side of the door. She sluiced off as much of the water as she could, wrung out her hair, and put her clothes—jeans and a T-shirt—back on, exiting the bathroom before she could talk herself out of it.

Too bad she hadn't taken the time to think about how it would feel to go pantiless. It felt . . . free. And a little naughty. Not the kind of feelings she'd intended to come out of a nice cold shower with. Not the kind of feelings that were going to keep her on her side of the bed. Especially with Daniel staring at her like that, intense, heated, noting she wasn't wearing a bra and liking it. She liked it, too, and the unfettered body parts he was currently focused on were advertising just how much she liked it.

His eyes lifted to her face and it felt like all the oxygen had been sucked out of the room. He eased to his feet and the same coiling, tingling heat in her nipples spread everywhere, making her shift restlessly, her hands curling against the urge to reach out . . .

She didn't have to. Daniel came over, and the way he was walking had nothing to do with his injury. She lifted her eyes over his abs and chest, up until their gazes met, having to tip her head back because he'd stopped only inches away from her.

He didn't say a word, didn't move a muscle, never took his eyes from hers. And still she felt like she'd been touched. More than touched. It went deeper than her skin, deeper than her pounding heart. Something shifted, something more than physical. Something . . . "Oh no," she said, backing off a step.

Daniel started a little, seeming to come out of his trance, too, and clearly not happy that he'd been in one to start with. And he was blaming her.

That was the least of Vivi's worries. They were in real trouble, she thought, collapsing onto the bed without any concern for the horrible diseases and pestilential vermin it might be harboring. A whole lot of trouble.

And it had nothing to do with sex.

DANIEL BOLTED TO THE BATHROOM LIKE A MAN IN drastic need of a life preserver. And there were Vivi's panties mocking him from the curtain rod. Game over. The ship was going down and he was sinking with it, drowning in a sea of hormonal stupidity. That's what sex with Vivi would be. Testosterone-based stupidity.

He didn't know where her loyalties lay. He didn't know anything about her, except she was a crackpot. But he knew himself, and if normal women weren't a part of his five-year plan, crackpots were definitely off the list. Even for casual interaction.

It took a lot more mental adjustment and a cold shower, but by the time he walked out of the bathroom he was able to act like nothing had changed. As long as he kept his eyes to himself.

"I have some questions," he said.

"Did something move under the bedspread?"

Daniel looked in her direction just in time to see her bound off the bed and slap at the bedspread a couple of times. He didn't see anything moving under the spread. Her shirt was a different story.

"You're wasting your time grilling me again," she said, going to lean against the nightstand beside the bed.

Daniel took the opposite wall. The distance couldn't hurt his concentration. "You're the common denominator," he said.

"Didn't tonight prove anything?"

"You waited until it was almost too late before you did anything."

"You told me to butt out."

"Now you're following instructions?"

"I was trying to prove there's no way I could have known those guys were going to show up." She pushed away from the nightstand, pacing like she did when she was agitated or frustrated. "They couldn't know they were going to fail the other day. If I knew they were going to hit again, or if they were using me to draw you out, they'd've had to be in contact with me. You already know that's not true."

"How do I know that?"

"My phone is tapped, and you've had agents on me every minute since the restaurant. I'm not working with whoever's trying to kill you."

"The spirits told you there'd be another attempt, Karnack?"

"I've saved your life three times, Ace." She stomped across the room and went toe-to-toe with him. "I practically destroyed my grandmother's truck and let me tell you, she probably knows it, wherever she is."

"Worried she'll come back to scold you?"

"It's only a matter of time," she griped. "What the hell is it going to take to convince you?"

"How about the truth? You're hiding something."

"Go to hell." She turned for the door, but he blocked her exit.

He didn't touch her. "I'm hungry, how about you?"

She eyed him suspiciously for a moment, then backed off a step before turning into the room. "I don't think this place has room service."

"I don't think anyone stays here an entire night," Daniel said, which was a mistake, because it turned his thoughts back in a direction he didn't want them to go. And, of course, his body followed.

To make matters worse, the couple in the next room chose that moment to prove his point. Very vocally, mixed with a nice rhythmic beat from the headboard. And if he and Vivi weren't going to follow their example, and they weren't going to eat, talking was the only thing left.

"I'm tired of talking," Vivi said, crossing to look out the window. "I'm tired, period."

"There are still a few things we need to clear up."

"Like?"

"How does this vision thing work, for starters?"

She turned back around. "I don't know. It just . . . happens."

"Is that how you knew I hated cauliflower?"

"Not exactly. It started with a vision, but my visions don't come with subtitles. I saw your face, and when I finally found out who you were, I looked you up on the Internet."

"My preference in underwear isn't posted on the Web."

She smiled faintly. "The rest was a combination of intuition, observation, body language, and human nature. No-body likes cauliflower. You're left-handed so chances are you sleep on the left side of the bed, most men prefer dogs, and when you slipped your hand in your pocket on the bachelor auction runway I could tell you weren't wearing tighty whities." When he got a puzzled look on his face, she added, "No lines. That left either boxers or boxer briefs, and you're a man who likes structure, control." Her eyes drifted downward. "No flapping in the breeze for you."

"It sounds like your vision is the least part of it. Are you sure you didn't read or hear something about the hit and then dream about it?"

"I wasn't sleeping at the time," she said around a huge yawn.

"Daydream then."

She climbed into bed, closed her eyes, and heaved a huge sigh. "Could we finish this interrogation in the morning?"

"It's not an interrogation. And you weren't exhausted five minutes ago."

She cracked an eye and narrowed it at him. "I've had a full day," she said. "Are you going to forget where you left off?"

If he got into that bed with her, there was a pretty good chance he'd forget his own name. But he couldn't let her know it. He eased down on the edge of the bed, giving up any hope they could stay on their respective sides when they immediately rolled together into the trough in the middle of the mattress. Vivi had started out facing the wall; she ended up with her face plastered to his neck.

"Uhhh," she said, which was probably consternation, but it sounded way too close to a moan, especially with her breath tickling warmth over his skin.

To make matters worse, she braced her hands on either side of his rib cage and boosted herself up, trying to get back to her side but ending up lying on top of him. Her breasts were squashed against his chest, her legs were tangled with his, and when he brushed her hair back her eyes were filled with humor and edged with heat.

"And I thought the mattress was lumpy," she said with a little shiver that rubbed her hips against his erection.

"It's not just me and the mattress." Daniel shifted his glance down slightly, heading for her pebbled nipples, but sidetracked by the orchid tattoo twining around her right breast, which reminded him of the one she had at the small of her back, which sent a burst of heat and need through him, strong enough to practically blow off the top of his skull.

Vivi stretched, her breath sighing out as a quiver ran through her, so slight he might not have noticed if every nerve ending hadn't been attuned to the tiniest sign she'd welcome what he wanted to do to her. And hopefully do it back to him.

Her gaze met his, but when she spoke her words didn't match the need he saw in her eyes. "Will you hold it against me in the morning?" she said in a voice that was a sexual assault on his ears.

There was a split second where he would have said no, where he would have said anything to get out of his clothes and into her. Instead he said, "Shit," clamped his hands around her hips, and lifted her off him. Because she was right. If she slept with him he'd wonder if she had ulterior motives.

When she tried to get out of bed, though, he pulled her back down and spooned himself behind her. She knew he wanted her. He could either run from the temptation or use it to prove something—to them both. "I can control myself if you can," he said.

"Making a point, Counselor?"

"Trying to get some sleep."

He must have sounded more convincing than he felt, or maybe she was just exhausted because she relaxed back against him with a soft sigh and within minutes she'd drifted off. Daniel spent a tense moment trying to figure out what to do with his arm before he gave in and slung it over her waist.

He knew he'd made the right choice, but it was going to be a hell of an uncomfortable night.

chapter 10

DANIEL HAD NEVER BEEN A TATTOO KIND OF GUY,
but there were moments during the long, sleepless night
when all he wanted in the world was to see the rest of that
damned tattoo at the small of Vivi's back. It didn't matter
that someone wanted him dead, or that his house was a pile
of rubble. The only thing on his mind was Vivi's body art.
True, that had less to do with the art and more to do with
the body, but curiosity was easier to accept than the rest of
what was going on inside him. A cold shower helped him
put his need for her away, for the moment, but he knew it
wouldn't stay buried forever.

Vivi stumbled out of bed when he exited the bathroom,
and it was all he could do to keep a lid on the lust. She
looked as groggy and irritable as he felt. That didn't improve
his mood. Clearly she hadn't slept well, either. Maybe he
would have done them both a favor by giving into his lust
last night. Or maybe she'd had other things on her mind that
were incompatible with sleep.

"I think I know a way to convince you to trust me," she
said, which was the last thing he wanted to hear.

What he wanted to hear was the name of the bastard behind the murder attempts so he could go home, rebuild his house, and get on with his life. While he still could.

Being a prosecutor wasn't what he'd expected it would be. In fact, being a prosecutor pretty much sucked. After his injury, he'd convinced himself that trying criminals wasn't that different from catching them. Same goal, same war, same bad guys, only he'd be the one making sure they went to jail for the rest of their lives. Except it wasn't quite that easy.

The evidence didn't always add up to a slam dunk, for one thing. Witnesses were reluctant, refused to testify at all, or lied outright. There were defense lawyers, juries that could be confused and misled, and judges that were more concerned about reelection than justice. End result? There weren't enough victories to keep him feeling like he was a force for good. And there definitely wasn't enough excitement.

Going head-to-head with a couple of hit men, not to mention the loony psychic, had reminded him of that. Danger was addictive. The flood of adrenaline, pitting his wits against a worthy opponent, the rush of getting out of it in one piece and bringing a bad guy down. The longer he was in the field, the harder it would be to go back to a job where he sat behind a desk most of the time.

"Did you hear me?"

"Yeah, you think you can convince me to trust you." He thought about asking her why it was so important, but she'd ducked that question more than once, and nothing had changed to make him think she was ready to answer it now. Because she didn't trust him.

He didn't know why his tired brain chose that particular time to figure out the obvious, but it was a lightbulb moment. It energized him, gave him a goal. It wasn't just about him trusting her, he needed her to trust him, too. She'd never come clean until she did. And she wasn't stupid; he couldn't make it obvious that he was only humoring her. He'd have to let her convince him. Gradually. "What did you have in mind?"

"Quincy Market."

"Quincy Market?" he repeated, his tone right in keeping with the first part of the gaining-Vivi's-trust plan. Not making it obvious he was worming his way in. And so what if the incredulity was real? It still got the job done.

"I'm going to do a reading," she explained. "I can't do it on you because I already researched you, and you won't believe anything I say. And there's really only one reading I can get from you anyway."

"I'm dead, I know."

"I could take you to my place, but you'd think there's some sort of setup that helps me cheat my customers."

"Marks," he said, because she'd expect his skepticism.

She had the predictable reaction to that, losing patience. "They're not marks. I could round up a dozen people who'd tell you that, but you'd probably think they were lying so anecdotal evidence won't do me any good. I'd be more comfortable at my place, but I can do a reading anywhere."

"Sounds like you have it all worked out."

"You're going back to your home office and hope those guys don't find you again, right?"

His eyes cut to hers.

Her gaze never wavered.

"I'm going to figure out who hired 'those guys,' then stop them," he said.

"You have a couple of leads, but if those don't pan out you're going to need your case files, and you won't show them to me unless you think I'll be of some use. So let me prove it to you."

"You're saying you can read my files and tell me who's involved in this thing?"

"It's worth a shot, isn't it?"

Play along, Daniel reminded himself, managing not to roll his eyes or give any other indication that he thought he'd be better off dumping what she was trying to hand him on his garden.

She took his silence for agreement, thankfully, since he didn't think he could bring himself to say yes.

"I don't have a cell phone," she said, "and I'm guessing you don't, either. There's no phone in the room, but maybe there's a payphone downstairs so we can call a cab."

"No cab is going to pick us up in this neighborhood."

Their eyes met, both of them coming to the same conclusion.

"We'll have to take Maxine," Vivi said.

Daniel nodded, starting for the door. "You drive."

QUINCY MARKET, ALSO KNOWN AS FANEUIL HALL Marketplace, sat on the Freedom Trail not far from City Hall and the Government Center. Once host to stirring, seditious speeches by the likes of Samuel Adams, the building was now a glorified food court, at least on the ground floor. Cafeteria-style restaurants were crowded cheek by jowl inside, selling everything edible from sushi to burgers. The patrons crowded around communal tables or sat on the low stone walls circling the trees planted outside while they ate.

Faneuil Hall was surrounded by souvenir stands, assorted stores, a Cheers pub re-created from the television show, and crowds of people. It felt a little exposed, but Vivi figured the hit men would never suspect they'd go to a place thronged with tourists.

As it was just after opening, and a weekday, there weren't a lot of men trolling for bargains. And since the ones who were there fit more into the categories of retiree mall walker, manny, or retail employee, Daniel kind of stood out. He was definitely getting a lot of attention.

Women were looking, appreciating, probably drooling, too. One poor woman walked into one of the kiosks dotting the walkways, fell on her backside, and popped back up, red-faced with embarrassment. But she never took her eyes off Daniel.

"Don't tell me," he said when Vivi laughed at his discomfort, "you knew that was going to happen."

"True, but there was no psychic ability involved."

He gave her a cranky look.

"You're not the usual kind of Wednesday-morning market patron."

"Can we just do this?"

She grinned up at him, but inside she was completely serious, her smile fading as she took a couple of deep breaths, cocked her head, and made the mental adjustment that opened up her mind.

At first it was like a radio tuned to static, a harsh punch of white noise before she began to get actual impressions, confusing snippets of feeling that didn't last any longer than the next could replace it. She shifted her attention to the crowd, focusing on the first face that crossed her path.

"That woman doesn't know it yet, but she's about to buy a pair of shoes," she said to Daniel as if she were talking about the weather instead of predicting the future.

Daniel rested his fingertips on the small of Vivi's back and steered her behind the woman she'd pointed out, a twentysomething wearing a trim business suit. She strolled down the sidewalk, slowing to look in the window of Nine West before she moved on. She made it almost to the door of the next store when she was sucked back into the shoe store gravity well, along with three other women in the vicinity.

"Care to tell me what she's going to buy?"

"Four-inch spike heels, black, with an ankle strap."

"A young, professional, unmarried woman buying fuck-me pumps," Daniel said, "who'd've thought."

"I'll mark that down under *not convinced*," Vivi said, turning to survey the other nearby shoppers. She stopped a young mother pushing a stroller, an older child of about four holding her hand, begging intensely for a soda pop. "Your daughter is about to throw up."

No sooner had the woman shifted her attention to the baby in the stroller than the four-year-old bent over and barfed at her feet.

Market workers converged on the scene of the toxic spill, and other shoppers detoured around the mess with varying degrees of disgust or sympathy. Vivi made a bee-line for a jewelry store not far up the way, going in to stand beside a woman who was trying to decide between two diamond cocktail rings.

"Get the bigger one," she suggested, "your husband is having an affair."

"I knew it," the woman said, storming out of the store, with the rings on either hand.

"Hold it!" the store manager yelled. "Security! Security!"

Daniel shook his head and followed Vivi out of the store.

"The bathroom's that way," she said to the first woman she came across. The woman thanked her and headed off in the direction Vivi was pointing.

"You can't prove that one," Daniel said when she turned to him, "and the others could have been good guesswork."

"Okay, then you try it."

Daniel wrestled with himself for a few seconds, but Vivi knew he wouldn't back down from a challenge. He made a slow perusal of their surroundings, then spun on his heel and headed back toward Victoria's Secret, stopping at the edge of the big front window where they could look in without being seen.

"Her," he said, indicating a customer flipping through a rack of thong panties and bra sets. "She's buying a gift."

"Nope," Vivi said.

"She's at least seventy years old."

"Yep."

The woman took the lingerie up to the sales counter, the clerk's face going through a gamut of expressions, most of which centered around shock and dismay. She took the woman to a rack of white cotton, talked furiously for a moment, then gave up and led the way to the fitting room.

"Strike one," Vivi said to Daniel.

"Okay." He took her by the hand, their fingers twining for a split second before he dropped her like a hot potato and set off along the brick walkway.

Vivi caught up to him and fell into step—three of hers to every two of his.

"That guy over there," he said, pointing to a potbellied man wearing jeans and a T-shirt. "Food court."

"Nope," Vivi said. Sure enough, the man bypassed the food court and joined the queue of people lined up in the blistering sun for one of the hourly Boston city bus tours. "Strike two."

Daniel stared down at her for a minute. His expression was inscrutable but his eyes were sparkling. He set off again, and since they went into Faneuil Hall she had no trouble keeping up with him this time. The problem was keeping her wits.

Faneuil Hall was crowded, to put it mildly, thronged with families and workers from the nearby buildings getting lunch, the single aisle bottlenecked around the lines at the ordering station of each food stall they passed. The noise level was out of control so there was no point talking, which was fortunate since Vivi couldn't have formed a coherent sentence to save her own life. Because Daniel kept touching her—or she kept touching him, arms brushing or hands bumping.

She could have predicted the heat she felt each time they touched, the way her breath came short and she wanted to press herself to him, skin to skin, to feel him hard against her like last night, to imagine him hard in her . . . which was a fantasy she had to ignore because if she took it any further there was a real danger she'd jump Daniel, right there in public with half the tourist population of Boston looking on.

What surprised her was the companionship she felt toward him. He'd relaxed for the first time in her company, and if she was stupid enough to want him when he was being prickly, at least she didn't have any illusions he'd want her back—in anything but the physical sense. This Daniel, though . . . she could build up real hopes about this relaxed and smiling man, and hope was just about the worst thing she could do to herself.

"No more predictions?" she said in an attempt to get them back on track.

"Devil worshipper," Daniel said about the first of a trio of little old ladies chowing down at one of the tables set wherever there was a square foot of spare floor space. "Porn star," he said, indicating the second elderly woman, "and that one is a dead ringer for J. Edgar Hoover."

Vivi smiled. "You can't prove any of those."

"Exactly."

Message received, she thought. She wanted Daniel to take her talent on faith, and she wanted it now. If he came to believe in her at all, it was going to take time, and no amount of pushing would get him there before he was ready.

"I'm hungry," she said, stopping at the next food place they came to, ordering one of everything on the menu.

She took the tray of hot food that was handed over the counter a few minutes later, and Daniel collected a sack of subs, pretending to stagger under the weight.

"The sandwiches are for later," she explained. "I never get to eat around you. I get to watch you eat, but somehow I keep missing meals."

She followed him to a table in the courtyard outside, Daniel taking the seat that put his back to a nearby tree. Vivi sat across from him, but she kept her eyes on the crowd. "Can you shut it off?" he asked, pulling a vegetarian sub from the sack.

"At first I couldn't, but I've learned how to control it," she said, digging into an order of nachos. "I can tap into it whenever I want to now."

"Tap into what, exactly?"

"Mostly it's feelings, like I told you before. When I'm doing a reading for one of my customers, I'll do an astrological chart, read the tarot, and generally there are specific questions the subject wants answered, so I interpret whatever I'm feeling with what they're asking.

"This kind of reading is more . . . You might call it a gut feeling but a lot stronger. Nausea when I looked at that little girl, suspicion and revenge with the woman buying the expensive jewelry . . ."

The old woman with the thong would have been the next logical part of that explanation, but Daniel didn't ask Vivi what she'd been feeling then. And Vivi didn't volunteer to tell him.

"That's how you knew you were being watched?" Daniel asked her.

"Yes, and I'm not too happy that your agents were in my place. Not to mention my underwear drawer."

Daniel refused to be sidetracked—except for a flashback to the lace panties hanging over the shower rod last night. She sounded convincing—she always managed to throw in an offhand little detail that made it seem like she actually had some sort of psychic ability. It was just as likely her shop was wired for audio, video, too, probably.

"You're the first time I had an actual vision."

"Of me dead," Daniel said.

She nodded, pushing her food away. "After you escaped at the Oval Room I thought it would be over, but then I had another vision."

"Me dead at Cohan's. And at my house?"

"And at your house. They're not going to stop."

Her eyes rose to his, and for the first time he thought about how traumatic it must be for her to have scenes of death playing in her head. If he'd believed her.

"I know you can figure this out on your own, but you'll get there faster with my help."

That, at least, was the truth. "I'm willing to work with you until this thing is settled," Daniel said, "but I'm asking you to respect some ground rules. No personal involvement being first and foremost. We aren't going to be friends, we aren't going to be compatriots, and there won't be . . . anything else."

"Maybe you should have that woven into a tie, Ace. Might save you from having to say it to every woman you meet."

"And don't call me Ace," Daniel said, going back to his boundary-setting without breaking stride. "This is a working relationship. Your part of it is research only, for lack of a better description. As soon as we figure out who's behind the contract, you take off and let me deal with it."

"You don't want me to testify?"

"Testify about what? Visions? Impressions? That kind of testimony would earn you a one-way ticket to the loony bin." And make him the laughingstock of the federal justice system. It was bad enough to feel ineffectual without looking it, too. "You don't want to testify anyway," he reminded her.

"No, I don't, and just for the record, I'm not interested in personal involvement."

"Yes, you are."

Vivi huffed out a slight, derogatory laugh. "Funny, I didn't expect you to be self-delusional."

"Maybe you should replay what happened in the motel lobby last night."

"Maybe you should replay what happened in the room, Ace."

Daniel didn't have a comeback for that. But really, what could he say?

"I think I can keep my hands off you," Vivi said. "And I'll keep my demeanor purely professional." Her gaze drifted down, below his waistband. "I wonder if you'll be able to say the same thing when this is all over."

chapter
11

THEY LEFT THE MARKET AND DROVE STRAIGHT TO
Daniel's house. It was still a crime scene, so he figured it
would be safe. Vivi wasn't so sure, but she didn't argue
with him since his purpose was to retrieve his files, which
hopefully he would let her look at. And she was driving, so
the minute she felt the slightest twinge of uneasiness she—
and Maxine—would decide what they were going to do.
Daniel wouldn't like it, but what was new about that? He
pretty much objected to everything she did.

Well, not everything. He'd seemed okay with her undie-
less state last night, judging by the way he'd looked at her.
He'd looked at her like it wasn't the absence of underwear
he'd liked so much as the fact there'd be less clothes to
work his way through—if he did more than look. She'd really wanted him to do more than look. Not a great memory
to be replaying with him only inches away, but at least she
was wearing her bra again. And she wasn't a complete
idiot.

Daniel hadn't suddenly decided he could trust her. He
was only going along with her for as long as it took to find

out what she was up to. And she was using that. He thought he had the upper hand, but while he was delusional she intended to worm her way into his trust, save his life, and then get the hell back out of his life again. There was no way they could have any sort of relationship, because she did have a secret, and it was a secret that would be a deal breaker on the relationship front for Daniel. Unless the deal included her in jail.

Once her game plan was firmly outlined, she felt a little better. Then they pulled up in front of Daniel's house and she could tell he was angry again, and the guilt came roaring back. "It's not like I had a choice," she said.

He glanced over at her. "I'm pissed at them, not you."

"You're a little pissed at me."

He shrugged, one shouldered.

"There were two guys with guns and only one of me."

"With no gun."

"You had a gun," Vivi reminded him.

"I was waiting for them to come in."

"They weren't coming in. They were making you into human kindling. You had two choices, come out and die or stay in and die. I gave you a third."

"How about choice number four: Distract the guy at the front door and give me a chance to get out. *Without* crashing through the wall of my house," he added, because the obvious comeback was that Maxine had distracted the hit man at the front door and supplied Daniel with an escape route at the same time.

Vivi considered asking Daniel how she was supposed to let him know about choice number four so he could escape once the gunman at the front door was distracted, but she couldn't see that line of discourse going anywhere good. He'd get more annoyed than he already was, and then she'd get irritated and say something sarcastic, and then he'd call her Uri Geller or ask her when the Mother Ship was coming for her. There'd be more sarcasm from her, which would result in silence from Daniel. But he'd make damn sure she knew how cranky he was because that was what it all boiled down to—feelings, and how uncomfortable it made him to know that even if he tried to hide his they were no mystery to her.

She could have told him it wasn't an issue anymore, and not because of his stupid "ground rules." As much as she hated to face it, she was beginning to have *feelings* for Daniel. Those feelings usually involved some level of exasperation, and there was generally an urge to roll her eyes at whatever came out of his mouth, but there was a definite attraction, too. There had been since his *GQ* strut down the bachelor auction runway, and no matter how condescending, patronizing, and chauvinistic he was, there were . . . feelings.

Being in love with Daniel would have been dangerous under any circumstances—not that she was in love with Daniel—but even mild affection was bad.

As soon as she got emotionally involved with a man, she stopped getting any readings on him. Her grandmother had told her it was the universe's way of making sure at least one part of her life was normal. Vivi thought it was bullshit. If she had to be a freak, it ought to at least work in her favor, not cut out when she needed it most.

"The spirits telling you knock-knock jokes?"

"Yeah, and the punch line is always about hit men."

"We should probably take the act inside. I don't think there's any real danger, but there's no point in pressing our luck."

"Fine," she said. "Right behind you."

Daniel ducked under the police tape, holding it up for Vivi to do the same. He didn't wait for her after that, and she didn't follow him too closely, taking her own time looking over the wreckage of his house.

The front, where her truck had gone in, was boarded up, and when she stepped inside, the living room was filled with glass and debris. Daniel was walking carefully through it, half bent over. She thought he was keeping an eye out for nails, but then he stopped and hunkered down, unearthing something in the pile of rubble where the passenger side of the truck would have been.

The something he dug out was his gun, and he wiped it off on the arm cover of his former easychair, which was currently providing a nice, comfy resting place for a large chunk of ceiling plaster. He stuck the gun in his waistband at the small of his back and continued into the kitchen without saying a word. Vivi didn't mind the silent treatment. Probably best he forgot she was there.

Everything in the kitchen was coated with a thin layer of dust, and the whole place reeked of smoke. The back door was singed, but still intact and serving its intended purpose.

"It's not as bad as I thought it'd be," Daniel said, so close behind her she almost jumped out of her skin.

It was a new experience, being snuck up on. Vivi figured she'd better get used to it, at least where Daniel was concerned.

"The impact of the truck must have blown out the fires," he said, turning for the stairs.

"Take your phone." Vivi plucked up the cell phone that sat in a charging base on the kitchen counter, and handed it to Daniel. "Just saving you some inconvenience," she said when he gave her one of his stares.

He took the phone and clipped it onto his belt, his expression shifting to no-harm-in-humoring-the-crackpot.

Vivi would have found that amusing, but unfortunately her radar was working fine where everyone but Daniel was concerned, so when his cell rang—an actual old-timey phone ring—she wasn't surprised, and there was no need to ask him who was on the other end.

He checked the readout, looking like he'd be running a finger under his collar if he'd been wearing a shirt and tie. Since he was wearing a T-shirt and jeans, he had to settle for a shoulder roll. He added a half-turn, as if that would keep the conversation private.

Under normal circumstances, Vivi would have given

him some space, but being kept ignorant was incompatible with having a pulse. And knowing he was talking to Patrice Hanlon was incompatible with her feelings, not to mention it added a whole other dimension to those feelings that she wasn't in the mood for.

"I know," Daniel was saying to Patrice. "I'm sorry to make you worry. I couldn't answer my phone last night, but I'm glad you called, and I'm glad you're feeling better." There was a pause. Daniel's eyes cut to Vivi, and she knew Patrice was asking if she was the reason Daniel hadn't answered his phone last night.

He didn't respond to that, although it would have been simple to explain that his phone hadn't been handy. Apparently Daniel had a nondisclosure rule where Patrice was concerned. Vivi liked that.

"I'm at my house getting some things," Daniel said into the phone, taking the stairs two at a time like the literal-minded guy he was.

Vivi trailed along behind him and found herself in a single room that ran the length of the house, one of the long walls notched out for the dormer windows she'd seen from the front. An entire office setup cluttered one end of the room: desk, computer, file cabinets, overflowing garbage can. An unmade bed and small refrigerator sat at the other.

"I have to go under for a while, and no, I can't tell you where I'm going, but I'll try to give you a call in the next day or so, let you know I'm okay." Daniel snapped the phone shut before Patrice could argue again, turned to Vivi, and said, "Let's get out of here."

He gathered up his laptop, then made a quick detour to the other end of the room to collect some clothing—all casual—out of a chest by the bed. He stowed the computer and clothes in a duffel, along with his gun, and headed for the stairs.

"Wait a minute," Vivi said, trotting along in his wake, "where are your files?"

In answer to her question, he lifted the duffel into the air.

"But—"

He was already out the front door, striding toward his garage. She had no choice but to follow, so she did, thinking, "Fine, let him run the show. Let him think he can make all the decisions without ever consulting her. He'd find out differently. If he lived long enough."

"WHERE ARE WE GOING?" DANIEL ASKED VIVI ABOUT five minutes after they left his house.

"You let me drive. I thought that meant it was my choice."

He'd decided to take his car, dented rear end and all, because there were a thousand similar vehicles on the streets of Boston while hers stuck out like a sore thumb, and not just because the windshield was barely intact and the other three windows were gone entirely. There weren't a lot of '52 red Ford pickups tooling around.

Once he'd made his intention clear, Vivi had called a friend of hers to have Maxine picked up for repair. Probably one of her customers, since the person on the other end of the phone call hadn't asked who she was talking about. Vivi left the keys under one of the floor mats, clearly not afraid the truck might be stolen. Daniel felt sorry for the unlucky bastard who tried to jack Maxine.

"I let you drive so I could watch for a tail."

"And shoot at them?"

"Only if they shoot first."

Vivi huffed out a breath and shook her head. She didn't answer his question.

Daniel kept his eyes glued to the road ahead. He'd be damned if he asked where they were going again. She hadn't put herself in harm's way three times to let him walk unsuspecting into danger now. Even when she was ticked off about something—

Okay, who was he kidding, he knew exactly what she was angry about: the ground rules speech, followed by him blasting out of his house and expecting her to follow along two steps behind like the good little soldier. Vivi hated violence, and doing what she was told wasn't high on her list of preferred activities, either. In fact, giving her the I'm-in-charge lecture and expecting blind obedience was not only self-delusional on his part, Daniel decided, it had been aimed at the wrong person.

The boundaries he'd been setting were for himself, because last night he'd seen some lace panties and Vivi's damp T-shirt, and he'd been inches away from fraternizing with the enemy. James Bond might sleep with women to get information. Daniel preferred to keep that option in reserve. As in, he'd rather walk into court naked than use it.

"I really need to know where we're going."

"My place," she said without hesitation.

"Nope, we're not going there."

"I guess I can wash my panties out every night, but I figured that would violate the Daniel Pierce 'No Personal Involvement' program." She glanced over, met his gaze. "Since you seemed to have issues with my panties last night."

He got hot just thinking about her panties. And she knew it. "We'll shop."

"I don't need new clothes. The ones I have are perfectly good. And I'm not exactly made of money. I'm not working, which means I'm getting further in the hole every day." Another sidelong look, this one full of temper. "Not that you give two cents about my finances."

"I'll buy you some damn clothes."

"You use your credit cards, or access your bank account, they'll trace it."

"So what? It's not like we're going to stand at the ATM and wait for them to show up."

"You're not buying me clothes."

"And going to your place is so much less risky?"

She didn't say anything, but her attitude was prickly at best, and since she claimed to know when it was safe, and he was letting himself be convinced of her talents, he decided not to argue. Besides, this time he was armed.

A half hour later Vivi pulled up in front of a brick row house not far from Quincy Market and got out of the car, Daniel tagging along behind her like an obedient puppy. That ended at her front door. He took the key from her, picked her up by the armpits, and plunked her down to one side, swiping her hair out of his face.

"You really need to do something with that," he said, pointing to the mass of curls falling to the middle of her back.

"I'll get right on it," she said, "as soon as you stop the macho crap."

"You want clean clothes? We're doing this my way."

She jammed her hands on her hips and glared at him, but she didn't argue.

Daniel unlocked the door and pushed it open, stooping to retrieve the pile of mail that had been shoved through the slot. Vivi tried to take it from him, but he lifted it out of reach and began to leaf through it.

"Tampering with the mail is a felony," she said.

"So is tax fraud."

"Huh?"

"Care to show me your books? I bet you're not declaring all your cash receipts."

"Most of my customers don't want receipts," Vivi said. "It's a kind of unwritten agreement. And anyway, no one who does a partial cash business declares everything. I'd go broke if I had to pay taxes on all of it, and then Uncle Sam wouldn't get anything at all."

"It's illegal," Daniel maintained.

Vivi held up her wrists and said, "Arrest me then," even though they both knew he wouldn't. And once she'd made her point, she plucked the mail out of his hand and brushed by him, taking it to a long, glass-fronted display case with a cash register at one end. She dumped the mail into a drawer, punched a couple buttons on the register, took out all the cash inside—which didn't appear to be very much—and tucked it into her pocket.

Just moments ago she'd told him it was costing her more than time to watch his back, but he'd written it off to anger and drama because altruism never set well with him. Now he had to admit she wasn't in this for the money— hell, she wouldn't even let him buy her clean underwear. But she wasn't putting her ass on the line for nothing. She had an agenda, and as long as she kept that agenda private, she couldn't be trusted.

To make matters more difficult, there weren't going to be any business records that would magically solve the puzzle by revealing a client connected enough to take out a contract on a federal prosecutor. All that left was gaining her trust and hoping she'd come clean. Or maybe he'd get lucky, and there'd be some clue in her shop, a business card laying around, or a name written on a pad of paper. He rolled his eyes. Maybe if he asked real nice Grandma would point him in the right direction.

The bottom floor of Vivi's building was retail space, consisting of a shop in the front that was filled with, as far as Daniel was concerned, New Age crap: polished stones, scented candles, books on astral projection and finding your inner peace. Daniel couldn't say he'd found his inner peace, but he knew it wasn't going to be lurking between the covers of a book written by some nut job. He didn't expect to find it floating in the depths of a crystal ball, either, but he went in search of one anyway. And where else would you find a crystal ball except behind a beaded gypsy curtain? Coincidentally, there was exactly such a curtain behind the counter.

He went through it and found himself in a small room containing a table and two chairs. And nothing else. Daniel had expected some sort of stage production, colored lights, spooky music, maybe a fan to waft ghostly breath across the back of the subject's neck. A deck of oversized cards sat on the table, and it was dark and cool, but otherwise the place was completely devoid of ornamentation.

"Kind of a disappointment," he said when he heard Vivi come up behind him. "You're giving psychics everywhere a black eye."

"You were expecting smoke and mirrors?"

"At least a levitating table. Give the tourists a show."

"I don't get many tourists in here," Vivi said. "My customers are mostly regulars, and they don't need a floor show to believe in what I do."

She turned away before Daniel could identify what he heard in her voice. Probably she was ticked off at him again. She was always ticked off for some reason.

It didn't stop him from following her back into the shop and through another doorway. This one opened onto a staircase, which led to Vivi's living space upstairs. Where the shop was fairly well ordered, the place Vivi called home was organized chaos. The furniture was well worn, each piece upholstered in a different pattern, as were the drapes. The walls were crowded with stuff, pictures in garish frames, mementos of vacations, the flotsam and jetsam of not just her life, but probably her grandmother's as well, judging by the cracked black-and-white photos and the Russian-looking knickknacks.

Daniel got the impression Vivi loved each piece, but the place made his head hurt. She'd gone through one of the doorways; he followed and found her in a bedroom, the walls a pale green, the furniture simple. She was tossing things into a leather backpack: clothing, frippery, lotions from the bathroom next door. And a deck of tarot cards.

She went back downstairs and circled the shop, plucking polished stones out of the bins along one wall. "Jade and black onyx," she said, tossing a chunk of each into her backpack as she named them, "amethyst, turquoise, carnelian, and clear quartz."

"What are those for?" Daniel asked.

"Most of them have protective qualities, some are for wisdom, good luck . . . And why am I bothering with the explanation? You don't believe in this anyway."

"True." But he read the label on the bin of the quartz. "Why do you need your psychic abilities enhanced?"

"A little extra boost never hurts . . ." She cocked her head and said, "Damn," her eyes meeting Daniel's.

"They're coming," he said.

"They're here."

She raced for the stairs just as the front and back doors opened. Daniel stayed in the shadows at the base of the staircase, wanting to get a look at the men who'd been trying to kill him. The guy at the front eased the door open, closing it behind him and limping into the shop.

The guy at the back tiptoed in, wearing a flowered neck brace. "I think they're gone, Hatch," he said to the limper. The lisp in his voice explained the flowers.

"They didn't come out," Hatch said. "Must be upstairs."

"My neck hurts," the other guy said. "My doctor doesn't want me doing anything strenuous."

"We don't get this done and we won't have to worry about strenuous ever again. We won't have to worry about breathing, either."

"They're not going anywhere. Just give me a minute to take one of my little blue happy pills."

"Shit, Flip, you take one of those and you'll be outside coming on to everything in a wifebeater."

"Nothing wrong with that."

"Unless you pick the wrong guy again and he beats the crap out of you."

Daniel felt hands at his back and nearly jumped out of his skin before he realized it was Vivi, and then he got antsy for an entirely different reason.

"What's the holdup?" she whispered, her lips all but pressed to his ear.

Daniel leaned back a bit and whispered, "Descriptions, names," except he must have said it too loud because Hatch swore and limped for the stairway. Flip rolled his eyes but he followed along.

Daniel wrapped an arm around Vivi's waist and hauled her up the staircase, pulling his gun as they went. He fired a shot down the stairs and was rewarded with some shouting, some swearing, and a couple of satisfying thuds.

"It won't hold them for long," he said to Vivi. "How do we get out of here?"

"There are windows, but the best bet is the door to the roof."

She took off, Daniel hot on her heels as she led him into the other bedroom. He caught a quick glimpse of garish fabrics before she tore open the door that led to the closet and pointed up. "That's the ladder to the roof, but I can't reach it."

Daniel shoved his way into the closet and pulled the door shut behind them, trying to ignore the feel of her small, curvaceous body pressed against his. It helped to remember there were two guys trying to kill them.

He pulled a cord and down came a narrow folding ladder. He boosted Vivi up and followed, blinking in the sudden bright sunlight.

"Now what?"

"Hush," Vivi said. Her eyes were closed and she was breathing evenly, or trying to.

"We don't have time for this."

"We'd better, because there's no way off this roof unless inspiration strikes, and inspiration requires calm." And she went back to the closed eyes, head cocked, deep breathing routine.

Daniel looked around, trying to assess the situation. Deep shit seemed the best way to describe it. The buildings to either side were at least one-story higher, and the fire escapes were too far down, at the level of the second-story windows.

"We're going to have to go back inside," he said. "Stay behind me and I'll—"

"Too late," she said, just as Daniel saw Hatch's head clear the top of the ladder. He fired off another shot, knowing it was only a matter of time before he ran out of bullets.

Then Vivi took his hand and said, "Run," and like a fool he sprinted headlong with her, straight toward the edge of the roof. And when she said, "Jump," he jumped.

chapter 12

DANIEL HAD MADE A CONSCIOUS DECISION TO jump. They were only two stories up, he'd thought. Probably they wouldn't die. Maybe break a few bones.

The world dropped out from underneath him, the rose-colored glasses fell off, and his predominant thought was *"Shit!"* His stomach gave a long, greasy roll and he was falling, legs windmilling, heart pounding, Vivi's hand in his oddly reassuring.

His life didn't flash before his eyes, but his sanity came into question. It was too late to unring that bell, though, and with the pavement rushing up at him, broken bones seemed like way too optimistic an outcome. They'd need a miracle to survive . . . Like a dump truck. Filled with something soft—not so soft that the landing didn't knock the wind out of him and send pain zinging through his bad leg. There'd be lots of bruises, but nothing felt broken.

He looked over at Vivi. She was grinning. So was he, jazzed on the adrenaline shooting through him, not to mention the part about cheating death again. He caught a glimpse of the hit men, two shocked faces peering at them from Vivi's rooftop, before the dump truck rounded a cor-ner and the only thing above them was the wide, clear blue sky.

"Still don't believe me?" Vivi asked, shading her eyes and looking all smug and superior.

Daniel knew what she was talking about. The back of a dump truck was big when you were inside it, but the chance they could have hit it from two stories up was pretty slim. Even if it was stationary. Jumping blind like they had . . . It had to be more than luck. But he wasn't prepared to admit that yet.

"We can debate the existence of your psychic powers later," he said. "Hatch and Flip are going to be looking for this truck, and it's easy to spot."

"Skeptics," she muttered under her breath, sitting up.

"I'm not a skeptic . . . completely."

"No, you're an idiot."

He gave her his most intimidating courtroom glare.

She rolled her eyes. "What would you call someone who's asked for proof and been given it—multiple times—and still refuses to believe what he sees?"

"A lawyer."

"There's always room for doubt, right?"

"This isn't about doubt. You're asking me to stake my life on your ability to pluck inside information from the ether."

"It's not just your life anymore. Starsky and Hutch know where I live, and now they've gotten a good look at me."

"Starsky and Hutch were good guys."

"They were cops."

Not the same as *good*, judging from her tone. But she was right about the rest of it. Hatch and Flip might be a comedy routine in the making, but that didn't mean they weren't paying attention. They'd tracked her to her house, and they'd staked out the place, which was why he'd ob-jected to going there in the first place. Okay, his reluctance ran more along the lines of not knowing her affiliation and possibly being led into a trap. But she already knew he still needed convincing, and since she'd been paying attention, she should know he was doubting more than her connection to the other side.

"We have to get out of here," she said, waving a hand in front of her face.

Daniel sat up. A pair of flies started buzzing circles around his head, and he realized it smelled in the dump truck. Really bad. Because the dump truck was filled with compost, laced with horse manure. Soft, but aromatic. "At least we have clean clothes," he said.

"I have clean clothes," Vivi corrected him. "Yours are still in the car."

"Not a problem," Daniel said. But getting out of the truck was.

He went up on his knees and flipped around, peering over the cab. A traffic light was coming up, but they motored through it on the green. The next one turned yellow as they got to it, the truck grinding to a halt with a shriek of air brakes and a lurch that nearly tossed Daniel face-first into the dirt. With no breeze to tone it down, the stench intensified to eye-watering proportions.

Daniel banged on the roof of the cab and got a "What the fuck?" out of the driver, which was good enough to reassure him the guy wouldn't put the thing in gear while he was trying to climb out of it. He'd hate to escape four murder attempts only to wind up a grease spot on the road by accident.

"How the hell did you get in there?"

"Hold on a sec," Daniel said to the driver.

Vivi draped a leg over the side of the truck, but since hers weren't as long as his, she couldn't quite reach the indent at the base of the dump truck's well without going on faith. But she was good at faith, he thought, watching her slither out until her feet found purchase. That was as far as she was getting without help, though, so he reached up, wrapped his arms around her legs, and let her slide down his body. Slowly.

"Um . . ." she said, sounding a little breathy, "my feet are on the ground."

And the rest of her was pressed against him, which suited Daniel just fine.

"You're welcome, asshole," the driver yelled as the truck took off, and Daniel and Vivi were left standing in the middle of the street.

Vivi tried to squirm away, but he kept his arm around her, just until they got safely to the curb. And then he still didn't see any reason for distance. If the hit men found them, he wanted to be ready to move in an instant, and if he needed to pick her up, he didn't want to have to chase her down first.

"If we act like a couple, we won't draw any attention," he said.

"I think it's too late for that." But she stopped trying to put space between them. Probably because the people around them were making faces, wrinkling up their noses, waving their hands in the air. "It's hard to blend in when you smell like a cesspool. And you are aware that we're walking back toward my place, right?"

"That's where my clothes are," Daniel said, "and it's the last thing the bad guys will expect us to do."

"Too bad we don't have time for a shower."

"That might be pressing our luck."

"When are you going to learn, this has nothing to do with luck?"

THEY WEREN'T FAR FROM HER PLACE, WHICH SHOULD have made Vivi feel better. All she could feel was Daniel, plastered to her side. She couldn't even smell the compost anymore. Her senses—all six of them—were too jumbled up by him.

"We need a place to stay," Daniel said, and her lower body gave a wholehearted throb of agreement, not over the practicality of his suggestion so much as the fact that there would have to be a bed wherever they ended up. Not that she needed a bed. Just about any horizontal surface would work—some vertical ones came to mind, too.

"Any ideas?" Daniel said.

She looked over at him and thought, "Oh, yeah." She had ideas, starting with the slightly sweaty T-shirt over all those amazing muscles and working her way down from there.

"If you keep looking at me like that . . ."

Vivi lifted her eyes to Daniel's and there was intensity, heat. Need. Her throat went dry, her palms went damp, and all of her wanted all of him. She opened her mouth to ask him to finish his threat, but what came out was, "Can I borrow your cell phone?"

Daniel didn't quite comprehend, caught up in her as deeply as she'd been caught up in him. Good for her ego but hell on her willpower.

"Phone," she repeated, holding out her hand.

He dug his cell phone out of his pocket, but he didn't hand it over. "Want to tell me what you're thinking?"

"Okay," she said, but only because she'd pulled her mind out of his pants. Unfortunately, it had landed in the gutter. "Eric Brophy."

Before she even finished saying Eric's name, Daniel was dialing, and it was no surprise when he said into the phone, "I need you to check someone out for me, Mike." He looked at her, eyebrows raised until she said the name again, then spelled it, Daniel repeating it into the phone. There were a couple of "uh-huhs," and then he snapped the phone closed. "Eric Brophy, forty-two, juvenile record but nothing as an adult. At least nothing he's been caught at."

"Except lying about his age." Vivi took the phone from Daniel and punched in Eric's number. "Vivi," she said, identifying herself.

"Babe," Eric said back, "long time no hear. You jonesing for some Eric?"

Vivi rolled her eyes. "Actually, I need a place to stay—"

"Say no more," he said, rattling off an address that wasn't far away. "Meet you there in a half hour."

" 'I?' " Daniel said when she'd snapped the phone closed and handed it to him.

"It's Eric's favorite pronoun," Vivi said. "He doesn't do so well with 'we.' "

"And when you show up with me in tow?"

"Trust me, it's better if I spring you on him."

ERIC'S BUILDING SAT DILAPIDATED AND EMPTY IN ONE of the older sections of Boston, six stories of brick, mortar, and steel that had probably housed dozens of Irish families during the 1800s. The inside was probably a holy mess, a jumble of original and secondary construction with a questionable infrastructure. The outside looked to be in decent shape. The architecture was plain, blocky even, but the brick had gone a soft pink and the masons had added some unique details to the façade. The place would have been plain for its time, but no one did work like that anymore.

If Eric was telling the truth, Daniel would have guessed the demolition permit wasn't just taking time, it would never come. There was no way the Boston Redevelopment Authority would let the owner tear this building down. It would cost a fortune to replumb and rewire, to upgrade the heating system, to make sure the place was structurally sound and create marketable spaces inside it, but the owner would be an idiot not to put in the time and effort. Condos in this building would be worth more than some glass-and-steel monstrosity that didn't fit the neighborhood.

Not that it mattered to Daniel. He and Vivi needed a place to lie low and this place looked like it fit the bill.

No sooner had they gotten a few feet from the car than a man came out of the building and down the front steps, planting himself in their path. "Vivi," he said, arms wide, swooping in for a hug.

Vivi took a step back. "Eric," she said, pasting on a smile that was as fake as George Washington's teeth. Eric didn't notice. "I could really use a shower."

"So I smell." He guffawed—that was the only way to

describe Eric Brophy's laugh, and apparently he found his own jokes hilarious.

"A pipe broke at my—our place," Vivi said. "We tried to fix it but—"

"Your place? Together? You and . . ." His gaze shifted to Daniel.

Daniel didn't supply his name. Neither did Vivi.

"Our place," Daniel said, slinging his arm casually around her waist.

Eric stood a little straighter and puffed out his chest. "I've been meaning to call you," he said to Vivi.

She rolled her eyes—and elbowed Daniel in the side, hard enough to make him realize he'd tightened his grip to near rib-cracking proportions. Eric, it appeared, wasn't the only one trying to prove something. Daniel chalked it up to his naturally competitive nature and put a bit of space between them. But he kept his arm where it was,

"I have to call a plumber," she said, "but in the meanwhile, we need a place to stay."

"Babe," Eric spread his hands, "you can stay with me."

"Are you sure? Because—"

"Both of you," he said, "and not with me, exactly. That would be awkward, seeing as you and I used to . . . well—" His attention shifted to Daniel. "I'm sure you already know Vivi wasn't a nun before you two hooked up."

Vivi gave him a dirty look. Eric was no match for it.

"Anyway, I got this building," he said, still talking to Daniel. "Well, it's not mine, exactly. I'm watching it for this guy, you know, making sure it doesn't become a homeless shelter while he's waiting for his demolition permit. There's plenty of room. You two can hang here until Vivi's place is fumigated."

"Does it have running water?" Daniel asked.

"All the amenities," Eric said.

Daniel searched for an excuse to say no, but there wasn't one, which meant his reason for turning Eric down was personal, not practical, and there was no room for personal when his life was on the line.

He turned on his heel, backtracking to the car, his hand on the small of Vivi's back to nudge her along beside him. Eric tagged along, too.

"Dude," he said to Daniel, "is that your car?"

Daniel glanced over at Vivi. She made a big show of studying her nonexistent manicure. But she was grinning.

"Yeah, it's mine," Daniel finally said.

"It looks like a hearse."

ERIC HAD BEEN RIGHT ABOUT THE WATER—IT RAN hot and cold. He'd hooked up electricity for them, probably not legal, but Daniel wasn't in a position to quibble, since he didn't have any other options.

He hadn't grown up in Boston, and he didn't have any family here. Probably one of the reasons he'd been posted to the U.S. Attorney's office for the district of Massachusetts. No connections equaled no conflicting loyalties. He couldn't turn to the job, either. They'd put him under police protection, and he wasn't having that—even if he thought it would work, which it wouldn't. Sooner or later the hit men would take him out, whether or not he was surrounded by cops. His best bet was to find out who was behind the contract and make sure it got revoked.

Eric lived on the ground floor; Daniel had opted for the third, far enough to keep from being overheard, far enough . . . Hell, he might as well admit he didn't want to be any closer to Eric than necessary. And since Vivi was staying with him, well, that worked out best for everyone. Except maybe Eric.

"So what's the story?" Daniel asked as soon as they were alone.

Vivi looked around. "Not much in the way of furniture," she said. Her eyes passed over a half-trashed, circa 1950 dinette set, stopping to take a good long look at the double mattress in one corner of what would have been the front room of the apartment. "It looks clean, and Eric said he'd get us a couple of fresh blankets."

"I wasn't talking about the amenities." In fact, he'd been trying hard not to think about sharing that mattress with her. "Eric," he said, adding before she could get the wrong idea from the rasp in his voice, "I have to be able to gauge the risk of staying here."

"I'd say it's pretty low," she said with a shrug in her voice. "Eric is slime, but only where women are involved. I dated him three years ago."

"Casual?"

She didn't say anything, so he turned around and watched her face. But her face wasn't giving anything away, either. "If you parted on bad terms, I'll need to factor in the possibility of revenge."

"If I wanted revenge, I'd tell my grandmother to deal with him. She's a Russian gypsy. She knows revenge."

She was also dead, but that wasn't Daniel's first thought. His first thought was that Eric was lucky his dick hadn't fallen off—and if he kept thinking that way, it was only a matter of time before he started reading tea leaves and slaughtering chickens so he could study their entrails. "When I said revenge, I was worried about Eric" was all Daniel said.

"First, Eric wouldn't know who to sell us out to. Not that you'd know it to hear him talk. He'd tell you he's connected to everyone and everything in this town, but his estimation of his own importance is sadly overrated. Second, he couldn't care less about you and me—except for the ego boost he'd get if he cut you out. The only terms he cares about are his, and as far as he's concerned, we parted amicably."

"In other words," Daniel said, "he cheated on you."

"There were other issues," she said huffily.

"I'll bet he wanted the lottery numbers, too."

"If my talent worked that way, I'd be living on my own private island somewhere."

"And I'd be dead."

Vivi studied his face. No sarcasm, no skepticism. She wanted to believe he was beginning to trust her—or at least her talent—but she couldn't let herself risk it yet.

"If you're done picking apart my love life, maybe we can focus on something more important," she suggested, "like the hit men. You've seen them for yourself now. Does that get us any closer to figuring out who hired them?"

"They're pretty average-looking, unless you count Flip's . . ."

"Fashion sense? I particularly like the flowered neck brace."

Daniel smiled slightly. "Aside from that, I didn't see any distinguishing features. And having their names isn't going to help much, either, since they're obviously nicknames. The accent is South Boston Irish, but anybody could hire a Southie, not just the Irish mob. In fact, it makes more sense for the mastermind to hire someone who's not from his own ethnic group. Throw me off the track."

"So we're back to your cases."

"Looks that way." Daniel's phone rang, and he held up a hand, his expression going flat when he looked at the read-out.

"More trouble," Vivi said.

"You having another vision?"

"No, it's just the way our luck is running."

chapter
13

"THE BUREAU IS PULLING YOU IN," MIKE SAID when Daniel finally answered his phone. "We don't have the budget to protect you, even if that would solve the problem. You'll go under for a while, and when the heat is off you can surface and take another post. California or Alaska maybe."

"Hawaii not available?"

"Lawyers," Mike snorted, "always want the cushy job."

"Actually, I'm pretty fond of Boston. I'm settled in and everything."

"Not your choice."

"The hell it's not. I don't work for the FBI anymore."

"You can't say this contract isn't payback for something you did when you were an agent."

"No, I can't, but I'm not going to run and hide now, any more than I did then."

"Circumstances are different."

"The message is the same," Daniel said, "and it's not one we should be sending. I run from this, I might as well paint a target on every U.S. attorney in the country. Guys like Sappresi won't hesitate to take aim."

"You think he's behind this?"

"No, but his lawyer will take advantage of the situation, and get the case kicked. And even if he doesn't, it'll take time for another prosecutor to get up to speed. If it goes to trial before the government's case is prepared, we'll lose. Either way, he's back out on the street."

"You don't know that."

"Like hell I don't."

Mike blew out a breath. "I've got no choice. Word came down from the top. You come in or you'll be brought in."

"Those same people decided I wasn't worth having around a few years back," Daniel reminded him. "I made a new life for myself, and they're not taking it away from me."

"You still work for the government, Pierce—"

Daniel snapped the phone shut, clipped it back on his belt, and turned to Vivi. "We're on our own," he said, ignoring his phone when it started buzzing at his waist. "We can't trust the FBI or the Boston P.D."

"At least they're not trying to kill you."

"They want to end my life, which amounts to the same thing."

"Maybe it's not such a bad idea to go in. You can lie low, take your time going over your cases, and they'll help you figure out who's after you."

"I thought I had help."

"Not professional help. Not the kind of help that shoots guns."

"That kind of help tends to find permanent solutions to things, including the people with the answers."

She went silent for a minute, her eyes on his. "You're hoping to catch one of the hit men and find out who they work for."

"The thought crossed my mind."

"And you think I'm crazy."

"You must be rubbing off on me."

They both went still, keeping their gazes off each other so they didn't have to acknowledge the "rubbing" comment and notice there was a bed conveniently handy.

"The odds of getting my hands on Hatch or Flip aren't very good anyway," Daniel said. "It's not like I can sit around waiting for them to show up."

"Even if they show up, your odds aren't very good," Vivi pointed out. "When they show up there's usually gunfire involved. The only way your hands are getting anywhere near them is if they're checking to see if you still have a pulse."

"So it's not a perfect solution. I've got a backup plan." He pulled the laptop out of his duffel and took it to the worn linoleum-covered dinette table. He powered it up, taking a legal pad for himself and putting one in front of the chair beside him. "We'll have to write fast," he said by way of invitation. "As soon as Mike tells the District office I refused to come in, they'll yank my ID. If I know Mike, he'll give me some time, but it won't be much, considering I pissed him off when I hung up on him."

Vivi stayed where she was, looking kind of shell-shocked and sick to her stomach. "You're going to list off your files, is that what you're telling me?"

"Before I lose my access." He nudged the pad closer to the empty chair. "Then you can do your thing."

"You're kidding, right?"

He stared at her, trying hard not to portray any level of kidding.

"I'm not Stephen King's version of a psychic," she said. "I didn't come out of a five-year coma with the ability to get movie-style visions on command."

"Huh?"

"*The Dead Zone*? Never mind. I can't tell you anything from a list of names we wrote down ten minutes ago."

"But I thought—"

"I need the files, mug shots, something the guilty party might have handled, at the very least."

"So that thing you did at the market?"

"I get my best readings from people. Living, breathing people."

Daniel pulled out his cell phone and tapped into his

wireless Internet connection. "You need people," he said, "let's find you some people. They might even still be breathing."

"SO...WHERE DO YOU WANT TO START?" VIVI ASKED, looking over at Daniel.

They'd been shoulder to shoulder, writing feverishly for the last thirty minutes. They'd managed to access most of Daniel's case files before the District office pulled the plug on him. And now that they weren't otherwise occupied, Daniel had plenty of time to notice how close Vivi was. And react to it.

He seized on the first name on his list so he didn't think about the nice, convenient mattress right across the room. "George Washington."

"Not breathing," she said absently, her eyes on his mouth.

Daniel stood up and stepped off. It felt like he was walking through quicksand. Or regret. "George Washington is still breathing—at least this one is. I prosecuted him for kidnapping. He snatched his stepdaughter and headed for Florida. Made it to Baltimore before he was caught."

"George is a disgrace to his namesake, but do you think he's the kind of guy who could hire hit men from jail?"

"Putting someone in prison doesn't end their ability to act in the outside world. Just like not putting them in jail doesn't guarantee they're not holding a grudge."

He'd staked his reputation on those he prosecuted being guilty, and just because they'd slipped past the reach of justice didn't mean there'd been no consequences. "Being accused of and prosecuted for a federal crime is no small thing. Even if the verdict is for acquittal, there's loss of face, loss of employment, divorce, any number of repercussions. And we're talking about people who only know one way of dealing with someone who's pissed them off."

"Okay, so we can't rule out any cases, won or lost. Take Anthony Sappresi, he seems like the kind of man who'd put out a contract hit on a federal prosecutor."

"What do you know about him?" Daniel said, watching her face.

"That he's your only active case at the moment," she said, not giving anything away.

"I already talked to him. He denied any involvement."

"And you believe him? He's the only one on this list who makes any sense."

"Do you know everyone on that list?"

"Well, no, but—"

"I thought you couldn't get anything helpful from a bunch of names."

"I'm not a crystal ball," she shot back, "I've got a brain, and it's telling me George Washington is a waste of time. A guy who preys on innocent little girls—"

"She went with him willingly. It was only illegal because she was fifteen and he took her across state lines."

"I'm not going to argue semantics with you," Vivi said. "My point is this: Does George have the kind of the connections it takes to put out a contract, or the kind of money to hire hit men?"

The obvious answer was no, but there was no way in hell Daniel was going to give her that satisfaction. Digging his heels in might be childish, not to mention foolishly dangerous for them both, but she'd pissed him off. Again. "I'm not looking at Sappresi. He's a lot of things, but it would take a complete moron to have the U.S. attorney prosecuting his case murdered. He'd be the obvious suspect."

"Maybe somebody is trying to frame him."

"That makes him the fall guy, not the perpetrator."

Vivi frowned, gnawing on her lower lip. "How about that man, the reporter at Cohan's?"

"Rudy Manetti? Tony wouldn't let him do anything stupid."

"Maybe Tony doesn't know he's planning something stupid."

Daniel wanted to shoot that idea down, but she had a point, and it was one he couldn't overlook.

"And how about Joe Flynn?" she asked before he had to admit as much.

"As long as I send Tony Sappresi to jail, Joe will be happy with me. He's hoping to unite the Irish families and move into the crime void Tony leaves behind."

"Won't the Italians have a problem with that?"

"Yeah, but I don't see how either faction would benefit from getting rid of me."

"Unless one of them has someone else in mind for your job. Someone . . . friendlier."

"Assistant U.S. attorneys are hired by the U.S. attorney, who is appointed by the president."

"You've never heard of bribery?"

"It would take a lot of money."

"Yeah. The kind of money available to the Italian Mafia or the Irish mob."

His first inclination was to deny the whole scenario; it just didn't make any sense for either Tony or Joe to put him up for a hit. They had a hell of a lot more to lose than they had to gain. But Vivi seemed so concerned, and she hadn't steered him wrong yet.

He paced across the room, torn between what he knew and how much trust he could put in Vivi's opinion . . . "Do you know any of this for a fact, or are you just spitballing from what you heard at Cohan's the night Patrice was shot?"

She took a breath, let it out. "I guess it's more that I know their reputations and I'm trying to make sure you've considered all the angles."

Daniel studied her for a minute, but if she'd been pulling out all the stops she'd have fallen back on her psychic ability to help convince him. Instead, she'd told him how she felt, she'd admitted it was only an opinion, and he had to respect her for that. He didn't have to agree with her, but he owed her the truth in return.

"I don't think looking at Sappresi again will gain me anything, and Joe Flynn is out, too. But you have a point about Rudy."

Vivi wasn't one hundred percent satisfied with his decision, but she accepted it.

"We can't do anything about Rudy tonight, so let's go over the list again. We'll look at the wins first, see if there's someone who might be connected enough to put out a contract on me."

He sat again—opposite Vivi—and pulled the legal pad over to him, writing a *W* or *L* next to each name.

Vivi came around the table and leaned over to watch him, giving a soft snort before he'd made it halfway through. "And you were questioning my stats," she said.

"These are high-profile criminals, and they can afford high-powered defense attorneys, the best in the business." And he was being defensive. "Yeah, my batting average isn't the best."

"If you were playing baseball, they'd ship you back to the minors."

It might come to that. If he didn't die first. Daniel took to his feet to walk off the frustration of . . . everything. Of course Vivi couldn't let it go.

"You know what your problem is, don't you?" she asked him. "You're color blind."

"What?"

"You know your cases inside out, you never skimp on the research or preparation, and the people you're prosecuting are nearly always guilty. But you don't see shades of gray. You only see black and white. It's not the best personality trait for a lawyer."

"Get out of my head, Mr. Spock."

"Dr. Spock was a psychologist, not a psychic."

"Not Dr., Mr." And when she only looked puzzled, he added, "*Star Trek*."

"Oh my God," she said with a laugh, "you're a Trekkie?"

"Every teenaged boy is a Trekkie," he said irritably. "Except maybe Flip."

"So you're saying you're more comfortable with aliens from another planet than earthlings with special talents."

"I'm saying I think you're from another planet."

"Don't you mean a galaxy far, far away?"

"That's *Star Wars*."

"Just checking," she said, still grinning.

"If you're done giving me career advice—"

"It's coming to me, it's coming—Wait . . ." she said, undaunted by the fact that he'd stomped back across the room and was looming over her. She closed her eyes and put two fingers to each temple. "You're going to run for the Senate, and you'll be elected! Yes, and you'll grow frustrated with the deal making and the graft and the inaction until one day you'll go onto the Senate floor, packing, and take out some of the more useless politicians."

"That would be pretty much all of them."

She turned her laughing, teasing face up to his and said, "You're a man of action."

She was damn right was all Daniel could think, hauling her to her feet and against him, and taking her mouth. Or trying to. Vivi wasn't a woman to be taken. She wrapped herself around him, one hand creeping up to fist in his hair. It stung a little. He liked it. Making love with Vivi ought to include a little pain, otherwise he could get seriously addicted . . . She dropped her mouth, her hot avid mouth, to his neck, twisted her incredibly built body against his, and he knew it was almost too late.

His hands were still banded around her arms. It took every ounce of willpower, and almost more strength than he had with his muscles shaking with need, to put her at arm's length. But he did it. He looked into her eyes, the haze of desire just clearing into confusion, and somehow managed not to finish what he'd started.

A few more seconds passed, or maybe an hour, and Vivi jerked her arms out of his grip and turned away. She was still struggling to catch her breath—so was Daniel—and neither of them spoke until they comfortably could. And even then they didn't look at each other.

"We'll start researching the wins first," he said, eyes trained on the street below their third-floor flophouse. "We can't go to jail and interview these guys, so we'll have to do some research first, look up known associates, family members, anyone who might be willing to talk to me."

"You mean us."

"I mean, you'll be doing your thing from the car."

She stomped over and jerked him around. "Let's get something straight. I don't take orders from you," she said, full of frustration and taking it out on him.

And better this way than the other, he told himself. Anger was so much less complicated than sex. "I'm in charge, that's nonnegotiable. You play this my way or you don't play at all."

"I know you think I'm a kook, but I'm not playing a game, Daniel." She turned and walked, as quietly as she'd spoken, back to the table, pulled the legal pad and the laptop over, and began to surf the Web.

There didn't seem to be any way to respond, so Daniel let it go. He had a feeling he'd be doing a lot of that where Vivi was concerned.

chapter 14

MORNING CAME EARLY. VIVI WOKE UP WISHING she could say the same about herself. They'd started the night on separate sides of the mattress, but they'd ended up plastered together, Daniel wrapped around her like a blanket. An electric blanket. With bare wiring that made her skin tingle, her nerves buzz, and parts of her get way too hot. She shifted, restless, not intentionally rubbing against Daniel, but she liked the feel of his long, hard body.

His hands clamped around her hips. "Don't do that again," he rumbled in her ear.

The feel of his warm breath made her shiver. So did the tone of his voice—for different reasons. The spike of lust and the little thrill of fear might have combined to overpower her better intentions. He didn't stick around long enough for her to find out.

Vivi stayed where she was until Daniel disappeared into the bathroom. And then she did a lot of thinking. The thinking started out being about Daniel, but that was counterproductive to the whole thought process so she tabled

Daniel, except in that the rest of the list related to him because he was the reason she was neck deep in hit men.

Her life was on the line, too, now, and if Sappresi was behind the contract, all he had to do was wait for her to step back into her routine and have her killed then. Because Sappresi knew right where to find her. And Sappresi had every reason to want her dead.

Back when her grandmother was still alive, and Vivi had just begun to take over the business, Tony had been one of her first clients, and he'd remained her best, until the day she discovered who he really was. And what he was using her predictions for.

Including the murder of an FBI agent.

She'd been the stupid one, naïve, wanting to believe in the basic goodness of everyone. So when she'd told Tony that a friend of his would betray him, and when she'd described the face of that friend, she'd never for one second guessed where that prediction would lead. Until she'd seen it for herself.

She'd lied to Daniel when she told him his murder was the first vision she'd had. Tom Zukey, the FBI agent Sappresi had ordered killed, had been the first. She hadn't understood what was happening then, though, and she'd written it off as a particularly vile nightmare. Until the next time Tony came in and she'd seen the truth of it on his face.

She'd refused to counsel him anymore after that, but Tony didn't go away without argument. So she'd used his superstition against him without a second thought. Tony believed in what she did, and he believed that harming her would turn the harm back on him. She'd made sure of it.

There'd been nothing she could do about Tom Zukey, though. Established law enforcement was notoriously resistant to help from psychics. Nothing would have been gained by going to the Boston P.D. or the FBI, except to sign her own death warrant if Sappresi found out about it. It made her sick to let him just walk away, but not as sick as knowing she'd helped him commit murder. True, she hadn't put the bullets in Zukey with her own hand, but she'd laid the groundwork. That made her just as guilty.

Daniel would surely see it that way, if he found out about it. She intended to do whatever it took to prevent that for as long as possible.

He came out of the bathroom, freshly shaven, his T-shirt and jeans comfortably worn and leaving nothing to the imagination. No saggy, homeboy pants for Daniel.

Vivi hightailed it into the bathroom and slammed the door before her thought processes clogged up with hormonal urges. By the time she'd brushed and washed and dressed, Daniel was waiting for her, everything he'd brought packed into his duffel. Probably didn't want Eric snooping. Vivi left her things there. It was no matter to her if Eric wanted to dig through them. All she'd brought was clothes, and Eric wasn't a pervert, he was a pain in the ass. Eric's only interest in a woman's clothing was in how fast he could get them off her.

RUDY MANETTI LIVED A COUPLE MILES AWAY, IN A building similar to Eric's. Rudy's building hadn't been rehabbed yet; it was still apartments. The mailbox at the front, communal entry said Rudy lived in 1A. Daniel and Vivi walked in from the alley entrance off the side street, counting off buildings and windows until they came to Rudy's apartment. Or, more accurately, Rudy's privacy fence, eight-feet tall, weathered wood, peek proof.

"It's locked," Daniel said after peering through the crack at the gate opening, "but not padlocked. I'll boost you over and you can open it for me."

Vivi didn't have a good feeling about the boosting program, but she didn't have a good feeling about any of this, and time was wasting. Daniel bent over and linked his fingers together, Vivi put her foot in the obvious place, and Daniel stood and lifted at the same time. The result was closer to a catapult than a boost. She went over the fence, but the landing wasn't pretty. The landing was five points—feet, hands, and ass—and she figured she was lucky it hadn't been her face.

"You okay?"

Vivi unlatched the gate and pulled it open. She chose to let her expression and the fact that she was rubbing her backside serve as an answer to his question.

Daniel didn't seem in the least repentant. Probably the smile on his face. "You go first," Vivi said, stepping back and gesturing him ahead of her.

Daniel stayed where he was, taking a moment to get his bearings. Rudy's apartment occupied one side of the building, and since it was the ground floor, he had a small backyard that was completely fenced off from the other side of the building. The reason for the fence escaped him. The yard was completely empty, no furniture, no flowers, no lawn equipment, which made sense because there was no lawn, just hard-packed dirt with some scrubby weeds.

Daniel went to the back door and tried the knob. "Locked," he said, glancing over his shoulder at Vivi.

"I opened the last one," she said.

"I'm a little out of practice."

"Break a windowpane out of the door, reach in, and unlock it."

"I was hoping we could get in without leaving tracks."

"He won't know it's us unless we stand here arguing about how to get in long enough for one of his neighbors to see us."

"There's a doggie door," Daniel said.

Vivi took a step back, her hands going to her hips. "You did not just suggest I crawl through a doggie door."

"I was only making an observation," Daniel said. "But now that you mention it, that's not a bad idea."

"No way. Absolutely not."

"You're small, you'll fit."

"If there's a doggie door, there's a dog. I don't want my face eaten off because you won't break a window. I like my face."

Daniel stared at her a second or two, the muscles in his jaw bunching. Then he hunkered down and pushed aside the rubber flap covering the opening. Vivi leaned in as close as she dared, looking over his shoulder, but she didn't see anything. Daniel dropped to his knees and stuck his head through the opening, taking a moment to study whatever was on the other side before he pulled back and stood up.

"There's a cat," he said. "Right up your alley."

Vivi rolled her eyes. "I'm not a witch."

"Semantics."

"Witches cast spells and perform rituals. Witches dance naked at the full moon. I don't do any of that stuff."

Daniel looked like he was stuck on the naked moon dancing. Hell, Daniel looked like he was undressing her with his eyes. If he kept staring at her like that, she might perform that task herself. And she wouldn't stop at her own clothes. "Fine," she said, squatting down on the top step and assessing the opening, about fifteen inches square. "I don't think I'll fit."

"You'll fit," Daniel said, sounding impatient.

Vivi took a deep breath, went down to her hands and knees, braced herself for trouble, and stuck her head past the rubber flap. Sure enough, there was a tabby cat sitting by the leg of a small dining table, watching her, tail lazily sweeping the floor.

Aside from the cat, the kitchen was about what she'd expected. Varnished cabinets, worn linoleum floor, fixtures from the sixties and, hello, decorated in Coca-Cola? She blinked a couple times but unfortunately her eyes weren't deceiving her. Coke trays hung on the walls, red-checkered Coke cloth covered the table and hung at the windows, Coke clock on the wall. Coke tchotchkes everywhere. Probably an old girlfriend with a coke addiction. And really bad taste in men.

Or maybe the dog had chased her off.

Vivi shot backward, winding up on her backside at Daniel's feet. "Shit. There's a dog," she said, looking up at him. "A big dog."

"You still have your face."

"And you're not in a fetal position, but that could change," she said, her eyes dropping to a vulnerable part of his anatomy. "Especially if you try to make me to stick my head in there again."

"If the dog wanted to eat your face off he'd come out the doggie door," Daniel said.

Vivi scrambled around behind him.

"Interesting," Daniel said. "You didn't think twice about crashing your truck through my house, or jumping off the roof of your building, but you can't handle a dog that isn't even threatening enough to bark."

"Easy for you to say, you're not the one about to end your life as a chew toy." But she scooted around to the doggie door again, and all right, she knew Daniel was psyching her into it, but she'd be damned if she let a dog get the better of her after she'd faced down armed hit men.

She stuck her head back into Coke Central and found the cat still lying by the table leg, still staring and swishing. And warm, stinky doggie breath washed over the side of her face. She froze, just her eyes sliding in that direction, and there was an open, panting dog mouth with big yellow teeth. A moist dog nose was above the mouth, and just behind that were a couple of dog eyes in a dog head attached to a large dog body.

"Hey, there," she said, going for nonaggressive. Come to think of it, eyeballing a dog was supposed to be a challenge. She switched her gaze to the cat and swore it rolled its eyes at her. "Sorry," she said to any animal that might have taken offense.

The cat started to wash its paws, and a huge dog tongue swiped up the side of her face. Several times. That tongue covered a lot of territory. If she'd been a Tootsie Pop, she'd have been down to the Tootsie Roll center in no time.

"What's going on?" Daniel called from the other side of the door, his voice sounding strained. "Why aren't you going inside?"

"Keep your pants on, Ace."

He muttered something she couldn't make out. Judging from the raspy quality of his voice, she decided that was a good thing. And she probably shouldn't push her luck any further.

She eased her arms and shoulders through the opening and inched forward past her waist before coming up short. She twisted, dipped one hip, then the other, and tried to wiggle them through, but her hips exceeded the doggie door limit.

"What the hell are you doing?" Daniel wanted to know. He still sounded raspy and strained, and she suspected it wasn't impatience. She suspected he was staring at her ass. Parts of her that shouldn't be went all warm and tingly, and the prevailing urge was to back out of the doggie door. And not because of the dog.

"I'm not getting any younger," Daniel said.

Or cooling off, apparently. It sounded like his voice had dropped into his crotch, right along with her thoughts. Vivi redoubled her efforts, trying to force her hips through with no luck. And she couldn't go back, either. She'd managed to wedge herself in, good and tight. "I'm stuck," she yelled back to Daniel.

He made a sound that defied translation into words but evoked a very definite physical response, and then she felt his hands on her hips. Her heart lurched, sending a jolt through her entire system. And while she was disoriented, he lifted, tipped, and shoved her through the doggie door on the diagonal. Her hips scraped the sides and then she was through, collapsing onto Rudy Manetti's Coca-Cola doormat, Rudy's dog panting hot breath into her face.

"Down boy," she said, climbing to her feet, her heart pounding for an entirely different reason. She'd just become a criminal, and having a federal prosecutor as an accomplice wasn't doing a lot for her hope of avoiding jail time.

"Well?"

"I'm thinking," she said to Daniel.

He stuck his head in the doggie door and glared up at her. The cat meowed and ran off. The dog paced over to stand in front of Vivi, facing Daniel. Its nose was all wrinkled back and it was growling.

"Aw," she said, "it's a smart dog. Don't worry about him, doggie," she said, patting it on the head. "He's harmless."

They had a stare down for a minute, Daniel trotting out his lawyer face. The dog looked up at Vivi, cocking its head.

"See?" she said. "Harmless."

The dog woofed, then plopped down on its belly and yawned hugely.

"Funny," Daniel said. "Let me in." And his head disappeared.

Vivi looked through the Coke curtains and he was standing there with a rock in his hand. "Now he's willing to break a window," Vivi griped to the dog. "I ought to leave him standing out there." She pulled the door open instead. "If you'd done that ten minutes ago . . ."

"What?"

"Nothing."

Daniel grabbed a Coke dish towel off the open door handle and wiped off the doorknob. "Did you touch anything else?"

"Just the metal strip around the doggie door when I was stuck."

His eyes met hers and she got a burning sensation. Everywhere. It was about fifteen degrees cooler in Rudy's apartment than outside, but there was a line of sweat trickling down between her breasts.

Daniel stooped and wiped off the metal strip. "Don't touch anything else."

Vivi gave him a look.

"Fine." He flipped her the dish towel, looking around the place for the first time. "Christ," he said.

"Yeah." Vivi wrapped the towel around her hand and pulled open the refrigerator door. Daniel looked over her shoulder. No Coke. "Weird," she said.

"You'd know."

And Daniel headed out of the kitchen. "How do you feel about birds?" he called back to her.

Vivi followed him and found herself in a small sitting room with a window looking out on the front of the building. There was a chair, a sofa, a table, and a lamp. And birds. Five birdcages were placed around the room, all of them holding at least one feathered, chirping thing. In the corner by the front window was a floor-to-ceiling leafless tree. At the top of the tree was a large parrot with multicolored feathers, beady little eyes, and a big mouth. "Raaaawk, Rudy's the man," he squawked.

"You don't think he'll rat us out?" Vivi asked Daniel.

"Raaaawk, Rudy's the man."

"I think his vocabulary is limited to ego boosting."

Daniel made a quick search of the room, finding nothing of interest. No personal papers, no unopened mail, no phone bills with interesting numbers. Vivi backtracked and did the same in the kitchen. "Nothing but kitchen stuff," she said when she joined Daniel again.

A short hallway led off the bird room, a bath on the front side, a bedroom to the back of the apartment. Daniel took the bathroom next. But there was really no storage. Hell, there wasn't even room for Vivi in there at the same time. So he moved across the hallway to the lone bedroom. He opened the door, then slammed it shut again.

"What's wrong?" Vivi wanted to know.

"The mailbox ought to say 'Ace Ventura.'"

"Uh-oh. What kind of animals are in there?"

Daniel cracked the door and peeked in. "I don't know, but there are aquariums."

"I can handle fish."

"No water in the aquariums," Daniel said, "so I think we can rule out fish. Probably can't say the same for lizards, iguanas, scorpions, or anything else you'd expect to find in a waterless aquarium. Including snakes."

Vivi blew out a breath, relieved, and slipped past him.

"You shied away from the dog, but you're not worried about snakes?"

"They're not wandering around loose in here," she said, "and I'm not sticking my head into the aquarium."

"I see your point." Daniel went into the room behind her. "You take that side," he said, "I'll take this one. Don't leave any fingerprints."

Daniel made his way around the room systematically, ignoring the creepy crawlies in their glass houses, searching every potential hiding space. The bottoms of dresser drawers, the pockets of suits hanging in the closet, between the mattress and box spring, and between the pages of the porn magazines by the bed. Vivi was glad she didn't have to touch those.

"His personal papers, bills and things, are in the bottom dresser drawer," Daniel said, "but there's nothing incriminating there. Except maybe his tax return. Rudy doesn't strike me as a guy who'd be a hundred percent honest on his 1040."

Rudy struck her as a guy who'd lie about everything from his bank balance to the size of his package. Rudy was a big talker. "Can we go now?" Vivi asked, feeling like she'd spent way too much time in Rudy's bedroom.

She headed for the door, but when she passed a fifty-gallon aquarium housing an orange, red, and white snake, she got an icky feeling—and it wasn't the run-of-the-mill snake phobia, either. She ignored the heebie-jeebies, stopping in front of the aquarium. More ick, still no specifics. It didn't feel lethal, so it probably wasn't aimed at Daniel, but she felt a need to tell him anyway, if only to see what he'd do.

"There's something hidden in the snake tank," she said.

Daniel went still, just his eyes cutting to the aquarium. "I don't see anything," he said after a long, tense moment.

"Trust me, Ace, there's something under the wood chips."

"So dig around in the wood chips and let me know what you find."

Vivi turned around, hands on hips, grinning. "You faced down armed hit men—and God knows what else when you were an agent—and you're afraid of a snake?"

"I wouldn't call it fear, exactly. More like caution."

"All you have to do is dig around in the wood chips," she parroted, "see if you find something."

"Easy for you to say," Daniel shot back. But he lifted the

screen top off the aquarium and, holding her gaze the entire time, stuck his hand in and rooted around in the wood chips. The snake came and curled around his wrist, probably liking the warmth. He ignored it. Vivi was watching and he had an image to maintain. And something interesting to find, as it turned out.

He shook the snake off and looked inside the envelope he pulled out of its tank. "Pictures of naked women," he said. "Taken without their knowledge, judging by the quality and angle." He tossed the envelope and its contents on the bed. "We're not finding anything tangible. What about you?"

"What about me?"

"Do your thing, Karnack."

"Funny," Vivi said, but she closed her eyes and shut everything out, the dog, the birds, the snake. Daniel. She wasn't getting anything, though. "Rudy's all talk," she said. "That's my professional opinion."

"That was my impression, too, and not only because we didn't find anything incriminating. Unless Rudy is a damn good actor, I can't believe he's involved with the mob, except for the family connection. Just doesn't feel right."

"Doesn't feel right," Vivi repeated.

"You got a problem with that?"

"No, Ace, but I thought you did."

Daniel chose not to follow that line of thought, the lawyer in him, Vivi figured. Instead, he went into the closet directly across from the bed, banged around inside for a minute or two, then came back out.

"What was all that about?"

"His camera suffered a puzzling accident."

"Too bad we can't do that to the rest of his equipment."

"Now you've developed a violent streak."

"I just needed the right motivation," Vivi said. "Let's get out of here."

Daniel started with a comeback, but Vivi grabbed his arm and said, "Now!" just as they heard the front door open.

Daniel dragged her across the hall and into the bathroom, shoving her into the tub, getting in with her, and pulling the curtain closed behind them. "It's Rudy," he said, as if Vivi couldn't hear him talking to the dog.

"Hey there, T-Bone," he was saying in that voice people used when they talked to an animal they loved. "How's my Boner, huh?"

Vivi met Daniel's eyes and wrinkled her nose, making a face that said, "Ewwwww." The corners of Daniel's mouth tipped up just enough so she knew he was sharing the moment, before his expression went hard again.

Rudy's voice floated back from the front room, still talking to the dog. "How'd you get my shoe?" he asked T-Bone, "I didn't leave the bedroom door open . . ." The next thing they heard was a click.

"Shit," Daniel whispered.

Rudy went into the kitchen first, coming back out before they could even hope to sneak out the front door. He opened the closet in the front room, did a quick walk through the bedroom, and then came into the bathroom. "I know you're in there," he said, the edge of the curtain inched back with the barrel of a gun.

Vivi froze, staring at that little black hole until spots danced in front of her eyes, and she realized even her involuntary bodily functions had frozen. She sucked in a breath, trying to think around the terror, instinctively looking to Daniel.

He wasn't going to be much help, she decided, watching his hands lift into the air. Vivi thought he was giving in kind of easy, and then he grabbed the top of the shower curtain, ripped it down, and wrapped it around Rudy, spinning him so that when the gun went off it blew out a chunk of tile in the corner of the tub.

Daniel gave Rudy a shove, grabbed Vivi, and hauled her out of the tub and down the hall. A couple more shots zinged after them, even though before she hit the kitchen Vivi looked back and saw that Rudy still hadn't fought his way free of the shower curtain. Another two seconds and they were out the back door, Boner nipping at Daniel's heels. They hit the alley, and Daniel slammed the gate in the privacy fence shut before the dog could come through.

They retreated down the alley, making the return trip at a fast walk so as not to arouse too much suspicion. They jumped into Daniel's car and locked the doors and sat there a minute, silent, both a little shell-shocked.

"Maybe we should take off before Rudy calls the police," Vivi suggested when she had some confidence that her voice wouldn't waver.

"He won't take the chance they'll find the camera."

"Good, because I left my fingerprints all over the tile in the bathtub." She was lucky that was all she'd left.

Daniel scrubbed a hand back through his hair, but he still didn't start the car. Not that she blamed him. After the close escape, going after another name from his list didn't hold much appeal for Vivi, either. Being in fear of her life for any longer than necessary held even less. She was tired of being scared, tired of walking on eggshells with Daniel, and tired of wrestling her libido down.

None of that was stopping until they neutralized the death threat, though, and the day was still young.

She heaved a sigh and buckled her seat belt. "Let's go see about George Washington."

chapter 15

GEORGE WASHINGTON'S EX-WIFE AND STEPDAUGH-
ter had closed up shop and moved to Seattle. George didn't
have any relatives in Boston, and if he'd had friends they
hadn't come forward to offer character testimony at the
time of his trial. Vivi couldn't put any logic to one of them
trying to have Daniel killed now.

For once he agreed with her. "How about Larry Hickman?" he asked her.

Vivi thought about Larry Hickman, but nothing was
coming to her. Her brain was empty except for the residual
aftershocks of having a gun pointed at her, and all she was
feeling was relief that she hadn't been shot. "I don't know."

"How about . . ." he waggled his fingers in the air, "your
Cosmic Telegraph?"

Vivi cocked her head, trying not to smile. "Nothing on
the Cosmic Telegraph about Larry. Not enough info."

"Well, we're here anyway," he said, steering his car to
the curb across the street from a rutted gravel driveway.
"We might as well check out Larry so we can cross him off
the list."

"He lives here?"

"His home is a six-by-eight cell in Allenwood Federal Prison," Daniel said, stepping out of the car. "His mother lives here."

"Alone, from the look of it." But Vivi hurried from the car. Much as she didn't like the prospect of what she might face—and she wasn't talking about the human inhabitants of the place—she didn't want to be left behind.

"Rundown" would have been an optimistic description for the small house where Larry Hickman's mother lived. The yard was a waist-high jungle, the house looked like it was defying gravity, and the whole place stank. It smelled increasingly more disgusting as they got closer to the house, an odor that seemed to be equal parts animal leavings, rotting vegetation, and some sort of fungus they would probably discover caused brain damage.

Daniel knocked on the door and it opened, letting out the stench of yesterday's fish dinner and revealing an old woman. Tufts of white hair barely covered patches of shiny pink scalp, and she was badly stooped, barely able to lift her head high enough to look at them. And it wasn't yesterday's dinner that smelled. It was last week's laundry, which the woman was, unfortunately for their noses, still wearing.

"My name is Daniel Pierce," Daniel said through the torn screen door. "You must be Mrs. Hickman."

She shut the door in his face.

He looked at Vivi.

She shook her head. "Too fast for a reading."

So Daniel went in anyway. Or tried to. The front door was locked, so he set out through the wilderness of her yard, Vivi following carefully in the swath his feet cut through the weeds.

Mrs. Hickman was in the kitchen at the rear of the house, another badly patched screen door the only barrier between her and the backyard—which closely resembled the front except that the stench was eye watering.

"We just want to talk to you about Larry," Daniel called

out—loudly in case her hearing was as decrepit as everything else within a hundred-foot radius.

"Fine," Mrs. Hickman said, "but I'll do the talking." The cast-iron frying pan she was holding when she came to the door was sending a pretty clear message, too. "My boy never did nobody no harm."

"He was a drug dealer," Daniel pointed out, pulling Vivi up beside him, and jerking his head in a way that told her to get on with it.

"So what?" Mrs. Hickman shouted, standing straighter and looking less like a dotty old woman and more like somebody it wouldn't be good to meet in a dark alley. "My Larry didn't force nobody to buy them drugs, and he didn't force nobody to take 'em, neither. He was a middleman, a whatchacall . . . entrepreneur."

"He was a distributor," Daniel explained for Vivi's sake, "part of the Corona network that kept the local street dealers supplied."

"'Xactly," Mrs. Hickman said proudly. "Boy couldn't read worth a tinker's damn, but he was a good son. He took care of me. He took care of this place, 'til you sent him to jail. And now I gotta live on Social Security. You ever try to live on Social Security, Mr. Jackass Federal Prosecutor?" And she shoved the screen door open and stomped out, standing straight, brandishing her frying pan.

Daniel backed off, trying to sweep Vivi behind him. She wasn't having any of that, but she stayed close to his side, one hand fisted in the back of his shirt, the other light at his waist. It might have been distracting if he hadn't been worried about death by skillet.

"I'm sorry to hear about your troubles," he said, still trying to buy Vivi enough time to rule Larry and his crazy mother in or out, "but I need to know if you've been in touch with your son lately."

"'Course I have, he's my baby," she snapped. "I visit him every chance I get. In that federal jail you put him in." And she lunged at Daniel, the skillet held high over her head.

He wrapped his arm around Vivi and skipped out of the way, carrying her along with him. The skillet came down on empty air, but Mrs. Hickman had already checked her forward momentum. And she could run. She'd given up all pretense of being a frail old woman. She came after them, full speed ahead, screaming threats and obscenities at the top of her lungs.

"Call the police," she shrieked, taking another swing. "Call nine-one-one." Too bad for her it wasn't the kind of neighborhood that had a watch group. Or anyone who gave a damn about what was going on next door.

Daniel took off for the car, hauling Vivi along in his arms and hoping like hell his bad leg would hold them both. He swore he could hear the homicidal skillet whistling past his ears. And to make matters worse, Vivi started to struggle.

"Hold still," he yelled at her.

But she wriggled even more violently. Her elbow slammed into his injured thigh, and Daniel dropped her to her feet, going down to his knees. He swore he felt the skillet whoosh by, close enough to graze the waistband of his jeans. He definitely felt the breeze, so he went into a tuck and roll, coming back up in time to see that Vivi had gained her feet. And Mrs. Hickman was standing over him.

"I know Pablo Corona," she bellowed, raising the cast-iron frying pan over her head again. "I'm going to call him and—"

Vivi popped her one, a nice right jab to the jaw. Mrs. Hickman went down like a sack of flour, the skillet clanging on the hard-packed earth of the front yard.

"I can't believe you did that," Daniel said as Vivi helped him to his feet. "You won't shoot the hit men, you won't run them over, but you'll coldcock an old woman."

"Yeah, well, she earned it," Vivi said, "but I'm not strong enough to put her completely out, and she's about as frail as a rottweiler."

Daniel climbed to his feet and looked down at her. Larry's mother was flat on her back, dazed but not unconscious, a bruise already blooming where Vivi's small fist had made contact.

Daniel wasn't feeling much sympathy. "Any luck?" he asked Vivi.

"Larry's not trying to kill you," she said, setting off for the car. "She'd know if he was, and she wasn't hiding anything."

"You got all that, huh?"

"It helped when I touched her."

"You mean punched her."

"Fine, I punched her, and if we're smart, we'll be long gone by the time she calls the cops."

"Man," Daniel said, "you really don't like the cops."

"Law enforcement personnel don't, as a rule, have much imagination," Vivi said dryly. "They tend to want to arrest me."

"You have to admit they have cause this time. You did sucker punch an old woman."

"To keep you from getting your head caved in. By an old woman."

Daniel refused to be embarrassed by that. "I'm just going to enjoy this for a while, if you don't mind."

"Okay," Vivi said, stopping at the passenger door and looking over the roof of the car at him. She was smiling, too. "And when you're done poking fun at me, you might want to ask yourself why we're all the way across the street, but it still smells."

VIVI WAS FINDING IT HARD TO BREATHE, BUT THERE was no stench involved. Daniel had peeled out of his shirt before he got in the car, took one look at the brown smear on the back of it, and tossed it into Mrs. Hickman's yard, where it immediately sank into the tangle of debris and disappeared.

He was sitting there, a foot away, like it was nothing to drive around Boston without a shirt. Vivi was sitting there, trying not to think about the fact that he was a foot away, bare from the waist up. And all of it was muscle, including his head most of the time. But she wasn't thinking about his head. She was thinking about his pecs, peppered with just enough dark hair to make her palms itch to touch it. The hair veed down over washboard abs and disappeared beneath the waistband of his jeans like an arrow pointing the way to . . .

"It's not Mrs. Hickman," Vivi said, dragging her thoughts back above his waistband and wiping surreptitiously at her upper lip. "She'd know about it if Larry was up to anything. She'd have tried to keep you at the house long enough for Hatch and Flip to take care of you, instead of attacking you with a skillet."

Daniel didn't respond, and she didn't dare look at him or she'd lose what little presence of mind she possessed, not to mention the tiny bit of willpower that kept her staring out the passenger window. And then there was the drooling. That would be really embarrassing. "I didn't realize Larry worked for Pablo Corona."

Corona the Butcher, rumored to be insane and known to be indiscriminately violent, was the Colombian drug lord who controlled a good portion of the cocaine trade in North America. There was a ten-million-dollar bounty on his head. It had yet to be collected, and not for lack of trying.

"Would Corona take out a contract on you?" she asked Daniel.

"Not over Larry Hickman. Pablo probably knew when Larry was arrested, but he would have seen it more as routine maintenance than anything else. The only person Pablo would've had killed was Larry, if he'd been stupid enough to talk. Which he wasn't."

"Then why did we bother with him?"

"Had to rule him out. Have to rule everyone out to be completely sure, either through research or personal knowledge."

Vivi made the mistake of looking over at him, and her mild level of exasperation was no match for the instant flare of lust. Worse yet, Daniel knew what she was thinking, or rather feeling. It amused him, she realized, narrowing her eyes on that little lawyer smirk on his face. She hated that smirk. Her palms stopped itching and the iron snapped back into her willpower. Parts of her were still experiencing a heat wave, but she wasn't caving in to that anymore.

"There are a lot of names on this list," she said, holding up the legal pad where Larry Hickman's name was now crossed off, along with George Washington's and Rudy Manetti's. "Are you saying we have to find every one of these people or their lunatic relatives?"

"The law of averages says we'll get the right person before we're halfway through."

Vivi didn't want to be overly pessimistic, but the law had never been a friend of hers. "I thought we were going back to the apartment," she said when Daniel pulled into the parking lot of a mom-and-pop-type restaurant.

"What for?" Daniel got out of the car and went around to the trunk, opening it and digging through his duffel. He pulled out a clean shirt and slipped it over his head.

"Are you sure this is a good idea?" Vivi wanted to know.

"You claim you never get a decent meal while I'm around."

"This place can't be decent. I know this neighborhood. An ex-friend of mine lives not too far from here." And Heather Wilcox definitely wasn't decent. At least she hadn't been when Vivi caught her on top of Eric "just having sex, babe." Not that it had been a surprise. She'd known Eric was a hound, but it had been right after her grandmother died and she'd needed . . . someone. Being alone, however, had turned out to be an improvement over having a toxic spill like Eric in her life.

The restaurant was on a main street, but the building had clearly once been a house. It sat on a patch of potholed macadam, a few weeds in the cracks the only spots of green on the property—if she didn't count the stuff hanging out of the Dumpster at the far back corner of the lot. The building itself was covered in aluminum siding, dented and faded to a dull gray.

"I know it doesn't look like much," Daniel began.

It looked like food poisoning waiting to happen.

"But you get your best meals at a place like this."

Vivi wasn't convinced, but he took her by the wrist and towed her to the front door, and when he opened it, some really fantastic aromas leaked out and beckoned her inside.

Something niggled at the edge of her mind, but Daniel was touching her and they hadn't had breakfast, so she walked in without further objection—and stopped just inside the doorway, taking a good look around and trying to figure out why she felt uncomfortable. She shook Daniel's hand off, which helped until he set his fingers at the small of her back and gave her a light shove.

"Take that back booth," he said, bending close so his breath brushed over her ear and the nape of her neck. She shivered and bypassed the sign that said, SEAT YOURSELF, walking obediently to the booth he'd indicated and sliding into the side against the wall.

Daniel hesitated, then sat beside her.

Vivi scooted as far into the corner as she could, trying to ignore the way their thighs brushed, and their arms brushed and the large, solid feel of him beside her, smelling faintly of dry rot. Even that made her hot because she remembered how he'd come to smell like dry rot, which made her laugh.

"What's so funny?" he wanted to know.

"Mrs. Hickman chasing you with a frying pan," she said.

He laughed, met her eyes, and laughed with her, and she fell just a little more for him. Worse, she could imagine having an actual relationship with Daniel now that he'd begun to loosen up some, one that could even last a lifetime if he ever came to trust her. Except she hoped he never trusted her completely. She was keeping a pretty big secret, and when he found out it wasn't going to be pretty, and if she didn't tell him now . . . "Daniel," she said, taking advantage of the friendly moment, going with instinct. "I need to tell you—"

"About them?"

Vivi looked where he was looking and saw two cops come into the restaurant. Two more came in about a minute behind, and they weren't the last. Before she knew it, the place was half full of uniforms, and the discomfort she'd felt when they walked in made perfect sense.

"Why are you shaking?" Daniel asked.

"Why don't you care that the place is full of cops?"

"They're all looking at you."

Which didn't make her feel any better. "What if they have our descriptions?"

"If they had your description you'd be under arrest by now," Daniel said, not liking the way several pairs of cops' eyes were plastered on Vivi with enough heat to set her on fire. Odd though that he was the one who was burning, not liking the way they stared at her, even though it kept their eyes off him, which was good as his was the more recognizable face—to cops at least. "The trick is not to draw attention to yourself." He took two of the plastic-coated menus from behind the condiments on their table, opened one, and handed it to her so it hid her face.

"Why don't we just leave?" she whispered from behind her menu.

"It would definitely get their attention if we walked out because half the Boston P.D. is in here," he said. And now that they couldn't see Vivi's face—or body—anymore, they weren't drawing as much attention. Daniel received an assessing stare or two, but he thought he saw envy rather than curiosity on those faces.

The waitress showed up, early fifties, frowsy blonde hair and a pink uniform with a white apron. Her name tag read JUNE, her eyes were on Daniel, and she wasn't blinking.

Vivi cleared her throat, she and June exchanged glances, and June said, "What'll it be?"

"Is there anything that's not fried?" Vivi wanted to know.

"Sure." The waitress leaned over Daniel, took her sweet time reading a menu she probably had memorized, then pointed to something Vivi couldn't see. "This . . . no.

Maybe—no. I guess everything is fried." And she straightened reluctantly, fixed Daniel with her adoring stare, pencil poised over her order pad.

"Bring us two cheeseburgers," Daniel said.

"Fries?"

"With hers. Onion rings with mine. Iced tea for both of us."

"Well." Vivi tucked her menu away. "Don't I feel all helpless and feminine. The rest of the customers rub off on you or something? Men on a power trip," she explained in answer to the puzzled look he sent her.

"They're not all on power trips."

"They are when you have a record," she muttered crankily.

"You only have one arrest on your record."

"Right, and it's a nonviolent crime, but that doesn't stop some of your coworkers from checking me for weapons any time they want."

Daniel knew exactly what she was saying. There were men on the force who thought a badge put them above the law they were sworn to uphold—a license to be complete assholes whenever the mood struck them. And the mood would strike any straight male who laid eyes on Vivi.

He felt a surge of hard, brittle anger, but there was a facet of territoriality that he didn't fight because it surprised him and he wanted to examine it. He didn't like what he found, and when Vivi reached over and put her hand on his, he felt another surge of emotion he really didn't like. Because it wasn't hard.

"Daniel."

He looked up and realized the waitress was there with their drinks and food. She dropped everything off, then went back to her position by the serving window between the kitchen and the counter, staring at Daniel with a little smile on her face.

He didn't really mind, until the cop sitting at the counter started to send him dirty looks. He hunched his shoulders and dropped his head over his meal, and when he risked another glance the waitress was taking food out of the window and heading off to serve it. The cop was still there, still looking at him, only this time his eyes were narrowed and he looked . . .

"Oh, my God," Vivi moaned, "this is amazing." She took another bite, eyes closed, looking like she'd just had really good sex.

"It's the grease," Daniel said, picking up his burger and concentrating on eating with every fiber of his being. The waitress came over to refill their glasses. He looked up, and jumping Vivi wasn't the only thing he had to worry about. It wasn't even top of the list. The dawning recognition in the cop's eyes was much more worrisome.

Daniel took a twenty out of his wallet, dropped it on the table, and got to his feet.

"What?" Vivi said, her mouth still full of cheeseburger.

"Time to go."

"I thought leaving would draw too much attention."

The officer glanced at Vivi's face when she spoke, did a double take, then turned his back and started talking furiously into the little radio at his shoulder.

"Too late," Daniel said.

Vivi folded the paper lining of the little plastic basket her burger had been served in, making it to go. She hesitated, then did the same with Daniel's, heading for the door behind him.

The cop stepped in front of Daniel. "Don't I know you?" he said.

"Nope," Daniel said, "never seen you before."

The cop turned to Vivi. "And you?"

"You're asking me that in front of your girlfriend?"

"Yeah," the waitress said from the other side of the counter. Her hands were on her hips and her expression was set to pissed off.

"Now, June," the cop said. His tone was condescending, even before he added, "this is official police business."

Daniel reached for Vivi, got a handful of onion rings, and wrapped his fingers around her wrist instead. He pulled her out the door, making it around the corner to the parking lot just as another police cruiser pulled up. Out popped Officer Cranston, who hurried inside.

"At a precinct on the other side of town, huh?"

"Just get in," Daniel said, starting the car and putting it in gear almost before she got the door shut. They pulled out of the lot, but not before they heard the unmistakable sound of a police siren winding up behind them.

chapter
16

DANIEL MADE A COUPLE OF QUICK TURNS AND pulled the car over to the curb, just as Vivi was about to make the same suggestion—strongly.

"I don't need you to tell me to ditch the car," he said.

And she didn't need him to tell her he was still skeptical about her abilities—although he seemed to be developing a sixth sense of his own.

He exited the car and went around to the trunk while Vivi wrestled with a lapful of food and argued with her still-growling stomach. As if she had a choice. She dumped the burgers while Daniel was busy removing his personal effects from the trunk. He took off on foot, not bothering to see if she was behind him. And why should he? she asked herself, trotting a little to keep up with him. She'd shoehorned herself into his life and resisted all efforts on his part to push her back out. And now he'd quit trying.

Somehow, acknowledging her part in this whole fiasco didn't mitigate the fact that he'd gone from trying to get rid of her to taking her for granted. And sure, maybe that represented the normal arc of most male-female relationships, but wasn't there supposed to some good stuff in between? Of course, the in-between stuff usually consisted of conversation, sex, and some level of commitment. And sure they had all those things. But their conversations consisted entirely of who was trying to kill them, their only commitment was to stay alive long enough to walk away from each other, and they'd done everything but let the hit men catch them to avoid having sex. But they thought about it a lot.

At least she did, Vivi allowed, especially now, when she was walking behind him. The man was muscle from head to toe, and most of it was flexing, especially his butt. He had a really nice butt. And she had a really big problem.

She stuck her hands in her pockets and made a concerted effort not to think about Daniel's butt and how much she wanted to grab it. Not actually that difficult when she remembered Officer Cranston and his eagerness to get his handcuffs on her. And not in a good way.

Their surroundings were improving gradually as Daniel cut between buildings and kept to back alleys and yards. The day was bright and sunny and they were dressed for it, Vivi in shorts and a loose tank, Daniel in jeans and a T-shirt. Vivi felt like she looked right at home. Daniel stood out like a sore thumb, and it wasn't just the fact that he was toting a duffel bag. Daniel carried himself with authority, and that just naturally attracted attention.

"You need to look like you fit in around here," she said, hurrying to catch up with him.

Daniel looked down at his jeans and T-shirt.

"It's not your wardrobe. And it's not your luggage."

"The rest of it is nonnegotiable."

Vivi rolled her eyes. Even his vocabulary marked him as a lawyer. "Try to slouch," she suggested. "Mess up your hair and stop making eye contact with everyone we pass. Jeez, did you forget everything from when you were a field agent?"

"I always had a cover story. People tend to believe what they're told."

"When they don't have a story they have to draw their

own conclusions from what they see. And what they see when they look at you is a lawyer."

Daniel shrugged.

"If Cranston stops to ask questions, it won't take him any time at all to run across someone who remembers seeing you." Not that it was going to be a problem for long because they couldn't stay off the main streets forever, and if Cranston had brought in reinforcements they were bound to stumble across a cop.

"I know where we are," Vivi told Daniel. She'd glimpsed a street sign and if she was right . . . She turned in a circle, and sure enough, there it was. "Come on."

This time she took off without waiting for him to concur about their destination. And she didn't look back.

"The former friend you mentioned? And why former?"

"It's a long story." Vivi stopped at the edge of the sidewalk between two buildings, checking the street for signs of a police cruiser or foot cop. When she didn't see one, she slipped out of hiding and jaywalked to the other side.

Daniel pulled her to a stop before she could open the door of a two-story redbrick house with cheerful striped awnings over the wide front windows. The windows were filled with dried flower bouquets, candles, and the other completely unnecessary doodads women felt a need to buy and scatter around their homes. It didn't seem to be a business in the usual sense that there was a name over the doorway and an open sign inviting pedestrians in off the street. The little sign on the front door that read BY APPOINTMENT ONLY confirmed his suspicions. Vivi's friend ran a business out of her home, but it wasn't a store.

"Give me a little background before we go inside," he said to Vivi.

She heaved a sigh, running out of patience.

"I used to be a field agent, remember? The first rule is never walk in blind." Which was an explanation that got him what he wanted without admitting that he knew he'd hurt her feelings and was guilty over it.

"Heather Wilcox, late twenties, blonde hair—last time I

saw her. No known connection to the Mafia or any other illegal organization."

"You left out her measurements."

"You can ask Eric. She used to supply my shop with
candles before she started supplying Eric with herself."

"And neither of them felt a need to let you in on their
extracurricular activities," Daniel interpreted.

"Brilliant deduction, Ace. I sent Eric packing, and then
I invited Heather to go with him."

"And you think she'd be willing to help you now?"

"We don't have much choice," Vivi said, her eyes
trained on the street corner behind Daniel.

He glanced over his shoulder and saw the front hood of
a cop car, the light bar just coming into view as it rounded
the corner and started in their direction. Vivi couldn't possibly have seen it coming, but she didn't resist when Daniel
pulled her through Heather's front door.

He almost went back out. The place reeked. The scent
of flowers made the air so heavy there was barely room for
oxygen. He went light-headed before he realized he was
holding his breath. He let it out, deciding there were advantages to being a mouth breather.

"Um, there's something else you might want to know
about Heather," Vivi said. "She has this thing about compe-
tition."

Daniel wondered what she meant, but that was before
Heather appeared out of the back. She glanced at Vivi, took
in the fact that Daniel was standing well within her personal space, and oozed across the room to drape herself
over him. "Most people settle for a handshake," he said,
prying himself loose.

"I'm not most people," Heather informed him. "I'm
friendlier."

"Only when it comes to men," Vivi put in. "I thought
you were dating Eric."

"On and off," Heather said, but her eyes stayed on
Daniel. So did her hands, and one of them was drifting
down his chest, heading for his crotch.

Daniel caught Heather's wrist before she discovered whether he dressed right or left.

Vivi smiled. At first he thought it was because he'd refused to let an attractive woman grope him to prove a point. Really it was the knock at the door, which clearly Vivi had been expecting. "Cranston?" he asked her.

She nodded.

"Who's Cranston?" Heather wanted to know.

"Just this cop who's following me around," Vivi said. "He asked me out a couple times, and he's having trouble taking no for an answer."

"Uniform cop?"

"Answer the door and find out."

Heather made a beeline for the uniform. Daniel and Vivi went in the opposite direction, up the narrow stairs that led to the second floor. They'd barely gotten out of sight before they heard Cranston's voice wanting to know if Heather had seen a man and a woman.

"Besides us?" Heather asked before he could get into descriptions.

Hand-dipped candles were hanging everywhere at the top of the stairs. Daniel, busy looking over his shoulder, blundered into them, setting them swinging and clattering together.

"What's that?" Cranston asked, the last syllable coming out as a yelp—Heather checking what Cranston had downstairs, presumably. "That could be construed as assaulting an officer."

"That's not assault," Heather said, "this is."

"Hey!" There was some more crashing around downstairs, and then Cranston said, "I'm going upstairs," adding reluctantly, "if that's all right with you."

"He can't come up here if she doesn't give him permission," Daniel whispered.

"She could be persuaded."

Sure enough, Heather's response was, "You can go upstairs if you promise to check out the bedroom first."

"Shit," Daniel said under his breath.

There were three doors leading off the small landing at the top of the stairs. Daniel could have pulled Vivi through any one of them and been completely out of sight, but then they'd be trapped in a second-story room with no way out, except in Officer Cranston's custody—protective in Daniel's case.

Vivi would probably have to go the mug shot, fingerprint, cavity search route. The Boston P.D. really had no reason to hold her, but there was no doubt in Daniel's mind that Cranston would find something to charge her with before he was forced to cut her loose. And Daniel didn't like the thought of Vivi being released without him around. The hit men knew who she was now, and she'd be a sitting duck.

He took a quick look around, nudging her into a tiny nook in one corner of the landing, then cramming himself in beside her.

"What are you doing?" Vivi said.

"We can't go into the bedrooms. Heather'll take Cranston in one of them . . ."

Daniel looked down at her and suddenly the bedroom sounded pretty good to Vivi. Then again, who needed a bed? The wall seemed to be just as good, especially when he braced his hands on either side of her head and leaned against her.

She pushed back, tried to put some space between them. He let her, but she knew what he was thinking. She was thinking it, too, but kissing Daniel was dangerous, even if it was just his mouth on hers . . . His hands slid down the wall, he gathered her against him, and her system took a second punch.

He hooked a hand behind her knee and lifted her leg up along his hip, pressing into her at the same time. Her head spun, her stomach spun, parts of her were tingling, parts were burning, and all the parts wanted more. Right now, bed or no bed.

"It's awfully quiet up there."

They broke apart, guilty, chests heaving, Daniel reaching for his duffel and the gun inside before it sank in that it was Heather's voice they'd heard.

"Either you guys learned how to fly," she called out, "or there's something else going on."

Their eyes met, held, and it was like the kiss had never ended. Vivi could still feel his hands on her, still taste him. She ran her tongue over her lips, his eyes dropped to her mouth, and she braced herself. But he only took her by the hand and pulled her to the top of the staircase. He let her go before they made it down more than a couple of steps, but Vivi knew it wasn't over.

Neither of them was going to walk away from what they'd started.

IT WAS EASY TO GIVE CRANSTON THE SLIP. THEY called in a mugging down the street and he had to respond since he was the closest radio car. Vivi figured they'd head back to the apartment, maybe pick up where they'd left off. She hadn't counted on Daniel's ability to compartmentalize. Or his reluctance to take their relationship to another level.

She ought to be feeling reluctant herself. What she felt was frustration. A lot of frustration. She'd would've liked to take it out on Daniel. Several times. But she'd be damned if she gave him the satisfaction of knowing she wanted him that desperately. Besides, he'd probably reject her. Damned self-control, she thought, glaring at him.

"Now what did I do?" he wanted to know, sounding as cranky as she felt.

"Nothing."

He gave her a look, anger with a little smolder around the edges.

"Just walk," she said, "back there." And she took off, making sure she was a couple of paces ahead of him because the last thing she needed was to see any part of him.

They were on their way to the nearest name on Daniel's list, and walking a couple of miles in the late-afternoon sunshine didn't exactly cool her off. It didn't help when he pulled her to a stop and bent his head next to hers. She turned her face to his, her breath wheezing out on a sigh as she waited, hoping . . .

It took her a minute to realize he was speaking, and then another few seconds for his words to batter their way through her disappointment.

"That's Dominic Furillo," he said, gesturing to a hot dog vendor just down the sidewalk from where they were standing. "He was charged with money laundering."

"Charged?" Vivi asked, turning her attention to the criminal, a much safer subject. Her body wasn't as quick to make the adjustment, but she figured a slow simmer was the best she could hope for anyway.

"Tried and acquitted," Daniel said. "He used to own a successful high-end restaurant, but he lost it to legal fees. My guess is he can't get a loan, so he's working his way up from the bottom."

"If he doesn't have enough money to open a restaurant, what makes you think he could hire hit men?"

"Suppose you go find out."

Vivi rolled her shoulders to work out the knots. She started for the cart, half turning before she'd gone two steps.

"Don't worry," Daniel said, "I won't take my eyes off you."

"That might be comforting if they weren't on my ass," she said.

He lifted his gaze a foot or so, grinning unrepentantly.

"Not better," Vivi said, heading off again to play inquisitor, which wasn't easy when all she could think about was Daniel watching her.

She made it to the cart before she'd come up with a way to get the information she needed. So she did what seemed natural and ordered two hot dogs, loaded. He started building them and her mouth began to water. "Smells amazing," she said, and then she looked fully into Dominic Furillo's face for the first time and felt a little tick of recognition, like a puzzle piece falling into place in her brain. "Didn't you used to own your own restaurant?" she asked him. "That place in the Leather District."

"Dominic's."

"Yeah. That was a great place . . ." She looked at the cart, then back at him, and she could see he was guessing pretty accurately at the direction of her thoughts. "You don't seem too broken up about being here instead of there," she said, senses wide open and not getting any regret or unhappiness, or animosity toward anyone for being in this situation.

"Shit happens," he said with a shrug, handing her the hot dogs wrapped in foil and sitting on a cardboard tray.

She picked one up and took a bite—mostly because he seemed to expect it—and then she closed her eyes and let all the various flavors mingle in her mouth. It was all she could do not to moan in ecstasy and not just because her stomach was happy to be getting sustenance. "This is incredible," she said around a second mouthful.

Dominic grinned full out. "It is, isn't it? You know, three years ago I would have told you I'd rather be dead than wind up here. But I think if I'd stayed where I was, running my restaurant and obsessing about being at the top of the game, I would have had a heart attack and I'd be dead right now."

Or the guys he'd been laundering money for would have killed him. Seen in that light, Daniel had done him a favor, because the mob wouldn't touch him now.

"Well," Vivi said, handing him a ten-dollar bill, which was all she had on her. "If you want my opinion, this is where you belong." She raised her hot dog in a sort of salute and headed back to Daniel.

She got a flash halfway there; her sixth sense was talking again, shouting more like. And what it shouted was "Run." Not a good idea, she decided, since running would be like painting a big red target on her back.

She picked up her pace, hustling around the corner only to discover the jig was up.

"Feds," Daniel said as soon as she'd joined him. "One's

by the hot dog vendor, the other is over there." He pointed to a spot across the street.

Both of the guys were watching them. Otherwise they were going unnoticed by the crowd, casually dressed, appearing to be sightseeing or taking a break in the shade.

"They don't have cover stories, and they're not having any trouble blending in."

"I didn't have any trouble picking them out," Daniel said.

"Me neither, considering one of those guys isn't exactly a stranger to me."

"Mike put him on you?"

"And I gave him coffee."

"Shit," Daniel said, which seemed to sum up their predicament pretty well.

"What do we do?"

"Lose 'em. But they're not going to be as easy to shake as Officer Cranston." Daniel took a bite of his hot dog and added, "Damn, this is good. Too bad we don't have time to eat," and he plucked Vivi's out of her hand and tossed them both in a nearby trash can.

"I'll make it up to you," he said when he caught the look on her face.

"It'll have to be something pretty amazing to make up for that hot dog."

"I think I can manage that."

Yeah, Vivi thought to herself, he could probably manage that. He could probably ruin her forever for all other hot dogs.

chapter
17

"HERE WE GO," DANIEL SAID.

Vivi watched, fascinated, as he shifted from sexual innuendo to dealing with the task at hand. His dark eyes went
from one kind of intensity to another. Not that it mattered
since both kinds were scary. It was probably good that they
hadn't had sex, because he was the kind of man who poured
all his skill and all his concentration into whatever he was
doing. Considering what he'd done to her with one kiss in a
stairwell, with the threat of arrest just feet away, that much
undistracted focus would probably kill her.

He laid a hand on her shoulder and she gave a little yelp
and shoved it off.

"Jesus, what's your problem now? One of your spirit
guides goose you?" He didn't wait for an explanation, wrap-
ping his hand around her wrist and towing her after him.

She stumbled a little, but the activity helped her forget
about his skin on hers, and when reality got through to her
she jerked her wrist free and crossed the street under her
own steam. Daniel led her halfway down the block, behind
a bus dropping off and picking up passengers.

"You're pulling the old bus routine?" she scoffed. "I expected you to have a little more imagination."

"I'm using it all up on you," he said, adding, "not in that way."

"I don't know what you're talking about."

"Right," Daniel said, "it was just me back in Heather's upstairs hallway."

Vivi chose to ignore that.

Daniel used the bus as cover to start running in earnest, threading his way through the pedestrian crowds, Vivi trailing along in his wake.

They'd headed away from the two federal agents, but the feds had been too close for the bus to put them off the trail for long. Both took up the chase, playing bumper tag with cars when Daniel led Vivi across the street mid-block. Worse, one guy cut left, the other went right, talking on a wrist unit.

"Calling in local backup," Daniel said.

"With my luck it'll be Cranston." But Vivi already knew she and Daniel were trapped because the entire block was wall-to-wall buildings, and there was a federal agent at either end.

Daniel didn't see it as a no-way-out situation. Daniel was an outside-the-box thinker. He ducked through the nearest doorway, a bakery, saying over his shoulder, "One of the agents will follow us, the other will stay outside. They'll coordinate through their wrist units."

"At least that means they're not talking to the locals," Vivi said, following Daniel straight through the bakery in blatant disregard of the objections of the hairnet clad woman behind the counter and the goggling customers. Since most of the customers were female, and they weren't goggling at her, Vivi didn't think the staring had as much to do with their effrontery as it did Daniel's backside.

Behind the bakery was an alley that ran the length of the block, and again the sidewalk openings would likely take them directly into the arms of an irate FBI agent, or any local backup that may have arrived. So Daniel repeated the process, back to front, with the business on the other side of the alley, which happened to be a massage parlor. Among other things.

They ran straight through, just like with the bakery. The similarities ended there. No one was wearing a hairnet for one thing. Several of them wore a lot less, and not just the guys on the table.

Vivi would have expected women in that profession to be a lot less sensitive about nudity, not to mention immune to performance anxiety. But they shrieked and covered various body parts Vivi was trying her best not to see and Daniel wasn't taking the time to appreciate.

They hit the front door without stopping, barely hesitating at the street. At least one car screeched to a stop to avoid hitting them. On the bright side, a quick look at either end of that block told her there weren't any cops—at least none in marked cruisers.

On the down side, the footrace was taking a toll on Daniel. His limp was getting more pronounced, and there was pain in his eyes. And things went downhill from there.

The fed who'd taken the shortcut behind them burst through the front door of the massage parlor, looking confused until he spotted them across the street. And then he looked confused again, and a little worried, because when Vivi tried to take off again all Daniel did was take her by the hand and wait for the agent to join them. The confusion was cleared up when Daniel punched him in the nose.

Blood splattered, bone crunched, and the guy went down to his knees. Daniel didn't wait to find out if he was getting back up. He dragged Vivi back across the street, back through the bordello/massage parlor—more shrieking and covering up—back through the bakery, where Daniel should have been on the menu. They completely retraced their steps until they wound up where they'd started, including the part where they didn't have a clue what to do next.

Vivi had her hand pressed to the stitch in her side. Daniel was rubbing at his left thigh, and taking stock. It was getting to be late afternoon, lots of vehicular traffic on the narrow streets, lots of foot traffic on the sidewalks.

"We need to split up," Daniel said.

"Do you think that's a good idea?"

"We stand out too much as a couple."

"Right," Vivi said, "you don't stand out at all by yourself."

"I can't help my height, any more than you can help your . . ." He passed a look over her body and let the rest of the thought trail off into the obvious. "You go that way," he said, pointing north.

"Where are you going?"

"Make a right turn at the end of the block, walk for five minutes, and make another right turn. Find a place to lay low and I'll meet you in thirty minutes."

Since Daniel started walking south, Vivi had two options: chase after him and argue or do as he said. She chose Door Number Two. For one thing, it didn't feel like a mistake. And Daniel hadn't left her much room for improvisation.

She went to the end of the block and followed Daniel's instructions. Five minutes of walking took her three blocks, she made another right turn and saw a Boston P.D. cruiser making a pass, driving slowly and searching the crowd.

Daniel was right, she had no trouble blending in. But being short didn't do her a whole lot of good if there wasn't any crowd to blend in with, and the pedestrian traffic was getting thin as everyone made their way to dinner.

Vivi slipped through the nearest door and found herself in a beauty parlor straight out of the '50s, including the eye-watering stench of perm solution and cigarette smoke.

"Can I help you?" she was asked by a woman with a two-pack-a-day voice. Her latest contribution to the ambience hung out of her mouth, ash an inch long quivering on the end. She looked to be in her fifties, she was built like Jabba the Hut, and her fingernails might have been lacquered from a freshly opened vein.

"I just wanted to get in out of the heat for a minute," Vivi said.

"Don't think I can bring it, huh?"

Vivi looked at the woman's hair, fluttering around her head like a big blonde haystack, circa *Desperately Seeking Susan*. "I, uh, really didn't plan on having my hair done, today. No money," she added with a shrug.

"This one's on me, honey," the woman said, curving one bony, slack-skinned arm around Vivi's shoulders and heading for a chair covered in cracked and faded turquoise vinyl.

"No, really, I can't. I'm sure you have a paying customer—"

"Who says you ain't paying," the woman said, handing Vivi a stack of business cards. "May not be cash, but honey, the advertising will be worth every penny."

NINETY MINUTES LATER, DANIEL WAS BACK AT THE rendezvous point. For the fifth time. He'd lost the feds, he'd lost the Boston P.D. He'd lost Vivi. He'd quartered the area for about a ten-block radius and found no sign of her. Not that he knew what kind of sign he was looking for; it wasn't like she'd left footprints or hung a piece of clothing on a street sign to point the way. Then again, if she took off a piece of clothing to hang on a street sign, he could just look for the crowd of men. She hadn't been wearing all that much.

He should have headed back to the loft instead of staying in that area, out in the open. But he couldn't quite shake the feeling that leaving would be the wrong course of action.

He had to do something besides stand there, though, so he took out his cell phone. Much as he hated to do it, he figured he'd call Mike, find out if Vivi had been picked up by any law enforcement agency. The only other possibility was that she'd eluded everyone—including him—in which case he'd go back to the loft and wait for her to make an appearance.

"Hey, mister, looking for some action?"

He glanced over his shoulder and felt the tension drain out of his muscles. "That's not an offer you want to make unless you're prepared to follow through," he said.

Vivi stepped up beside him, half-smiling. "You weren't supposed to recognize me."

It was her eyes that gave her away. One look in the amber depths and he'd know her anywhere, even with her hair straightened and streaked, blonde and red among the darker strands. It should have been garish but it suited her—and it served to prove why women everywhere colored their hair. They said it was for a change of pace, or to make them more attractive, but really it was to make every man who looked at them wonder which color was the real one. And think about how much they'd like to find out.

"You're taking all the fun out of this," she said.

"It's not supposed to be fun."

"C'mon, it's a little fun."

He tried not to smile, but he couldn't quite hold it back. And then he could. "We've got company," he said quietly.

He felt Vivi tense beside him, just as the second federal agent who'd been chasing them materialized out of the evening crowd, too close to make a break for it. Especially as he hand his hand beneath the light jacket he was wearing.

"Are you going to shoot us?" Daniel asked him.

"You broke my partner's nose."

Vivi nudged Daniel.

He ignored her. "I could have done a lot worse."

"Why don't you come along quietly, make this easy for everyone."

"Including the hit men, since they'll know just where to find me."

Vivi nudged him again, but when he looked over at her, she was staring into oncoming traffic. Daniel followed suit—and maybe if he hadn't been using most of his concentration to make himself believe his own eyes he might have spent a few seconds figuring out how to capitalize on it.

Vivi came up with a game plan first, but then Vivi didn't have to waste any time on mental adjustment. Bizarre was Vivi's stock-in-trade. She took a step forward, hands up, in apparent placation mode.

The fed took a step back. "Stay where you are, ma'am."

"I'm not going to jail for him," Vivi said, "and I'm not a ma'am."

She took another step, the fed backpedaled again, putting him at the edge of the sidewalk.

"I'm not letting you take me in, either," Daniel said.

"There's nothing you can do to stop me."

"I don't have to stop you, Maxine will."

The guy was clearly baffled by that. He looked at Vivi, then back at Daniel, who was waiting for the inevitable question, and when it came, when the guy asked, "Who's Maxine?" Daniel pointed to the 1952 red Ford pickup truck that jumped the curb and hit the fed. It didn't hit him hard enough to cause internal bleeding or rupture his spleen or anything, just enough to take him out of any footrace for the next eight weeks or so.

"My leg is broken," he wheezed out through the pain.

Daniel wasn't paying attention to him, mostly because a teenage boy had catapulted himself out of Maxine's driver's seat and attached himself to Vivi.

"It's not my fault," he babbled, both hands wrapped around her wrist tight enough to cut off circulation. "I don't even know what happened. My boss told me to take the truck for a quick drive, make sure nothing rattled."

"He must work for George—he's the glass guy," Vivi explained for Daniel's benefit.

Daniel took another look at Maxine and sure enough the glass had all been replaced. The bullet dings had been bumped out smooth and repainted. The fed hadn't left any damage behind, so all in all, Maxine looked pretty good, considering what she'd been through in the last couple days.

The kid was still hanging on Vivi, still talking a mile a minute. "I was just driving around," he said, "not even thinking about where I was going, you know? But then the steering wheel got stuck and I ran into that guy and am I going to jail? Because I really don't want to go to jail. I want to go to Harvard, and I don't think Harvard lets in criminals."

Daniel inserted himself between Joe College and Vivi, one look enough to make the kid let her go. "I suggest you take off," he said.

The kid reached for his back pocket. "Shouldn't I give you my information?"

"I don't think having a criminal record is the only thing standing between you and Harvard."

"Huh?"

"If you don't want to go to jail, you should probably keep your name and license number to yourself. I'm not calling the cops and Captain Ahab here doesn't give a rat's ass about you."

The fed confirmed that by not taking his eyes off Daniel. Good thing his mission wasn't dead or alive because Daniel didn't think he'd be standing around long enough to make one-legged jokes.

Vivi pointed to the guy on the ground. "Look, he's calling nine-one-one," she said to the kid, "you'd better go."

The kid took off, losing himself in the crowd without a backward glance.

"He's not calling nine-one-one," Daniel said. "He's calling for backup."

"Then we should probably go, too," Vivi said.

"Yeah." Daniel looked around, then met her eyes. She was standing by the truck, arms crossed, foot tapping. "Shit," he said, "okay."

"You can get in."

"I'm not sure Maxine is ready to play nice."

"She already ran over one guy today," Vivi said, "but you might want to stay away from her tomorrow."

"You sure she doesn't want to go for the hat trick?"

"What's a hat trick?"

"Hockey," Daniel said, his eyes on the crowd. "Three goals by one player . . ."

Vivi stared in the same direction as Daniel, and there were Hatch and Flip. "I think they'd probably get out of the way this time. Or maybe not," she said, because Flip spotted Maxine just then. One hand went to his neck brace, the other slipped into his pocket, and then he spotted Daniel. But his eyes passed right over Vivi.

"At least somebody is fooled by my hair."

"Nice to know the hour and a half was worth it," Daniel said.

"It's not me they're recognizing."

"I wouldn't be here to be recognized if not for the hair."

"Who told you to hang around?"

"My pesky sense of responsibility."

"You're not responsible for me," Vivi shot back. "I can take care of myself. And I can take care of this." And she sauntered down the sidewalk, toward the hit men, swinging her hips, smiling at every guy she passed and leaving them staring in her wake.

She was aiming for Hatch, and as she passed him she hunched suddenly, crossing her arms over her chest, shrieking, "Hey!" and swatting at him.

Anyone who wasn't already staring at her turned to see what the ruckus was, and every guy who wasn't with a woman decided to defend Vivi's honor.

Hatch was making like Jackie Chan, arms and legs going a mile a minute. He fought silently, with absolute concentration, his eyes like black holes in an otherwise expressionless face. Not feeling any pain, would probably keep fighting ten minutes after death. It wouldn't be a good idea to take him on one-on-one, but a whole crowd of guys was too much for even a homicidal freak of nature like Hatch.

Flip was yelling, "Not the face, not the face," and cowering by a nearby storefront.

Vivi had circled around, coming up behind Daniel again. "We should probably be going."

"Give me a minute," he said, grinning.

"See, you are having fun."

"Yeah, now I'm having fun." Enough to make up for having to interact with Maxine again. Almost.

chapter 18

"YOU'RE GOING TO PARK HERE?"

Since here was right in front of Eric's building, Vivi didn't think Daniel's question deserved an answer. In the interest of maintaining the peace, she gave one anyway. "It's the only open parking space on the block."

"Everyone who's chasing us knows this truck. They've all been wounded by it. We should park it somewhere else. Somewhere not so obvious."

"You think Hatch and Flip are driving around looking for Maxine?"

"I think Hatch and Flip are somewhere sticking pins into a voodoo doll of you."

"And nursing their bruises."

Daniel didn't look like he appreciated her levity.

Vivi turned, laying her arm along the back of the seat, and fastened her gaze on his face. "What are you really angry about?"

"I'm not angry."

She tipped her head to one side, searching his face. "I think you're angry."

"How about Grandma? She have an opinion?"

"You don't want to know Grandma's opinion." Neither did Vivi, which was good since the only real opinion she had was her own, Daniel still being a psychic blackout zone. But he didn't need to know that. "If it helps, Grandma always hated passive-aggressive," she said, keeping up appearances.

"You want active aggression? Fine. It was stupid of you to walk straight at two armed hit men."

"I knew they weren't going to shoot me."

"I didn't know it."

"You would if you trusted my abilities."

Daniel ran both hands through his hair, fisting them until the pain cut through the red haze of anger. Not to mention the rest of the emotions he didn't want to acknowledge, including what it might feel like to see Vivi get hurt because of him.

The head pain didn't help much, but he flexed his thigh by mistake and *that* pain was enough to keep him focused for the rest of his life. It was definitely enough to clear his head, and the clarity produced some pretty interesting ideas, like why hadn't the hit men shot at Vivi? Hell, why hadn't they shot at him? It wasn't the crowd, and it wasn't having witnesses; the street in front of Cohan's had been curb-to-curb people and that hadn't stopped them.

It was because they hadn't wanted him dead.

The thought just popped into Daniel's head, which kind of spooked him, seeing as he was still sitting in Maxine and there was a possibility the truck was some kind of psychic hot zone. And that was beside the point, not to mention paranoid.

The hit men had switched from murder to capture—okay, death would have been the ultimate goal, but they'd only been trying to get their hands on him today. And maybe he could use that.

"We should go inside," Vivi said, "before it starts to rain."

And she was already cranky enough, Daniel could hear it

in her voice, and he could sympathize. It had been a sucky day, and now he had to top off all the suckiness with twelve hours of inhabiting eight hundred square feet of loft that was empty of just about everything except Vivi and a bed. He had a feeling cranky would be the high point of his mood.

"I'm tired, and I'm hungry," she said when he didn't respond. "Getting drenched would be the perfect capper to my day, but if you don't mind, I think I'll pass. Feel free to move the truck yourself, if it's that important to you."

Daniel ignored the keys she held up. "Looks like Eric is going out."

Eric exited the building, looking like a bad '80s clubbing cliché. Shirt unbuttoned to his navel, gold chains, tight jeans, no socks, one-day beard scruff.

"You up for a night on the town?" he asked Vivi. "You, too," he mumbled in Daniel's general direction.

"I'm exhausted," Vivi said, brushing by him to go inside. "We had a busy afternoon. You go out and have fun."

"Um, staying in sounds like a great idea, too."

"You never stay in on Saturday night."

"Yeah, well, I think I'll order in," Eric said, trailing inside after them. "You guys want some pizza?"

"Pepperoni and bacon," Vivi called as she started up the stairs.

"Green pepper and chicken," Daniel said from right behind her.

"Half and half," Eric muttered as he turned to go back into his ground-floor apartment.

"And some bread sticks and sauce."

"And salad," Daniel added. Then to Vivi, "He certainly knows the way to your heart," as soon as Eric was out of earshot.

"I never missed a meal when I was dating Eric."

"Maybe not, but I don't think it's your heart he's interested in."

"I'm going to take a shower" was all Vivi said.

She grabbed her backpack and made good on her intentions, but she must not have lingered under the spray because she came back out in less than fifteen minutes. To Daniel's disappointment, she wasn't damp at all.

"No towels," Vivi said. "I used a T-shirt to dry off." And she'd made an effort not to get her hair wet. The ends were a little damp, and the humidity of the shower took it from straight and sleek back to curly and out-of-control, but she felt like a human being again.

She spread her T-shirt out to dry, and when she straightened up Daniel was staring at it. She knew what he was thinking, and not because she'd read his mind. Because he met her eyes and she could see he was wishing she had that wet T-shirt on. And nothing else.

Vivi wished he'd take himself into the bathroom before she made his wish come true. Minus the T-shirt. And then she'd rip his clothes off and find out if he was better than all the hot, lurid thoughts running through her mind. Better might just kill her, but hey, what were her odds of getting out of this in one piece anyway? Might as well have her way with Daniel before Hatch and Flip got their way with guns.

Her gaze lifted to Daniel's and held. She wanted to cross that room more than anything she'd ever done, but she didn't move. Neither did he.

They might have stayed that way, or they might have given in to temptation, but a gust of wind rattled the window, and the connection was broken. Daniel headed for the bathroom, poker face back in place, acting like nothing was going on.

Well, two could play that game, Vivi decided. He wanted to pretend there was no heat, no sexual tension between them? Fine. He could go to hell. She felt like she was already there, wanting to crawl out of her skin, to scream if she didn't get some—

"Food's here," Eric called out from the hallway.

She opened the door, took the boxes, and shut the door in Eric's face.

"Hey!"

"Thanks," she yelled, "we'll catch you tomorrow."

After a minute, she heard him clomping back down the stairs. She dropped the boxes on the table, shoved the salad over in front of Daniel's chair, and opened the pizza box. She closed her eyes, breathing deeply. Nothing like satisfying one physical urge to make her forget about another.

"Did you save me some?"

Vivi held up the salad and kept her eyes to herself.

"You ought to have some of that," he suggested.

"Already had my vegetables today," she said around a mouthful of pizza.

Daniel took the chair across from her, opened the salad, and dug in. "You're going to give yourself a heart attack eating like that."

"The only thing I'm going to die of around you is starvation. Or lead poisoning."

DANIEL WAS SURFING THE WEB. VIVI SAT CROSS-legged on the mattress, meditating. Both of them were putting off the moment when they had to face the matter of sleeping arrangements.

After a while, Daniel got to his feet—and almost went down to his knees. "My thigh," he muttered, rubbing at it.

That wasn't the part of him Vivi had been wishing was stiff, but she could still do something about it. "Take your pants off and lie down on the mattress," she said, digging through her backpack. "I took a massage class," she explained when he only stood there staring at her, lines of pain around his eyes and mouth. "Mostly I use it when I get a tense client. But I can use it on any muscle, not just shoulders."

Daniel mulled that over for a minute, then he reached for his zipper. Vivi decided her self-control wasn't up to the challenge of watching him shuck his jeans, so she continued to search her backpack, all but stuffing her head into it, long after she'd found what she wanted. By that time Daniel was on the mattress, staring up at the ceiling.

Like she was putting her hands and face that close to trouble. "On your stomach."

He turned over almost before the words were out of her mouth. Apparently his self-control wasn't at full strength, either. It didn't take her long to forget about her libido.

The skin of his left thigh was a twisted, scarred mess, and there was a round, knotted scar just under his left shoulder blade. Even though Daniel was an emotional black hole to her, she could still feel his pain. "How did this happen?" she wondered, not realizing she'd said it aloud until he answered.

"I trusted the wrong person."

That explained a lot. "You were shot?"

"One bullet almost killed me, the other shattered my femur," he said. "It took half a dozen pins to put it back together."

"I'm sorry," Vivi said softly.

He glanced over his shoulder at her, then quickly away. "It's not your fault."

No, but she was paying for it. He didn't trust her. True, her situation was unique, and it would take a lot for a man who believed in tangible evidence to accept her definitely intangible talents. But she'd started at a disadvantage, because Daniel came from a job that taught him caution first, and the one time he'd strayed from that rule, he'd paid a heavy price.

She squeezed out some lotion, warmed it between her palms, and put her hand on his thigh.

He jumped. "What's that?"

"Lotion. I don't have any massage oil."

"It smells like you."

"It could be worse." She began to rub, and Daniel began to squirm.

"Not really," he said.

Her hands slipped off him for the fourth time. "You need to lie still. I can make it stop hurting—"

"That's not where it hurts."

"Fine." Vivi sat back on her heels, exasperated. "Where does it hurt?"

Daniel rolled over and pulled her down on top of him.

Vivi braced her hands on either side of his head. She didn't do anything about their contact from the waist down. "This is a bad idea," she said while her brain was still in charge.

"You knew we were going to end up here."

There was only one answer to that. She kissed him. Daniel kissed her back, and her knees went to water. Need shot along her nerve endings and . . . nothing else. Daniel was still kissing her, pausing only long enough to peel off her tank, which was the right kind of progress. But something was wrong. Maybe she was thinking too much—hell, why was she able to think at all? She pulled back, then slipped to one side and sat up. Daniel didn't stop her, and she could tell from his eyes that he wasn't concentrating. At all. "What's wrong with you?"

"Aren't you supposed to wait until we're done before you start criticizing?"

"If you're going to be distracted the whole time, I think I'll save us both the trouble." She had to climb over him in order to get off the bed. She was straddling him when he put both hands around her waist and stopped her.

"I feel like we have an audience," he said, looking over her shoulder.

"You think the spirits are listening in?"

"No, I think your grandmother is."

Vivi snorted out a laugh. Probably not a response that was going to get her what she wanted, but she couldn't quite believe what she was hearing. "You're having performance anxiety? A man who prosecutes major criminals in open court, a man who has to think on his feet and make split-second decisions with guns pointed at you."

"Yeah, but I'm not naked for that stuff."

"You're not naked for this," she pointed out.

"Not yet, but I'm going to be."

"Not at this rate," she pointed out. "I can't believe you're going to let an imaginary granny run you off."

"You don't believe she's imaginary."

"But you do." She got off the bed, picked up her shirt, and whipped it back over her head, mimicking, "I knew we were going to end up here," to herself. "Just like a lawyer, all talk and no action—"

Daniel grabbed her from behind, spun her around, and put her against the wall, not hard enough to knock the breath from her, but she lost it all the same because he just stood there for a minute, his body hot and hard on hers. His eyes were hot and hard, too, staring into hers with an intensity that had every nerve ending in her body humming so that when he put his mouth on hers she nearly shot to orgasm.

She ran her hands up under his shirt, across his nipples, and then down into his briefs, so she could close her hand around him.

He threw his head back, the muscles in his neck corded, looking like he was in pain. "Stop," he gasped out.

"Make me," she said, taking her mouth to his neck, his jaw, any exposed skin she could find, using her teeth and her tongue—and her hand—until he was groaning with the effort of holding back, until his chest was heaving and he caught her wrist and made her stop.

The look in his eyes went beyond intense, became a threat, a promise to make her suffer just as much. She sent him a look back, raised brow, half smile, a look that said, *Bring it on*. And he did, pulling her bra down around her waist because he was in too much of a hurry to unhook it. Not that she minded when he took her breast into his mouth, working the peak with his teeth and tongue, slipping his thigh between her legs at the same time, high and tight so her own restless movements helped shoot her to peak.

When she could breathe again, when the last aftershocks had faded and her eyes focused, he was there, watching her, still intense as he unsnapped her jeans. He peeled them off, along with her panties, slowly, never taking his eyes from hers as his hands slid the denim down her thighs. His fingers lightly brushed the backs of her knees and made her quiver, the more so when he bent to slip her feet free.

He stayed there for a moment, on one knee, his hands bracketing her hips, his breath washing over her, warm and heavy, and she knew if he took his mouth to her there the pleasure would be too much.

He stood, cupping her bottom and lifting her in one smooth motion, slipping into her before she could do more than gasp in a breath at the feel of all that hardness, that heat. And then he began to move and the world narrowed down to Daniel, his hands, his mouth, his body on hers and in hers, every part of him stroking every part of her until pleasure built again, not as fast and explosive as the first time, but more intense. She slid over the second peak, felt it flow through her until she imagined the glow coming off her was enough to light half the city. She dropped her forehead to Daniel's shoulders as he drove himself deep one last time and stayed that way, pulsing inside her and setting off just an echo of her orgasm.

There was no getting to the bed that way, but he moved his hands and let her feet drop to the floor again, probably afraid he'd drop her since she could feel his muscles quivering. She thought he'd want distance—if what they'd just shared had been half as intense for him as it had been for her, Daniel would need to reestablish his boundaries. But he only stood there, curled around her, his forehead against the wall as his breathing began to ease.

Vivi was in no rush to move, either. Her muscles were as shaky as his, her knees felt like they might buckle at any moment, and it took all the strength she could muster to keep her arms locked around his waist.

"Maybe we should . . . I think we ought to move to the bed," he said, so uncharacteristically hesitant that Vivi felt a need to lighten the mood.

"Just to sleep, right?" she asked him. "Because any more of this and I won't survive."

"I did all the work."

"You keep wanting to be in charge, so I let you."

"I'm not complaining."

"It sounded that way."

Daniel chuckled, taking her hand and pulling her across the room, toward the bed. "Any time you want to be in charge—when we're having sex—just let me know."

chapter 19

"MIKE SENT ME AN E-MAIL," DANIEL SAID THE NEXT morning.

Vivi dragged herself out of bed, trying not to groan. She was stiff all over, and not just from the wall. Daniel had let her be in charge. Twice. He claimed his thigh was still sore. He didn't look sore this morning. He looked . . . satisfied, relaxed. Smug.

"I guess my massage did the trick," she said, coming up behind him, bending until her head was close to his so she could see the laptop screen.

"Right, it was the massage." He looked over his shoulder at her, which put their faces about an inch apart. He could have kissed her. He didn't.

There was the boundary she'd expected last night, Vivi thought as he faced forward again. Daniel was all business again, focused on the task at hand. She knew there were still people trying to kill him—kill them. Not right at the moment though. You'd think he could take a minute to . . . What? Tell her that it wasn't just sex, that he had feelings for her? That she was good in the sack? What kind of reassurance did she expect from him? she asked herself. Hell, they weren't even dating, and once this thing with the contract played itself out, and if they were still alive, they'd both go back to their old lives. And their old lives didn't intersect. She'd known that all along.

It still took her a minute to focus on the e-mail Daniel brought up on his computer for her benefit. "One broken nose, one broken leg, no more agents. You're on your own." By the time that sunk in, Daniel had his cell phone to his ear.

"This is a good thing, right?" Vivi said to him while he was waiting to be connected. "No more feds after us."

"I have some questions," Daniel said into the phone, and since she couldn't give him any answers about the e-mail she figured Mike what's-his-name had come on the line. Daniel confirmed it by turning the phone so Vivi could listen in. She didn't need him to make the universal signal for "be quiet" to know she shouldn't talk.

"Didn't you get my e-mail?" Mike said, gruff, short-tempered. "Took me ten minutes to type the damn thing."

"Got it, understood it," Daniel said. "You left a few things out."

"Didn't take a genius to know what you'd do next," Mike told him. "We had the cops alerted to let us know if anyone connected to your old cases made a complaint."

"Mrs. Hickman called the police, the police called you, and the hit men heard all about it because they were listening in on the police band."

"Which is a large part of the reason we called off our operation. We're trying to protect you, not play informant for the bad guys."

"What's the rest of the reason?"

"You're being a pain in the ass."

"Nothing new about that."

"Except you don't work for me anymore. You stay on the street you won't have to worry about the job you do have."

Vivi felt Daniel tense. It didn't show in his voice. "Nothing will happen until Sappresi's in jail," he said. "They won't jeopardize a case involving a dead FBI agent."

"Nope, but after that they'll cut you loose. And yeah," Mike added, "this time we might have contributed to the hit men finding you, but the longer you're on the street the higher the probability they'll take you out." And he disconnected.

"You caught all that, right?" Daniel asked Vivi.

"I caught it."

"I need you to think long and hard about what you're doing."

"Still trying to get rid of me?"

"I'm giving you the facts and asking you to make a choice," he said. "I'm done running."

"In other words, you're going to make yourself into bait and go fishing for a hit man."

"Something like that." Except the bait usually got eaten, and Daniel had every intention of coming out of this in one, uninjured piece. And there was no way he'd let Vivi get hurt. It was enough to have Patrice on his conscience. "It's only a matter of time before the hit men catch up with me. Mike is right about that. If I sit around and wait, it'll be on their terms. I intend to make sure I'm in control when the time comes. It's not going to be easy, and I can't watch your back and mine at the same time."

"How will you even find the hit men, let alone get one of them to spill his guts?"

"No idea."

Vivi crossed her arms. "No, game plan is my thing. It sounds like I better stick around and show you how to do it, Ace."

"Fine with me," Daniel said, "just as long as you know who's in charge."

"Oh, I know who's in charge." And she walked away, leaving Daniel to wonder if he was the one in the dark. And deciding that he was.

If he had any sense he'd sneak out and handle the operation on his own. Then again, if he took off she'd only hunt him down again. Thank God she wasn't working for the hit men . . .

Daniel turned around and pointed his finger at her. "You," he said. "You're the key. You could figure out what I was going to do long before we met. Why can't you do the same with Hatch and Flip?"

"I was having premonitions about you," Vivi reminded him. "It took me forever to figure out who you were and where the first murder attempt was going to take place. I don't even know Hatch's and Flip's real names."

"Then let's find out."

"Just like that?"

"You wanted me to have a game plan," Daniel said, "this is it, take it or leave it."

Vivi mulled that over for a minute. Her response wasn't what he'd expected. "Does the game plan include letting me read the rest of your e-mail?"

The game plan didn't have a lot of actual details yet, but Daniel was pretty sure laying open his private life wasn't going to be on the list.

"Patrice wants to know why you haven't been around to see her, right?"

Then again, private was a relative term where Vivi was concerned—relative, as in nonexistent. "She's worried."

"Of course she is."

"She knows what's going on, and she hasn't heard from me in a while."

"Two days is a while? Is that the legal definition?"

"You're pissed off about the 'take it or leave it' crack."

"I'm not even surprised by the 'take it or leave it' crack, and I hope Patrice is feeling better. Feel free to take Maxine."

"I already told her I couldn't go to see her until this thing is over."

"You didn't tell her about me, did you?"

"She already knew."

Vivi went into silent thinking mode again. It was unnerving.

"What?" Daniel asked her.

"Nothing." Vivi started to turn away, then spun back

around. "It's just . . . Did you ever wonder . . . Is it possible . . ."

"If you have something to say, just spit it out."

She laughed a little. "I bet that's something you thought you'd never say to me."

"It was definitely on the list," Daniel said. "And now that you remember how to finish a sentence, maybe you can tell me what's on your mind."

"Nothing." Vivi waved a hand and said, "Nothing," again on the way across the room to rifle through her backpack.

Daniel was pretty sure there was "something" bothering her, but she wasn't telling him until she was ready—and he had no doubt it would be at the most inopportune time. And probably when it was too late for him to do anything about it.

THE BEST WAY TO GET HATCH'S AND FLIP'S ATTENTION, Daniel decided, was to call the cops and report a sighting. He was told, politely but firmly, that there was no longer an APB out on Daniel Pierce.

His next call was to Officer Cranston. "How'd you like another crack at the two guys who invaded the Oval Room?" he asked Cranston.

Vivi pulled the phone away from his ear. "Are you sure this is a good idea?"

Daniel ignored her. "Meet me at Boston Common," he said into the phone. "I'll be over by the baseball diamonds off Charles Street."

There was a pause, Cranston talking some sense into Daniel, Vivi hoped, then, "You can tell your sergeant about it if you want," Daniel said, "but it may come to nothing."

Daniel did some more listening, then disconnected. "Cranston is off duty in a half hour," he told Vivi. "He'll meet us there in plainclothes."

"Even if Hatch and Flip show up," Vivi said, following Daniel out of the apartment, "how are you going to get one of them alone?"

"We'll have to play it by ear."

"Wow, first no game plan and now play it by ear. What happened to the anal retentive part of your personality?"

"It doesn't want to get killed either. Get in the truck."

"But—"

"There's no way of knowing when they might show up," Daniel said, clearly running out of patience. "That makes it kind of hard to plan ahead. Unless you can tell me where and when to expect them."

"I don't have any connection to Hatch and Flip."

"You have a connection to me," Daniel said.

Which was exactly the trouble. Vivi had stopped getting any readings from Daniel days ago. It was nice not to see him dead every other night, but it was hell when it came to preventing her fears from turning into reality.

"You knew there was going to be an attempt at the Oval Room," Daniel reminded her needlessly. "You knew there was going to be another attempt at Cohan's, and then at my house. You knew Patrice was going to get hurt."

"What's your point?"

"You should be able to tell me where the next attempt will be."

"Those attempts were preplanned," she explained, thinking off the top of her head. "This one isn't."

"Or maybe they're not coming."

"That's possible, too, but if you're playing it by ear, then they don't know when or where they'll strike, and if they don't know, how can I?"

Daniel's brow furrowed.

"We don't have to do this," Vivi said. "Walking around with a target on your back isn't the best idea you've ever had."

"The target wasn't my idea, capitalizing on it was."

She heaved a sigh and gave up. He wasn't going to change his mind, and she wasn't going to let him stake himself out like live bait without being there to watch his back. "Get in the truck," she said.

He did, and so did she, getting behind the steering wheel

and turning the key. Maxine started right up, running rough as always.

"The Common is going to be crowded with people, even on a weekday," she said, steering the truck away from the curb.

"It's a big place. I think we can avoid the tourists."

"We aren't the ones the tourists need to worry about. It's Flip and Hatch. Or are you forgetting the Oval Room and the crowd outside Cohan's?"

Daniel gave her the I-haven't-forgotten-anything-ever look, including the stuff she'd done to irritate him. "Hatch and Flip didn't shoot at me in the crowd the other day. Something has changed."

"You could have told me that earlier," Vivi snapped. At the very least, it would have saved them an argument.

"I think they want to capture me instead of kill me outright," was all Daniel said. "Whoever is behind this must want some interaction before I die."

"What sort of interaction do you think they want with me?"

"As little as possible, if they're smart. And we're going to give them what they want."

There didn't seem to be anything left to discuss, so they made the rest of the drive to Boston Common in silence, both busy with their own thoughts.

"Leave Maxine in plain sight," Daniel instructed when they got there. "Cranston is going to call in a sighting. The dispatcher will tell him to ignore me, but it'll go out over the radio, and hopefully Hatch and Flip will hear it. I want them to know where to find me."

Vivi found a parking space on Charles and maneuvered Maxine into it, then turned sideways in the driver's seat. "Are you really going to let Officer Cranston arrest Hatch and Flip?"

"No."

"How are you going to manage that?"

"I'll figure it out when the time comes."

She crossed her arms, raised a brow.

"If they get arrested they go into the system," Daniel explained. "They'll lawyer up, and I won't be able to question them. Cranston can have them when I'm done."

"When we're done, you mean."

"Fine, when we're done. But this all starts with you staying out of the way."

"Okay," Vivi agreed with a shrug.

"You're not going to argue?"

"You have Officer Cranston for the takedown. My part comes in later."

Daniel didn't look like he believed her, but he'd be singing a different tune when she told him who was behind the contract.

BOSTON COMMON WAS FIFTY ACRES OF GREEN SPACE that had once been pastureland but was now dotted with memorials, trees, and the homeless sacked out on park benches or staking out patches of grass surrounded by all their worldly goods. The Common had seen public hangings, British army encampments, eighteenth-century food riots, and twentieth-century protests for peace. None of it surprised Vivi. The place was cluttered with so much psychic noise she could barely think.

She'd tried to tell Daniel, but he'd gone into a zone, channeling the field agent that still lived inside him, macho attitude and all. The Common suited his purpose, and that was all that mattered to him. Vivi and Officer Cranston had their roles, as far as he was concerned, but it was his "op," and he was running it his way.

Officer Cranston was the catalyst, Maxine was the tell, Daniel was the bait. Charles Street cut through the Common to the east of the Public Garden. Daniel chose to go in that way because Charles had on-street parking, and he could leave Maxine parked nearby like a big red X-marks-the-spot. And there were a lot of places to stash Vivi so she could stay safely out of the way, yet be handy when he decided she was useful.

Cranston's Daniel Pierce sighting had already gone out, which meant Hatch and Flip should have heard it on the police band by now. They should be on their way to scope out the Common, and hopefully when they got there they'd see Maxine and go looking for Daniel, only instead of them finding him, Daniel would find them and capture one or both of them. And in case they didn't immediately spill their guts, he'd expect Vivi to race in and produce some sort of psychic miracle to get him the information he needed.

And if any part of his foolproof plan went awry, Vivi figured Daniel would blame her. The jerk. He didn't even believe in her abilities, but if she didn't produce results, he'd get all cranky and moody and not talk to her for hours. That would be better than when he did decide to talk to her, because when he decided to talk to her he'd accuse her of being a fraud again.

And if she couldn't shut out some of the ambient spiritual chatter, she'd prove him right.

She leaned back against the tree Daniel had threatened to tie her to if she didn't stay put, closed her eyes, and tried to shut out everything. The cloudy, grumbling sky, the pickup softball game on the diamond not far away, Daniel watching it like he didn't have a care in the world.

First she filtered out the background noise, like she'd done at the market. Normally she would have focused in on her target, but Daniel was a closed book to her. She lifted her eyes to the heavens and made a mental comment about the fairness of *that*. The heavens didn't apologize. Apparently the heavens had decided that falling in love with a man was enough of a gift—the kind of thinking, Vivi decided, that meant God was definitely male. A female deity would have known Vivi needed every advantage she could get.

Since she wasn't getting divine help, and Daniel wasn't a useful resource, all she could do was "listen" to what was going on around her—again, just like at the market. Could be she'd get a whiff of nefarious intent, and if she could narrow it down she might be able to warn Daniel when Hatch and Flip arrived. It was a pretty big *if*. There were a

lot of people in the Common, and no guarantee Hatch and
Flip would be the only ones planning mayhem. But it was
all she had.

They'd been there about a half hour, Vivi following instructions, staying under the cover of one of the trees
planted along Charles Street where she wouldn't be immediately visible. Daniel was wandering back and forth between
the sidewalk not far in front of Vivi and the baseball diamond, where Officer Cranston had joined a pickup game.
Cranston was in the outfield, which let him blend in while
leaving him relatively free to keep an eye on the goings-on
with Daniel. After watching him play for a few minutes,
Vivi figured it was also in keeping with his skill set.

She didn't appreciate being shoved to the sidelines, but
she had to admit the setup was pretty good. It probably
would have worked exactly as intended—if Daniel had
been the target.

She'd been open, looking for even the weakest hint of
trouble. What came to her was so strong she stumbled a bit
mentally, and when she did realize what she was feeling,
her stomach took a long, greasy roll.

Daniel had made his way back to the baseball diamond,
a good ways off. She waited until he glanced in her direction and then waved her arms. To anyone else in the park, it
would look like he hadn't even marked her presence. To
Vivi, the look he sent spoke volumes. Stay put, he was saying, don't give away your position. Great advice, if her position had been a secret.

She followed the direction of her mental red alert and
saw Hatch, walking with purpose, coming in from the north
end of the Common. Flip appeared almost simultaneously
at the south end. He was walking with purpose, too. Vivi
was pretty sure the purpose was her. The only mystery was
what would happen if they accomplished their purpose. The
possibilities made the sick feeling in her stomach spread.
Thankfully, it hadn't spread as far as her vocal cords or feet,
and she put both to good use, racing from her hiding place
and yelling for Daniel at the top of her lungs.

Daniel might not be too happy about her abandoning his game plan, and Cranston would probably stand there and cheer while she was gruesomely murdered, but they both wanted to get their hands on the hit men, so it was no surprise to see them come running. It was just her luck that they were too far away.

Daniel was pointing to Hatch and shouting something. Probably wanted her to try to get a read on him. But she was too busy freaking out to get anything. And there was no way she'd get within a foot of Hatch if she could help it. Hatch was scary.

And anyway, Daniel was on an intercept course for Hatch, so maybe she'd mistaken his reason for yelling and pointing. Cranston was just realizing the plan had been hijacked, and apparently he was a can't-walk-and-chew-gum-at-the-same-time kind of guy because his feet had stopped moving while he looked at the four other participants of the drama and struggled to make a decision about what he should do.

There wasn't a whole lot of decision-making necessary for Vivi. She cut left and headed for Flip. Flip probably had a gun, but it wasn't in plain view—and it was hard to be scared of a man wearing a flowered neck brace, even if he was armed.

Turned out it wasn't the gun she needed to worry about. Flip had even scarier weapons.

"Sappresi's psychic, right?" he said, coming to a halt about ten yards away. "That's what the boss told us."

Momentum took Vivi the rest of the way. Desperation had her reaching for Flip's throat. She didn't want to kill him, exactly, just shut him up. Fast. Choking someone with a neck brace, she discovered, was impossible.

"We just want you to come with us," Flip said, backing off a couple steps, hands up, looking harmless and sincere.

But Vivi was in full-blown panic mode, not thinking, acting out of sheer terror that Daniel would hear her secret. She threw herself at Flip again, searching him for a gun. He fought her, but she had abnormal strength, Russian weight-lifter strength. The kind of strength that allowed an ordinary mother to lift up a car and save her trapped child. Flip was no match for it.

She found the gun at the small of his back, and she heard Hatch yelling his partner's name and then a bunch of other stuff. She couldn't make out what Hatch was saying, but she couldn't take any risks. Flip had gotten to the gun while she'd been sidetracked, so she kicked him in the kneecap, wrenched the gun out of his hand, and pointed it at him.

"Oh, puh-leeze," he said, hopping on one leg and holding his injured knee, "you're not going to shoot me."

"No?"

They did the Mexican standoff thing for a minute, then Vivi said, "Crap, you're right," because her hand was shaking, and there was no way she could trust herself to pull the trigger. She might hit Flip, but she might hit someone else altogether. "Aren't you at least worried I'll shoot you by accident?"

"There's no reason for violence," Flip said. "We just want to talk. We're not going to hurt you, honest."

No, but Daniel would if he found out about her connection to Sappresi, not to mention Tom Zukey. And he could hurt her worse than any physical pain Hatch and Flip could inflict.

"Why me instead of Daniel?" she asked Flip.

"Don't know. We were told to bring in Sappresi's psychic." He glanced at the gun, then met her eyes again. He said he didn't believe she'd shoot him, but there was enough doubt to have him opting for verbal persuasion over physical enforcement. "Like I said, we just want to talk to you. And maybe you'll learn something useful if you come with us. Maybe you should ask Pierce what he thinks."

Suddenly it wasn't so hard to shoot the gun. In fact, Vivi heard a bang and realized she'd pulled the trigger. Thankfully, when she looked down the gun was pointed at the ground. But that shot had served its purpose.

Daniel stopped and immediately turned to her, Hatch

took off running. Flip was standing there, mouth open, eyes wide, legs crossed.

Vivi considered throwing the gun at him, but that would be counterproductive to not becoming a kidnap victim, so she shoved it in the waistband of her pants. And then she couldn't remember if the safety was on. Flip was limping in her direction, and she didn't want to wrestle with him since the car-lifting strength was gone, and when they grappled for the gun she'd probably get shot in the backside. Getting shot in the butt would be a great distraction, but there was the pain and bleeding and potential hospital stay to worry about. Not to mention the definite possibility that Hatch or Flip would spill the beans while she was writhing on the ground in agony.

Something prompted her to reach into her pocket, and there were the stones she'd stuffed in there earlier. Quartz, turquoise, jade, carnelian, and a nice knobby chunk of amethyst. Just about all of them had protective powers. Vivi was more interested in their earthly purpose. She started winging the stones at Flip, and about the third one he zigged when he should have zagged.

"Ouch," he said, clapping a hand to his eye and taking off.

A minute later Daniel raced by her, but Flip had a pretty good head start, and it was clear that Daniel's leg wasn't going to hold up much longer. Thankfully, for both of them, it didn't have to. A newer Impala screeched to the curb. Hatch was behind the wheel. Flip jumped in and they took off.

Daniel turned around and began to limp back. Even from a good distance away Vivi could tell he was angry.

She met him halfway. Nothing to gain from putting off the inevitable. "Did you get the license plate?" she asked, making a useless attempt to side track him.

"No, and there are a million of those cars on the road. What the hell were you thinking? If you were going to shoot the damn gun," Daniel said, keeping his voice down, "why didn't you hit something?"

Vivi gestured to the small crowd of innocent bystanders that had gathered. "Like one of them?"

"Like Flip. He was a foot away from you."

"He was also six inches taller and fifty pounds heavier. I was afraid he'd take the gun away and use it on me."

"So you threw stones at him instead."

She looked away. "It got rid of him, didn't it?"

"That wasn't the point of this."

"No, the point of this was to capture him alive, remember?"

Daniel didn't say anything. He was busy wrestling with his temper.

"Go ahead," Vivi said, "spit it out."

He stepped away, then whipped around and came toe-to-toe with her, keeping his comments between the two of them. "You had a gun in your hand. All you had to do was point it at Flip until I got here."

"I was a little panicked," she said, knowing she sounded convincing because it was true. She'd been a lot panicked that Daniel would get his hands on Flip, and Flip would spill his guts about her past involvement with Sappresi. "I'm sorry."

"At least tell me you were able to get something from him."

"All he said was that he wanted me to go with him. I was . . . surprised." Again, not a lie, even if it worked in her favor. "I didn't— There wasn't time—" She did a palms up. "He's a threat—to both of us—but I can't tell you anything more that that."

Daniel took a few seconds to absorb that. "He wasn't supposed to come after you," he finally said, sounding like he was on the downhill side of the anger roller coaster. "Did he give you any idea why he did?"

She shook her head. "It's a complete mystery."

"Great," Daniel said, completely disgusted, "I was getting tired of the last one."

Cranston finally showed up, huffing and puffing. "There wasn't supposed to be any shooting," he said between gasps for breath. "Now I'll have to write a report."

"Go ahead, write a report," Daniel said, "make sure you

answer all those pesky questions that are sure to arise, like why were you running an undercover operation your sergeant didn't know anything about."

Vivi had to give Cranston credit, he thought about it for at least half a minute and then he muttered, "I knew this was a mistake," before he held out his hand.

She reached behind her, pulled out Flip's gun, and gave it to him.

"I'm a police officer," he said for the benefit of the gawkers. He looked the gun over and added, "It's only a starter's pistol folks. Nothing to see here."

People began to wander off in ones and twos.

"You're holding the gun with two fingers," Daniel said to Cranston. "Still hoping for fingerprints?"

Vivi made an apologetic face. "They're probably all mine, since I had to wrestle it away from Flip."

Cranston sighed and stuck the gun in his pocket before he shuffled off.

"He's not too happy with me," Vivi said.

Daniel headed for Maxine. "Neither am I."

chapter 20

THE GAME PLAN AT BOSTON COMMON HAD BEEN pretty simple. Go fishing. When one of the hit men bit, reel him in and have a serious conversation. Problem was, he'd used the wrong bait. So instead of answers, he'd come back with more questions. First and foremost: Why had the hit men gone after Vivi instead of him?

"Your guess is as good as mine," she said out of the blue.

"I thought you couldn't read minds."

"It doesn't take a psychic to know what you're thinking."

"Too bad, I could use a psychic about now. Not to mention earlier today."

"Why are you getting pissy with me?"

Daniel took it for a rhetorical question, but when he didn't respond Vivi got to her feet and stepped into his path. "No, you know what, Ace, never mind. I'm done." And she stalked across the room, grabbed her backpack, and started jamming her things into it. It didn't take long.

"If you think I'm going to stop you, you're mistaken," Daniel told her.

"Emotional blackmail only works on someone who has emotions," she shot back.

"I have emotions."

"Stubborn isn't an emotion, neither is stupid."

"Those aren't the ones I was referring to."

"Oh, you mean the ones you ignore."

Daniel gave her one of his lawyer looks. She rolled her eyes. The lawyer looks had lost all effectiveness on her. Apparently, a bad attitude was what it took now.

"You've been trying to get rid of me since the Oval Room," she said, zipping her backpack and shouldering it before she turned to him. "You win."

Daniel caught hold of her as she brushed past him, then looked at the hand around her wrist—his hand—as if it belonged to a stranger.

She was right, he'd been trying to make her go away since day one. He didn't need her to get through this thing. She was just dead weight . . .

Vivi tore free and headed for the door.

Daniel got there first. "Where are you going to go?"

"Home."

"Those guys were after you today," he reminded her. "They know where you live."

"I can take care of myself."

"You'll have to go out a window to prove it."

She took a survey of the windows, contemplated the possibility of climbing out one of them and getting safely to the ground two stories below, and came to the conclusion she was stuck. "You're just an ape in a suit," she snapped at Daniel. "You can dress up the brawn, you can give it a corner office, but underneath the expensive suit and fancy law degree you still want to muscle your way through things."

"You're ticked off because you want to do something stupid, and I won't let you."

"And you're stewing because you couldn't get your hands on one of the hit men, and now you're getting off on pushing me around."

"I'll let you know when I get off."

"If there's a God I won't be anywhere in the vicinity when you get off."

That wiped the smirk off his face.

"Don't talk to me anymore," she snapped before he could say something else to inflame the situation. "You're being a jerk."

"And you're being a pain in the ass."

"Get out of my way and your ass will stop hurting."

"My ears would be happier, too, but I guess my ears and ass will have to put up with you for a while longer."

"Gee, that was such a lovely invitation, but I'll have to say no."

"No isn't an option. If not for me coming to your rescue today—"

"You! I wrestled the gun away from Flip—"

"The powder puff hit man," Daniel said. "Maybe you should have sicced your grandmother on them. Flip probably would have run away screaming."

"The gunshot did that," she snapped at him. "My gunshot."

"It was about damn time you did something useful. You keep saying you're here to save my life, but you won't take action until yours is in danger."

"I almost committed vehicular manslaughter to keep you safe. I jumped off a roof for you."

"Don't forget trashing my house. I especially enjoyed that one."

Her mouth flew open and she sputtered for a minute without forming any actual words.

"Speechless," he said. "My life's work is done."

Vivi stalked over and drilled a finger into his chest.

Daniel caught hold of her wrist, but he wasn't quick enough to clamp his hand over her mouth.

"You're a—a—stubborn, pigheaded, tunnel-visioned, failure of a federal prosecutor," she yelled at him.

"And you're a crazy, irritating, sideshow freak of a psychic."

"Idiot."

"Stalker."

"Jackass."

"Lunatic."

One minute they were in each other's faces, the next in each other's pants. Hands were everywhere, clothes came off. Daniel wasn't wasting time getting to the bed. He scooped Vivi up, his hands supporting her backside, and slid into her, hard and fast, making her gasp and throw her head back. A hollow thud sounded, since she was against the door. She didn't seem to notice. She braced her hands on his shoulders, dropped her mouth to his neck, and the world narrowed down to the feel of her lips and tongue on his skin, the heat of her body against and around his, her soft moans and the tension building in her until she snapped like a bowstring.

Daniel could have followed her over the edge, but what good was self-discipline if he couldn't hold off long enough to feel her convulse around him, to hear that final moan trail off into a contented sigh. Her body went soft, curling into his as he made those last strokes that took him to where she was. Pleasure flooded in and tension drained out, taking his strength with him.

He staggered to the bed, barely able to support his own weight, let alone Vivi's. Not surprisingly, when they got there, strength came roaring back in. He figured it had something to do with Vivi lying there without a stitch of clothing on, a blissful expression on her face. And nothing whatsoever coming out of her mouth.

She opened her eyes and looked up at him, one eyebrow rising lazily. "Finally, something we can agree on," she said, pushing him over onto his back.

Okay, she was taking control, and it was going to get

him what he wanted. But he couldn't let her get away with it scot-free. "Maybe I want to be on top," he said.

"Maybe you should just lie there and let me run the show for once."

"Every time I let you make decisions, someone gets hurt."

"True, but it hasn't been you."

"Not yet."

"You want to do this, or would you rather argue about it?"

Daniel pretended to consider his choices.

Vivi pretended to get out of the bed. Or maybe she wasn't pretending, since when he caught her around the waist she wasn't all that cooperative. At first. He cupped one of her breasts and ran his hand across her nipple and she stopped trying to pull free. He tugged her back down on the bed and kissed the side of her neck, working his way up to her ear, and she relaxed beside him. He raised up on one elbow, and she shoved him onto his back.

She straddled him, braced her hands on both sides of his head, and took him in. And he didn't object. Not that he was letting her do all the work. Especially since her breasts were right there, just inches away from his mouth.

She went a little wild. That crazy, no-holds-barred personality of hers took over and Daniel rethought his decision to let her be in control because the wilder she got the less control he could find. He flipped her onto her back and picked up the pace, his hand slipping down between them. She cried out, hands fisted in the sheets, back bowed, abandoning herself to the climax as completely as she threw herself into everything else.

Daniel felt the pleasure rip through her, and when she opened her eyes, he saw it and felt it for himself. He swore he did, swore there was a split second before his own orgasm hit that he was feeling her pleasure, as if she'd shared it with him when her gaze met his and she lay herself bare.

He shifted to his side and gathered her against him, her back to his chest. Vivi snuggled her head into the crook of his shoulder, wiggled around until she was comfortable, and gave a little, contented sigh.

Daniel had the sudden urge to read the paper. Of course, he'd have to go out to buy a paper first, and maybe pick up dinner. There was a great Chinese place across town . . . And if he tried hard enough, he could stay away for the rest of the night—and then he wouldn't have to deal with what he was feeling. But he'd have to admit that Vivi was right— he ran away from his emotions. It worked for him though, and he saw no reason to change it.

"I think I'll take a shower," he said to Vivi. It was only another way to run, but at least he didn't have to get dressed and go out. Or defend himself to her.

"I don't think I can move," she mumbled, sounding half-asleep.

Daniel got to his feet, pulling her up with him, surprising himself more than Vivi. "C'mon, a shower will make you feel better," he said.

He was right, too. She felt impossibly better in the shower, wet and sleek and hot, gliding to peak more gently this time. He fell over with her, sliding into an orgasm that wasn't as explosive but seemed to go on and on, until every nerve ending in his body hummed with it.

Even then he wasn't completely satisfied. He wanted more, and wanting more was always a problem. Worse, it wasn't only about sex. Holding her in the afterglow had felt pretty damn good, and that just complicated matters all to hell. But then, nothing about this situation had been simple.

IF IT HAD BEEN VIVI'S INTENTION TO SIDETRACK Daniel from the fiasco in the Common, sex wasn't the answer. Sex burned off the leftover adrenaline and relieved the tension, but it didn't distract either of them. Daniel went right back at the problem at hand, worrying it like T-Bone with one of Rudy's Italian loafers.

"I don't know why they went after me instead of you,"

Vivi said for at least the fourth time. "It makes no sense."
Unless Sappresi was behind the hit. Sappresi was the only
one who would want her taken out because he was the only
one who knew that she could hurt him. And Sappresi was
the only one who would know she was helping Daniel.

"Maybe we should go over it one more time." Daniel was
prowling the apartment, mind working deep into steamroller
mode. There was no way to get through to him when he was
like this, working through a problem, refusing to let it go until he had an answer. Worse, he was still in phase two. Phase
one was fact-finding mode, peppering her with questions.
Phase two was repeating the process to see if there were any
details left out.

Since it was after midnight and she'd had a full day,
phase two was pissing her off. So she decided to add some
details she'd left out the first time. Okay, they were impressions not details, and they were unflattering to Daniel, but
he was keeping her awake. And not in a good way.

"Well, first you were a pigheaded jackass who made all
the decisions," she said, "including the part where I was
staked out in clear sight halfway across the Common from
you and Officer Jelly Donut." She was lying on the bed,
eyes closed, and not only because she was exhausted.
Imagining Daniel's reaction was always the safer bet.

"You were supposed to stay beside the tree and keep out
of sight."

"I was hiding, just like you ordered me to. You went off
to the baseball diamond."

"I was trying to stand out. And I wanted you near the
truck . . . in case."

Vivi snorted. "What, you thought Maxine would protect
me?"

"Let's just say the two of you always seem to scrape
through trouble. Maxine leaves a path of damage big
enough to name a hurricane after, but you don't get hurt.
You're in the eye of the storm."

"I'll tell her you said so. She'll be flattered."

There was silence. Vivi cracked an eye and found Daniel watching her, arms crossed, eyebrows raised, waiting for her to continue the narrative.

"We were at the part where you were supposed to be blending in," he prompted helpfully. "Try to keep the sarcasm to a minimum if you want any sleep tonight."

"Fine. I was trying to blend in," Vivi said, "but you also wanted me to get a reading. That meant I had to shut out everything physical in the Common, so by the time I saw Hatch and Flip coming and realized they were headed for me instead of you, it was too late. I tried to get your attention . . ."

Daniel made a dismissive gesture with his hand. Vivi couldn't tell if he was repeating what he'd done earlier or if he was blowing her off again. Probably the latter since he didn't say anything for a couple of minutes.

"Did you get anything from Flip?" he finally asked.

"I got the gun."

More silence from Daniel, the kind that had an attitude and the attitude was "not amused."

"I was busy panicking," she said. "There was a lot of confusion and a lot going through my mind." Like blind terror. "I'm sorry, maybe if I'd had more time . . ."

"Tell me what Flip said to you."

"We covered that already."

"The exact words. Try to remember the exact words."

It was Vivi's turn to go silent.

"You can get back at me later," Daniel said.

"I'm not getting back at you, I'm trying to remember." Not to mention factor in what she'd told him earlier. Lying was never a good idea, especially when you had to repeat what you'd told when you were exhausted to begin with. "Everything happened so fast," she stalled. "Hatch and Flip were coming from opposite sides. You were coming from the baseball diamond, but I knew you wouldn't get there in time, and I figured Flip would be easier to deal with than Hatch."

"You did okay," Daniel said.

She opened her eyes and raised up on one elbow. "Was that a compliment?"

"That was an observation. I thought you were going to kill him with your bare hands."

"Panic and terror. He had a gun, and I decided I should get to it before he used it. We were fighting over it when it went off."

"Too bad you didn't shoot one of them, even accidentally."

"I'm just happy I didn't shoot anyone else accidentally," she said. "Anyway, Flip just said he wanted me to go with him, that they weren't going to hurt me. Yeah," she added when she got a load of the look on his face, "I didn't believe him either."

"I think they wanted to use you to get to me," Daniel said.

"I guess they're not aware of the probability you'd thank them instead of rescuing me."

"I think there's a higher probability they'd give you back after being stuck with you for a few hours. Unless they know who you are, and they know you're helping me. If that's the case, they were just saying they only wanted to talk to you in the hope you'd go along peaceably. Then they'd probably drive you to the nearest landfill."

Daniel went back to pacing and thinking. Pacing and thinking weren't going to do him any good since nothing had been accomplished by their conversation, but pacing and thinking seemed to make him feel better.

Vivi was beyond thinking. She was busy being scared. Flip knew who she was. *Sappresi's psychic.* And if Daniel had his way, if he captured Hatch or Flip, it wouldn't be long before they spilled the beans, and Daniel learned the whole ugly truth of her involvement in Tom Zukey's death. No matter her naïvete, Daniel wouldn't understand. Daniel wouldn't forgive her. Daniel would walk away.

Not that he'd need her anymore, Vivi reminded herself,

because if Daniel captured one of the hit men, he'd find out who was trying to have him killed, and he could make sure the murder attempts stopped without her help. And if he never saw her again, it wouldn't matter to him.

But it mattered to her.

chapter
21

VIVI WOKE FROM A DEAD SLEEP, HEART POUNDING, eyes wide, a scream echoing in her straining ears. Her scream in the vision, she realized, already checking to see if Daniel was still in bed with her. Because in her dream he was dead. And it was her fault.

He stirred behind her, one arm slipping around her waist, his breath warm at her temple. It should have been comforting to feel him wrapped around her. But it made her feel trapped, claustrophobic. She'd forced herself into Daniel's life, but somehow he'd wormed his way into her affections. It was a recipe for disaster, even without the life and death stuff.

What she did was a part of who she was, and even if he'd been interested in having a relationship that didn't involve guns and possible death, she couldn't hook up with someone who didn't believe in her one hundred percent. Not to mention the upcoming betrayal. Daniel was a black-and-white kind of guy; even if he'd felt something for her besides amused tolerance and reluctant need, finding out about her history with Sappresi would destroy it.

She extricated herself from him, but the open window across the room wasn't enough, so she went out of the apartment and down the stairs, picking up the pace when she went past Eric's door. Eric had a guest—a very vocal and enthusiastic guest, and she was in full agreement with whatever Eric was doing. Either he'd found a self-starter or he'd learned a few things since their time together. Whatever the case, they were having a good time, considering the solo had become a duet. Life should be so simple as an orgasm. Vivi thought, with a kind of soft sadness, that it would never be that way for her.

Then again, would she want it to? It was great in the moment, but when the moment was over she wanted to able to have an intelligent conversation. Not that her conversations with Daniel were all that intelligent. Mostly they were contentious. But it worked for them.

It had been cloudy during the day and it still was, the city lights staining the overcast night sky a dull, blackish orange. Vivi dropped down to sit on the steps. It was still warm, but the wind had come up and she rubbed her arms, chilled.

"It's going to storm," Daniel said from behind her.

Vivi hadn't heard him come out, but she wasn't surprised. "Seems right, somehow," she said. "You can't do anything about a storm, you just have to ride it out."

Daniel sank down on the step beside her, close enough for her to feel his warmth without actually touching her. "You can carry an umbrella."

"Sure, you can keep yourself dry, and you can stay away from the high ground, but there's no way to predict when and where lightning will strike. If your fate is to die by a freak of nature, you might as well kiss your ass good-bye. All the precautions in the world won't save you."

"I don't believe in fate."

"I know."

"Want to tell me what this is all about?"

"No," she said, and meant it—for all of ten seconds. "I had another vision."

"That's what all the thrashing around and mumbling was about. Not to mention the scream."

"That was Eric's friend."

"It wasn't that kind of scream. And it wasn't loud enough to wake anybody but me."

Vivi would have apologized, but she wasn't all that sorry.

"I take it I was dead in this vision," Daniel said.

"I guess your head isn't as hard as I think it is."

"No room for error, huh?"

Vivi grimaced, trying to forget the staring eyes, the trickle of blood from his temple.

"A few hours ago that would have made your day."

She hunched her shoulders. Sarcasm might help, but it was hard to be quippy when you had a corpse in your brain. Especially a corpse you were in love with.

Yeah, she thought with a sigh, it was love all right. No problem admitting it anymore. She was just too mentally exhausted to shut it out.

If Daniel had been privy to her thoughts he probably would have run screaming, but since he didn't have her kind of insight, he just sat there, deep in problem-solving mode, from the gist of his next question. "Any idea where this took place?"

It was the last thing she wanted to do, going back into the vision, but she drew her knees up and wrapped her arms around them, then took herself back. "Cars," she said.

"A parking lot?"

"No, broken-down cars."

"What make?"

"I can't tell," she said, pulling back from the cars, past Daniel's staring eyes, and out of the vision. "Some of them didn't even have grilles or bumpers."

"Sounds like a garage, or maybe a dealership repair facility," Daniel said.

"What difference does it make? We've been down this road already. Three times."

"And we've defied your predictions three times."

"And then I have another prediction. You dead again. I'm beginning to see a pattern."

"You think?"

"I don't know what to do anymore."

"So you're just giving up?"

"It was different this time," she said, resting her chin on her drawn-up knees. "You were protecting me."

"I thought you couldn't get any premonitions about yourself."

"That's what I thought, but getting close to Flip today . . . Maybe I channeled him somehow." She sighed, reliving the main event in her head one more time, just to be sure her interpretation was accurate. It was. Regrettably. "All I know is every other time I was a spectator. This time I was somehow involved in your death."

"And now you're going to tell me that you leaving will prevent it."

Vivi huffed out a breath, lifting her head to glare at him. "I didn't concoct this to convince you to let me go."

Daniel did his silent mulling thing. This time he added steepled fingers. He didn't, however, share the outcome of his musings.

"You said yourself the hit men were probably trying to use me to get to you," she reminded him. "If I'm not around, I can't be a liability."

"You can't be an asset, either."

"You don't think I've been an asset anyway."

"You've come in handy a time or two. So has Maxine," he added. And he was definitely smiling.

It shocked the hell out of her.

"That's the second time I made you speechless."

"Yeah, once for each time you complimented me."

"I'm just stating the facts. Don't get all flummoxed."

Flummoxed was an understatement. Her cheeks heated, her pulse bumped up a couple of notches, and she had to fight to keep the stupid smile off her face. So he'd complimented her. It was only a matter of time before she did something to tick him off again. Or worse. "Me being the reason you get killed is a fact, too," she said.

"It's not the first time you've seen me die in one of your visions."

"This time feels different," she said. "With the others I felt like I could change the future by sticking around. This one . . . It feels like I need to take myself out of the game."

"No."

"No? That's it? Just no?"

"You can't go home," Daniel said. "They know where you live."

"I'll get out of the city, somewhere they won't be able to find me."

"What makes you think that will save my life? These guys aren't going to give up because you're gone."

"That doesn't mean I have to make it easier for them."

"In other words, you don't care if I die as long as it's not your fault."

It took her a minute to fully absorb that. "Is that what you really think?" she asked him.

Daniel exhaled heavily. "No."

"You should go to the FBI," Vivi said, "work from that angle to figure out who's after you." And she'd go to Sappresi, make some sort of deal to keep Daniel safe.

He tapped a finger on her temple. "I don't know what's going on in there but we started this thing together, and we're finishing it together. Whatever the outcome."

"So I guess I should have kept going when I walked out a little while ago."

"If you were really serious about leaving you would have."

Vivi shoved both hands back through her hair, rubbing her sore head. "I don't know what to do."

A car whooshed by, the wind blew, and sounds drifted to them from the bar down the street. Daniel was silent.

"What, you have nothing to say?"

"You get mad when I tell you what to do," Daniel said.

"But you're not going to let me leave, are you?"

"Leave?"

They both shifted around in time to see Eric come strolling out of the building. His shirt was unbuttoned. So were his jeans, and the zipper was down way too far. On Daniel, unzipped jeans and no underwear would have been sexy as hell. On Eric, it violated the too-much-information rule.

He stepped around Vivi and went to the bottom of the steps, leaning against the rusted wrought-iron railing in front of Vivi. The jeans gapped more. Vivi kept her eyes above waist level.

"You going somewhere?" Eric asked, and when they only stared he added, "I heard you guys talking out here."

"Amazing you could hear anything, considering the brick walls and the competing noise factor.

Eric cracked a smile. "Jealous?"

"Revolted," Vivi said. "Why are you here?"

"Just getting some air," a woman said from behind them, "same as me."

Daniel turned around again. Vivi didn't bother. She knew that voice, so it was no surprise when Heather oozed her way down the staircase, her hand ruffling through Daniel's hair on the way by. She took the railing opposite Eric, lounging with her back against it. She was wearing one of Eric's T-shirts. And nothing else. Unless Vivi counted the smirk on her face when their eyes met. It wasn't, however, a relief when she looked away because her gaze landed on Daniel and didn't move.

"I thought you two broke up," Vivi said to her.

"This is just a casual thing," Eric said. "Me and Heather hook up now and then, and we do business once in a while, too."

"You're into potpourri and candles now?"

"Diversity, babe. It's the name of the game. Don't want to get bored."

"I couldn't agree more," Heather said, shifting closer to

Daniel. "Maybe we should diversify our activities for the rest of the night. You know, change partners."

"Been there, made that mistake," Vivi said.

"Well, it's not really about you," Heather replied, her eyes still on Daniel.

"I'm sorry I called you a stalker," Daniel said to Vivi. "You don't have the focus for it."

Vivi leaned her elbows on the riser behind her, and watched Daniel scowl at Heather. She didn't even try to keep from grinning.

Eric must have decided he should step in before Heather pushed her luck too far. "So . . . how's your plumbing?" he asked.

"The plumber told us he couldn't do anything until the end of this week," Vivi said. "Is that a problem?"

"Oh, uh . . ." Eric looked up at the building. "The owner claims he can't get a permit to demolish this place, so I guess they're going to rehab it."

"We can go if you need us out," Daniel said.

"Not necessary. I expect to get a call any time telling me they're going to start work, but 'til then, hey, me casa, you casa."

"I'll find a way to pay you back," Daniel said. "I always pay my debts."

Eric went kind of pale. Vivi didn't blame him. Judging by the tone of Daniel's voice and the look in Daniel's eyes, he wasn't offering future favors.

"Honest, dude," Eric said, "I don't want anything from you."

"I'll take you up on your offer," Heather said.

"I didn't make an offer," Daniel said. It was more of a threat.

Heather shrugged. Very dramatically. "Too bad," she said. "You might like to walk on the wild side once in a while."

Daniel chuckled. "You think you're wild? You're not even close."

Heather didn't take that well. She jammed her hands on

her hips, her mouth dropped open but nothing came out. Apparently she was searching for a suitably nasty comeback and coming up empty—which was surprising since Heather excelled at nasty. In the end, the best she could come up with was a vague threat.

"You'll be sorry," she said, and then she slinked her way back up the steps and went inside.

Eric went with her.

"There's something going on there," Daniel observed.

"If you're talking about Eric, he's harmless," Vivi said. "He might sell us out to make a buck—if he had any clue who to sell us out to."

"What about Heather?"

"Heather was concentrating elsewhere. It's hard to read someone in her state."

"What state would that be?"

"Horny," Vivi said bluntly. "Until just before she went inside. Then I caught something . . . malicious."

"I insulted her," Daniel said. "She'd probably key my car if she could find it."

"It felt stronger than that."

"I'll run a check on her first thing in the morning." Daniel got to his feet and held out a hand to Vivi.

"I'm coming," she said.

"Yeah, you are."

She stood, but she didn't climb the steps. "I thought you weren't going to tell me what to do."

"I'm not telling you what to do," Daniel said. "I'm just agreeing with you."

chapter
22

ERIC WAS ACTING WEIRD—WEIRDER THAN USUAL, and that set off Daniel's trouble radar. He was expecting something to happen, but he wasn't expecting to hear his phone ring about five minutes after he and Vivi got back to the third-floor apartment.

"There's a bomb in the building," a strange voice said when Daniel answered. "It's armed and set to go off in five minutes."

"This isn't Flip, so it must be Hatch," Daniel said.

Vivi froze halfway across the room, then went racing back, dragging Daniel's head down to hers so she could hear the conversation. What there was of it.

"Four and a half minutes. Come out or blow up."

"And I just take your word for it?"

"The bomb is under the floor of the apartment you're staying in." And Hatch disconnected.

Daniel felt Vivi sag next to him, but he didn't have time for weak knees. He wrapped a hand around her wrist and headed for the door. "You wrestled Flip's gun away from him," he reminded her. "You can handle a bomb."

Daniel thought she was resisting when she pulled free, but she only curled her hand into his and followed him down the stairs. They went into the apartment directly under theirs, and there, duct-taped to the ceiling right beneath where their bed would be, was a bundle of wires and what appeared to be dynamite, wrapped with more tape. A cheap timer ticked off the minutes and seconds in glaring red. Just under three minutes.

"Do something," Vivi said.

"I'm not an explosives expert. I'm just as likely to set it off as turn it off."

"Two and a half minutes," Vivi read off the display. "What do we do?"

"We go out," Daniel said.

"And get captured?"

"No choice." It was one of the common-sense rules of being a field agent: Always have an escape route. He'd checked out the building when he and Vivi had first come to stay there. It was a warren of apartments. They could get lost in the place long enough to call for backup, but there was no way they could escape a bomb without getting captured. "Two hit men, two doors," he said for Vivi's sake. "Same goes for the windows since they're only front and back. And I doubt the fire escape would hold up to a heavy wind. The only way out is through the front door."

"How about the roof?"

Daniel took her by the hand and pulled her out of the second-floor apartment. "Even if we had time to get up there, it's too big a risk. The bomb may not have enough firepower to damage more than a floor or two—"

"Eric and Heather!" Vivi raced down the stairs ahead of Daniel and began to bang her fists on the door to the apartment Eric was using.

Daniel joined her, both of them pounding and yelling. Heather shouted something back that sounded like, "You had your chance," so Daniel backed up against the wall opposite the door and gave the doorknob a good shot with his good leg. The old wood of the jamb splintered and the door crashed in.

"There's a bomb upstairs," he yelled through the opening, "get out or die."

Eric stared at him, brow furrowed, having trouble processing the danger. Heather was already on her feet. "Jesus," she said, ditching Eric and racing out the door.

Vivi stuck around, trying to make Eric understand he was about to die. Daniel heaved her over his shoulder and raced for the exit, Eric hot on his heels. The place exploded just as they went through the front door, a punch of heat and noise, and a blast of air that tossed Daniel face-first onto the sidewalk, Vivi on top of him. Everything went gray and fuzzy, but somewhere in his groggy brain he got the sensation of movement, and when his brains unscrambled he found himself in the back of a van, hands and feet secured by the plastic ties that were replacing handcuffs everywhere.

Vivi lay next to him, completely still. He nudged her, but she was out cold. At least he thought she was out, but when the van came to a stop she rolled over and looked at him.

"Waterfront," she said.

The doors opened and sure enough Daniel smelled water and heard it slapping against a man-made structure, probably a dock or wharf. Neither of them were gagged, so they must be in an area where they couldn't be overheard in the event a little recreational torture was planned before the main event. Unfortunately, that didn't help much since they were hauled out of the van, carted onto a boat, and taken down to a tiny galley belowdecks.

The boat barely looked seaworthy, an older model with a wooden hull and decks that hadn't seen varnish in a couple of decades but appeared to be no stranger to dry rot. The general theme continued in the galley. Lots of wood accented with brass, musty smell, not well maintained. The postage stamp–sized table had a tarnished brass railing to keep things from sliding off in rough seas. It was also convenient for securing prisoners.

Flip took a length of chain, ran it through Daniel's wrists, and padlocked it around the railing. He took another plastic tie out of his pocket, looped it through the one around Vivi's wrists, and tethered her to the porthole hinge on the opposite side of the galley from Daniel.

The boat motored away from dry land, but it was pitch-black out, which made it impossible to tell where they were headed. Daniel figured it was Boston Harbor rather than the Charles River or Fort Point Channel, and they were probably going out far enough for Hatch and Flip to toss their bodies into the ocean once the deed was done.

It wasn't long before the boat stopped, the motor cut out, and Flip appeared in the hatchway. He looked a little green around the gills. "Everybody comfy?" he sang out weakly.

"Aside from being bounced off the pavement a little while ago," Vivi said, "this sea air is hell on my hair."

"Sure, but the wild, curly thing suits you much better than that straight, streaky mess."

"How do you think it will look soaked in blood?" Daniel asked Flip.

"Well, blood is never a good look."

"Neither is having a building fall on your head."

Vivi was silent. Probably hadn't had time to process everything, what with being abducted and facing the prospect of her own death. Judging by the expression on her face, it had all come crashing back in.

She swallowed audibly. "Eric . . . Is he . . ."

"That place folded like an accordion," Flip said, "but nobody got hurt. Eric and his little chippy girlfriend got out. Huh, if they had any brains they wouldn't have been there at all after they gave you up."

"Eric's not connected, huh?" Daniel's comment was directed to Vivi, but Flip answered.

"That putz? He's nobody. We knew where she lived."

Flip hooked a thumb in Vivi's direction. "When the orders changed from killing you to getting her, we went back to her neighborhood and asked around. Didn't take us long to run across Heather, and Heather brought us to Eric. The rest is history."

"More like felony," Daniel put in. "Several felonies, if we're keeping track."

Flip shrugged.

"Why didn't you use a fake bomb?" Daniel asked him.

Another shrug, one-shouldered this time. "We knew who we were dealing with. You were armed, so we couldn't go into the building after you. We had to get you to come out."

"Why not just wait?" Vivi wanted to know. "We would have come out eventually, and there wouldn't have been any reason to . . . to . . ."

"He still would have been armed, and you'd have come out during the day, most likely."

"It's not like you were worried about innocent by-standers getting hurt before," Daniel said.

"We were worried about witnesses."

"So you decided to plant a bomb and arm it in the middle of the night?"

"We didn't think you'd be fooled by a fake one, so we had to use a real one."

Daniel knew the rest, but he took a minute to fit what Flip had told him into the overall puzzle. No lightbulbs popped on over his head, and there was no aha moment. In fact, he wasn't any further ahead than before. "Why did the orders change from killing me to getting her?"

Daniel was watching Flip, waiting for a response, but Flip's cell phone rang—"Gypsies, Tramps and Thieves" by Cher—and he went above to answer it.

"Now's your chance," Daniel said to Vivi.

"My chance for what?"

"Do your thing, get a premonition, tell me how to get out of this."

"It's not that simple," she said. "I can't just turn it on and off like a light switch."

"You did at Quincy Market."

"This isn't exactly the market. We were almost blown up a half hour ago, and now we're trussed up like garbage bags out in the middle of Boston Harbor with a gay hit man who's nursing a bad case of whiplash and a black eye because of us."

"If you don't put it out of your mind and concentrate on getting us out of here, we're going to be at the bottom of Boston Harbor. And if we're lucky, they'll kill us before they tie cement blocks to our feet and dump us overboard."

"You're not helping," she snapped.

"Compartmentalize, damn it," he snapped back.

She gave him one last glare then closed her eyes and made a face that looked more like constipation than concentration. It was no surprise when her breath burst out of her and she shook her head, her eyes meeting his. "It's no good."

Daniel lost it, just a little. Okay, he lost it a lot. He had enough presence of mind to keep his voice down, but mentally he was nose-to-nose with Vivi, shouting at her. "You keep jawing about how you can help me solve this thing, and every time I ask for help you've got some excuse why you can't."

"They're not excuses. This isn't exactly a science, you know. Stress—"

"Stress, my ass. You make a big deal about being a psychic and talking to the spirits, but what it's really about is you getting off on being different. You cock your head and shut your eyes and spout some bullshit prediction that has more to do with observational skill and a good grasp of human nature than anything else."

"You really think I like being this way? I've been an outsider all my life—in kindergarten, for God's sake. Do you think a five-year-old wouldn't give anything to fit in, to not be teased every day? I don't have any friends, I can't have a normal relationship with a man because they're all so afraid I can tell what they're feeling. People think it's cool having psychic ability, but they don't want to hang around with someone who can do what I do."

"I—"

"No, it's my turn to talk." Vivi tried to take the argument to Daniel. She was brought up short by a couple of plastic garbage ties, but she managed to get her point across. "I'm sick of hearing about how you don't trust me, and you don't believe in my ability—until you need a miracle, and then you expect me to race in and save the day."

Daniel snorted. "If I didn't trust you and believe in your ability I wouldn't be asking you to save the day, but you can't even drum up a halfway credible premonition."

"Because I love you, you jackass."

They both froze, just their eyes cutting to each other.

"Uh . . ." Daniel wheezed.

"That's right, you moron, I love you," she yelled at him. "That's what happened to my ability to read situations like this. It's supposed to be a gift, so I can have a regular relationship, but it doesn't seem like such a gift to lose my insight so I can be stuck with a pigheaded throwback like you."

"Uh . . ." Daniel said again, his mind racing but nothing coming out of his mouth.

"Speechless," she said, her voice dripping sarcasm, "now my day is complete."

"It's not exactly what I was expecting to hear," Daniel said when his vocabulary reappeared in his brain. "Give me a minute to process it."

"I'm tired—"

"You're going to be dead, and so am I, if you don't get your sixth sense tuned back in."

"Again, not helpful." She'd been about to say she was tired of beating her head against the emotional wall he kept between himself and the entire world, but heartbreak shouldn't be her focus right now. Becoming a permanent addition to the bottom of Boston Harbor was more the issue.

Flip returned before they could come up with a way to get free, short of chewing off their own wrists wolf-style. "The boss will be here soon." He put one hand to his stomach, the other to the wall to brace himself against the pitching of the boat. And he was beyond green. "At least I hope it's soon because the wind is kicking up and I'm not such a good sailor. I like a good sailor," he added without much real enthusiasm, "as long as we're on dry land."

"What's going to happen when your boss gets here?" Vivi wanted to know.

"I'm sure you can imagine," Flip said. His cheeks puffed out and he swallowed several times, fighting his stomach back into submission. "I hope to hell Tony Sappresi never finds out, although the way I feel now, death would be a relief."

"What's Sappresi have to do with this?" Daniel asked.

"Clearly he's behind the hit," Vivi said, "just like I've been telling you all along."

"Oh, puh-leeze," Flip said. "If Tony the Sap was behind this why would I care if he finds out?"

"Good point," Daniel said. "So why do you care?"

Flip rolled his eyes, then pressed a hand to his stomach. "Isn't it obvious? Everyone knows he's the most superstitious bastard on the East Coast. If we put a bullet in Tony's personal psychic and he finds out, our lives won't be worth spit. Especially since you won't be around to put Tony in jail." The boat listed heavily from one side to the other and Flip escaped above deck, both hands over his mouth.

Daniel didn't say anything. His eyes had locked on Vivi. She could feel him staring at her, and that wasn't all. The temperature in the galley had gone up several degrees, or maybe it was his anger burning through the no-insight rule.

"Sappresi's psychic," he ground out.

Vivi winced, and not just because he sounded like he was chewing rock. His eyes, when she forced herself to meet them, were so dark and cold. They'd never been that cold before, even that first day when she'd interrupted the bachelor auction.

"Is it true?"

"Yes," she said, giving him points for not just taking Flip's word about it. "I used to read for Tony Sappresi."

"Used to?"

"I quit when I discovered he'd had an FBI agent killed."

Daniel went silent, so she took the chance to tell him the story and hoped to hell he was listening. "Tony was one of my first regular customers," she began, "back when I was barely out of high school and I'd just begun to work with my grandmother. I didn't have much control over my ability then. I couldn't watch the news or read the paper without some . . . emotional overflow, and Tony wasn't as high in the Mafia as he is now. I didn't know who he was or what he did. As soon as I found out, I refused to read for him anymore."

"He just let you go?"

"He wasn't happy—Flip was right about his superstition level, but it actually worked in my favor. I convinced him my readings would be worthless if they were forced."

"You lied to him," Daniel said.

"No. I meant it. I can't force things, and reading for someone like Tony . . . Knowing what he'd done . . . The readings would have been negative, and there was no way I could have been sure if I was seeing what I wanted or the real future."

"Why didn't you come forward when Zukey was killed?"

"Right, you would have believed me," she said. "You would have put me on the stand to testify against Tony."

"Of course not, but—"

"But what? You'd have patted me on the head and sent me on my way—that's if you didn't have me put in the cell next to Tony's for being in cahoots with him."

"Cahoots?"

Vivi rolled her eyes. "You still don't entirely believe me and God knows I've given you enough proof. No one would have believed me except Tony." And he'd have had her killed. Vivi knew Daniel was thinking it, just as she knew he wouldn't say it and justify her . . . omission of the truth. And her death would have been for nothing, since the U.S. attorney's office never would have indicted Sappresi on the word of a storefront psychic.

"I warned Tony that a friend would betray him," she said. "I gave Tony his description. I know I didn't pull the trigger, but I felt like I was responsible for that man's murder.

"Once I started getting visions about your death, and I realized who you were, I couldn't just ignore the situation. I guess in some way, I felt like saving your life would atone for my part in Tom Zukey's death."

"So you did all this out of guilt."

"At first, yeah." "No" would have been the safe answer, but despite the third degree she was feeling pretty good, not eager to let weight settle back on her chest now that she'd gotten it off. "I'd like to think I would have sought you out and warned you regardless, but knowing you were prosecuting Tony for the murder definitely made it more pressing to keep you alive."

Daniel's eyes rose to meet hers, and she felt a chill, down to her very bones.

"You should have told me," he said.

"No, I did the right thing."

"You didn't exactly prevent my death."

"You're not dying tonight," Vivi said. She expected him to ask her how she knew that. He didn't. She'd betrayed him, lied to him, consorted with the enemy. Any one of those put her on the wrong side of the law-and-order line, as far as Daniel was concerned with his uncompromising, black-and-white point of view. He'd shut her out completely, and if they survived this boat trip, he'd cut her from his life like a tumor.

Well, Vivi thought, the hell with him. Better a clean, surgical separation.

"Where'd Flip go?"

Vivi flinched, the sound of his voice cutting through a

silence cold enough to raise gooseflesh. "Upstairs to wait for the boss, I guess."

"Who's not Sappresi."

"Which I'm beginning to regret," she said. "I could probably talk Tony into keeping me alive. But you'd be toast."

chapter
23

THE WIND CONTINUED TO SHARPEN, MAKING THE boat dip and sway. It wasn't long before Vivi heard Flip groaning between bouts of retching. Aside from Flip's gastrointestinal distress, and the slap of the waves against the wooden hull, it was quiet in the tiny galley belowdecks. Deathly quiet.

Daniel was sitting with his hands on the table curled into fists—wishing they were around her neck, Vivi figured. He wasn't talking, but she could feel his fury: a still, cold pool of black water that was a lot scarier than the rolling expanse of harbor outside the boat.

The muscles in her arms were screaming, and she realized she was straining against the plastic tie around her wrists. There was no way it would break, she told herself. She bought it, but it took another minute before she could relax, her fingers tingling as the blood rushed in. As long as she stayed loose, the tie wasn't tight enough to cut off circulation, but she couldn't slip a hand free.

The clinking of metal caught her attention. She looked over and saw Daniel holding the length of chain.

"It's about time you decided to do something besides sit there sulking."

Daniel ignored her, studying each of the eighth-inch-thick links. She didn't know what he was looking for, but he apparently didn't find it because he moved on to the brass railing it was looped through. Each section of railing was bolted to the table, which was a slab of wood about two inches thick. Daniel tested each section, grasping them one by one and giving a good experimental shake or two to see if there were loose bolts. He put some muscle into it, too, biceps cording, jaw knotting. Nothing budged, and nothing relaxed on Daniel. He looked like he was an inch away from chewing his way through the side of the boat. All he needed was a little more incentive . . .

"No ideas?" she said, loading her voice with sarcasm. "Next you're going to ask me to do something, right?"

His eyes shifted to hers. She wasn't fazed.

"I lied to you, I betrayed you, you shouldn't have trusted me, blah, blah, blah. Since you're going to hate me for the rest of your life, it'd be a real shame if your life only lasted a few more minutes."

He didn't reply, but Vivi could tell he was seeing red. Good, she thought, he'd need the anger.

"I didn't tell you because I knew you wouldn't listen to my explanation," Vivi said, poking at what she knew must be a sore spot. God knew it was one for her. "You would've walked away and now you'd be dead."

"Right, it would have been terrible to miss this experience."

"If it wasn't for me you wouldn't have lasted this long."

"Save the propaganda. I just want to get out of here."

"Away from me."

"As far as I can get."

"Then do it," she shot back. "You always want to muscle your way out of things. Now's your chance."

Daniel surged to his feet and took hold of the chain, white-knuckled, on the edge of a full-out, Mel-Gibson-against-the-Redcoats berserk episode. Perfect. Of course he might turn on her once he was done tearing the boat apart, but it was a chance she had to take.

"You can't keep waiting around for me to save the day," she said.

Daniel lost it, straining against the chain for all he was worth. Vivi heard the shriek of metal—the railing, she thought—pulling away from the table. Instead, the entire table ripped away from the side of the boat with enough force to spring a couple of the dry-rotted seams in the ancient wooden hull. Daniel, his wrists still tied together, dragged himself up the hatchway to the top deck, dragging the chain and the table along behind him.

Vivi stood there for a minute, staring open-mouthed at the water leaking between the boards, feeling it pool around her bare feet like the cold hand of death. Then she yelled for Flip. Sure, he had a gun. But he hadn't used it yet, and drowning was pretty much a sure thing.

It was Daniel who showed up in the doorway, hands free.

"Go away," she said, yelling for Flip again.

"Flip is still draped over the railing, adding to the poor water quality of the harbor. On the upside, he's a lovely shade of chartreuse."

"Once he realizes what's going on, he'll get me out of here."

"I've got his pocketknife."

She ignored him.

"You're pissed at me?" he said.

"You're being unreasonable."

"I'm not the one who's been lying about everything."

That hurt, because she knew he was saying he didn't believe she loved him, either. "My lie helped keep you alive."

"All you did was postpone the inevitable."

"Flip," she shouted, her eyes never leaving Daniel's, "Pierce is escaping. Come down here and shoot him."

"Now who's being unreasonable?"

"I learned it from you."

Daniel heaved a sigh and slogged through the water,

now ankle deep on him. "I ought to leave you here," he muttered, attacking the plastic tie around her wrists with a pocketknife.

She twisted around as far as possible, putting her body between him and her wrists. "Just give me the stupid knife and go away."

"Stop fighting me or I'll have to knock you out."

"Going to use the Vulcan death grip?"

"I was thinking something more earthly. Like a bullet. Or a pocketknife."

"Convenient."

"Save it—unless you think your tongue is sharp enough to cut you out."

Vivi didn't like it, but she had to let him at her plastic-tied wrists—him and his pocketknife, which must have been pretty dull since it took a solid two minutes and three nicks before he sawed his way through.

The boat was foundering pretty badly and listing to port, or maybe starboard, by the time she was free. Daniel waded over to the hatch and heaved himself up the steps. He reached down for her, but she made it to the deck under her own steam.

"There's no point trying to start the engine," Daniel said.

Vivi was already climbing over the side of the boat.

"What are you doing?"

"Swimming to shore," she said, stopping mid-climb, one leg over the railing.

"What about Flip?"

She shrugged. "What about him?"

"He's in no shape to swim."

"Just leave me to die," Flip moaned, looking like he meant it.

"See? He wants to die. And you wanted me to shoot him. Several times. So it works out for everyone."

"We can't just leave him to drown."

"We?" Vivi gave a slight, derisive snort of laughter. "There is no *we*, Ace."

He didn't say anything, not about their partnership any-way, and his silence on the subject was all the confirmation she needed.

"Your life is on the line, too," he reminded her when she swung her other leg over the railing. "Flip can tell us who's behind the murder attempts."

Vivi jumped over. She didn't give a damn about the murder attempts anymore. She probably would tomorrow, but for the moment, all that mattered was distance. Time would be the real healer, but that wasn't within her power to change.

"Where are you going?" Daniel yelled from the deck, which was all but underwater now.

"I'm swimming to shore," she yelled back.

"It's at least a mile. You'll drown."

"Well, that'll make your day."

There was a splash behind her. She spun around and there was Flip, jammed into a life preserver, floating list-lessly in the water. Daniel dove in, grabbed hold of the rope around the preserver, and began to sidestroke, Flip bobbing along behind him like a paisley cork.

"Shouldn't you be holding the rope in your teeth?" Vivi asked Daniel. "It's more macho that way."

He didn't look amused. "You could help."

She rolled onto her back, kicking lazily with her feet, preserving energy. "You'll make it. I'm sure."

"I thought you couldn't get a reading . . ." he trailed off.

Their eyes met, held. Daniel looked away first. She could have told him she'd only meant that she knew he'd get to shore because he wouldn't let himself fail, but best just to let the matter go, she decided.

That was surely what Daniel intended to do.

BY THE TIME DANIEL GOT HIMSELF AND FLIP TO THE wharf, Vivi was long gone. She hadn't even left a water trail. True, there was no way to know where she'd actually climbed onto shore, but it still ticked him off.

He hauled himself out of the water and dragged Flip out, both of them flopping on the littered, weedy wharf. Daniel just needed a few minutes to catch his breath. Flip probably would have preferred death. He was flat on his back, propped up by the life preserver under his armpits, listing to one side with noxious fluids running out of his eyes, nose, and mouth, thanks to the regular, weak heaving of his stomach. Not going anywhere until Daniel was ready to carry him. Daniel not only didn't want to carry him, Daniel was inexplicably torn between getting answers from Flip and leaving him on the wharf like storm-wrack so he could track Vivi down.

It wasn't a tough choice—hell, it was no choice at all. Vivi would still be around when—if—*when* he went looking for her. If he left Flip alone, he'd be gone as soon as he could drag his perky ass off the dock.

And yet there Daniel was, the answer to his problem not three feet away, and what was he doing? He was carrying on a debate between getting those answers and going after Vivi. She'd lied to him, and why had she lied to him? Because she didn't trust him. After all her big talk about blind faith, she'd had none in him. Otherwise she would have told him about her history with Sappresi. Sure, Daniel thought, he'd have been angry, and sure he'd have been suspicious, but . . .

He sat up and slicked his dripping hair out of his face. How about that bomb she'd dropped on the boat, he said to himself. He could be pissed off about that, right? Her claiming she had feelings for him was just a cheap ploy to get around her utter failure to predict what was going to happen . . .

His house. She'd destroyed his house. And smashed up the back of his car, not to mention getting his laptop and phone blown up . . .

Nope, no matter how he looked at the whole stupid fiasco, he couldn't make any of it Vivi's fault. Sure, she was irritating and stubborn and probably crazy, not to mention overly emotional. Then there was her tendency to lie. Even in extreme circumstances and with the best of intentions, that was a deal breaker for Daniel, especially when the lie involved a tie to organized crime.

Still, she hadn't put him in this situation—she'd put herself in, but his involvement was someone else's idea. And if he was being honest, he had to admit his life had been a damn sight more exciting in the last two weeks. Of course, that was due more to the murder attempts than to Vivi. It didn't change the fact that they were better off without each other. It didn't change the fact that going after her now would be a mistake. And it didn't change the fact that the life and death stuff needed to end.

Best, he decided, to concentrate on the part of that list he could actually do something about. That meant getting Flip to rat out his coconspirators. Daniel would be out of danger then, and so would Vivi, which meant she'd be off his conscience and his mind.

Easier said than done.

First he had to get Flip to Washington, D.C. The Boston P.D. would have been a lot more convenient, but he didn't have any clout with local law enforcement, and there'd be all that jurisdictional crap to wade through. It would take days to get Flip transferred to FBI custody, not to mention the wear and tear on his patience, waiting for the two factions to stop marking their territory and start acting like they were on the same side.

It meant touching Flip, not a pleasant prospect since Flip was wearing a good portion of his last three meals. Daniel hauled Flip to his feet, shimmied him out of the life preserver, and braced his shoulder in the other man's armpit. Flip slid down to the concrete, wet noodle–style. Daniel took hold of his collar and started to drag him.

"Hey," Flip protested weakly, "these are designer jeans. You're scuffing the label."

Daniel stopped walking. He didn't let go of Flip's shirt. "Get to your feet or there won't be any label left. Or skin on your ass."

Flip waved him off and crawled to his hands and knees,

then wobbled his way upright. It was slow going, but Daniel prodded Flip along until they found a payphone that worked. A half hour later, a government car showed up. Black and boring, Vivi would have pronounced it. Daniel was more interested in the method of propulsion. He would have preferred a helicopter but he had to take what he could get and be grateful. On the downside, a car meant wasted hours. On the upside, it had a comfortable backseat, so Daniel showed up in Washington at least partially rested. Flip showed up cuffed, smelly, and sullen.

"Jesus," Mike Kovaleski said when Daniel walked into his office. He put his arms up like he might hug Daniel, then thought better of it and settled for a crushing handshake. "Man, we thought you were dead."

"The bomb?"

Mike nodded, taking his seat behind the desk in his cluttered little office. " Your personal effects and the woman's were found in the rubble, and since it'll take time to excavate . . ." He spread his hands.

"You figured we were dead," Daniel finished.

"Yeah, so what happened?"

"It's a long story." Involving a nymphomaniac, a two-bit hustler, and a psychic. Some day Daniel figured he'd laugh about it, but it was going to be a while. Thankfully, he had something else to concentrate on. "The guy I brought in, you've got him on two counts of attempted murder and two kidnappings, at the very least. I need to know who hired him, and I don't care if you have to make a deal."

"Too late for that. A lawyer arrived about an hour before you did, knew this clown was coming in. Already has a gag on him."

"Who hired the lawyer?"

"Won't say, claims it's confidential. And don't ask me to crack their records. You know more about that attorney/client privilege bullshit than I do."

Daniel sat back, searching his personal repertoire of case law and coming up empty. No judge would let them breach confidentiality on a fishing expedition. If he didn't have a solid suspect, he wasn't getting a warrant for the lawyer's records. "What about the boat?"

"Any idea where it went down?"

"Only generally."

"We can send down a diver, but I wouldn't hold out hope that the registration will do us any good. It's probably stolen."

"Run Flip for known associates," Daniel suggested.

Mike sighed and fired up his desktop, feeding in the name Frances Llewellyn Ipswich.

"No wonder he goes by Flip," Daniel said.

Unfortunately, nothing came up, no wants, no warrants, no previous arrests.

"Shit," Mike said, "this guy hasn't even lifted a pack of gum. And it's not like there could be two people with that name."

"Either he's never been caught, or he's new at this."

"I'd go with the latter—for him and his pal—since they're complete fuckups. Lucky for you."

"Yeah, lucky for me," Daniel said absently, his mind already worrying at the problem of how to get something useful out of Flip.

Mike was on the same page. "We'll find a way to get him to talk," he said. "You do your lawyer thing, start digging and keep digging 'til you find out what kind of toilet paper this jackass uses. Something's bound to pop along the way. You know the drill."

"Right," Daniel said. "Too bad we can't use one of those on Flip."

"Yeah," Mike said with another sigh, "the good old days. On the other hand, we can send him someplace really choice, give him a couple of days in the general population, and see how he likes that."

Daniel snorted. "Hell, for Flip, prison will probably be a lot like a singles' bar."

chapter
24

MOST OF A WEEK HAD PASSED SINCE VIVI HAD LEFT
Daniel swimming for shore, towing Flip behind him. She'd
hung around, lurking in the shadows of an abandoned warehouse, long enough to make sure they made it to shore, and
then she'd gone home.

Daniel hadn't called. Not that she'd expected him to. He
wasn't still angry over her betrayal; he'd put her in his past.
It was how he operated. Well, the hell with him. She refused to waste any time mooning over Daniel Pierce. Unfortunately, there didn't seem to be anything else to do,
what with the weekend a couple days off. There wasn't a
lot of foot traffic in her neighborhood on weekdays, and
since her few regulars didn't realize she'd come back, they
weren't showing up, either. She could have called them,
but she was sadly lacking in initiative. Which was not
mooning behavior, no matter what anybody else might think.
It was self-defense. Calling him would only be asking for
rejection.

No way would Daniel want her around after discovering
her connection to Anthony Sappresi. Right was right, for

him, and wrong was wrong. And she was wrong; he'd been waiting for her to prove it all along, and she finally had.

She could still see the grim, closed-off look on Daniel's face when Flip had spilled the beans. She could still feel the heaviness settle on her chest, the sadness that he could write her off so easily— And, okay, maybe she was mooning, just a little, but that was because she didn't have anyone to commiserate with. Because she was alone. Again. Being a psychic meant she didn't have any corporeal friends. Those who weren't leery of her talents wanted to use them for their own gain. So she found it best to steer clear of close friendships. She had neighbors and acquaintances, but you couldn't cry on an acquaintance's shoulder. And since there'd been nobody to tell about Daniel, there was nobody to call and trash him to, nobody to get drunk with so she could forget about him for a little while. She could get drunk by herself, but that would be pathetic. And she couldn't go to a bar and get drunk with strangers, that would be asking for trouble, even without a couple of hit men to worry about.

Of course, it was only an assumption that the contract had been terminated—a pretty good assumption, knowing Daniel. When he set his mind to something, it was succeed or die trying. True, while she'd been his wingman she'd purposefully sabotaged the mission. But only that one time at Boston Common, and she hadn't put him in danger. And eventually he'd gotten what he wanted. By now Flip had probably spilled his guts, which meant Hatch and his boss were keeping Flip company in federal lockup.

But it didn't feel that way to Vivi. It felt like there was still a threat. Probably the fact that Daniel hadn't bothered to let her know she was safe. Jackass. He owed her that much, at least, but apparently one little lie—that she'd told for his own good—was enough to cancel out the lifesaving portion of the relationship.

Well, the hell with him. If he'd left it up to her to make sure she didn't end up on a morgue slab, she'd do it her way.

Vivi went downstairs and flipped the sign in the front
window to CLOSED. Not that there were people clamoring
to see her on a Thursday morning. She just didn't want any
interruptions. She went into the back room where she did
her readings, took a few moments to center herself, and
opened her mind. Nothing. No visions, no nudges, no ex-
trasensory activity of any sort. Wherever or whatever her
insight came from, it wasn't talking.

"This is no time to cut out on me," she said to the room
in general.

The room had no response, which equated to "You're on
your own, kid."

She sat back in her chair and spent a moment sulking
about that, but sulking wasn't going to get her out of trouble.
And what the hell, she'd always wondered what it would be
like to be normal. It probably wasn't the best time to experi-
ment with normal when her life was on the line, but sitting
around doing nothing wasn't a viable option, either. And really, she had all the information she needed. All she had to
do was substitute logic for intuition, right?

A little help wouldn't hurt, either, she thought a few
minutes later when logic wasn't delivering, going over the
facts one more time while she swallowed her pride.

ANTHONY SAPPRESI HAD ALREADY BEEN RULED OUT,
and Rudy Manetti was only a pervert. Joe Flynn was the
only one left. Daniel had already discounted him, but Vivi
wasn't so easily convinced.

She could go to Cohan's, see if Joe showed up there
again. But putting herself in a mob hangout, with a man
who might have tried to kidnap her once already, didn't
hold much appeal. If she was going to be used against
Daniel, she'd damn well be sure the person using her was
the one they were looking for. And there was just one resource left to her.

Tag Donovan had given her his phone number the day
he'd been tasked to follow her, and they'd wound up hav-

ing lunch instead. It wasn't that much easier to call him than Daniel, but at least there weren't any personal feelings involved.

Alex answered. They exchanged greetings, and Vivi said, "There's something I need to tell the two of you. Are you free for lunch?"

"Maybe. We're having lunch with Tag's family. If his mother mentions marriage, I'm allowed to leave. Chances are I won't actually get to eat—although Tag says she promised to be on her best behavior."

Vivi laughed. "Then do you mind if I talk to Tag for a minute?"

Alex didn't say anything, but she must have handed the phone over to Tag because the next voice Vivi heard was his. "Hey," he said, sounding glad to hear from her. "How's tricks?"

From anyone else that comment would have Vivi rolling her eyes. Tag's cheerfulness was completely contagious, though. "Not bad," she said, "considering I've been kidnapped, held hostage, and nearly drowned."

"I heard about that," Tag said. "I also heard you used to do readings for Anthony Sappresi, and when Pierce found out about it he tore a boat apart with his bare hands."

"He was pretty mad," she said. She could have set the record straight, but Daniel wasn't the bigger issue here. "How about you?"

"I haven't heard your side of the story," Tag said, sounding grim.

Vivi didn't want to tell Tag about her role in Tom Zukey's death any more than he wanted to hear it, but it had to be done so she took a deep breath and dove in. Tag didn't interrupt her once, and when she'd finished, it took him a couple beats to say anything, and then his question took her completely by surprise.

"Did you give Sappresi Tom's name?" he wanted to know.

"Well . . . no."

"Then why are you blaming yourself?"

"Aren't you?" she asked Tag.

"If you want to know the truth," he said, "I'm blaming Tom. He should have told me he was taking a meeting with Sappresi. By the time I found out and got there, it was too late to save him, and I almost died on top of it. And while we're passing out blame, Sappresi gave the order."

It was Vivi's turn to be speechless.

"Trust me, I know how you feel," Tag said into the silence, "but it's just a waste of time to beat yourself up."

Tag had been assigned to work on the case that had brought him into Alex Scott's life, Vivi knew, when what he'd really wanted to do was find the man who'd killed his partner, Tom Zukey, because Tag had felt like he'd let Zukey down. So when he said he understood, he really did. Vivi wasn't sure she was ready to let go of the guilt she felt over her part in Zukey's death, but she was willing to put it aside for a little while. "Thanks, Tag," she said. "Can I ask . . . Is everything okay . . ."

"Pierce is still alive, if that's what you want to know. I figured you already got that much out of the agents."

"What agents?"

"The ones assigned to watch your place."

"There are agents on me?" she asked, but she didn't hear Tag's answer. She hadn't been out of the house for most of a week, and okay, maybe she'd been a little shell-shocked, considering everything that had happened. Definitely too caught up to notice the attention focused on her. "Did Daniel . . ."

"I don't know for sure if Pierce made the arrangements, but that would be my guess."

"Well, who asked him?" she said before the little spark of warmth inside her spread. So Daniel had cared enough— No, *care* was the wrong word. If anything, it had been concern for her safety, most likely to save his own conscience. And since there was concern, there was still danger.

Tag had wisely chosen not to comment. She didn't want to speculate on what was going through his mind.

"Can I run something else by you?" she asked instead.

"Sure."

"If you thought someone was guilty of something, how would you go about finding out for sure?"

"You're not going to do something stupid, are you? I could stick around a couple days if you want. Alex, too. She's pretty good in the trenches."

Vivi's first reaction was to tell him to butt out, but that was more of a knee-jerk reaction to the way Daniel had treated her, so she reined her temper in. "I just need some advice."

"If it was me, I'd start by going through everything that happened," Tag said, "beginning from day one. Get it down on paper, that'll help since this is your first time. Once you've done that, see what jumps out at you. There's no such thing as a coincidence, keep that in mind. Every thread has to be pulled. One of them will lead you to the person you're looking for."

"Then what?"

"Then you have to decide the best way to handle it."

"What would you do?"

"Call the authorities."

She had to give him credit, he hadn't even hesitated over his answer. But she wasn't fooled. "I asked you what you'd do."

"Take the fight to them," Tag said with a shrug in his voice. "You wait, they have the upper hand. But that's me. You're a civilian. You should call . . . I'll give you Mike Kovaleski's number," he amended because he knew she wouldn't go to Daniel.

"Thanks," Vivi said, taking down the number he gave her. "Good luck on your trip." And she disconnected, her mind already spinning with possibilities.

If she was going in search of Joe Flynn, she'd have to wait for the dinner hour, anyway, so it wouldn't cost her anything to try Tag's suggestion.

She dug out a legal pad and a pen, and made herself a cup of herbal tea, which she hated but which also promoted clarity of mind. She drew a line down the middle of the paper from top to bottom. The left side was for a list of names, the right for the high points of each incident.

She began with the bachelor auction, putting a quick note on the right side of the sheet for what she considered important moments of the evening—the arrival of the hit men pretty much covered it. The left side stayed empty. There were too many people to list, even if she'd known their names.

Then she remembered that Daniel thought the reason for the contract was personal, so Vivi wrote down Patrice Hanlon, Alex Scott, and Cassandra Hobbs. They'd all been present at the auction, and they all had a personal relationship with Daniel. And since those names made some other points of the evening seem important, she added Daniel's deal with Patrice to buy him, and the helicopter showing up to rescue them on the right side. No coincidences, Tag had said.

Next was the incident at Cohan's. Again, Patrice's name went on the left, along with Rudy Manetti's and Joe Flynn's. The right side had only three entries. Daniel had been there because he had a dinner date with Patrice, Joe Flynn had shown up, and so had the hit men.

She took a short break to make herself lunch and kept going while she ate, writing down whatever seemed to stick out, no matter how inconsequential it seemed. The car that had almost trapped them in Daniel's cul-de-sac after she'd trashed his house to save him from the fire—a BMW, which in retrospect seemed out of place in the mostly working-class neighborhood. The fact that the hit men hadn't really shot at Daniel after that because, Daniel had rightly concluded, they'd wanted to capture him instead. Before they'd switched to trying to capture her . . .

Tag had told her to go over the facts to see if something jumped out. Well, something was jumping—or more like someone.

Patrice Hanlon.

Somebody must hate Daniel pretty badly to want him dead, Vivi thought. If she'd hated somebody that much, wouldn't she want to see the takedown?

Patrice Hanlon had been there at the first two attempts

to kill Daniel. Patrice had made sure she didn't touch Vivi the one time they'd met. Fine, she'd been shot and flying on painkillers, but Vivi knew Patrice hadn't missed the part about her being a psychic—a psychic who was helping Daniel. It wouldn't have taken much for Patrice to connect Vivi to Sappresi. And it was after that last phone call Daniel took from Patrice that the hit men knew who Vivi was and began to focus on her.

Suppose Patrice thought there was more than a collaboration going on between them, Vivi postulated? Daniel thought the hit men wanted to use her against him. Maybe that was another thing he was right about. Maybe whoever wanted him dead, also wanted him to suffer first. Whether or not Daniel felt something for her— Okay, it was a big *not*. But the murderer wouldn't know that, and no matter what was between them, he would still put himself in danger to save her. Saving her was the right thing to do, and he was all about "right."

It was a lot of maybes and ifs, but when Vivi looked at all the pieces she felt like she was getting a pretty complete picture. Tag would have gone after Patrice, but that didn't feel right to Vivi. She didn't have the skills to take on a woman who had a homicidal maniac like Hatch at her beck and call. Allegedly. Tag had suggested she call Mike Kovaleski, but Mike had never been her biggest fan. Mike would also want proof, and she didn't have any. So she called Daniel and tried her theory out on him—or rather she blurted out, "Patrice Hanlon hired the hit men."

Daniel didn't buy it. Big surprise.

"Why would Patrice want me dead after all these years?" he wanted to know.

Vivi hadn't gotten over the fact that he'd answered his phone after seeing her number on the display, let alone that he was actually carrying on a conversation with her. Making a good argument was currently beyond her ability. "I don't know" was all she could come up with.

"You don't know, or is this more of your psychic rambling?"

"*This* has nothing to do with my psychic ability. Patrice was there at both of the first two attempts on your life."

"The bachelor auction was publicized, and anyone could have seen me at Cohan's. I was there a couple hours before Hatch and Flip showed up. Plenty of time for someone to call them."

"You just don't want to believe your judgment is that bad, Ace. If you put your personal feelings aside—"

"Are you sure my personal feelings are the issue? Maybe you're jealous. And don't call me Ace."

All the breath leaked out of Vivi's lungs, and she rubbed a hand over her chest in a futile attempt to ease the ache there. He didn't want to talk about her feelings, but he'd use them as an excuse to bury his head in the sand so he didn't have to examine his own feelings where Patrice was concerned? Fine. It was his life.

"Think whatever you want. *Daniel*. The facts are right there in front of your face. If you choose to ignore the truth that's your business."

"The truth as you see it."

"You don't want to believe me because I lied to you, I get that. You can ignore the possibility and hope I'm wrong, or you can do what I did. Look at everything without your feelings getting in the way."

"It won't matter without a reason," Daniel said. "Give me a motive, and maybe I'll consider that a friend I've known for years wants me dead."

"Fine," Vivi shot back, and disconnected. Mr. Show Me wanted a motive, she'd get him one the only way she knew how. By making a little social call on Patrice Hanlon.

chapter
25

VIVI THOUGHT PATRICE WAS TRYING TO KILL HIM. Daniel thought Vivi was a nutcase. If Patrice hadn't tried to kill him after her brother was murdered in prison, why would she want to kill him now? It made no sense. Hell, none of it made sense. The whole thing had been a cluster fuck from day one. Every lead was a dead end, every ploy he attempted turned into a *Three Stooges* routine, and even when he got a break, nothing broke. This last claim of Vivi's was just the icing on the cake. Trying to steer the investigation in Patrice's direction was like saying Bambi's mother had shot herself to make deer hunters look bad.

The trouble was, he was fresh out of ideas. He didn't have a clue where to look next. Flip was in federal prison, keeping his mouth shut—at least in the interrogation room. Hatch was still at large. The puppet master was lying low.

Daniel had gone home, mostly because he refused to run anymore. But it wouldn't have hurt his feelings if there'd been another attempt to kill him. Hell, he was practically begging for it. The house was anything but secure. Repairs had begun, the front wall framed in but covered only with flimsy plastic. Squirrels and raccoons might have issues with the plastic, but Hatch should have no trouble coming in after him. And Daniel was ready.

There were weapons stashed all over the house, and if all else failed, he could use his fists. Vivi thought only the weak-minded resorted to violence, but she'd never seen him this way, all but choking on frustration and impatience, not to mention the other things that were bubbling around inside him, emotions he didn't want to admit to feeling in the first place. He wanted this thing over with, wanted to get on with his life. But a nice, sweaty fistfight would have gone a long way to working off some of the pressure.

There hadn't been any more murder attempts. He didn't believe the threat had passed, but if he couldn't flush out the soldiers and get one of them to lead him to the mastermind, he was doomed to spend God knew how much time looking over his shoulder.

And then Vivi called with her wild theory. Much as he hated to admit it, she was right—but not about Patrice. Vivi was right about going back through the case, removing himself and all his preconceptions, and looking at the facts again. Maybe some new angle would present itself—and okay, he was going to look at Patrice while he was at it. But only to rule her out.

It still felt ridiculous. Patrice had no criminal record, no ties to organized crime—except her uncle, Joe Flynn, who had absolutely no use for her, since she fraternized with the enemy. And after all the years and all the kindnesses Patrice had shown him, Daniel thought, here he was wondering if she wanted him dead. If she found out, his suspicion would be a worse betrayal that what Vivi had done to him.

But what if Vivi was right? He hated the thought, and he wasn't too happy with Vivi for planting it in his head. But the agent part of him kept whispering that trust was a mistake, and the lawyer part of him agreed. And since the guilt-ridden part of him knew he couldn't be objective until he ruled Patrice out, he headed for the only resource that came to mind. Flip might be acting like he took a vow of silence, but Daniel was prepared to do the talking, starting with the big question.

"Ever heard of Patrice Hanlon?" he asked, barely waiting for Flip to settle into his chair in the little interview room at the prison.

Flip just sat there, sullen, nonresponsive, clearly not faring well in jail, judging by the black eye and split lip. He kept his gaze level, but Daniel swore he saw a flicker of . . . something in Flip's eyes. He picked up his cell and called Mike.

"Yo," Mike said. Mike wasn't big on small talk.

Neither was Daniel at the moment. "Run Patrice Hanlon," he told Mike, his eyes on Flip, waiting for him to blink. "Maiden name Patrice Flynn. You won't find a criminal record, but I'm looking for something else. Call me with the results."

Flip blinked. He fidgeted, too, cuffs and shackles rattling. "She's my cousin," he said. "Second cousins, actually, on my mother's side."

"Hatch?"

"What about Hatch?"

"How does he know Patrice?"

"He doesn't," Flip said. "And anyway, what does Patrice have to do with anything? I thought you were looking for the guy behind the contract on you."

Daniel sat back in his chair, asking himself the same question Flip had asked him, and wondering the same thing Flip was wondering. What did any of this have to do with Patrice? Unless she'd suddenly developed a split personality, he still had no clue why she'd want him dead.

"So who is behind the contract, and why does he want me dead?" Daniel asked Flip. But he'd lost his momentum, given Flip time to get his composure back, and to remember what was at stake for him.

Flip crossed his arms over his chest and kept his mouth shut.

"You're really going to spend the rest of your life in jail for someone else?"

"At least I'll have the rest of my life."

"You're forgetting this is a federal crime. Massachusetts may not have the death penalty, but the U.S. government hasn't made as much progress."

Flip turned pasty.

"Your new complexion doesn't really go with prison orange," Daniel said. "But don't worry about it. They have a nice doctor on staff here. He'll be happy to put you out of your misery."

"Tell them not to put a poem on my gravestone," Flip said, looking like the bravado was making him feel better. "I hate poetry."

"Funny."

"And nothing too heavy for my last meal. There're few things sadder than a fat corpse."

"Who's behind the contract?"

Flip shrugged. "The one-armed man? Ma Barker? Maybe Jack the Ripper stopped in for a visit— No, Jack likes to do his own dirty work."

Daniel half rose from his seat, hands fisted. And his phone rang. He kept his eyes steady on Flip's while he pulled his phone from the holder on his belt, glanced down at it, and let it go to voicemail. He didn't recognize the number, but he was grateful to whoever it was since the call had kept him from throttling Flip. Throttling Flip would have been satisfying, but Flip's lawyer would have a field day with it, and the balance of power would shift away from Daniel.

Not that Daniel had all that much power. His only real ace in the hole was the death penalty, and that wasn't working. Yet. A few more days in prison and—

His phone rang again, the same unfamiliar number. This time Daniel needed the distraction, so he stepped out into the hallway to answer it. He listened very carefully, just as the caller instructed, then clipped the phone back on his belt.

The guard was getting ready to escort Flip back to his cell when Daniel entered the interview room again. Daniel shoved Flip back down. Flip missed the chair.

"Police brutality," he shrieked, hauling himself back to his chair. "My civil rights have been violated. I'm going to sue you and the government. I'm going to be a millionaire."

"For falling on your ass?" Daniel snorted. "You'll never win a lawsuit with that. Especially since you don't have any witnesses."

Flip looked over at the guard, who'd resumed his station by the door.

The guard held Flip's gaze for a beat, then turned his head to stare off into the far corner. If he'd covered his eyes, it wouldn't have made the message any clearer.

"Now," Daniel said, placing his hands palms down on the table and leaning forward, "you're going to answer my questions."

Flip rolled his chair backward until he hit the wall. The guard headed for the door.

"Stick around," Daniel said to him, keeping his gaze level on Flip's. "Somebody needs to make sure I don't kill him."

PATRICE LIVED IN BEACON HILL, IN A REDBRICK AND wrought-iron, ivy-swathed town house along a steep, narrow street with brick sidewalks and perpetually burning streetlights. Louisburg Square was within walking distance, and there were tasteful boutiques and highbrow cafés along the main thoroughfares. The entire neighborhood would have breathed a collective gasp of horror if Vivi had tried to open for business anywhere within five miles of Beacon Street. As it was, she half-expected someone from the historical commission to race up and tell her only tourists and residents were allowed to infiltrate the enclave. And the residents were only tolerated as a necessary evil, as long as they didn't dare to change more than the baking soda in their refrigerators.

She hated to admit it, but Daniel would have been right at home in this neighborhood—the nine-to-five Daniel, anyway, the Daniel who wore designer suits and patronized charity events with a view to running for public office.

The Daniel who preferred to solve his problems by shooting, beating, or exploding his way out of them would as soon cut off his right testicle as live in Beacon Hill. But that Daniel was only a temporary throwback.

Maybe she should call Mattel, see if there were any licensing possibilities. Barbie might stick with Ken, but real women everywhere would take one look at a Daniel doll and probably have catfights in the doll aisle of the toy store. And if she was any judge of female behavior—and she was—it'd be FBI Daniel rather than Federal Prosecutor Daniel that was to blame for the bitch slapping and hair pulling. And speaking of bitch slapping . . .

Vivi climbed the steps to Patrice's front door, which probably cost as much as her entire house. The sidelights were stained glass, the appointments were polished brass, and the statement was pretentious. Patrice, when she answered the door, looked anything but. She wore jeans, a sleeveless cotton sweater, and a pristine white bandage on her left upper arm, and her feet were bare. Her hair was pulled back into a ponytail, and with her freckled face almost completely bare of makeup, she looked like the she ought to be the maid or babysitter.

Her carriage and tone, when she spoke, were lady of the manor, all the way. "Can I help you?" she asked politely. And then the recognition came into her eyes, and everything about her sharpened. "Aren't you . . ."

"Vivienne Foster. We met at Cohan's the night you were, uh . . ." She made a vague gesture.

Patrice's right hand flew to the bandage on her left arm. "I was a little out of it when Daniel introduced us."

"Not so out of it that you missed the part where he said I'm a psychic."

Patrice took that in, one eyebrow inching up. "Why would that matter to me?"

"That's the sixty-four-million-dollar question, isn't it?"

"I think you should come in and sit down, Ms. Foster—"

"Vivi."

"Vivi. This promises to be a very interesting conversation."

Patrice led the way into a sitting room beautifully appointed with antiques. Vivi preferred her worn, mismatched furniture; at least it meant something to her.

"I haven't seen Daniel in a couple weeks," Patrice said, taking a seat on a Queen Anne chair. "I haven't talked to him, either, except that once, and then he rushed me off the phone. I'm a little hurt."

"He's been busy trying to stay alive," Vivi said, dropping onto a Chippendale love seat.

Patrice gave a soft breath of laughter. "I can't believe he hasn't ended that nonsense by now . . . You're working with him, right?"

Vivi shrugged. She could have told Patrice the truth, but the pretense that she and Daniel were still a team had to be maintained. "Does it bother you that Daniel is confiding his problems to me?"

"Not at all. I was actually wondering if he—if you have any suspects."

"As a matter of fact, *we* do."

Vivi didn't miss the way Patrice pressed her lips together.

"So he trusts you. In a matter of days?"

"Has it only been days?" It felt like a lifetime. "I know it doesn't seem fair—"

"Fair!" Patrice sat back, hands white-knuckled on the arms of her chair, fighting her temper. Her temper won. "Is it fair for some tattooed bimbo to sashay into Daniel's life and take over after I spent the last seven years getting him to open up?"

"Open?" Vivi glanced around a room that looked like it

was kept in order by a maid with OCD. "I can see how a repressed social climber like you would think that."

"I put in all the work to gain his trust."

"So you could kill him."

Patrice made the you-must-be-crazy face.

"That would be really convincing for anyone else," Vivi said. "You covered your tracks pretty well, but you're going to tell me everything."

"Suppose I'm not in a talkative mood."

Vivi took a deep breath and closed her eyes. "Let's start with family," she said after a moment. "Your uncle Joe, specifically."

Patrice made a non-drawing-room-approved noise in the back of her throat. "Joe Flynn is a big, dumb Mick who thinks he knows what's going on. I'm running circles around him." A small, humorless smile curved her lips. "And now you'd like to trot off to Daniel to tell him some interesting fairy tale you concocted in your strange little mind. He won't believe you."

"No, but he'll believe you."

"I don't have anything to say to Daniel."

"Not even that you've got me tied up somewhere, and if he wants to see me alive again, he can come and get me in person?"

"You've been watching too much television."

"You got this idea from television?" Vivi said. "And here I thought you came up with it all on your own. I'm so disappointed."

"What the hell are you doing?"

"Forcing your hand. I know you're behind the contract."

"You know . . ."

"And I know you want to get your hands on Daniel too much to let me walk out of here."

"If that were true, it would be really stupid to take you prisoner with the FBI listening in."

Vivi lifted up her T-shirt.

Patrice raised an eyebrow. "Nice bra," she said.

"It's one of those Victoria's Secret ones. I have trouble finding my size, but this one is perfect."

"And not hiding a wire. How about the jeans?"

"I'm not taking my pants down for you. I'm no fan of law enforcement, so why would I put my life on the line to help them?"

Patrice took a moment to consider that. "I don't get it. If you're so sure I ordered a man killed—a man I truly like, by the way—why would you come here, unarmed and with no backup?"

Vivi shrugged. "Daniel wants to know who's trying to kill him. I'm giving him the answer."

"Because you have no proof."

"Not at the moment, but I've already planted the suggestion that you're behind this."

"Daniel trusts me."

"Do you believe that? Or do you think he'll eventually take a good, hard look at you? Not to mention he could ask Flip."

Patrice thought that one over, lips pursed, mulling over the probability that Flip would keep his mouth shut, *and* that Daniel would trust her enough to ignore Vivi's warning. It was too much to take on faith. "Hatch," she yelled.

Hatch came out of the depths of the house, two hundred pounds of muscle barely regulated by severely underutilized brain cells. He grinned at her—at least Vivi thought it was a grin. His teeth were showing, but his eyes were still cold and dead.

Patrice stood, and Vivi took a deep breath. This was where it got dicey. She'd known she was walking into danger, but facing it now was scarier than she'd imagined.

"You know what to do," Patrice said to Hatch. "I'm off to make a date with Daniel."

"Big mistake," Vivi said, hoping she looked as calm and confident as she sounded. "He'll be ready for you."

"How? He doesn't know where you're being held."

"He'll figure it out."

"Very good. That almost sounded convincing."

Vivi laughed. "If you think I have any doubt, then you haven't been paying attention." But she was worried. She was taking a hell of a chance with her life, not to mention Daniel's. But it was the only way to end this thing so that he had a fighting chance. And it was Daniel's risk to take. He didn't have to come after her.

But Vivi knew he would.

chapter
26

DANIEL WAS SITTING IN HIS CAR, IN HIS DRIVEWAY, staring at the plastic-shrouded front of his house and thinking it was a pretty good metaphor for his life at the moment. He was bare-assed in the wind, with just enough knowledge to make him feel secure when really there was nothing between him and complete disaster—and that included self-control.

His hands fisted around the steering wheel, he struggled to breathe and keep his chest tight at the same time, to hold in the anger and the fear, the complete and utter impotence that wanted to explode out of him in a burst of sound and fury directed at anyone or anything that got in his way. He needed the anger, and the fear, needed to focus them on the right person at the right place and time. And he'd make sure there was a little left over for Vivienne Foster.

If she was still alive to yell at.

She had a gun to her head, aimed by her own hand. And his. He had to face that. She'd called to tell him about Patrice, and he'd been stupid enough to throw a challenge in her face. *Get a motive,* he'd said. Might as well tell her to jump off a bridge. Or a roof, because hell, he was jumping after her, wasn't he?

Wanting a motive, or a shred of proof, before he believed one of his few friends was trying to plant him wasn't the stupid part. Saying it to Vivi was. She didn't think like other people. Not to mention she had something to prove to him, and since he'd made it clear that he wouldn't accept paranormal confirmation, she'd gone to get it the only way she could. She'd let Patrice take her hostage. And the gun that was aimed at her head? It was in Hatch's hand, and the guy didn't seem particularly sound of mind. The guy seemed like he held a grudge, and if Vivi thought Daniel enjoyed violence, she was in for a real eye opener with Hatch.

That thought led to another red-hazed, heart-pounding struggle for control that Daniel might have lost if the phone on the passenger seat hadn't buzzed. He flashed back to the jail cell, to the last call he'd taken. From Patrice.

He snatched up the phone. It took a few precious seconds to focus on the readout, and then another second to rein his frustration back in before he answered it.

He managed to sound almost calm.

"Mike told me you were leaving Boston today," he said to Tag Donovan by way of greeting.

"Alex and I are at Logan Airport, waiting to board," Tag said back. "She has an assignment to do her photojournalist thing in Iraq. I'm going along to make sure she doesn't have an unfortunate run-in with a sniper or suicide bomber. Speaking of which, I'm glad you didn't get blown up. Alex, too."

"Nice to know I'd be missed," Daniel said. And it was interesting to know it mattered to him, when he'd always told himself it didn't. "You've been talking to Mike."

"I've been talking to Vivi."

Not a news flash that gave Daniel the warm fuzzies. "Sappresi—"

"She told me about that," Tag said.

"Zukey—"

"And that. And that you two were on the outs over it. You don't really think she's to blame?"

"Don't you?"

"I think Tony Sappresi is to blame, and since you're putting his ass in jail, problem solved."

"It's not a matter of blame," Daniel said, "it's a matter of trust."

"So I guess that means you don't want to know that Vivi asked how I would go about figuring out who was behind the contract."

"And you told her . . ."

"I told her to go back through the events, see if anything popped. And then she asked me how I'd handle whatever popped."

"Jesus," Daniel said, not needing to ask the obvious. Tag was an FBI agent. There was only one way to handle this kind of situation. "Why didn't you call me sooner?"

"Why? What's going on?"

"I give myself up or she dies."

"Shit," Tag said, making the leap from his conversation with Vivi to hostage crisis. "You give yourself up and you die," he pointed out to Daniel. "Her, too. You know the score. And you know the protocol."

"The protocol doesn't mean squat when it's someone you . . ."

"Yeah," Tag said into the silence. "Been there, done that."

Tag had been in a similar situation, with Alex held at gunpoint. He'd pulled a Rambo and gotten her out. The difference was, Alex had been the target in that scenario. If Tag had waited, she'd be dead.

Vivi was only a hostage. Daniel should have called the FBI, he should have stepped out and let them handle it. But Patrice wanted him. Anyone else showed up, or she even got wind the authorities were involved, Vivi was dead.

Flip hadn't rolled, either. His lawyer—or rather Patrice's lawyer—had arrived in the nick of time and put a muzzle on him, good and tight. Since there was nothing but Daniel's word to prove Patrice had anything to do with Vivi's disappearance, she'd walk. And he'd wind up dead sometime in the near future.

"You still there?" Tag wanted to know.

"Yeah," he said, disgusted, angry, but mostly exhausted. He was fucking worn out trying to keep up with Vivi, mentally and physically.

"When and where?" Tag asked.

"Tomorrow morning, early. They'll contact me and set up the meet."

"It'll be somewhere deserted, a place where a murder, and probably torture, wouldn't be noticed. Why tomorrow?"

"So I can sit around and wonder what's happening tonight."

"Which you're not going to do—sit around, I mean. Whoever you're up against is stupid enough to give you the time to get ahead of this thing. Work whatever leads you have and figure it out. You have leads, right?"

Daniel exhaled heavily. "Just the one Vivi gave me. Patrice Hanlon."

"Ouch."

"You don't sound surprised."

"Alex doesn't like her," Tag said, sounding like a shrug went along with the observation.

"Another sound reason for thinking the woman is capable of murder."

"Maybe not to you," Tag said, "but I've learned to trust her judgment."

Truth be told, it carried weight with Daniel, too. He hadn't known Alex Scott as long—and certainly not as closely—as Tag. But she was one of those people who just seemed to know. Alex didn't talk a lot, but she listened, carefully, and her bullshit meter seemed to be pretty damn accurate.

His own judgment wasn't proving quite so sound or reliable. He'd trusted Patrice and doubted Vivi right down the line. Sure, he had good reasons, but that was little comfort at the moment because, looking back, he could see what he'd purposefully ignored all along. Patrice Hanlon had every reason to hate him, and all the time she'd been pretending to care, she'd been easing her way into his trust and biding her time. And yeah, it had taken him years to completely trust her, but he still felt like a fool.

He had to thank her for the perspective, though. Compared to Patrice's betrayal, what Vivi had done was nothing.

"You should call Mike and have him activate a hostage team," Tag said.

"You and I both know that isn't going to fly," Daniel said. "It'll be come alone or Vivi dies, and it won't be an idle threat."

"Then take Patrice out today."

"I called already. Her housekeeper says she's out of the city for a couple of days. She's gone under."

"The guy in jail—"

"Patrice is his cousin, but that's all I could get him to admit to before his lawyer showed up and shut me down. Once Patrice finds out he told me that much, he's going to suffer an unfortunate accident in the jail yard."

"Sounds like she's pretty well covered," Tag said. "I can change my flight."

"No point," Daniel replied, "unless you can help me figure out where Vivi is being held."

"Can't do that, but I know someone who can. Her name is Harmony Swift, and when she shows up at your door it will help if you trust her."

"Not another woman," Daniel groaned. "I'm plagued by women. No offense, Alex," he added since he knew she was listening in.

"None taken," Alex said, and he could hear the smile in her voice. "I feel pretty much the same about men. Present company included."

"I hate to break up the act," Tag said, "but our plane is about to board. Pierce, you're not going to get official assistance, so you're going to need the unofficial kind. Harmony Swift is in analysis. She's dying to get in the field, reads every file she can, listens in on all the wiretaps, and she's a whiz at research because a large portion of her job is tracking violators on the Internet. If anyone can find Vivi, Harm can, and she'll keep it on the q.t."

"She'd be willing to do that for me?"

"She'd be willing to do that for me," Tag said.

Daniel thanked him and disconnected, deciding it would be a good time for him to bow out of the conversation. Tag was the one who'd been stupid enough to confirm Alex's opinion of men. Tag could face the consequences.

Daniel had his own woman troubles to deal with.

ALL IN ALL, VIVI THOUGHT, SHE WAS PRETTY COM-fortable. Okay, her hands were plastic-tied again, but her feet were loose and there was no chance of drowning. She was sitting on a car seat, a really nice car seat, butter-soft leather, lumbar support, and a headrest with built-in speakers that were, unfortunately, out of commission since there was no car and therefore no radio in the immediate vicinity. There were lots of cars nearby, not to mention trucks, semis, taxicabs, and one school bus. They were all in various stages of disassembly, chop-shop style, which explained her carless car seat . . .

Then it dawned on her, or rather it flashed across her mind. Daniel, lying on the ground with staring, lifeless eyes. And in the background, there'd been a wide assortment of vehicles in various stages of disassembly, chop-shop style.

It took her a minute to get past the horror of that vision, the complete and utter terror that she suddenly found herself in the place Daniel was supposed to die, and the fear that maybe she'd gone about this thing all wrong and she wouldn't be able to prevent it.

She could have escaped, since her feet weren't secured, but there was Hatch, leaning against the side of a Jaguar chassis about twenty feet away. He held a gun loosely in his right hand, index finger lying straight along the trigger guard. He'd been told to watch her, and that's what he did. His eyes, dark, empty holes in his otherwise nondescript face, never left her. She didn't think he even blinked.

So she might as well make the best of it. "Where are we?" she asked Hatch.

Hatch didn't answer. Not a multitasker. All his focus was going into watching her. Talking at the same time appeared to be too much to ask. Walking and chewing gum was probably out, too, but she had a feeling shooting was as natural to him as breathing.

"How long are we going to be here?"

No response from Hatch again.

"Patrice didn't waste her time telling you what's going on," she said. "I guess you're just a weapon to her, and you don't have to keep the weapons informed."

That got a rise out of Hatch. His eyes became even colder and harder, with an edge of violence that had a thin layer of control over it. He looked completely crazy, serial-killer, stalker crazy . . . Okay, now it made sense. Hatch had feelings for Patrice. Mental note, Vivi told herself: Don't say anything negative about Patrice or her relationship with Hatch.

"Would you mind loosening my wrists?" she said instead. "This tie thing is cutting off the circulation, and it's not like I'm going anywhere with you standing over me holding a gun."

Hatch was back to silent staring.

"And while we're on the subject, I'd like to lie down. Since we have to be here all night there's no reason we both have to lose sleep. My butt is going numb—"

"I can put you out of your misery," Hatch said, cocking the gun and putting it at her head.

"Never mind."

AN HOUR AFTER HE TALKED TO TAG, DANIEL'S DOOR-bell rang. He answered the door and there was a leggy blonde standing there, with an expression that was way too cheerful for an FBI agent. "Harmony Swift," she said, "but you can call me Harm. Everybody does. And you're Daniel Pierce."

He nodded. "Are you from California, by any chance?"

"Yes, why?"

"You have one of those California names." And she looked like she should be strolling down Rodeo Drive, all tanned skin and long legs and blonde hair, wearing one of those skimpy designer dresses and cuddling a ridiculous, Thumbelina-sized dog in her arms.

"Tag Donovan sent me. He said you have a problem." She indicated the plastic-covered front wall of his house. "Is that it?"

"That's just a symptom of the overall disease."

"Not as ugly as chicken pox—lacks the oozing, scabby quality—but I still don't think it will catch on."

"Design by Ford Motor Co. It's a long story."

"And I hear your problem has an expiration date."

"Is that why you broke land-speed records to get here?"

"Air-speed records maybe," Harm said. "If there was an air-speed limit."

"Mike sent you on a helicopter?"

"I sent myself on a helicopter."

"Kind of unusual, isn't it?"

She shrugged, smiling with pep. "It's easier to do my job if I occasionally . . . circumvent procedure."

Daniel decided not to question her rule-breaking habits, especially since it was to his advantage.

"Maybe we should get started," she prompted.

Daniel stepped back, taking the computer bag off her shoulder as she came inside, and leading the way to his upstairs office. "There's water and cold drinks in the refrigerator. Or I can make coffee."

"All I need is the Internet."

"Wireless," he said, setting her shoulder bag on one end of the desk.

"Tag said there's a contract out on you, so I checked the organized crime situation in Boston, since that's the most likely source of a hired hit. It appears that someone is marshalling the individual factions of the Irish mob into one organization," she said, sounding all business, the incarnation of looks-can-be-deceiving, "and it's not Joe Flynn. His name is on all the wires, and the confidential informants are talking about him, but his actions don't fit the circumstances."

"What are the circumstances?"

"A sharp increase in the typical crimes: vehicle theft, protection in the South End and branching out, probably drugs as well, but that's a little harder to quantify in the early stages. And then there's the contract on you."

She sat in the chair Daniel pulled over for her, took out her laptop, and got it running. "There's been a team of agents on Flynn for the last six months. He does a lot of schmoozing, talks to a lot of people, but it seems like the conversations all run along the lines of the one he had with you."

"At Cohan's? I'm on FBI surveillance?"

"Yeah, but don't sweat it, you're not even close to the most interesting person he's been seen with. Flynn spends a lot of time talking to politicians, community leaders, federal prosecutors . . ." She smiled over her shoulder at him. "What we don't see is him with any known criminals, and he practically never drops off the radar, so—"

"He's a front."

"Yep. There's someone else calling the shots, someone who's happy to let good old Joe take all the bows while they stay behind the scene and run the show."

"This is all really interesting, but it doesn't solve my problem."

"Right, kidnapped psychic. Hey, if she's a psychic, why didn't she predict her own kidnapping?"

"She arranged her own kidnapping," Daniel said. "It's a long story."

"It sounds like an interesting story, and we've got all night."

"We've got until two A.M. to figure out where Vivi is being held," Daniel corrected her. "I need to go in before they're expecting me, and they're expecting me at four."

"Slave driver," Harmony said, but she lifted her hands,

surgeonlike, and wiggled her fingers. "Let's see what we can find out on the World Wide Web."

"Start with the name Patrice Hanlon. Joe Flynn's niece," Daniel added.

Harmony twisted around to look at him. "That's a little too coincidental—I know, it's a long story." And she turned back around and set to work.

When two A.M. rolled around they hadn't made a lot of progress. No surprise there. If Patrice was forward-thinking enough to start gaining his trust seven years in advance, she'd be covered everywhere else. But it wasn't her criminal activities that interested Daniel.

"I compiled a list of her real estate holdings, like you asked," Harm said. "They're scattered all over the city and the surrounding area. Quite a number of them are suitable for conducting criminal activities—or holding someone prisoner—without risking exposure."

"Give me a hard copy of the properties," he said evenly. Inside he was roaring in frustration, but having a meltdown wasn't going to help him find Vivi.

"There are way too many to check out before your four A.M. deadline."

Daniel didn't feel a need to respond, seeing as that was obvious.

"Well," Harm said, "this was fun. Give me a call the next time you need help not figuring something out." She took one look at his face and lost her sunny California smile. "I'm sorry, Daniel. I wish there was something else I could do."

Daniel let out his pent-up breath, and got out of his own head for the first time since he'd found out Vivi was being held hostage. "You found properties the IRS would have missed. Finding Vivi is my problem—you're not a field agent—"

"Don't rub it in."

Since that comment seemed weighted with things Daniel didn't want to disturb, he decided it was best to let it pass. He took Harm's bag and escorted her out to her car, which was still waiting at the curb, the driver kicked back and sleeping in the front seat. But as he opened the car door, a flash of chrome and red paint caught his eye. He handed Harm her bag and crouched down so he could see below the branches of the huge red maple at the edge of his driveway. And there, parked in front of his neighbor's house, was Maxine.

"Was that truck sitting there when you came in?" he asked Harm.

"I don't remember. Why?"

"No reason," Daniel said. "Have a safe trip."

Harm got in the car and the car took off. Daniel was already on his way next door. Vivi had left the truck. There was no other explanation. She'd figured he'd still be mad at her, so she'd parked it far enough away to not be apparent, but close enough so he wouldn't miss it in the morning. The question was why?

chapter 27

DANIEL LOOKED INSIDE MAXINE, BUT THERE WAS no note, no clue to Vivi's whereabouts. And how could there be? Vivi'd had no idea where Patrice was going to stash her.

So why had she left Maxine parked outside his house? Because she was asking for a little faith? If that was the case, she was asking a lot. Maybe he'd had enough experience with Maxine to know there was something strange about the truck, but possessed and able to navigate around the city by itself? Too much of a stretch for someone who barely trusted real live human beings.

And yet Daniel went back into the house, collected his gun and Harm's list, and returned to the truck. Okay, so he was willing to take a chance. In giving herself up to Patrice Hanlon, Vivi had done the same. And yeah, he realized she'd done it to force his hand, but it was still a sacrifice, and she was counting on him to rescue her. Or show up and help her rescue herself, at the very least. What difference if he took his car or her truck?

Maxine's keys were under the driver's floor mat, right where Vivi usually left them. And sure, there was a bit of a hesitation when Daniel put the key in the ignition. "C'mon, I need a break here," he said. "Let's go find Vivi." He was too frantic to feel weird about talking to Maxine, not to mention relieved when she started right up.

Harm had given him the entire list of Patrice's properties. He wouldn't be able to check out all the locations, but he could hit the most likely. The problem, he realized when he'd reviewed the highlighted addresses, was that they were all likely. All of them were deserted and secluded, and they were scattered around Boston and the neighboring cities, from warehouses down at the waterfront to buildings like Eric's that were waiting to be rehabbed.

He chose a place not far from his house, but it didn't feel right when he drove by, which made him roll his eyes because it was something Vivi would say. Of course, she'd actually have something concrete to back up that sentiment. If you could call ESP concrete. He consulted the list again and aimed the truck toward the next nearest address. Instead he found himself driving around, knowing the task was useless and searching his mind for some other way to find Vivi. He needed help, but all his usual sources were tapped out, and he was . . . He consulted a street sign and realized he was almost to Savin Hill, which wasn't near any of the likely addresses on Harm's list.

That was when his panic began to burn off and his brain kicked back in. Anthony Sappresi lived in Savin Hill. When they'd spoken after the first murder attempt, Tony had told him he needed something to trade. That implied Tony had information. Vivi had been reading regularly for Tony before Tom Zukey was murdered, and Tony hadn't been happy when she quit. Voila, Daniel thought. He could trade Vivi for the information he needed to find her. She wouldn't be happy about reading for Tony again, but hey, she'd still be alive and maybe so would he.

He pulled up in front of Tony's house, all prepared to make the deal. He rousted Tony out of bed by pounding his fist on the front door and leaning on the bell, and his resolve didn't waver. Tony was wearing a robe that had been purchased about fifty pounds ago, and Daniel suspected that he slept alfresco, but Daniel ignored the danger to his eyesight and told Tony what he needed. And when Tony asked the obvious question, "What are you going to do for me?" Daniel went blank. Okay, the words were on the tip of his tongue, but he couldn't bring himself to throw Vivi under the bus. Even to save her life.

"I'll step down from your case," Daniel said instead.

"My mouthpiece tells me it won't matter whether you're on the case or not. It ain't looking too good for me."

"Your lawyer is preparing you for conviction?" Daniel scoffed, laying it on thick. "You need to get a new lawyer."

"The evidence ain't gonna change if you're off the case."

"True, but a new prosecutor will need time to get up to speed. Your lawyer—your new lawyer can argue that a continuance violates your right to a speedy trial, maybe get the date moved up so the new prosecutor isn't ready. It bumps up your odds of acquittal, which is a good thing since your odds of acquittal are currently zero."

Tony thought about that for a minute, then shrugged. "I'm a gambling man. And I ain't letting no broad take over my turf."

Daniel stuck out his hand, Tony took it, and the deal was struck. It gave Vivi the best possible opportunity to get out of this alive, and get her life back.

But for Daniel, there was no turning back.

TONY MOBILIZED HIS WISE GUYS AND SENT THEM OUT to Patrice's properties, and when Vivi wasn't at any of Daniel's top picks Tony sent his goons to the rest of the places on Harm's list. There were dozens. Daniel had to give Tony credit: He accomplished in less than an hour what it would have taken Daniel days to do alone.

"Here you go," Tony said at a little after three A.M., handing the list back.

Daniel took it, having to calm himself down because he was trying to read so fast he couldn't focus on anything. "All the addresses are crossed off except three," he said when he could finally read it.

Tony shrugged, which was dangerous considering the bathrobe situation. "You told me not to send my guys inside."

Because there was no telling what would happen if two warring crime factions ran into each other with Vivi in the middle.

"Those are the places they couldn't scope out without going in," Tony finished.

And he had less than an hour left to figure out which one of the three Vivi was at: an abandoned warehouse on the waterfront, a strip mall in Jamaica Plain waiting to be torn down, and a salvage yard.

"This one," he said to Tony, pointing to the salvage yard. "Any idea what it is?"

"City Salvage," Tony said, "as in vehicles are salvaged from the rightful owner and sold piecemeal to struggling repair shops all over the city."

Patrice Hanlon as Robin Hood, Daniel thought, except the part where she pocketed all the profits. And then it dawned on him. *Chop shop.* That meant cars, some of them stripped down to bare chassis. Just like in Vivi's last vision of him.

He didn't remember leaving Tony's house, or getting in the truck. There was only blind elation mixed with the fierce relief that came with finally being able to *do* something. Remembering he had less than an hour to spare took the air out of his sails.

By the time he got there he was down to thirty minutes, and while the temptation was to go in with guns blazing, he had no idea where in the place Vivi was being held. But he knew she was inside. Gut feeling, he assured himself, nothing to do with any extraneous perceptions unsubstantiated by science. And it had nothing to do with Maxine.

Just to be sure, he parked the truck at the far edge of the lot, and then he had to wait about a minute for Maxine to thrash herself to a stop. She didn't want to be left out of the fun, he caught himself thinking—not the craziest notion he'd had all night.

City Salvage sat amongst rundown warehouses and empty storage buildings, a big, cement-block rectangle with a semisized roll-up door in one of the long sides. Even if the door wasn't locked, and he could open it by himself, the hinges were rusted and would make a hell of a noise. There were small windows up high in the walls and no outside lighting. Perfect for illegal operations, not so perfect for breaking and entering without being caught.

The surroundings didn't offer much help, either, mainly because the surroundings consisted of an expanse of asphalt so old there wasn't a square foot of it that wasn't cracked, heaved, or potholed. A lone Dumpster sat almost squarely below one of the small windows, which was propped open.

Daniel did a circuit of the building on foot and that was it. Cracked asphalt, some trash blowing across it by the wind from the harbor, and that lone, conveniently placed Dumpster. Too conveniently—unless his luck was just running that good, and there was no way his luck was running that good. The Dumpster and the open window were a trap. And he had no choice but to spring it.

He hauled himself up onto the Dumpster, and discovered it left him about a foot short of the window. He had to jump and catch the sill, then brace his feet against the rough cement block. His leg protested the entire program, but he ignored the pain and muscled himself up high enough to look in the window.

He couldn't see Vivi or Hatch. Hopefully that meant they couldn't see him, and he wasn't Spider-Man anyway. It was impossible to suction himself to the side of the building indefinitely. It was either up or down.

He chose up, and his muscles weren't entirely prepared to defy gravity. Funny, he thought, how out of shape he'd gotten sitting behind a desk. Sure, he worked out almost every day, but gym-fit and street-fit were two different things. Mentally and physically. If he hadn't had the advantage of surprise, and if Hatch had put up any kind of fight, he doubted he'd have gotten the better of the man.

As it was Hatch almost got the better of him, before Daniel got in a lucky punch.

"Thank God he has a glass jaw," Vivi said.

Daniel pulled one of the plastic ties Hatch favored out of the other man's back pocket and secured his hands and feet. "You could have helped," he said to Vivi.

"Whenever I try to help you get mad at me."

"I get mad when you interfere."

"In your book those two are the same."

Daniel stood there, nursing his temper for a minute, even though he knew time was growing short.

"Care to let me free?" she prompted.

"Why are you in such a hurry now? You wanted to be here."

"Because you didn't believe me about Patrice."

"And you couldn't give me five minutes to get used to the idea, to verify her guilt and decide how to deal with it? It made more sense to put us both in a life-and-death situation?"

"You said to get you a motive!"

"And how is this getting me a motive?"

"You can talk to her—"

"I could have talked to her without you being held at gunpoint."

"Not if you didn't think she was guilty."

"I would have gotten there if you'd given me some

time—Jesus." Daniel scrubbed his hands back through his hair and jumped off the verbal merry-go-round. "I should walk away," he said. "You and Patrice deserve each other."

"Well, this is entertaining. And gratifying."

Patrice Hanlon's voice. Daniel traded a look with Vivi, both of them coming to the same conclusion even before they heard the sound of a gun cocking. Daniel turned around. The gun was pointed at Vivi.

"I've been practicing," Patrice said. "A lot. I'm pretty good."

Daniel dropped Hatch's gun.

Patrice came over and kicked it across the floor, then plucked the pistol from the back of Daniel's waistband and bent to check each of his ankles. He was tempted to kick her in the head, but she never took her eyes off him. And she kept the gun pointed at Vivi.

"I knew you'd come early," she said as she stood and stepped back. "I knew you'd find out where we were holding the kook somehow."

"I'm not a kook," Vivi said.

"Really?" Patrice said. "That's what you're worried about right now?"

"We're not going to die, so yeah, I don't like being called names by a two-bit mobster wannabe with no imagination."

Patrice's hand tightened on the gun, and for a second Daniel thought she might pull the trigger. She laughed instead. "Still trying to psych me out, I see."

"Just calling it like I see it," Vivi said.

Hatch decided to join the party by retrieving his gun from where Patrice had kicked it, and pointing it at Daniel, his hands and feet tied together awkwardly. Patrice stepped in front of him. Hatch didn't like it.

Patrice didn't realize how close she came to ending up a casualty. Or maybe she did, because she took the gun—carefully—from Hatch and set it on the hood of a Mustang behind her.

"I appreciate the gesture," Daniel said to her, "but aren't you going to kill me?"

"I have to," Patrice said. "The sacrifice is necessary."

Vivi caught Daniel's eye, then looked at Hatch. Hatch, red-faced and pissed off, was staring at Patrice. Patrice cut the ties around Hatch's wrists and ankles, but she kept his gun, and she stayed between him and Daniel, and they all knew why. Patrice had feelings for Daniel. Sure, those feelings were warped and mixed up, but they existed.

"I'm here now," Daniel said, "there's no reason to hurt anyone else."

"There's a very important reason," Patrice said. "Hurting her hurts you."

"Right," Vivi put in, "he's going to be all broken up if something happens to me."

Patrice ignored her. "I find it interesting," she said to Daniel, "that you would sacrifice yourself for a woman who was a nuisance just a few days ago."

"That's why Flip and Hatch went after her at Boston Common. I was the original target—"

"But as soon as they told me you were protecting her, it was irresistible." Patrice gave Vivi one of those down-the-nose superior looks. "She was easier to get to, for one thing. She won't pick up a gun, for Christ's sake."

"I picked it up," Vivi said, "I shot it, too. Just not at anyone."

"Which only proves my point," Patrice shot back. "God knows why you care about her, Daniel, but you do, and you're going to have to watch her die, just like I lost Bobby."

"Who's Bobby?"

"Her brother, Bobby Flynn," Daniel said to Vivi. "Long story short, I caught him selling drugs, he shot me, he went to jail."

"And one of those animals in federal prison stabbed him to death," Patrice said. "I spent all this time working my way into your trust, Daniel, so that when the time came, I could make you pay."

"You're avenging your brother's death."

"I'm finishing what he started," Patrice said. "My father

was killed by Sappresi's goons, and it was left to Bobby to avenge his death and unite the families. But Bobby never could do anything right."

"And Joe Flynn was just a figurehead."

"Joe Flynn couldn't strategize his way out of bed in the morning, but the families are run by men. So I let Joe do what he does best, which is talk. But I put the words in his mouth."

"Let's see if I have all this," Daniel said to Patrice. "Avenge your brother, unite the mob, take over the city."

"You forgot the part where I kill you."

"That falls under the vengeance part of the program."

"Oh, it does more than that. Taking out a federal prosecutor, especially one I'm known to be friends with, gives me credibility."

Daniel moved a couple feet away from Vivi, and leaned against a half-stripped pickup. "You definitely take the prize for forward planning," he said.

"Timing is everything," she said. "I knew this moment would come, and I wanted to be ready."

"Pull that trigger and you sign your own death warrant. At least two people connected with the FBI know you took Vivi hostage, and Tony Sappresi helped me find this place. He'll trade you for a plea agreement in a heartbeat. Hell, he'd be happy to do the time. Fingering you would make him a hero to his bosses, instead of a disgrace."

Patrice lifted one shoulder in an elegant shrug. "Tony can say whatever he wants. It'll be hard to prove without a body." And she cocked the gun.

Daniel's first instinct was to put himself in the line of fire. He shifted away again. Patrice swung the gun his way, but Vivi jumped in.

"Hatch is really looking forward to pulling the trigger," she said.

"I know," Patrice said, "but it has to be me. It should have been me all along. I have to prove I can do my own dirty work before I can expect others to do it for me."

"Well, I have to give you credit," Vivi said. "It can't be easy for you to murder someone you're in love with."

Hatch shifted ever so slightly, his gaze sliding from Patrice to Daniel.

"She's just saying that to upset you," Patrice said to Hatch. "It's not true."

"Really?" Daniel put in. "So all those times you wanted me to spend the night, you were lying?"

"Yes."

"Every time I dropped you off, and you kissed me good night—"

"On the cheek," Patrice said, her gaze shifting between Daniel, Vivi, and Hatch so quickly she had to be getting dizzy.

"But you pressed yourself against me, and, while I'm no expert on women, I figured out how to tell when a girl likes me in the seventh grade."

Hatch went for his gun.

Patrice stepped in front of him again. "They're just trying to make you irrational so I'll send you away."

"If we're just trying to make Hatch irrational, deny it," Vivi said.

"Shut up and go stand over there," Patrice said to Vivi, pointing to a large, grease-stained tarp laid out on the floor about ten yards behind Daniel. There was nothing around the tarp to get splattered with blood, Daniel noticed. Not a good sign for anyone without a weapon. And he and Vivi were still in the direct path of Patrice's gun.

But for once Vivi's stubbornness was working in his favor.

"No way," she said to Patrice. "If I go stand over there you're going to try to shoot me."

"I'm not going to just try."

Vivi crossed her arms and held her ground.

"Hatch."

Hatch jumped at Patrice's command, but Vivi wasn't co-operating. She didn't run, not with a gun aimed at her, but she was agile, ducking and jumping out of the way whenever Hatch reached for her. Finally he snatched her up, carried her over to the tarp, and plopped her down.

"You have to get out of the way," Patrice said to Hatch. "She'll run."

"Not after I shoot her."

Patrice was focused entirely on Vivi, and Patrice was juggling two guns. Daniel dove aside, away from Vivi. Patrice claimed she knew what she was doing, but she wasn't going to pull a Wyatt Earp and blast away with both guns. Her first shot whiffed past him, and he was on her before she could squeeze off another.

Since he had her by sixty pounds or so, it was no contest, and Daniel wound up with all three guns. Unfortunately, he also wound up with Patrice and, unlike the guns, she wouldn't stay where he put her . . . And where the hell was Vivi anyway?

He finally saw her running through the place like the villain in that James Bond movie, ducking through stripped car bodies, jumping over dollies and toolboxes, catapulting off bumpers, trying to keep some large piece of equipment between her and Hatch at all times. Hatch lumbered along behind, shoving obstacles aside instead of going around them, two hundred thirty pounds of muscle guided by a pea-sized brain that was tunnel-visioned on Vivi.

"Hey," Daniel yelled.

Hatch didn't even break stride, but Vivi was distracted long enough to fall back within arm's length just as they got to the tarp. Or maybe she let Hatch catch up. Either way, it was his downfall, literally. He lunged forward, his fingertips feathering through the ends of her long hair at the same time his feet slid on the grease-covered tarp and flew out from underneath him. He slammed flat on his back, his breath grunting out, three or four long, black hairs clutched in his right fist. He didn't get back up.

Vivi turned around and took in the sight of Daniel holding a gun on Patrice. Her hands went to her hips, and she smiled full out, nodding once in satisfaction at a job well done.

"He would have let you go as soon as he saw that I had Patrice at gunpoint," Daniel said to her.

She looked down at Hatch on the ground, his eyes rolled back in his head, wheezing in shallow breaths. "My way works, too."

chapter
28

THE BOSTON P.D.—LED BY OFFICER CRANSTON—
arrived to shut down the stolen car operation. The FBI collected Patrice and Hatch. Daniel went along to make sure
they were incarcerated with Flip. Vivi tried to make a quiet
retreat and found herself flanked by men in black suits, one
of whom she recognized. Not to mention his nose was still
taped.

"I gave you coffee," she said to him.

"And now I'm going to give you a ride," he said, looking more like it was revenge than repayment.

Probably he'd gotten in trouble for getting his nose broken. And failing to keep her under surveillance. Probably
he wouldn't make that mistake again. "Why am I being arrested?"

"You're not being arrested," the coffee drinker said with
tangible regret. "You're being debriefed."

The man was going to need a lesson in stoic if he ever
expected to be a really good agent. Maybe Daniel could
teach him.

"I'm really tired," Vivi said, not to mention heartsick.

Daniel hadn't even given her a second look. He'd just walked away like she'd never been anything to him. And who was she kidding besides herself? If she'd ever meant anything to Daniel, her tie to Anthony Sappresi and her lie about it had destroyed it. "Can't we do this next week? Just about any day works for me."

The coffee drinker and his partner each took an elbow and started walking. Vivi had two choices, go along peaceably or be dragged. She chose Door Number Three, digging in her heels, not going willingly.

They lifted and kept walking with her suspended between them. They weren't even putting a lot of exertion into it. That was just adding insult to injury. "This is chauvinistic," she said. "This is police brutality. I bet you don't haul around drug lords like this."

"Drug lords can have us killed."

"I can put a curse on you," Vivi shot back. "How'd you like to go bald?"

Their eyes cut to each other, and they put her down. Of course they were at the car by then, and the threat of hair loss didn't keep them from bundling her into the backseat. The coffee drinker got in beside her and made sure her seat belt was good and tight. Vivi figured she was lucky he didn't handcuff her to the shackle bolts set into the door. Or gag her.

"I can already see how this is going to go," she said when the other agent put the car in gear and it glided silently away from City Salvage. "And not because I have special powers of insight."

SHE WAS RIGHT, TOO. THEY DIDN'T BELIEVE A WORD she said, not when everything she knew had come to her psychically, and she was dealing with guys who were almost as fanatical about proof as Daniel.

She'd covered the story twice, and they weren't letting her go. She was in a D.C. hotel with an agent stationed outside the door, and since the information was only flowing in one direction she had no idea what they had planned for her. When the phone rang, she figured it was one of two things: either they were going to ask more questions or they were going to have her arrested. It was neither of those. It was something she'd never even considered.

"Vivi?"

"Daniel," she said back, managing to get his name out while the shock of hearing his voice equated to numbness. That split second passed, her heart shot up into her throat, and it felt like somebody was banging on cymbals about two inches from her head.

"Still not calling me Ace?"

Since that was obvious, she didn't figure it needed a response. Not that she could talk anyway.

"How's it going?" he asked.

Vivi put her head between her knees, waiting for the clanging and nausea to pass, and when it did the pain came rushing in, nearly as debilitating. But at least she could talk.

"You there."

"Yes."

"Say something."

"You called me." Not the most original or scintillating comeback in the world, but at least she got it out in a credibly even voice.

"Mike tells me you're still being debriefed."

"Did you call to gloat?"

"Actually, I was wondering why you hadn't left."

"What would be the point? Unless I'm planning to put all my belongings into a bandanna tied around a stick and haunt the train yards."

"Not taking Maxine on the lam with you?"

"Maxine expects a regular diet of gas and oil, and in order to satisfy her appetite I need money. Money means customers, and that means going home. And the minute I hit my front door your buddies will arrest me again."

"They're not my buddies."

She ignored his disclaimer. "And they'll think I took off

because I have something to hide," she said, which was true if she considered her feelings for Daniel—although as far as she knew that wasn't a jailable offense. As it was she'd left that out of the narrative. Falling in love had nothing to do with hit men and mob activity. It didn't really have anything to do with her anymore either, except it would take longer to get over than the fear of death. "I figure they'll ask me to recap the events at least one more time, two tops. Then they'll let me go, and I won't have to worry about the FBI again."

"Including me?"

"You didn't waste any time saying good-bye," she pointed out.

"The place was crawling with cops and feds."

"That's what happens when you call and tell them you were almost murdered by a high-ranking mob figure."

"Debriefing brings out your sarcastic nature."

Sarcasm had more to do with getting her through the phone call. Speaking of which . . . "Did you want something? Besides asking useless questions and telling me things I already know?"

"I thought I'd tell you some things you didn't know."

He must be talking about the case because Vivi knew everything there was to know about Daniel. Okay, the phone call had surprised her, but the phone call had exhausted Daniel's capacity for mystery.

"Let me guess," she said. "Flip is still in jail and Hatch is keeping him company. And Patrice is in a different jail."

"That's the bottom line," he said.

"Well, thanks for letting me know."

"Vivi . . ."

She waited, every sense straining, but that was all he said. Just her name. Her ears didn't pick up anything more, and her noncorporeal senses still hadn't kicked back in where Daniel was concerned. She doubted they ever would.

"Good-bye, Daniel," she said, and she disconnected.

In her entire life, Vivi had never had a quiet moment.

She'd been accidentally tapping into other people's thoughts for as long as she could remember. She'd always thought silence would be the closest thing to heaven, but silence from Daniel, that kind of silence, was just too much to bear.

DANIEL HAD HIS OWN DEBRIEFING SESSION, CONSIDER-ably shorter than Vivi's since he had no trouble being believed. The feds were a bit dicier about his decision to go off on his own. So was the U.S. attorney's office. Those problems were solved with his resignation, at least as far as he was concerned.

He could have stayed on at the U.S. attorney's office; he was a hero for putting a halt to the mob uprising. But he'd made a deal with Tony Sappresi, and while he could have justified breaking a deal with a mob boss, he found he didn't want to.

He'd solved the case. Sure, Vivi had been a big part of the solution, but he'd have gotten there eventually—and he'd saved his and Vivi's lives. He still felt like a failure. He'd been a good agent, but he'd had to give it up before he was ready. He was a good lawyer, too, top of his class in law school. But that was just about grades on a transcript. When it came to trying cases, he didn't have a very good track record. Probably because his heart wasn't in it.

Not that he wanted to think about his heart at the moment. What he wanted, or rather needed, to think about was his future—as in not having one. He wasn't worried about his ability to keep breathing and walking around. It was the direction that bothered him. He'd always had a purpose, and his purpose had always involved getting the bad guys off the street.

Problem was, he couldn't be an agent, and he couldn't be a lawyer, and vigilantes were frowned upon, not to mention completely against his ethical makeup. All that left was superhero, unless he suddenly started getting messages from the great beyond. The only image he was getting with any regularity was Vivi's, and there was no mystery where those images originated. What to do about them, now there was a mystery.

Step one, he decided, was to have a face-to-face with her. The phone call had been a complete bust. She'd sounded a little shaky in the beginning, but then her voice had been so steady he thought he'd imagined that first part. He didn't have her skill at reading people, but Vivi wasn't all that good at hiding her feelings, so here he was, knocking on her front door.

She pulled it open and stepped back in invitation. She didn't bat an eye. She hadn't batted an eye when he left her, either. No tears, no pleading, no questions. The woman claimed to be in love with him, and she didn't even want to know when she'd see him again. Apparently, none of that had changed.

"You have a reason for being here, I'd imagine," she said, her voice as empty of feeling as her expression. He held up a white takeout bag. "Burgers from that little mom-and-pop place."

She ignored the bag, but he saw her swallow a couple of times, her lips twitching like she wanted to lick them. He was damn glad she didn't because there were things to be cleared up between them, and if he had to watch her lick her lips he wasn't sure he could keep his hands off her long enough to remedy anything but his great and irresistible hunger for her. Vivi didn't look like she'd be receptive to physical interaction until the emotional part of the program was fixed, so she'd probably kick him out and then he'd be back to square one, waiting for her to cool down while his need to be with her, even if it was just to talk, grew to even more astronomical proportions. And since bribery wasn't working, he fell back on hubris, barging in and shutting the door behind him—not that Vivi tried to stop him.

She didn't make any sort of protest at all, just backed away, her eyes never leaving his face. Even in the gloom Daniel swore he saw desire in them. But there was vulnerability there, too, and it got to him like nothing else could. She'd always been so sure of herself, so confident the world would behave exactly as she expected—predicted—it to. Except him, she said she couldn't read him. Because she loved him. Strangely enough, knowing he was as much a mystery to her as she was to him put Daniel almost totally at ease for the first time since he'd met her. Almost. Dealing with Vivi had never been easy. He didn't expect that to change now.

"Mike tells me you got a lawyer and refused to answer any more questions," he said, getting on with the matter of putting their professional affiliation in the past so they could both move on with their lives.

"I answered their questions," Vivi said, "so did you, I assume. And since they actually believe you, what did they need me for anyway?"

"Corroboration. The case has to be properly assembled, and they can't do that without your statement. There was no reason to bring a lawyer into it. They'd have let you go by now. All you had to do was sit tight and let the situation play out—and what am I saying? You never could do that. You have no patience, and no faith in anyone but yourself. You always have to do things your way."

"I let you rescue me, didn't I?"

"You let me . . ." And here was the argument he'd been expecting. She drove him crazy like no one else could. "You're saying you could have gotten free any time you wanted?"

"You set me free, remember? And you got Patrice to take away Hatch's gun. And I didn't do anything because I knew you had a plan, and your plan probably included me being incapacitated. Hatch and Patrice thought I was a nonthreat, too. I could have done something once my hands were free, ran away, stomped on Hatch's foot, whatever, but suddenly jumping in like that would have messed everything up."

"Suddenly jumping up would have resulted in immediate gunfire," Daniel said, somewhat mollified—and surprised—by her logic. And what it said about her.

"Exactly. And since they had all the firepower, we'd be dead."

"So . . ." Daniel ventured farther into the store, encouraged by the general thaw. "You trusted me?"

Vivi bumped up a shoulder. "You came even though I said you would die trying to protect me. My vision—"

"We managed to prevent every one of those visions."

"We?"

"We."

"That would be a really nice ending to all this, except you don't believe in my visions."

And Daniel didn't want an ending. But he couldn't just blurt that out. He had to work around to it. "If I don't believe in your visions, how did I know to jump the other way instead of trying to protect you? And how did I know where to find you?"

Vivi stopped halfway to the front counter, turned, and looked at him. "How did you know?"

He shrugged, as if it were every day he collaborated with a Mafia capo. "Tony Sappresi. I agreed to step down from his case if Tony would send his guys out and check Patrice Hanlon's properties. They narrowed it down to three. One of the three was a salvage yard, and you said there were cars in your vision."

"Tony? What made you go to him?"

"Maxine."

She snorted out a laugh. "Really?"

"You left Maxine at my house for a reason."

"I left Maxine because I thought she might come in handy. Like if you didn't want to take your car."

"Well, she came in handy. Patrice has a lot of property. I figured Hatch was watching you, and the only way to get you out in one piece was to surprise him. But there was no way to check all the places in time. I was just kind of driving around, trying to figure out what to do, and I realized I was almost to Tony's place. The rest you know."

She took a moment to digest it all. "Why did you do it?" she finally asked. "Why did you throw your career away for me?"

"You put your life on the line to save mine," Daniel said. "I owed you."

Wrong answer. Vivi crossed her arms over her chest, squeezing tight to ease the pain. She finished crossing the room and went behind the counter, feeling better for having the bulk of it between her and Daniel.

"Well, debt paid," she said. "You can sleep with a clear conscience tonight."

"I didn't mean—"

"Me, too," she said over him. "I helped save your life, that makes up for what happened with Tom Zukey. No more sleepless nights, and no more visions." She hoped.

"And that's it?"

"Well, I finally got someone in law enforcement to believe in me," Vivi said. "So it's not a total loss."

Daniel crossed the room, stopping on the opposite side of the counter. He laid his hands on the glass top, taking some time to gather his thoughts.

Vivi could tell something had changed, and she had a feeling she was about to find out the real reason Daniel had come calling, because she knew it wasn't to rehash the case. Her heart began to pound, black spots crowding the edges of her vision before she realized she'd stopped breathing.

She sucked in a breath, trying to make sure Daniel didn't notice his effect on her. She probably should have stepped back so there was more than the width of that narrow counter between them, but making her shaky muscles behave was more than she could manage.

"So," Daniel said, "I guess we trust each other."

Vivi nodded. It was the only safe response.

"You could say we like each other, too."

Another nod.

"You might even say we're friends. In fact, we could be more than friends. We could be business partners."

Vivi froze, even her shaking knees locked as her eyes shifted to his. "Huh?"

"I'm going into private work," he said. "Mainly cases

that are long cold. I thought maybe you'd be able to help. It'll take a while to get a rep—"

"Hold it!" This time she had no trouble moving her feet, backing away from Daniel, not to mention the notion they could work together. And nothing else. "I don't think—"

"I do." Daniel came around the end of the counter, stopping when Vivi backed off again. "Like I said, it'll take time to build a reputation. Things will be tight for a while."

He looked around, and she knew he was thinking hardship would be no change for her. "I do all right," she said.

"I'm not asking you to give all this up," he said, with a crooked smile. "I was just thinking I might be able to use a psychic. Especially one who wants to do more than tell people about their marriage prospects and if they're going to be successful in business."

"You're really asking me to work with you?"

"Absolutely."

Vivi was flabbergasted, to say the least. She was also deflated, disappointed, and pissed off big-time. She didn't know what she'd expected him to say . . . That was garbage, she knew exactly what she'd expected him to say—or at least what she wanted him to say. And she was an idiot for holding out hope of anything emotional where Daniel was concerned.

"I told you I love you, you idiot."

"You did."

"And you have the nerve to show up here and talk about everything but that?"

"Well . . ."

"You offered me a job!"

"Yeah, but I brought dinner, too."

"Get out!" She gave him a two-handed shot to the chest that didn't move him an inch but sent pain singing up to her shoulders.

Daniel wrapped his arms around her and pulled her against him, and the pain shot to her heart and stuck there.

"I was asking you to be my partner," he said.

"I got that."

"There are all kinds of partners."

Vivi's heart began to thump again, but she was breathing fine this time, and the pain in her chest seemed to ease up some. She took a deep breath and lifted her eyes to Daniel's face, braced for the worst, hoping for the impossible. "You're going to have to be more specific than that," she said. "You know I can't read your mind."

He kissed her, a soft, gentle kiss that spoke of more than sex but when she tried to ask him what exactly it did mean, he swept his tongue inside her open mouth and she thought, "Oh, good, no matter what else happens between us, there'll be sex." She gave herself up to the kiss, to the feel of his hands moving over her, and by the time they pulled a scant inch apart they were both breathing hard. And if Daniel was feeling half of what she was, he wouldn't waste any more time on words. But he did, and they were the kind of words that melted parts of her that had nothing to do with sex. Like her heart.

"I love you, Vivi," he said, his eyes intense but sincere on hers. "I'm not promising there won't be arguments, and probably some of them will be over your psychic ability and my tendency to doubt it, but I trust you and I think we can make it work. And I promise you'll never miss another meal," he finished, retrieving the hamburger bag from the counter where he'd left it and holding it up, a hopeful expression on his face.

She pretended to consider it, letting her gaze shift to the white takeout bag. "Those are some pretty incredible burgers."

"So I've heard."

"I bet they're so incredible they're even good cold."

"I don't know . . ."

She took the bag from him and set it back on the counter. "I wouldn't mind missing a meal this one time," she said slipping her hand into his.

"Nope, I made a promise." And he dropped her hand, reaching for the bag.

So she kissed him, poured everything in her heart into

it, backing him toward the stairs leading up to her living quarters the whole time. "Let's get this partnership going," she said when his heels bumped the bottom step.

Daniel caught her hand, pulling her up the stairs with him. "I thought you said you couldn't read my mind."

"It's not your mind I'm reading, Ace."